T0304901

Suzanne Wright lives in England with her husband and two children. When she's not spending time with her family, she's writing reading or doing her version of housework – sweeping the house with a look.

She's worked in a pharmaceutical company, at a Disney Store, at a primary school as a voluntary teaching assistant, at the RSPCA and has a First Class Honours degree in Psychology and Identity Studies.

As to her interests, she enjoys reading, writing, reading, writing (sort of eat, sleep, write, repeat), spending time with her family, movie nights with her sisters and playing with her two Bengal kittens.

To connect with Suzanne online:
Website: http://www.suzannewright.co.uk
Facebook: https://www.facebook.com/suzannewrightfanpage

Suzanne Wright

THE
MONSTERS
WE ARE

PIATKUS

PIATKUS

First published in Great Britain in 2025 by Piatkus

3 5 7 9 10 8 6 4 2

A CIP catalogue record for this book
is available from the British Library.

Hardback ISBN 978-0-349-43463-6
Trade paperback ISBN 978-0-349-43465-0

Typeset in Garamond by M Rules

Printed and bound in Great Britain by
Clays Ltd, Elcograf S.p.A.

Papers used by Piatkus are from well-managed forests
and other responsible sources.

Piatkus	The authorised representative
An imprint of	in the EEA is
Little, Brown Book Group	Hachette Ireland
Carmelite House	8 Castlecourt Centre
50 Victoria Embankment	Dublin 15, D15 XTP3, Ireland
London EC4Y 0DZ	(email: info@hbgi.ie)

An Hachette UK Company
www.hachette.co.uk

www.littlebrown.co.uk

For Steve,

You'll be missed.

Chapter One

"Ew, I just licked at the cotton candy sticking to my upper lip and got a taste of my face paint." Anabel shuddered, sticking out her tongue. "Tastes like chalk."

"Why did you choose to have your face painted in that stereotypical green witch style anyway?" Wynter Dellavale asked, eyeing her coven member curiously.

"Well, this *is* an 'It's almost Halloween' party."

"And you're dressed in a blood-stained cheerleader's outfit. The face paint doesn't go with the look."

"Yes, but everyone will now assume that the boils and hairy warts on my face are fake."

Wynter felt her brow crease. "No, they still look real." They wouldn't be there at all if the blonde didn't use herself as a trial subject when she created new potions. Some caused all kinds of aftereffects. Rashes. Hallucinations. Bad guts. Perhaps even the belief that you were the reincarnation of Bloody Mary ... unless Anabel's claim to be exactly that was in fact true. Her soul *did* have the ability to retain all her memories from her past lives, to be fair.

Wynter sighed. "If you'd just stop experimenting—"

"I know, I know," said Anabel with a flap of her hand.

"And yet, you keep doing it."

The blonde's back straightened. "Excuse me, I'm not the only person here who has bad habits."

Xavier's brow knitted. "What's that supposed to mean?"

Anabel sniffed at him. "It means *you* lie all the time for no real reason. Hattie is always asking random people embarrassing questions about sex. Delilah keeps cooking up self-proclaimed karma potions that will one day get her shanked. And Wynter keeps coming back to life every time she dies—part of being a revenant, yeah, but it's still freaky. So, you know, I don't think any of you should be throwing stones at my glass house."

"I'm sensing you're expecting us to be fair," said Xavier. "Why?"

Anabel plucked at her skirt. "I guess I thought it would be a nice change."

"You reached too high," he told her, scratching at his head with a grimace. "Christ, could no one have warned me that the hair chalk makes your scalp itch like a mother?" His usual tousled brown hair had been slicked back and colored lime green to go with his outfit.

"You think chalk is bad, try wearing a veil," grumbled Hattie. "I forgot how uncomfortable they are."

"One would think, after the amount of times you've been a bride, that you would have remembered," Delilah said to her. "But then, one would also think that you'd have chosen divorce over murder, even if you do insist on the first being a sin while the latter is somehow excusable."

Hattie shrugged. "Divorce is too lengthy a process. It was quicker to just . . . help them pass on."

Snorting, Wynter shook her head. The woman spoke like she'd arranged for her ex-husbands to die peacefully in their sleep but, yeah, it hadn't quite played out that way. Which was why it was weirding Wynter and the others out that Hattie was dressed like a bride right now.

Wynter and her group hadn't been a coven for very long, having only met for the first time when they'd been kidnapped by bounty hunters who she later killed. Well, to be more exact, it was the monster that lived inside her who was responsible for the deaths.

The position of Priestess hadn't been something Wynter ever coveted. She'd resisted for a while, just as she'd resisted officially proclaiming them a coven—one that Delilah had named the Bloodrose Coven. But it had been a pointless resistance. Still, they were more of a family. A family with rather dysfunctional dynamics and a streak of crazy that couldn't be tamed.

Hearing squeals, Wynter looked to see a mechanical hand zooming across the floor, scaring the dancers. She fingered her renaissance-style gothic gown as she glanced around. She had no idea whose idea it was to temporarily convert the warehouse into a cemetery-themed bar, but she saluted them. The dim lighting and dry ice machine made the place feel dark, chilly, and unwelcoming. Fake tombstones, dead flowers, hanging cobwebs, and open standing caskets revealing rubber skeletons added to the creepy factor.

Most patrons were in fancy dress, and many had had their faces painted. Most had also plied themselves with alcohol. They stood around in groups, danced on the manmade dancefloor, tackled iconic Halloween songs on the karaoke—most of which were from the 70s and 80s—or even played bowling with pumpkins at the other side of the warehouse.

The building normally stored vehicles—all of which were now parked in driveways or at curbs around the town that was smack bam in the middle of no man's land. Woods, lakes, and mountains bordered the town. Varying types of houses were situated around it. Stores, bars, and restaurants could be found at the pretty plaza. Beyond those were warehouses, utility structures, and pastureland.

The town was vastly different from the medieval city below them, where many residents lived, including the Ancients—seven beings who'd founded Devil's Cradle. Beings who could also grant people all sorts of things in exchange for their soul. Not weird at all.

The badlands landscape surrounding the town was wild and untamed with the hills, spires, and crooks. So very different from the lushly forested town of Aeon—a place she'd once lived before the immortal beings that ruled it unfairly decided to end her life . . . at which point she'd cursed the land with a wasting disease before fleeing.

It could be said that she was somewhat unforgiving.

Wynter took another sip of her warm cider. "Gotta say, as special events go, this is way better than that midnight 5k fancy dress run we did last night."

"I agree," said Hattie, reaching beneath her veil to adjust her fading red hair. "That race was brutal. My feet are still killing me."

Wynter frowned at the elderly woman. "I don't see why they would be. You didn't run, you flew in your crow form. And you only completed half the race."

"I got lost."

Delilah snickered. "What happened to your avian navigation skills?"

Hattie shot the Latina a scowl. "I turn into a crow, not a homing pigeon."

Wynter chuckled. The old woman hadn't gotten lost during the race at all. Nope. She'd headed home so she could finish her book, and they all knew it.

Dancing on the spot, Delilah said, "Damn, I love Halloween."

So did Wynter. And, as it happened, so did most of Devil's Cradle—something she'd learned when a schedule of events was posted through the letterbox of their cottage in the underground city. The residents didn't wait for the 31st of October to come crawling around; no, they began their celebrations on the first day of the month. All kinds of weird and wonderful events took place during the run-up.

Well, preternatural beings tended to like Halloween. It was a day for monsters, after all. And Devil's Cradle was full of various species of preternatural, which was why it was also known as "the home of monsters". Not a comforting nickname, no, but it didn't stop people regularly coming here to seek the Ancients' permission to stay.

Wynter and her coven—all of whom had a price on their head— had done that very thing. It wasn't at all unusual for Ancients to give refuge to fugitives and outcasts. The seven immortals were outcasts themselves. They were banished from Aeon many moons ago after another breed of immortal they resided among had slaughtered their kind and dumped the only survivors here.

The price for sanctuary at Devil's Cradle was steep. Residents had to sell partial rights to their soul to one of the Ancients, who would then brand them and provide them with shelter and protection.

Wynter wore such a brand on her palm—a "C" surrounding a triangle that had a snake slinking through it. The "C" stood for Cain, an Ancient who not so long ago marked her a second time when he claimed her as his consort. The seal looked as if it had been stamped on her inner wrist with a hot iron, so there was nothing subtle about it.

As of late, Cain no longer owned only partial rights to her soul. She'd sold all rights to him in exchange for immortality so that she could live a full life with him. It also meant that her soul was now once more anchored to this realm.

She had lost said anchor when she'd died as a child. If a deity hadn't back then turned her into a revenant—a sort-of-undead witch that hosted a monster and was essentially an instrument of vengeance—Wynter's soul would still be in the netherworld. Otherwise known as purgatory for preternatural beings.

"Apparently, there's a crazy build up to Halloween every year," said Xavier. "Some residents considered skipping it this time round, since things aren't exactly great between the Ancients and the Aeons right now. War could be declared on us at any moment. But the majority of the townspeople figured that that was all the more reason to take the time to celebrate everyday stuff."

"I half-expected people to resent that we're all stuck in the middle of the immortals' bullshit, but they don't," said Delilah. "They're wholly pissed at the Aeons for invading their town. Twice. Our side won, sure, but people still died. Everyone's pretty much hoping that Adam will retaliate so they can get rid of the threats once and for all."

It would indeed be beyond wonderful if Adam met his doom like the other three ruling Aeons had recently done—it was a long time coming, in Wynter's fine opinion. "I think he'll come. He's got to be *pissed* that not only is Abel dead but he was returned to Aeon in pieces." Ha.

Cain had almost killed Abel once before long ago, but it wasn't so easy to end the life of an immortal, and a healer had gotten to Abel in time to save him. It hadn't worked that way the second time round.

"If he doesn't come, do you think the Ancients will storm Aeon?" asked Anabel.

They likely wished they could, but the truth was that they were stuck here. The four ruling Aeons had formed an invisible cage surrounding the previously barren land that was now known as Devil's Cradle.

The Aeons were actually Cherubim, but most people weren't aware of that. Similarly, they weren't aware that the Ancients were Leviathans. Both breeds were—along with the now-extinct Behemoths—the first creations of God. He'd assigned the four lesser deities Kali, Nyx, Nemesis, and Apep to watch over them. But . . . the deities had taken their eye off the ball, and many deaths had followed when the three breeds of immortal turned on each other. *Twice.*

The result? God turned his back on *all* of them, including the deities. And so he'd done nothing to free the Ancients from their jail. And why had the Aeons imprisoned them in such a way?

Short answer: They were assholes.

Long answer: They didn't like it when people were more powerful than they were, and so they'd find all sorts of reasons to justify why they might then erase their existence.

Their main motivation was that they believed Cain had no right to exist. His parentage was . . . a dark matter, to say the least. He wasn't merely a Leviathan, he was the son of Satan. Yup. She was the consort of the honest-to-God's Antichrist.

Words he'd once spoken to her flitted through her mind . . .

"I am in fact one of the biggest monsters that will ever live. That, baby, is the Curse of Cain. And you, pretty witch . . . you now share in that curse, because I've claimed you as mine. And I'll never fucking let you go."

That was fine with her, though, because she didn't want him to.

"I'm not sure what they'll do," Wynter prevaricated, unable to share much of the information that Cain had trusted her with.

Once, she'd believed that the Aeons and Ancients were the same breed of immortal because they were not only all part of the first civilization but were similar in many ways. They lived underground, were weaker if out in the sun, possessed impressive abilities, could sleep for long periods of time, and had long ago lost the ability to procreate.

But she'd recently learned from Cain that although the two camps of immortal were similar, they were actually two very different breeds. Hence why the Aeons didn't share the Ancients' ability to purchase souls. Though most people tended to believe the false rumor that the Ancients only possessed the ability because they'd sold their own souls to the devil.

Hattie sniffed and swept her gaze over the room. "On a more important note, I don't see any butlers in the buff."

"Why would you?" asked Delilah. "It's a run-up-to-Halloween party. People tend to wear scary outfits."

"Butlers can be scary."

"Not with their asses hanging out."

"I'd happily be the judge of that."

Delilah nudged her playfully. "You need to stop being such a perve. It's not like you don't get sex on the regular."

A wicked grin curved Hattie's mouth. "My George should be here soon. We agreed to try some roleplay again later. I'm going to be the poor helpless woman who's hypnotized by a vampire who then drinks her blood and ravishes her. Should be interesting."

"Well, I'm hoping to score tonight. It shouldn't be too hard while I'm wearing this getup." Delilah gestured at her Catwoman outfit. A private joke, really, since she could turn into a black cat of any size—including a monstrous beast with iron claws. "It does wonders for my figure."

It did indeed. It had snatched the attention of many males. But then—with her curvy figure, flawless dark skin, and long legs—Delilah did that no matter what she was wearing.

"The dude at the bar has been eye-fucking you for about twenty minutes," Xavier told the Latina.

Delilah glared at him. "And you're only telling me this now? Why?"

Xavier shrugged. "I'm the Joker tonight. The Joker's an asshole. Ergo ..."

Anabel leaned into him. "The woman who's dressed as Harley Quinn keeps looking at you."

"She's the new werewolf in town, right?" Delilah hummed, twirling one of her short, tight curls around her finger. "I've heard that werewolves are kind of wild in bed."

Xavier's eyes lit with interest. "Really? Well then, maybe I'll go introduce myself in a little while."

"As Xavier, or as whatever name you come up with at the time?" asked Anabel.

He lifted his shoulders. "Does it matter?"

"It *should*," said the blonde. "But I don't suppose you'll ever quite get that."

The song changed, and Hattie perked up. "What a classic. Back in the day, I would play this song at home over and over. Reggie got so sick of it he threatened to snap the record in half if I didn't stop listening to it so much."

Wynter tilted her head. "And who was Reggie?"

Hattie's lips thinned. "Husband number three. Serial cheater. Highly temperamental. Threw a porcelain cup at me once."

Wynter frowned. "What? Why?"

"He realized I'd poisoned the tea he just drank."

"Huh," said Anabel. "It's not entirely surprising that he threw the cup, then."

"No, I suppose not," said Hattie.

Anabel jumped as a scream came from the speakers. "Jesus *Christ* my heart can't take this."

Wynter felt her mouth twitch. The music might be loud, but it wasn't always loud enough to muffle the sound effects of caskets creaking open, owls hooting, wolves howling, voices screaming, and the wind moaning. In general, Anabel possessed a nervous disposition, so the freaky sounds were easily getting her all worked up.

"Hey, Wyn, your man has arrived," Delilah announced.

Wynter tracked the Latina's gaze, and her stomach fluttered at the sight of the tall, lean figure of male perfection heading their way. Hooded eyes that were a striking lustrous black locked on her. A pleasant little shiver worked its way through her.

She vaguely registered that another Ancient, Azazel, was with him. Wynter only had eyes for Cain. His intense, unblinking, laser-focused stare made her think of a snake. So she hadn't found it terribly surprising to learn that Ancients were in fact serpentine creatures—another thing that very few people knew. Sometimes, those eyes of his could look as empty as an open grave. Other times, they could be practically aflame with emotion.

Delilah let out a dreamy sigh. "Damn, Wyn, I know he's yours and everything . . . but I'm gonna look occasionally. Because he's *so* worth looking at."

It was truly ridiculous just how unbelievably sexy he was. There was something so decadently predatory about him. Wicked. Utterly sinful. There was an edge of raw danger to him that warned any in his path that they were looking at the penultimate alpha male.

Hattie leaned into Wynter. "Do you think we'd ever get him to be a butler in the buff?"

Oh, the woman didn't possess an ounce of shame. "No. No, I really don't."

Reaching Wynter, he boldly swallowed up her personal space, his lips canting up in a hint of a smile. "Evening, little witch," he said, his voice deep, rumbly, and carrying a note of authority—a note that intensified ten-fold in the bedroom.

"Well hello," she said, sliding a hand up his chest as she drank in the sight of him. A face so flawless should be somewhat annoying, but every single feature was a pleasure to behold. "I didn't think you were coming."

"You were taking too long to come to me. I missed you." He dropped a soft kiss on her mouth. "Enjoying yourself?"

"I am, yes." She let her fingers sift through his short hair. The strands were a deep, rich black that were impossibly dark in a very preternatural way. "I might even have a nice buzz going on, thanks to the drinks I've been knocking back. Don't tell anyone."

"Wouldn't dream of it." He looked down at the corset of her dress. "I have so many plans for what to do to you later while you're wearing this outfit."

She smiled. "Always happy to be an inspiration." Wynter went to say hello to Azazel, but his rich blue eyes were on Anabel.

"What's with the boils and warts?" he asked her.

Anabel cleared her throat. "I'm allergic to crowds."

He sent her a look that called her a liar. "You've been experimenting on yourself again, haven't you?"

"Wow, I'm failing to see how that's your business," Anabel sassed. "And stop talking to me. Why do you always talk to me?"

Azazel shrugged. "I like to make people feel uncomfortable. You're an easy target."

The blonde blinked. "At least you're honest."

Xavier turned to Azazel. "Yeah, what's that like?"

Cain put his mouth to Wynter's ear. "I thought you said Hattie would be wearing a scary nun habit."

"She told me she would be," said Wynter. "I have to admit, I got nervous when she walked into the living room wearing that wedding dress. But she's promised me she doesn't intend to go marry George or even drag him into a handfasting. As long as there's no such union, he's safe from her black widow inclinations."

Cain hummed, sliding a hand down Wynter's back to rest just above the swell of her ass. "How long before I get to whisk you out of here? I want you to myself."

"You want me naked."

"That, too," he admitted without apology. "First, though, I mean to hike that gown up around your waist and fuck you hard. Can't do that here." His eyes blazed with possession. "I don't want anyone else seeing or hearing you come."

Really, the dude was far more territorial than she would have thought he had the potential to be. Ancients just seemed so unmoved by so many things. Which would be natural if you'd been around since the beginning of time and there was little you hadn't seen, done, or heard.

She hadn't expected that the one night she shared with Cain would turn into a relationship, or that he'd one day grow to care for her. He hadn't ever given her those three little words, but she didn't need them. All she needed was—

A loud booming sound came from outside the warehouse and seemed to reverberate in the air.

Wynter jerked her head back. "Was that thunder?" It *sounded* like it, yet it seemed too close, and there'd been no build up.

"Yes." Cain exchanged an odd look with Azazel. "But I don't believe it's a natural thunder."

"What, why not?" Wynter frowned as the two Ancients headed for the exit. "Hey, wait!" She trailed after them, signaling for her coven to come along.

"What's happening?" asked Xavier.

"No clue," replied Wynter as they shrugged through the crowd now surging toward the exit, no doubt curious about the ongoing cracks of thunder. "But I'm gonna find out."

Outside, she sidled up to Cain as she glanced up at the sky. Her mouth fell open. "What in the ..." A cloud had formed, a face flickering within it like a static holographic image. A face Wynter recognized and would truly like to rearrange with a shovel someday. Her inner monster stirred, opening its eyes, not liking what it saw.

"D'you think it's God?" asked Hattie.

"No," replied Delilah. "I think we're looking at something *far* from holy."

11

Anabel grasped Wynter's hand. "So this is how we die."

Oh, for heaven's sake. "We're not going to die, and it's not God."

"Then who is it?" asked Xavier.

"People of Devil's Cradle," a booming voice crackled as the mouth of the face within the cloud moved. "For those who do not know me, I am Adam, the last ruling Aeon."

Anabel's eyes went wide. "Wait, he's here?"

"No," said Cain, though his gaze remained on the cloud. "Think of this as a news broadcast. We see him. He doesn't see us."

"I'm no doubt the last person you all wish to hear from," Adam went on, his voice both compassionate and reasonable, "but I did not trust that this message would reach you unless I delivered it personally. The Ancients tell you only what they want you to hear."

There was some truth in that. Actually, there was a lot of truth in that. But the Aeons were just as bad for only revealing what they wished to reveal, so . . .

"I do not want war," Adam added. "I never did, in truth. All I originally wanted was for the witch who cursed my land to be handed over to me. Simple. Easy. Fair."

He wouldn't know what fair was if it slapped him in the face and force-fed him a cracker.

"Imagine if your own town was rotting," he continued. "You would want the person responsible to undo their curse, would you not? It was all I asked; it was not unreasonable. But your leaders refused to surrender Wynter Dellavale to me, and so blood was spilled in your town. I want no more of that. Enough people have died on both sides, including my son." The latter word reverberated with anger and grief. "But I *will* bring pain and suffering to your town if my needs are not met—I want Cain and Wynter to surrender themselves to the custody of my people. If they do, everyone else will then be left alone."

Her stomach lurched. She looked up at Cain, but his eyes were fixed on the image in the sky.

"Until they appear at Aeon, I will punish the town of Devil's

Cradle itself at random times, and others will die," Adam went on. "You may wonder what I mean by that or how exactly I would achieve it. You will never have to find out if my terms are met. My offer is a kindness. Two individuals are not worth the lives of so many."

Wynter noticed in her peripheral vision that plenty of people were glancing her way. Hopefully they weren't contemplating doing as Adam requested. Because she'd otherwise have to kill them, and that would be a bummer.

"I do hope for your sake that Cain and the witch make the right choice," Adam went on. "But my feeling is that they will not, and so you may well have to take the matter into your own hands. I will pay one million dollars to anyone who delivers either Cain or the witch to me *alive*."

Son of a bitch.

"Give me both, and I will award you two million," Adam added. "Give me neither, and you will all pay for that mistake."

The image of Adam's face flickered and wavered. Eventually, it winked out, and then the cloud slowly dissipated.

Swiping a tongue over her lower lip, Wynter turned to Cain. "Well, this could be a problem."

Cain sighed. "Yes, yes it could."

Chapter Two

As the seven Ancients sat around Cain's dining table a short time later, he and Azazel relayed the incident that brought the night's celebration to a screeching halt. Cain kept his voice cool and calm, pushing down the rage that threatened to fog his thoughts. It was no easy thing when said rage relentlessly crawled through his blood and simmered low in his belly.

Beneath the table, he flexed his fingers. A bounty. Fucking Adam had put a bounty on Wynter's head. Again. Like once hadn't been enough.

Cain supposed he couldn't complain *too* much about the first bounty. After all, it had pushed her to seek sanctuary. It had brought her to Devil's Cradle, brought her to *him*. Cain could never lament that. Selfish, maybe, but he was often that way where his consort was concerned. She thankfully let it slide much of the time.

He wouldn't have imagined that he'd ever wish to claim a consort. But then, he never would have thought that anyone—man or woman—could make themselves indispensable to him. Wynter . . . she was vital to him. As necessary as breathing. Something he would never give up.

He'd been so numb before her. So detached from the world that he'd ceased to want things. Nothing had entertained, intrigued, or brought him any true satisfaction. Wynter had walked into his world, sliced through the listlessness, and settled into his life as easily as if it had been preordained.

He liked to believe that the latter was true. Liked to believe that she'd been made specifically for him. Because it often felt like she was.

She suited him in every imaginable way. She delighted his senses and appealed to him on every level. More, she enraptured his monster in such a way that its possessiveness of her wasn't shallow.

The creature didn't covet Wynter as if she was a pretty bauble. It *saw* her, recognized the witch as a person in her own right rather than a collectible item, and it coveted the entirety of her. Hence why it wanted to bind itself to her—something Cain hadn't yet run by Wynter. He had no idea if she'd go for it, but he had hope, given that she'd sold him all rights to her soul and given up her mortality for him. That depth of commitment was nothing to sniff at.

Even back when so many secrets had ran riot between them, they'd still gradually built something. Something true and solid and long-lasting. And, despite what he'd feared, the revelation of his own secrets hadn't destroyed what they'd built.

Wynter accepted him anyway. Accepted that, as a Leviathan, Cain was a gateway to hell for souls. Accepted the presence of his monster, despite that it was a thing of nightmares. More, she'd accepted that he was the only son of Satan—the darkest and most corrupt of the Leviathans who now dwelled in the depths of hell. Which wasn't exactly easy to digest, let alone make peace with. But Wynter hadn't pulled away from Cain for even a moment.

Really, she was a true marvel to him. He was quite certain there was no one like her. And not simply because she was far from a normal revenant.

It was fortunate that Adam had no clue just how important she was to Cain, or he would have placed an even bigger price on her head—one so high that it would have been all but irresistible to most who resided in Devil's Cradle. Because Adam wouldn't merely plan to use her to lift the curse on Aeon, he'd plan to torture her until the end of time.

Of course, the bastard wouldn't find it so easy to keep her contained. The deity who'd marked and regularly watched over her would never permit it. Kali would free her somehow if Wynter didn't manage to free herself. That brought Cain no real comfort, though.

15

Because the thought of her in Adam's custody for merely five minutes was too much to stomach. Especially when Cain would have no way to physically track and save her, courtesy of his fucking cage.

"I don't understand," Ishtar said to no one in particular, giving a slight shake of her head. "The things Adam said do not make much sense."

Cain's inner creature snarled at the sound of the Aeon's name. It didn't want to be there in that dining room with the Ancients. It wanted to be back in their bedchamber with Wynter, who'd agreed to wait for Cain there. His creature wanted access to the only thing that had the ability to calm it.

"What would be the point of putting a price on Cain's head?" Ishtar went on, her cornflower-blue eyes cloudy with confusion. "Adam knows that even if someone did miraculously manage to subdue Cain, there is no way they would get him out of Devil's Cradle—we are all trapped here."

"Yes, we are," said Azazel beside her. "But the majority of our residents don't know that, do they? In their eyes, Cain could easily give himself up to keep them safe. And when he doesn't, they may turn against him. I think that is what Adam hopes for. These people came to us for protection, after all. If they believe we're neglecting their safety, they may choose to leave. And if our population lessens, we'll have less manpower in the event of an attack."

Sitting on Cain's left, Dantalion gave a slow nod, an angry flush staining his bronze skin. Like Azazel, he was mistaken by humans for a demon. Perhaps it was due to the many dark tales about him, or maybe it was due to the danger and callousness that he so blatantly exuded. "It would seem that Adam has decided to play the long game. He means to ensure that we are vulnerable before he makes his move on us. And in the meantime, he intends to finally get a hold of Wynter."

"That won't happen," Cain stated firmly, and his creature rumbled a sound of agreement.

"I doubt the residents would expect you to surrender her to

Adam, given that we vow to never hand over those in our service to outsiders," said Dantalion, scraping a hand over his shadow of blond stubble. "*But . . . they might expect her* to make that sacrifice to protect the town. And when she instead stays here, they may not be happy with her."

"Then we'll have to make it clear to everyone that the town wouldn't actually be safer if any of Adam's terms were met," said Cain. "We can explain the situation. Or most of it. They'll place more weight in our words than they ever will in that of an Aeon."

Given that Ishtar would truly love nothing more than to have Wynter out of the picture, Cain expected his mouthy, jealousy-ridden, ex-lover to suggest that his consort give herself up. But Ishtar stayed suspiciously silent on the matter, absently playing with her blonde curls.

Maybe the hand her sister had placed on her arm was what kept her quiet. Or just maybe he'd finally gotten through to her that Wynter was here to stay, but that was probably wishful thinking on his part. It seemed more likely that Ishtar was merely biting her tongue *for now*. Perhaps because she sensed just how furious Cain was due to the threat now hovering over his woman.

"Even so, the price on Wynter's head *will* be a problem," said Azazel, folding his arms. "You need to be prepared for that, Cain. No one will try to cash in on the bounty that Adam put on you—they won't go up against an Ancient. But a revenant that they're not truly convinced is a revenant? Some might decide to accept Adam's offer and take her to him. At the very least, they'll be tempted."

Directly opposite Cain, Lilith nodded, making strands of her long red hair tumble forward. "Her being your consort will make people hesitate. But there are some who will be both stupid and greedy enough to consider cashing in on the bounty."

Under no illusions about the people who resided at Devil's Cradle, Cain was quite aware of that. There were plenty of criminals and dark-natured characters here who'd done far worse things than snatch and hand over a witch to claim a reward.

Cain forced his back teeth to unlock. "If anyone tries it, they'll die. She's more powerful than any of them realize."

"Yes," began Lilith, "but if she's killing people left, right, and center—even in her own defense—it might create resentment among the residents. Many belong to packs, covens, conclaves, and fey courts, etc. They wouldn't take kindly to losing members of whatever their group might be."

Wynter didn't kill for shits and giggles. Her monster, though? Well, that was a whole other story. It *ate* people left, right, and center. Hence why his inner creature found the monster so intriguing and wanted to "meet" it. Which would be a bad idea since, according to Wynter, the thing that lived inside her wanted only to kill—something it would do indiscriminately.

"I want to make something very clear," said Cain, sweeping his gaze over every person seated at the table. "If my consort is attacked by any of your people and forced to kill them in her own defense, there will be no repercussions for her." Generally, it was ruled that no resident could kill another unless either it was a matter of self-defense or they had the permission of the Ancient who owned the person they wished to execute.

Azazel flapped a hand. "That goes without saying."

The others at the table echoed the sentiment and assured Cain that Wynter would face no ramifications in such an event—even Ishtar.

Lilith sat back as she exhaled heavily, her green eyes glimmering with annoyance. "I knew there was a chance that Adam would hesitate to immediately go to war, given that the other attempts to wipe us out by Aeons were unsuccessful. I knew he might well feel the need to be cautious and so take a little time to gather his forces. But I'd counted on him being so filled with the need for vengeance that he would be helpless to do anything but ignore common sense and immediately wage war on us."

"Of course you did," said Dantalion. "We all did. Why would we not have, considering we sent Abel's hacked-up body back to him?" He thrust a hand through his short blond hair.

Seth shifted in his seat on Cain's right, his amber eyes narrowed in thought. "I feel like we're missing something."

"In what sense?" asked Inanna, the older sister of Ishtar, speaking for the first time. The siblings looked much alike, only Inanna's hair was sleek and straight rather than curled, and she didn't have Ishtar's pointed chin. Inanna also possessed a poise and elegance that her sister lacked. Ishtar was more sensual and sultry, considering herself to be the ultimate seductress. "What troubles you?" Inanna prodded.

Seth replied, "Adam has essentially prioritized getting his hands on Wynter. Someone as prideful, arrogant, and bloodthirsty as he is doesn't just *table* vengeance so easily."

"No, they don't," agreed Cain. The Aeon was good at controlling his emotions, but not when it came to wounded pride. His self-restraint often then went out the window. Adam's ego was a fragile thing. "Vengeance has to be a drumbeat in his blood right now. He'll want me dead more than he ever did before. Adam has lost the prominent members of his family in one way or another, and he'll blame me for each of those losses."

Seth's brows lifted, his expression going pensive. "Ah, yes. He lost me when I sided with you. He lost our sisters when they died during the first war—it won't matter that the Aeons launched the attack, he'll tell himself that there would have been no need for war if it hadn't been necessary to eradicate you. Although he emotionally lost Eve a millennia ago, he lost her physically when she came here for sanctuary recently with Abel's twins. To add to all that, Adam then lost Abel when you killed him during the last battle. Adam will for sure hold you accountable for all his 'suffering.'"

"The latter loss will be the one he feels the hardest," said Cain. "Abel stroked his ego by wanting to be like him, by striving to please him, by being under his complete control until that last moment when he went against Adam's orders and came for us."

"Which will be another thing that Adam likely blames you for." Seth sighed, stroking a hand over his blond layered buzzcut. "You always were his favorite scapegoat. But despite all he'll be feeling, he's temporarily settling for turning our people against you in the hope of lessening our numbers. I truly do feel like we're missing something."

Poking his tongue into the inside of his cheek, Azazel looked at Seth. "You said that Adam's prioritizing getting his hands on Wynter. That's not entirely accurate. He's prioritizing lifting the curse on Aeon. We have to wonder why." He paused. "I couldn't get Saul to confess why it was that he believed it essential that Aeon didn't fall. But he swore it must not happen."

"I can't imagine that Eden is once again using the underground city as her Resting place," said Dantalion, referring to God's consort. "I don't see what else would make it special."

"I, too, struggle to see why the fall of Aeon would be such a dire event," said Azazel, scratching at the back of his head, making strands of his short dark hair spike up. "But maybe there really is some great reason why the Aeons believe it can't happen. And just maybe that's why Adam is willing to put the wellbeing of Aeon before seeking vengeance."

"Or," began Ishtar, "maybe Adam simply insinuates to the other Aeons that the place must not fall so that they will not want to leave; so that they will believe there is a purpose to staying there—it is probably how he got them to stay for so long. Well, *that* and telling them that the rest of the world is a terrible place. But, really, what difference does it make? He is clearly going to make us wait, and there is absolutely nothing we can do about it. We are stuck here, and that is that."

"You know, I've been thinking," said Seth. "Three of the Aeons who caged us are dead. The cage will have weakened. Not enough for us to shatter it, but maybe we could at least punch a hole through it. A hole big enough for us to exit through."

Ishtar slid him a bored look. "That is a very nice thought, but it will not work."

"You don't know that," said Seth. "We haven't tried. We won't know unless we do."

"Three of our jailors might be dead, but their power is still incorporated into the prison," Ishtar reminded him.

"Yes," Seth allowed. "But it's no longer so potent now that they're in the afterlife."

"It does not matter. Until Adam too dies, the walls of the cage will remain strong. The Aeons used our blood to power it, remember? It was the only way they could seal it."

"But they didn't use Abaddon's blood, since they didn't believe he would live," said Seth, speaking of Cain's uncle—an Ancient who, unknown to most, lay at Rest in Cain's garden. "He could potentially open it. With our help, that is."

Ishtar's brow creased. "Are you forgetting that he is in some sort of coma?"

"No. But we could try waking him, couldn't we? We never did before, because there didn't seem much point when he would likely lose his shit at being confined."

Who wouldn't when, for them, it was only yesterday that their children and brothers were slaughtered in a war? "He wouldn't be so furious if he woke to hear that three of our jailors are dead," Cain mused.

"But he *would* be if we didn't manage to form a crack in the cage," said Ishtar. "Which we will not."

"Don't be so sure," said Seth. "All Hallows' Eve is coming up. Our power will be stronger then. Always is. We could take advantage of that and try to pierce our prison on that very night. If we have Abaddon's aid, I think it could work."

Cain pursed his lips. "It's certainly worth a try." Especially since *someone* had repeatedly called out to Wynter in her sleep and led her in the direction of the temple where Abaddon rested. Cain and Azazel had speculated that, even in sleep, Abaddon could be somewhat aware of the goings-on around him. If that was true, he might not be so hard to wake.

As if recalling their speculations, Azazel caught Cain's eye and nodded. "I agree."

Seth gave both Cain and Azazel a look of gratitude for taking him seriously. "It might pay to have Eve and the twins add their power to ours—they're Aeons, after all. Strong. And each of them has a blood-link to either one or two of our jailors."

They did indeed. The twins were actually fathered by none other than Abel. They'd helped Eve flee to Devil's Cradle after learning that—in an effort to provoke Cain and throw him off his game—Adam had planned to kill her and then dump her body on the border of the town.

"Their contribution could therefore be truly helpful," Seth added.

Ishtar gave him a look that called him slow on the uptake. "If they are here on behalf of Adam they are hardly going to aid us in such a way."

"But they might not be here on his orders," Seth pointed out. "We all recently agreed that they are likely not, remember. They certainly weren't here on Abel's behalf—he was prepared to see them dead."

Ishtar let out a haughty sound. "I am still not inclined to trust them."

"I'm not suggesting that we should." Seth spoke to everyone as he continued, "But consider that they've made no move against anyone since coming here. They also didn't take advantage of our distraction during the battle with Abel to pull any kind of stunt. We all agreed to allow them to come and go from my Keep as they pleased because we wanted to see what they would do with their freedom. My people tell me that they haven't done anything that could be considered remotely suspicious."

Cain's hirelings had reported the latter as well. The Aeons, unbeknown to them, were being closely and covertly watched by the hirelings of various Ancients.

Lilith absently doodled circles on the table with her fingertip. "According to my aide, they only venture out when they wish to go shopping. They haven't tried squeezing information out of residents. They haven't tried getting near Wynter's cottage. Nor have they tried to sneak into Keeps or go nose around the manor."

Dantalion sank deeper into his seat. "My hirelings said the same."

"As did mine," Ishtar snippily admitted, "but I am still not ready to trust the Aeons."

Seth's eyelid twitched. "As I said, I'm not asking you to."

"Assuming they are here with no ulterior motive, would they agree to be of assistance in this matter, Seth?" asked Inanna. "They were not happy that we once considered them suspects when it became clear we had a traitor in our midst. And we have not exactly made an effort to right that wrong."

"Eve will offer her aid," said Seth with utter surety. "She doesn't hold what we did against us. She's seen enough of what we suffered at the hands of other Aeons to understand why we had assumed another betrayed us."

"What about Noah?" asked Dantalion, referring to Abel's son.

Seth hesitated. "He's practical enough to understand why he came under suspicion but still appears hurt by it. I don't know if he would be willing to help. As for his sister . . . She's holding our distrust against us, unwilling to see why she might have once been a suspect—Rima has a chip on her shoulder."

"Then the siblings are not likely to do us any grand favors." Inanna cut her gaze to Cain. "It might help matters if you appear to lower your guard around them. Eve desperately wants your trust, and I believe that the twins would also be responsive to it."

"I've visited them a number of times at Seth's Keep." Given that Eve had been out of his life since the day he and the other Ancients were first caged, it was still strange for Cain to have her around. She'd been clear that she wanted to "rebuild" her relationship with him. Really, though, they'd never had one—Adam saw to that.

"But that is not an indicator of trust." Inanna paused. "Unless . . . did you take your consort with you?"

"No." Although Cain had come to believe that the Aeons likely had no ulterior motives for seeking sanctuary here, he wasn't confident enough in that belief to allow them near his consort. He'd made it clear to the aides watching them that they should intervene if any of the trio attempted to approach her.

"I know you are highly protective of your consort," began Inanna, "and I can understand why you would wish to keep her away from the Aeons. But introducing her to them would go a long way to soothing any insult they feel. They would see it as a gesture that you are coming to accept and trust them; that you view them as family. They would then be more likely to help us escape this prison. And that is our ultimate goal, is it not?"

Ultimate goal or not, Cain felt absolutely no urge to introduce his consort to the Aeons. "I can smooth things over with them myself. I don't need to pull Wynter into it."

Dantalion snorted. "You have plenty of charisma, Cain. But they will be suspicious if you abruptly train it on them or act any differently. Inanna has the right of it—you need to appear to be lowering your guard around them. Actions speak louder than words, as the saying goes. Allowing them to officially meet your consort—"

"We might not need their help," Cain clipped.

"But it's possible that we will." Azazel raised his hands. "Look, I don't trust them around Wynter any more than you do. But if we are to pierce the prison, we need to take advantage of All Hallows' Eve. That means we have one shot—this year, at least. I would prefer that the Aeons are there when we act. And think of it this way: We all want to know if they are here on Adam's orders. If they agree to aid us in escaping this prison, it will tell us that they are not—he would never under any circumstances wish us to be free."

Sighing, Cain swiped a hand down his face. Before he could respond to Azazel's comment, Seth turned to him and spoke.

"You, Wynter, the Aeons, and I could all have dinner at my Keep tomorrow evening," Seth suggested. "Wynter would be safe, Cain. If anyone was going to make a try for her, it wouldn't be while you and I were present, would it?"

"And she's not exactly helpless, is she?" Dantalion tacked on. "Can you honestly say, hand on heart, that you believe introducing her to them at Seth's Keep during what will seem like a family dinner could lead to an attack on her life?"

In truth, the more Cain had spoken to and observed Eve, the more he'd come to trust his gut instinct that she meant Wynter no harm. He wasn't so sure about the twins yet, though. He was certain of one thing—Seth was right; they wouldn't dare make a move on her while two Ancients were present.

Cain would still much rather skip the introduction altogether. But it *would* be a gesture that'd help settle any ruffled feathers. And if the Aeons agreed to help, it *would* finally prove once and for all if they were here for Adam or not. Cain would rather know for sure if they were a danger to his consort.

"I'll talk to Wynter," Cain told Seth. "If she's willing to meet with them, we'll go ahead with that dinner you mentioned. I doubt she'll object."

Ishtar examined her nails. "The help of the Aeons will not be enough to fracture our prison. We will need Abaddon if we have any real hope of accomplishing it. Personally, I doubt we will manage to wake him."

"We have nothing to lose by trying," Dantalion pointed out.

Ishtar folded her arms. "And if Abaddon does wake and we do manage to fracture the cage, then what?"

Cain looked at her. "Then we take the war to Aeon, and we destroy every inch of the fucking place."

Chapter Three

Walking into his bedchamber shortly after the meeting, Cain saw that the crimson drapes had been drawn, and the candles around the room were all lit. Just as she often did, his little witch had curled up on the armchair with a paperback in hand, completely relaxed ... as if the last ruling Aeon hadn't just put a price on her head. Typical. Much like her coven members, nothing daunted her for long—if at all.

The tension slipped from his shoulders as he drank her in. His woman. So beautiful. Deadly. Confident. Powerful. Fierce. It was a devastating combination that delighted both him and his monster. She was their own personal catnip.

Some people around the town were put-off by her magick being dark. For Cain, it was a draw. Darkness was familiar to him. Comforting. Even enthralling.

In any case, he would never be repelled by anything about Wynter, but he understood why the tone of her magick would make some people nervous. Not everyone could handle darkness. They tended to shy away from it.

Luckily for him, Wynter wasn't one of those people or she'd have attempted to leave him by now. Since he had no intention of allowing that, it was truly a good thing she hadn't tried. The scene wouldn't have played out well.

Her thickly lashed quicksilver eyes lifted to Cain, and she studied him carefully. "You're not feeling any calmer, huh?"

He raised a brow. "Did you think I would?"

She set her book down on the armrest, and then her slender form uncurled from the chair. "A girl can hope." Wearing only one of his tees—and possibly her panties, he couldn't quite tell—she strode toward him, so feline and stealthy and fluid. Wynter never took tentative steps. She was always sure of herself, of her movements, of where she needed to be.

Reaching him, she looped her arms around his waist and pressed a kiss to his throat. Cain slid his own arms around her shoulders and nuzzled her neck, breathing her in. That staggeringly feminine scent that was *all* Wynter rushed into his system, along with the addictive smell of her magick. *Jasmine and black pepper.*

"I can feel how worked up you are," she said. "I don't like it. I don't want Adam to have any hold over your emotions like this."

What did she expect? Lifting his head, he met her gaze. "In case you've forgotten, he put a bounty on you."

"And on you." Fury flared in her eyes. "Are you *sure* you don't want me to kill him for you? Because it'd be my total fucking pleasure."

Cain's chest squeezed. *For you*, she'd said. It wasn't the price on *her* head that most angered her. No, it was the bounty on his. She was as protective of him as he was of her.

And she loved him.

It was something he savored even as the surprise of it left him feeling off-balance. He didn't know how she could possibly feel that depth of emotional devotion for him; how she couldn't be repulsed by the reality of what he was, what he could do, and how he came to be born.

But then, Wynter knew what it was to be different, to be unnatural, and to have to hide parts of yourself from everyone around you. She was more accepting than anyone he'd ever met.

He wanted to be able to claim he loved her in return—she deserved to have those words from him. But he didn't believe he'd felt the emotion since he was a child. He couldn't recall *how* it felt. The ability to experience it as an adult eluded Cain somehow. He resented that, even though Wynter gave no indication that it mattered much to her.

"Obliterating the bastard would be my pleasure as well," he told her. "But I promised my monster that it could finish Adam. It's holding me to that promise."

She let out a petulant grunt, like a child being deprived of its favorite form of downtime—which, for Wynter, was wreaking vengeance. She looked so fucking cute right then, all sullen and dour, that he couldn't help but nip the juicy swell of her heavy lower lip.

Generally, Cain didn't find people "cute". But he supposed it would be fair to say that he didn't notice others on the same level that he did Wynter. He wasn't "moved" by them as he was her—only she had that influence on him.

He didn't know how to describe what he felt for her. It wasn't soft. Wasn't sweet. Wasn't fluffy. It was more like a dark storm that raged inside him.

She was so much more than the addiction she'd once been. She was no longer a simple obsession. She was ... everything. There would never be any walking away from her. She might not have official rights to his soul the way he did hers, but she owned him just the same. And he point-blank refused to lose her.

"From here on out, you need to be exceedingly careful, Wynter. Some people will be tempted by Adam's offer. A million dollars is a lot of money." Cain cuffed her arm with his hand and looked down at the seal on her wrist that branded her his consort. "I'm not sure if even this symbolic reminder that you are not to be touched will be enough to keep you safe from any residents who think to cash in on the bounty."

She sighed. "I know. Especially since Adam made out like he only wanted me to undo the widespread decay. There'll be people who tell themselves, *hey, it wouldn't be so bad if we did it because it's not like the Aeon means her any harm.*"

"Which is why I plan to give a speech to the residents tomorrow. I'll make it clear that Adam means us *all* harm."

She gave a sharp nod. "Good idea."

"You should know that I intend to put guards on you."

"Yeah, that's not gonna happen."

He felt his face tighten. "Wynter—"

"No, hear me out," she said, raising her hand. "If I was up against an Aeon here in Devil's Cradle, I'd agree to it, just as I did when Saul wanted to get to me. But this is different. Adam is nowhere near me. And putting guards on me would send the wrong message."

"It would send the message that you're under my protection. How is that 'wrong'?"

Wynter shot him a look. Her Ancient was not dumb. In fact, he was ace at strategy. So either he was purposely being obtuse here, or his overprotectiveness was clouding his judgment. "Because it would communicate that you don't trust in my ability to protect myself. That would only embolden anyone thinking of accepting Adam's offer."

Cain clamped his lips shut. He clearly wanted to argue. Badly.

Before he had time to formulate a bullshit protest, she continued, "It would also make people wonder if just maybe those who doubt I'm a revenant are actually right to have such doubts. I can't prove that I am a revenant without showing everyone my monster. That's not something I can do as it would attempt to kill the nearest people just because it can. So I need to send the message that I don't need protection from them."

"It might not be enough."

"No, it mightn't," she reluctantly conceded. "Someone might still make a try for me. They'd dramatically fail. And then I'd send a whole other message."

He gave her a look that said, "I'm listening".

"Revenants are something to fear. Fear is what will encourage people to leave me be. Not guards. Not threats. The best way to ensure that no one fucks with me is to let others see what happens when people do."

Cursing beneath his breath, he tipped his head back.

She couldn't blame him for wanting to do things *his* way. He'd never had anyone in his life who it would severely pain him to lose.

He didn't always handle that well; it sometimes skewed his thought processes.

If having guards would truly help her, Wynter would agree to it even if only to give him piece of mind. She didn't like it when he was all knotted up inside. But she genuinely didn't believe that his approach to the situation was the answer, so she wasn't going to back down simply to make him feel better. It would come back to bite them both on the ass.

She hugged him a little tighter for a brief moment. "Besides, would you truly trust that any guards you appointed wouldn't think to try to take me to Adam?"

Cain let out a long breath. "No," he admitted after a few moments, his gaze once more locking with hers. "The only person I wholeheartedly trust is you."

She felt her expression soften. "Then trust me on this. You know I'm right. It's not like *you'll* appoint yourself guards, is it?"

"I'm an Ancient."

"But not invincible. *I* could end you."

His lips canted. "I know. I like it."

"God, you're so disturbed."

"Probably." He didn't seem all that concerned about it.

She rolled her eyes. "On a whole other note, how did your meeting with the other Ancients go?"

He absently played with her hair as he gave her a brief rundown of the conversation.

Her interest seriously piqued, she asked, "Do you think you really have a chance of piercing the cage?"

"If we have Abaddon's help, yes. Without him? Not so much."

"How difficult will it be to wake him?"

"If he's the one who keeps leading you to the garden while you're sleeping, perhaps not so difficult."

She bit the inside of her cheek. It was still strange to think that the male voice she'd heard in her dreams could have been not only real but his uncle. "When are you going to try?"

"Tomorrow evening."

"Alone, or with the other Ancients?"

"All seven of us will try as a unit. It may take several attempts to pull him completely out of sleep. It may even be something that takes days or weeks. On the other hand, it might not work at all, but I don't wish to dwell on that."

She hummed as he nuzzled her neck again, his nose brushing her skin, his lips grazing her pulse. "Seth's idea to try punching a hole through the cage on All Hallows' Eve is a good one. Especially since there'll be a blood moon then. I'm totally up for meeting Eve and the twins. I think the other Ancients are right, it would help smooth things over." And she was interested in observing them, in making her own judgments about them. "I agree with Seth, I think Eve will definitely want to help puncture your cage."

"Maybe. But I'm not so sure that either Noah or Rima will." Cain captured her gaze. "Never let your guard down around Eve or the twins, no matter how innocent you believe them to be."

"I wasn't planning to. So, when am I supposed to meet them?"

"We will all have dinner together at Seth's Keep tomorrow evening. Why are you pulling that face?"

"I get the feeling it'll be a fancy affair. I'm not fancy. I don't know dinner etiquette. I can wave a sword around and impale people and all that jazz. But sit up straight, put a napkin on my lap, and make sure not to pick up the wrong fork? I just get uncomfortable."

His consort was so competent and self-assured that there were times Cain forgot that, like everyone else, she occasionally felt out of her element. "Seth is old-fashioned in many ways, so he'll likely aim for 'tasteful.' But that doesn't mean you won't *fit* in that environment. And fuck etiquette. No one will care what you do with your napkin, what fork you use, or if you slouch in your seat."

"I know, but I'll still feel out of place among all that elegance and shit."

"You have your own grace—it's predatory in nature, and it makes my dick hard."

She snorted, humor lighting her eyes.

Cain caught her face in his hands. "You won't be out of place. Your place is with me. And trust me, there is nowhere you could go where you wouldn't fit; where you'd appear to 'lack' compared to others—you're perfect as you are."

He stroked her prominent cheekbones with his thumbs. He loved to look at her. Loved knowing that this stunning face would never physically alter; that she was frozen on a cellular level and he wouldn't lose her to the aging process. Watching her age and wither away . . . no, he couldn't have handled that.

Immortality had changed her. She was stronger, faster, more durable, boasted better reflexes, and healed faster—it was all part of the package. But she'd changed in other ways too. Power sometimes thickened her voice, which never failed to make his inner creature stir in delight. The hum of dark, chaotic magick surrounding her now held a static quality, as if amped up and eager to be released. And her predatory air was so much more apparent, more threatening.

He doubted she could ever again pose as harmless and submissive the way she had when they first met. He hadn't bought her act. His gut had warned him that there was much more to this witch, and it had been correct. Wynter had been hiding plenty from him but, bit by bit, she'd revealed many of her secrets.

There were few secrets left between them now. She'd had to withhold some things at Kali's insistence. He didn't blame Wynter for that, but he didn't like it much. More, he didn't like that he had no idea what the deity wanted with or from her.

In creating a revenant that could age, live as a normal person, and return from the dead over and over, Kali had gone *far* off-script. She'd essentially shaped Wynter into a weapon, an instrument of vengeance, and his gut twisted each time he found himself wondering just what Kali would one day ask of his witch.

Cain slid his hands from Wynter's face into her hair. Black as a crow's wing, it was soft and long and shiny. A pleasure to fist while he moved in and out of her. "When are you going to move your things here?"

She blinked, seemingly taken off-guard by the abrupt change of subject. "Some of my things *are* here."

"Only the bits and pieces you'll need for staying overnight on a regular basis. I want you to officially move in with me. You said you would. We held off for a while to give you and your coven enough time to properly settle here. Well, they're settled. So are you."

"I know. And I'll move into the Keep soon, I swear."

"So you've repeatedly said. But you're procrastinating."

Wynter opened her mouth to object but it would have been a lie. Generally, she wasn't one to procrastinate. Once she made a decision, she forged on ahead and made shit happen. But in this instance, she felt so torn. She wanted to move in with Cain, but . . . "My coven is still so new. The thought of moving out and leaving them alone like that still makes me feel like I'll be neglecting them."

"Most covens don't live together in one house," he patiently pointed out. Well, of course he was patient; he probably had no doubts that he wouldn't get his way eventually.

"I dread what they'll get up to without my supervision." The four of them were mentally unstable in one way or another. Correction, in *several* ways. Sometimes, she was honestly wowed that they'd lived this long.

"You moving in here wouldn't mean they'd be without your direct supervision. You'd see them as much as you do now, since you'll still need to go to the cottage every day to work. Things won't really be any different for you or for them than they are at the moment, except that you'll hopefully agree to have dinner here more often rather than always eating with your coven at the cottage. I'd offer for them to move into the Keep so you'd have them close, but I doubt they'd accept."

"They'd appreciate the offer, but they wouldn't accept. They love that cottage. But thank you for being prepared to make the offer." She dabbed a soft kiss on Cain's decadently carnal—and it had to be said, highly skilled—mouth. "I'll move my possessions here a little at a time, okay? The slow transition will make it easier."

Releasing her hair, he dropped his hands to her hips and gave them a little squeeze. "For you or for them?" he teased, his mouth hitching up. "Is separation anxiety kicking in?"

She narrowed her eyes and poked his shoulder. "Hey, *you* try being responsible for four highly unhinged people and then tell me how simple it is to leave them unsupervised for long periods. I'm genuinely surprised that they haven't gotten themselves executed yet."

His smile widened. "I must admit, I share in that surprise." He slipped his hands beneath the long tee she wore to cup her ass, his fingertips tracing the lacy edge of her black panties.

"Oh, and when I do fully move in here, you can't complain about all the witchy stuff like crystals and plants that will be set around this ever so masculine room." It wouldn't look so masculine, then.

"Why would I complain about being surrounded by things that represent who and what you are?" He sobered. "Be honest. Are you reluctant to take this step? To live with me?"

She felt her brows snap together. "No, of course not. I'm sorry if I've made you feel that way. I'm not leery of taking *any* step with you. Surely the seal on my wrist proves that."

He only twisted his mouth.

She fisted his shirt, giving him a severe stare. "I'm one hundred percent committed to you. To what we have."

"I know that."

She tilted her head. "You don't look all that pleased about it."

"I'm far more than pleased, I assure you."

"Then why did you frown?"

He sighed. "Because my monster is jealous."

She double-blinked, confused. "I'm sorry?"

"It wants you to be just as committed to it as you are to me. That sounds petulant, I suppose, but my creature is very attached to you."

Wynter figured she should probably find that disconcerting, given how very nightmarish his creature was. Instead, she was kind of touched. Well, she was weird like that.

She bit her lip. "Okay. Well. I don't want it to feel left out. Or jealous. But I don't see what I can do to make it feel better."

He let out a low hum. "There is something you could do."

Something about his tone made her skin prickle. "What?"

"My creature wants to bind itself to you."

Wynter felt her nose wrinkle. "That sounds very . . . permanent." A memory tickled her. "You mentioned something about this before. You said it would be a way to stop me from aging but that it would be too dangerous for me."

"A mortal wouldn't have survived my creature's bite. That doesn't apply to you anymore." His gaze sharpened. "And the binding *would* be permanent. Everything about us is permanent."

She rolled her eyes at the note of warning in his voice. "Like I didn't already know and, what's more, *agree* to that." Meaning to fold her arms, she went to take a step back, but the hands on her ass held her tight to him. "Now, what would it mean for me to bind myself to your creature?"

"It would mean that your life-forces would be tied."

"Tied? But wouldn't that make your creature vulnerable? It would die if I died, right? *You* would die." Her stomach lurched at the thought.

"It doesn't quite work that way. A soul is the core of a person. Their life-force is the energy that the soul generates. When a person's body dies, their soul moves on, along with their life-force. The latter doesn't die. As the soul remolds parts of itself for rebirth—like in the netherworld, where it's beaten down to be purified—its life-force also transmutes right along with it, until it becomes a different energy."

"Okay," she said.

"As such, if you died, your life-force and that of my monster would remain intertwined. The break would only occur if your soul and life-force altered for rebirth. Which wouldn't happen, since Kali would only send you back."

"But what if She didn't? What if, for some reason, I didn't come back and then my life-force altered? Then what?"

An intensity gathered behind his eyes. "Then I'd fucking find a way to rain fresh hell on Her."

Wynter barely resisted the urge to roll her eyes again. "Don't get all snarly, I'm not saying She wouldn't send me back." Though there was always a chance it could happen. Deities were unpredictable, to say the least. "I'm speaking of a hypothetical situation here. What would happen to your monster if I died for real?"

"It would feel immense physical pain. I would, in turn, be weakened by the severance of its link with you. But I wouldn't die. My creature and I would survive, and we would free your soul so that you could be reborn just as I promised you."

She narrowed her eyes. "Just how much would it weaken you?"

He hesitated. "I would likely have to Rest for a decade or so. But that would be for the best in any case."

"Why?"

"If I didn't, I would eventually begin to . . . mentally deteriorate."

"Go insane, you mean?"

He slowly dipped his head. "Wynter, both my monster and I would lose our sanity if we lost you irrespective of whether you were bound to my creature in some way or not. We need you. The only thing that would keep us going would be the knowledge that you were out there somewhere for us to find."

Which was sweet and all, but it didn't erase her concerns. "Would there be other consequences to your creature's life-force being tied to mine?"

Cain shook his head.

"Then I don't really get why your monster would be so keen on this. I mean, it gains nothing from it."

He tapped her nose gently. "Wrong. It will have the satisfaction of knowing you're committed to it. And . . ."

36

"And, what?"

"And you will carry its venom inside you. As you already know, my creature wants that. It resisted before now because if you had died you'd have returned fully healed and so its venom would no longer flow in your veins—the whole thing would have been for nothing. But now that you're immortal, you'd survive the bite. The venom would then live in your blood."

"So it's the venom that forms the binding?"

Cain dipped his chin. "Once it has been absorbed into your bloodstream three times, you and my monster would be forever tied."

"And how would you feel about that?"

His brows inched up. "What do you think?"

"I don't know. That's why I asked. You have very few vulnerabilities. Letting your creature entangle its life-force with mine would make it and, by extension, *you* vulnerable to an extent." She didn't like that part at all. "I don't want to ever be a weakness to you."

He pinned her gaze with his own. "You could *never* be anything but my greatest strength. As for how I'd feel about all this . . . I wouldn't have a single issue with it. I want you bound to me in as many ways as possible. I don't know if I'll ever feel that I own enough of you; that you're as tied to me as I need you to be."

She frowned. "You own my damn soul. Need I remind you of that?"

"Oh, pretty witch, it's not at all necessary to remind me of that—it's not something I would ever forget or take for granted. I treasure it, much as I treasure that you trust I'd never abuse that hold I have over your soul." No one else had ever had that level of faith in Cain; none had ever expected "good" things from him until Wynter.

"But?"

"There's no 'but'." Cain dropped a kiss onto the tip of her nose. "I just mean that, despite owning your soul, I very much like the thought of also being preternaturally tied to you." Wynter always felt slightly out of his reach due to her partly belonging to a deity.

Which was another reason why owning her soul satisfied him so thoroughly—his claim to her now ran deeper than Kali's ever could.

Also, it gave him a sense of security that he didn't like admitting he needed. But when you were the son of Satan, it surely wouldn't be so surprising that you didn't have complete faith in your ability to keep the people who mattered to you close.

"So you really want this, then?" she asked.

"I do." He wanted to know she accepted him to such an extent that she also wholeheartedly accepted his monster. She'd assured him that she did, and he wholeheartedly believed her. But her agreement on this would prove and cement it, and Cain found that he needed that.

Her brow flicked up. "And how much of that is because you'd then feel I was officially trapped in this relationship?"

Cain licked the inside of his lower lip. "I don't want you to ever feel 'trapped' with me but, as I said before, I want you bound to me in as many ways as possible."

"You think I might one day leave you?"

"Haven't we been over this before? You might try, but you'd only find yourself chained to my bed."

She gave him a droll look. "Ah, yes, I did forget that." Pausing, she twisted her mouth. "Was Lilith's consort bound to her creature before he died?"

"Yes. It would have allowed nothing less." When it came to Wynter, neither would Cain's own creature. And, not viewing itself *as* a monster, it didn't see why Wynter wouldn't agree to make such a commitment to it. But Cain did, so he added, "You don't need to make a decision now. Give it some thought. Can you do that for me?"

"Yes, I can do that."

"Good." He gave her a quick kiss. "Now let's shove aside all serious discussions so we can enjoy the rest of our evening."

"I'm absolutely up for that."

"Thought you might be." He let his gaze drop down her body.

She might only be dressed in a t-shirt and panties, but ... "You're wearing far too many clothes."

"You know, I was just gonna say the same to you."

"Hmm, well, I think we should both do something about this little situation."

She smiled. "You know what? Sometimes, it's like one mind."

"Strip for me. Slowly." He took a step back and folded his arms, expectant. "I want to take a good, long look at what's mine before I ravish you."

"Ravish, huh? Awesome. Because you're rather good at it."

"Why, thank you. Now strip." He narrowed his eyes when she swiftly whipped off the tee. "I said *slowly.*"

"Oh yeah, I forgot."

"Did you? Did you really?"

"No. No, not really." A slow grin curved her mouth. "Why, you gonna punish me?"

"I'm going to fucking defile you."

A delicious wariness flickered in her eyes, calling to the predator in him.

"Define 'defile'," she said.

He smiled. "I'd rather just show you."

Chapter Four

After eating breakfast with Cain the next morning, Wynter strode through the arched hallways of his Keep as she made her way to the exit. The tall, cylindrical building was seriously impressive. A fusion of the old and the new. It boasted many state-of-the-art features, but she was more wowed by the imperial staircases and domed, frescoed ceilings that made her think of cathedrals.

She was also a fan of the stained glass windows that came in different shapes and sizes. It was difficult to tell from the inside, but the Keep was constructed of black stone. The shimmer of magick embedded in said stones prevented the exterior from looking dull.

Wynter skimmed her eyes over one of her favorite paintings as she passed it. Cain had long ago told her that he was an avid collector, but she'd sensed that much from the display of rare books, artwork, and sculptures in his Keep. Of course, the fact that he'd been so intrigued at the thought of having rights to an undead soul also gave her a clue.

Exiting through the Keep's thick wooden doors, Wynter then walked through the bailey, passing several buildings such as the brewery, bakehouse, and stables. People hung around said buildings or stood in the courtyard, talking. The fine hairs on her body lifted at the odd looks some slid her way. Others avoided meeting her eyes altogether. Lovely.

Yeah, she'd figured that Adam's claims, threats, and very generous offers would garner her such attention. That asshole needed to have his insides ripped out.

Wynter notched up her chin and kept moving. She strolled through the arched opening in the stark walls that surrounded the Keep and bailey. Her home was thankfully only a short walk away.

Lots of residents were out and about, heading to work and getting stores ready to open. There was no denying that the medieval city was something to behold. Though it was modernized, there were no phones, no computers, no TVs. But that was part of what Wynter liked most about it. It wasn't so much a place of technology as a place of preternatural power.

Venice-style canals networked through the city. Each of the Ancients had their very own Keep, and all were sporadically dotted throughout the place. There were also many houses, and no two looked exactly alike. They came in all styles.

Some were rustic and whimsical, like magical country hideouts. Some held a fairytale feel, such as the very singular gingerbread house. Others were old fashioned, featuring wattle walls and timber frames. Some were cute and enchanting, much like the cottage that Wynter and her coven occupied. Beyond all the buildings were rivers, mounds, forests, and caverns.

Residents could shop at the stores, eateries, baileys, or the market near the town hall. Most people spent their downtime going horse-back riding, socializing at the taverns, or playing games such as golf and football in the large park.

Artificial sunlight shone down upon the city, but it didn't stem from the aqua blue stalactites that hung from the cavernous ceiling. It came from the combined power of the Ancients. Beneath the hustle and bustle noise were the artificial sounds of birds cheeping and the flapping of wings. The slight breeze was equally fake yet more than refreshing.

Simulating real-life, the sunlight would gradually fade and eventually be replaced by moonlight, just as the daytime sounds would be replaced by the hooting of owls and chirping of crickets. As such, one could easily forget that the city was underground.

Wynter walked along cobbled path after cobbled path, doing her best to ignore the looks being slanted her way, letting her gaze roam over the Halloween props outside each house—scarecrows, skeletons, ghosts, door wreaths. But some people so very rudely stared at her that there was no ignoring them. They were always the first to look away when she met such bold stares, though.

Striding down her street toward her home, she saw that many of her lycan neighbors were stood around. They didn't offer her odd glances or glares. They gave her nods or simple greetings. That was the thing about lycans, they were so territorial that they considered their closest neighbors under their protection, irrespective of whatever else might be happening. It was a comfort to know that none would be considering cashing in on the bounty. They'd instead be pissed about it on her behalf.

A relieved breath left her lungs as she finally reached the gate to her front yard. When she'd first seen the thatched-roof cottage from the outside, Wynter had thought it looked like a magical retreat. That "feel" had only deepened since the coven had added more and more personal touches to the exterior—hanging bells, garden gnomes, fairy castle sculptures, a wicca welcome mat, cauldron planters, and hanging baskets spilling with fern.

Of course, the current Halloween-y stuff only made it better. A row of witch hats bordered each side of the path. Synthetic cobwebs were attached to the doorframe. Pumpkins lay on straw either side of the doorstep. Fake ravens were dotted around the angular lattice windows. Hattie had rested some of the brooms from her very vast collection against the stone wall. And then there was Xavier's contribution—a hand holding a red apple that he'd stuck to the front door near the knocker.

Wynter unlocked and then pushed open the thick door, strangely comforted by the familiar scraping sound it made as it scuffed the floor. Hearing voices coming from the kitchen, she made her way through the living area, pausing to kick a rumple out of the Moon tarot card rug.

The cottage's interior was charming with its curved walls and wooden ceiling beams. Synthetic vines and maple leaf garlands were twined around the tree-trunk columns. A crescent moon mirror hung above the arched, brick fireplace. Pretty throw pillows adorned the plush sofa and single armchair. Triangular vases of fig and ivy hung from the walls.

A triple moon trunk sat beneath the corner altar, to which they'd recently added some symbols of late fall. So now skulls, pumpkins, acorns, and dried leaves sat with the athame, bell, candles, and cauldron.

The scents of coffee and freshly baked goods washed over her as she entered the kitchen. Xavier and Delilah sat at the barn wood dining table, empty plates in front of them. Hattie was pulling a loaf of bread out of the oven, humming to herself. Anabel stood at the counter sprinkling herbs into her cauldron; her tools and other jars of ingredients were close at hand.

They glanced Wynter's way with a smile and said brief hellos. Then, as one, they frowned.

"What's wrong?" Xavier asked her.

Wynter began to clear the table, stacking plates. "I don't much like that so many people felt the need to stare at me or look at me all weird just now."

He grunted. "Assholes."

"Some were probably simply wondering how willing you'd be to answer some questions about what Adam said last night during his little broadcast," said Hattie.

Wynter placed the dirty dishware in the sink. "Cain will be making a speech sometime this morning. He'll clear everything up."

"That's a good thing." Xavier stretched out his long legs beneath the table. "I hope he also makes it clear that people had better not dare try taking you to Adam."

She had no doubt that he would, but . . . "We all know some will be up for it. A million is a *lot* of cash."

Pushing out of her seat, Delilah let out a little growl. "I could honestly murder that son of a bitch."

43

Anabel slid Wynter a quick look. "From now on, you need to take healing potions with you wherever you go."

Wynter nodded. "Will do." Being immortal now, she was harder to injure, but she could still be gravely wounded.

"Want tea?" Delilah asked, rooting through the homemade mixtures in the cupboard near her cauldron, which was at the opposite end of the kitchen from Anabel's. "I was just about to make myself a cup—ooh, wrong tea balls. They're for pain relief."

Hattie smiled. "They have a nice 'kick' to them, don't they? I always feel all floaty after I drink those. Like I'm in subspace."

Wynter almost jerked back. "What do you know about sub—you know what, I don't want to know."

A wicked glint lit Hattie's eyes as she cackled. "No, you really don't."

"Anyways, it would appear that the lycans have my back, which is nice." And useful, because they made excellent backup and there were *two* packs on this street. That was a whole lot of claws and teeth.

Xavier snorted. "Lycans aren't nice."

Wynter sighed. "I thought Elias had stopped provoking you," she said, referring to the Alpha of one lycan pack.

"He has, but now the Beta of Diego's pack is being rude to me all the time."

Wynter felt her brow crease. "Why?"

"Stewart doesn't like that I had a one-night stand with a vampire."

"Well, you know how lycans feel about vamps." There was some bad history between the two species. "In Stewart's mind, since the lycans consider us 'theirs,' it was a betrayal on your part."

"*Not* my issue," said Xavier. "When I told him to stop being an asshole, he grinned and said he had way too much fun tormenting me. He won't be grinning by the time I'm done with him."

Wynter tensed. "What does that mean?"

"It means he'll be reminded that payback is a bitch."

Which would be fine, if Xavier's idea of payback didn't tend to be fatal. "Xavier—"

"Don't worry, I'm not going to take him out."

"*Or* invoke a demon and have them do your dirty work for you?"

He only scratched his jaw.

"For God's sake." Wynter plopped herself onto a seat with a weary sigh. With Xavier, disliking someone was *all* the reason he felt he needed to end their existence. Something she blamed on his previous coven, who had very few scruples. "You'll need to find another way to deal with the Beta. Not only because it's wrong—and no, I don't expect you to give much of a shit about that—but because you'd be executed for murdering him *unless* you can first gain permission to do it from the Ancient who partially owns Stewart's soul."

His lips pursed, Xavier nodded. "I can do that."

"*Without* lying that he's done a bunch of things he actually hasn't done."

"I wasn't gonna." He looked appropriately offended that she'd think otherwise.

Wynter snorted, not whatsoever fooled. Was it really any wonder that she hesitated to move out of the cottage when they were all a danger to themselves? On that subject ... "I should probably tell you that Cain is pushing me to move in with him soon."

"I'm not surprised, he's not a dude who'd be okay with his woman dragging her heels over something like this." Delilah handed her a steaming cup of tea. "You need to stop stalling."

Yes, she did. "You know why I am."

The Latina rolled her eyes. "It's not like we'll burn the cottage down without your supervision, *Mom*."

Flames erupted out of Anabel's cauldron, giving off a weird green smoke. Coughing, the blonde wafted her arm through the air. "Mother*fucker*." She emptied a vial of liquid over the flames, and they slowly died down.

Delilah cleared her throat. "If—no, *when*—you move out, you'll still be here as often as you are now."

Wynter sipped her tea. "That's pretty much what Cain said."

"And he's right." Delilah heaved her box of for-sale bespelled cosmetics out of the cupboard. "Look, you can keep your room here. Not that I think that things won't work out between you and Cain in the long run. It would just be a symbol that this is still your home. In spirit. If that makes sense."

"It doesn't," said Xavier.

Delilah threw him a dirty look. "I wasn't talking to you."

"Can't say I care." Xavier jolted in his seat. "Dammit." He shot a glare at thin air and rubbed at his nape. "One thing I don't like about this time of year is how active the spirits get. They can be seriously annoying at times."

Delilah used her hip to bump a cupboard door shut. "I still say we should hold a séance."

"Nu-uh," said Wynter, shaking her head.

"But it could be fun," said Delilah. "And Xavier's an expert at communing with the dead."

"Providing he has a corpse he can use as a conduit," Wynter reminded her. "I am so *totally* not going there."

"It's probably for the best that we don't," said Hattie, fussing with the little plant pots on the windowsill. "A lot of the spirits here seem angry and melancholy. Probably can't get a ticket out of hell. Poor bastards. I'll be heading there for sure myself."

"I wouldn't worry about that," Xavier told her. "Personally, I think the devil is gonna freaking dig you."

The old woman smiled. "Well thanks, darlin'."

Delilah turned to Wynter. "Back to the whole you moving out thing—" She stopped as Wynter raised a hand.

"I told Cain I'd move my stuff to his place little by little. And I will." As for whether or not she'd bond with his monster ... well, she didn't see any harm in it. But she needed a little more information before she made an official decision one way or the other.

"Good," said Delilah. "You shouldn't hold yourself back. Especially out of some cute but silly need to watch over us. We'll be fine."

A crackling sound filled the room as purple smoke ballooned out of Anabel's cauldron. The blonde hissed. "Motherfucking *fucker.*"

Wynter sighed. "If you say so, Del."

A blaring sound came from outside followed by a monotone voice announcing that Cain would be making a speech from the city's tallest tower in exactly thirty minutes.

"There's no point in us opening our shop yet, then," said Xavier.

Wynter nodded and took another sip of her tea. "We might as well wait until after the speech."

"It gives you time to go pack a few things to move to Cain's Keep later." Delilah gave her a pointed look, daring her to put up a protest.

Wynter sniffed. "Fine." Her mug in hand, she headed upstairs to her bedroom. Taking a good look at the space, she couldn't help but heave a sigh. Other than the books, raven bookends, and maybe the African violet plant, not one thing here would fit well in Cain's chamber. Still, she wouldn't leave any of it behind. Aside from the furniture, of course—it all came with the cottage.

Setting her cup on the nightstand, Wynter wandered over to the ancestor altar that she'd set up on the top of her dresser. She constructed the altar every fall to honor those she'd lost. It was a tradition most witches followed.

This time, she'd used a red cloth that looked much like the one she'd left behind at Aeon when forced to go on the run. Normally, she would have placed photos and belongings of her deceased loved ones on the altar, but she'd had to leave those behind as well. Instead, she'd drawn pictures of them—they weren't fabulous, but they held a real likeness to her mother, grandmother, and mentor Rafe—and placed items she'd found in local stores that much resembled family heirlooms. There was also a chalice, candles, and pumpkins.

The altar would for sure look out of place in Cain's chamber, as would her collection of crystals and the astrological-themed throw on the armchair. She'd leave them here for now and take them to the Keep at a later date.

By the time Wynter had bagged up a few things and drank

her tea, it was almost time for Cain's speech. Together, she and her coven went to stand in their front yard. From there, she could clearly see Cain standing at the top of the city's tallest tower. The other Ancients stood behind him in what appeared to be a gesture of solidarity.

The streets were packed with people, many of whom lived on the surface and had no doubt come here to be present for Cain's speech. It wasn't long before he raised a hand, gesturing for a silence that immediately fell.

"I know you'll all have questions," said Cain, pure power amplifying his voice. "Several, probably. What do the Ancients make of Adam's announcement? Does the Aeon truly not want war? Did Wynter Dellavale really curse his land? Do she and I intend to give ourselves up? What will Adam do if we don't?

"I will answer those questions. You should also ask yourselves another: Why would Adam not come here for vengeance? Strange that he didn't, don't you think? In relatively short order, the three other ruling Aeons were killed, including his son. Abel's dismembered body was dumped at Aeon for Adam to find. Yet, he proclaims he doesn't want war. Personally, I find that exceptionally hard to believe."

Glancing at the sea of faces around her, Wynter saw that Cain wasn't the only one.

"The opinion of myself and the other Ancients is simple: Adam fears coming here," Cain continued. "He fears facing us and all of you. If the last ruling Aeon falls, the place and its inhabitants will be vulnerable. And so he concocted a plan that would weaken us. That plan? To remove the most powerful Ancient from the equation by placing him in a position where he must give himself up for the safety of his people."

Anabel leaned into Wynter. "So he's really the most powerful?" she whispered.

Wynter only nodded.

"Here's the thing," began Cain, "it would not save you if I did.

Adam would still come—he would *never* overlook what happened to his own people here. Never. And if I'm not at Devil's Cradle when he does come, you will be down one Ancient. We all know that one Ancient can make all the difference."

Wynter watched as people digested that. It was clear that not all of them had looked at the situation that way before.

"As such, it isn't an option for me to surrender myself to the Aeons," Cain went on. "It would only make Adam come here that much sooner. To leave would be for me to neglect the promise I made to the people in my service—that being the promise to keep them safe."

Ah, it was clever of Cain to put it that way. No one would expect him to hand himself over now.

"I made another vow," Cain added. "The vow to never hand people over to any outsiders who may come for them. As such, to give Wynter to Adam would be a betrayal on my part. And I think you can all understand why I would never surrender her to him in any case. To address the question I'm sure most of you have, yes, she did curse the land of Aeon."

Wynter tried not to tense as people glanced her way. She'd agreed for Cain to give the residents more information on what happened back then, but she didn't much like that her private business would be aired this way. *Fuck you, Adam.*

"She was unfairly exiled, as was her mother many years before," said Cain. "Except, in truth, Aeons don't exile you. They have one of their keepers toss you over the falls. Wynter didn't learn that until a keeper tried to do that same thing to her. She escaped, cursed the land to avenge herself and her deceased mother, and then left. I doubt anyone here would blame her for that."

Maybe they wouldn't, but they were clearly weirded out that she'd been able to infect the place with a blight that couldn't be combatted—it was written all over their faces.

"Adam is well aware that I won't surrender either myself or Wynter to him," Cain added. "That isn't a losing situation for

49

him, though, as he believes people will subsequently turn on me and choose to leave Devil's Cradle. A lesser population means a lesser army—one that's far easier for him and his own troops to take down.

"Some of you may in fact decide to leave, particularly when he starts using his ability to manipulate the natural elements to punish the town. That is your choice. An understandable choice. Adam has done his best to scare and confuse you. I don't doubt that that has worked on some. Playing mind games has always been a forte of his, after all."

Wynter felt her lips twitch at the use of reverse psychology. It certainly worked on many of the crowd. Eyes narrowed. Chins lifted. Backs straightened. They clearly weren't happy that Adam believed he could play them.

"Those who wish to stay will naturally wonder what the other Ancients and I now plan to do about Adam." Cain paused. "Twice now Aeons have invaded our town and tried to destroy it. We intend to return that favor. We intend to strike before Adam has the chance to step even a single foot in our direction. We will make our move sometime soon and rid ourselves of this last threat to our home."

Satisfaction began to gather in the air. People nodded or smiled, clearly up for getting some payback against the Aeons.

Cain swept his gaze over the crowds, very briefly settling it on Wynter. "There may be some of you who are tempted to act on Adam's offer and cash in on the bounties. I don't think I need to tell you how ridiculously stupid that would be." Menace thickened his voice. "Not simply because neither I nor my consort are easy targets, but because there would be no reward. Adam would do no favors for any of you. He would only view you as part of the army that led to his son's death.

"He would kill you. But not quickly. Not cleanly. You would suffer. And, let's face it, you'd deserve it for betraying your people, for making them vulnerable at a time of war, and for shitting all over a place that is a sanctuary for many—including you."

Wynter noticed some people nod, including her coven.

"So think on that," advised Cain. "Don't let greed override your common sense. If you do, the consequence would be simple: either Wynter would kill you, her monster would kill you, I would kill you, or—in the unlikely event that you made it to Aeon with a captive in tow—Adam would kill you. In short, no matter the case, you would die. And it would be as far from painless as painless can get."

Well.

Chapter Five

As Wynter had anticipated, the meal at Seth's Keep *was* a fancy affair. Not simply due to the gourmet food and vintage wine. Every place at the table had an elegant little name card featuring a calligraphic font.

There were multiple knives and forks of various sizes and styles—all so shiny they could double as mirrors. The pretty crystal dishware looked so expensive she'd honestly hesitated to touch it. The classical background music made her miss her regular background dinner noise, even if it was the sounds of her coven members squabbling like kids.

The room sure smelled good, though. The scent of the beeswax candles on the table laced the air, along with the scents of food, pungent wine, and the freshly cut flowers that formed the centerpiece.

The other people seated at the long, mahogany dining table seemed perfectly at ease. Still, conversation was sort of . . . stiff at times. The silences weren't always comfortable.

Being introduced to Wynter had seemed to pleasantly surprise both Eve and Noah. They'd even seemed a little touched, though more Eve than him. As for Rima? She still behaved somewhat aloof toward Cain and Seth, clearly intent on holding a grudge over the surely-not-so-hard-to-understand fact that she'd once been under suspicion of freeing Saul—like his sister Lailah, he had been one of the four ruling Aeons who'd imprisoned the Ancients. The siblings were now dead.

As she'd talked with and studied the Aeons at the table, Wynter had reached the conclusion that Cain's assessment of them was correct. Although she'd once lived at Aeon, she'd never spoken a single word to Eve or the twins before now; hadn't even exchanged nods with them. Mortals simply held little to no interest for Aeons. They were easily ignored and just as easily sentenced to death, much like Wynter and her mother.

Not that Wynter held that against *these* particular Aeons. They'd had nothing to do with what happened to her or Davina. Abel and his consort, Lailah, were to blame—both had paid for that with their lives. Something which often made Wynter smile.

She actually felt sorry for Eve and the twins. They were permitted to stay at Devil's Cradle, but they weren't fully trusted or welcomed by its residents and so hadn't yet integrated themselves into society. Wynter knew what it was like to stand apart like that. Knew how lonely it could make a person feel. Her old coven had treated her as though she were an outsider for most of her life.

Opposite her, Eve looked up from her meal with a smile and said, "Living at a Keep must be quite strange for you, Wynter. Modern-day houses are quite different, even at Aeon. I never left there until coming here, but there were ways for people to see how the rest of the world looks. I saw houses made mostly of glass, saw some that were like palaces, and even buildings that were higher than any tower I could ever imagine seeing."

Wynter knew that the woman had "viewed" the outside world by utilizing preternatural methods such as fire-gazing. Cain did it often using the font in his temple. Wynter had found it pretty fascinating to watch as images flickered to life within the flames, providing a kind of satellite view of the globe. He could zoom in on any spot to get a better look. Aeon, however, could not be seen—the Aeons had ways to block it from view. But, just the same, those assholes couldn't see Devil's Cradle.

"Modern houses are very different from Keeps," Wynter confirmed. "But I can't say that living at Cain's Keep feels strange." Nor could she truly say she officially lived there yet, but she saw no need to have that conversation with his family. "I'm not sure I'd love it so much if it was situated above the town where it's not so easy to regulate the temperature all-year round, though." Castles weren't exactly simple to keep warm.

"Yes, there's a bit of a chill up above now, isn't there? I don't like wandering around the town. I'm quite happy exploring the city. Many of the Halloween decorations outside the houses are quite something."

"I tried urging Cain to include a few inside and outside his Keep, but he vetoed it. He's kind of boring that way." He wouldn't even agree to prop some pumpkins around the front entrance.

Beside her, Cain arched a brow at Wynter. "Boring?"

"In general? No," she replied. "But when it comes to celebrating holidays? Oh, absolutely."

"Only because many are now so commercialized," he said.

Wynter playfully gave his arm a soothing pat. "I get it, old man."

Humor danced in his eyes. "You'll pay for that later."

Eve chuckled. "You two have a sweet dynamic." She lifted a slice of fresh bread and bit into it. "This bread is truly delicious."

"My staff purchased it from the shop that's run by the Bloodrose Coven," Seth informed her.

Her eyes widening in a delighted surprise, Eve looked at Wynter. "Really? You baked it?"

"Not me. One of my coven, Hattie, does the baking," Wynter clarified.

Rima lifted her glass of red. "And you enchant weapons with dark magick." There was an accusatory and slightly pompous note to her voice that was *all* provocation.

Pfft. As if Wynter would be put on the defensive so easily. No one—least of all a practical stranger with a serious attitude problem—would ever make her feel shame for her magick being dark. It wasn't as if she'd *turned* it dark somehow. It changed when she died. Death never failed to leave its mark.

Having felt Cain tense beside her, Wynter placed a hand on his thigh and smiled at Rima. "I can do many things."

The other female went to speak again, but Noah quickly said, "I think your ability to enchant weapons is impressive. I heard you can deactivate the runes at will. Is that true?" he asked, seeming merely curious.

Wynter dipped her chin.

"Which then enables you to prevent your own work from being used against you," mused Noah, his lips kicking up. "Smart." He paused. "It's so strange that no one at Aeon ever realized you're a revenant. It's as if Kali made sure that you flew under the radar."

"It is," agreed Rima. "Why?" She tossed out the word in challenge.

Wynter gave a lazy shrug. "You'd have to ask Her."

"I'm not sure I'd want to be in frequent contact with a deity, even if there is honor in being Favored, but it has to be interesting at times." Noah cocked his head. "I don't understand why Kali made you so different from other revenants. You really don't need to feast on flesh and blood to survive?"

"Darling Noah," began Eve, a fond smile plucking at her mouth, "that is not something one should ask at the dinner table."

His cheeks pinkened. "Sorry," he said to Wynter. "Just curious."

"It's fine," she assured him. "And the answer to your question is yes, I truly don't have that particular diet."

"Why?" Rima repeated.

Serious eye roll. "Again, you'll have to ask Kali."

Rima folded her arms. "I'm asking you."

"Enough," said Cain. The word was low. Soft. But pure frost.

"Like Noah, I'm merely curious," Rima defended, though she dropped her bad attitude in an instant.

Her brother gave her a hard look. "You're being rude, and you know it."

Rima drew in a breath and then turned back to Wynter. "I apologize," she said, sounding genuine.

"Then let's have no more rudeness," pressed Eve.

Rima cut her gaze to Cain. "Why did you lie to your people?"

It wasn't a demand or said with any hostility. It seemed to be a genuine query.

He blinked. "Excuse me?"

"You told them that you plan to soon invade Aeon," said Rima. "Only that isn't possible. So you lied. I don't understand why."

"It was the truth." Cain sliced into his fillet mignon. "We fully intend to take the war to Adam."

Rima's brow creased in confusion. "How?"

Seeing an opening to raise the subject of how he might get the aid of the three Aeons at the table at one point, Cain replied, "We believe it's possible that we can cause a fissure in the prison." He felt it safe to reveal his plans, since there was no way the Aeons could get the information to Adam even if they were in league with him. "Three of its creators are dead, so the power they instilled into it is no longer so potent. That means the cage has essentially been weakened."

Rima's brow furrowed. "But the blood of each Ancient was used to fortify it, yes? I'm not sure how any of you could still damage it unless several of you died."

"We could do it with help from another Ancient." Or so Cain hoped.

"But there are no others."

He forked a piece of meat and put it in his mouth. "Not true. One other was dumped here with us. The Aeons didn't bother to take or use his blood to power the cage because they didn't believe he would live—they only brought him here because they knew that watching him die would be difficult for me."

"You're referring to Abaddon?" asked Eve, stilling in surprise. "He lives?"

"He's in a coma of sorts." Cain lowered his cutlery to the plate and lifted his glass. "We've never attempted to wake him before—he for sure would have lost his mind while confined and unable to avenge his children." He'd been deep in grief at the time.

"Children?" echoed Rima.

Seth nodded, his face solemn. "Many children were slaughtered when the Aeons sprung an attack on us all those years ago."

Eve's gaze turned unfocused. "I could hear them screaming, but I couldn't get them help. Adam had confined me to my room after I told him that I wouldn't fight against my son." Her eyes sharpened as she looked from Seth to Cain. "Do you really believe you can wake Abaddon?"

"If the Ancients act as one when we attempt it, yes," replied Seth.

"Will his contribution truly be enough to cause some sort of crevice in the prison?" asked Eve.

Seth tugged at the collar of his shirt. "I'd like to think so. We won't know until we try. Which we plan to do on All Hallows' Eve with or without him, but hopefully with him. Do you have no idea at all why Adam proclaims that Aeon cannot afford to fall?"

Eve shook her head.

"Maybe he just hasn't given up hope that Eden will one day use Aeon as her Resting place again," Noah suggested. "If Aeon is gone, so is that hope. I personally cannot envision God ever entrusting us with the safety of his consort again. For some, it is too painful a pill to swallow."

"If Aeon continues to rot, no one can use it for anything. Do you intend to undo the curse after Adam is dead?" Rima asked Wynter.

"I would if Cain asked it of me," Wynter replied.

"Which I won't." Cain took one last sip of his wine and then set down his glass. "Hundreds of my kind were butchered there, including my father and an uncle who gave his life to save mine. Their blood stains that ground." It needed to be razed.

"So does the blood of many Aeons," Rima reminded him.

"Only those who chose to join Adam in unjustly attempting to wipe out my race." Every single one of those Aeons deserved what they got.

"I don't dispute that. My concern is that there are other Aeons there. Ones who were not part of the war. They will be without a home. They won't understand this world."

Cain gave a delicate shrug. "I doubt they will need to learn, since it is highly unlikely that they will survive the upcoming battle."

"Most of the Aeons who wronged you a millennia ago died in the war. Others fell recently, and Adam will soon meet that same fate. Why punish the last living Aeons?"

Cain felt his face harden. "Not all died in those wars. Many survived. Don't try to tell me differently. It would be a lie, and you know it."

Rima allowed that with a slight incline of her head. "Some are still alive, yes, but they don't make up the majority of the population."

"Perhaps. But none of that population will be spared because they will not *ask* to be spared. They have been raised to loathe the Ancients and consider us evil. Raised to believe that this cage is necessary; that we can't be allowed to live unless confined this way. Why? Because Adam needed to be sure that no one would be tempted to free us. He needed to be sure that we would be eliminated if we ever managed to escape."

Rima looked down at the table, biting her lip.

"And when we appear at Aeon, every one of them will fight to defend their home from the bogeymen they believe us to be." They'd do it fervently. "None will wave a white flag. None will choose not to join the battle. None will care about our plight. Am I wrong?"

Noah exhaled heavily, making the flame on one of the candles dance to the side. "No. No, you're not. It would be pointless to even consider the possibility that you could form a treaty with any survivors. As you say, they will unite against you for certain. They fear and loathe you in equal measures."

Seth sat back in his seat. "Which is another reason why we will not go to Aeon offering a truce to any who would consider sitting out the battle. We can't—won't—take the chance that their true plan is to later mount an attack on us. We cannot chance that they would attempt to shove us into yet another prison."

"I understand that," said Rima, raising one hand in a placatory gesture. "I do. But what if they were to agree to be confined to Aeon?"

Seth slanted his head. "Tell me, Rima, how did you fare when being confined to my Keep for a few months?"

Her shoulders sagged. "I hated it."

"So did I," mumbled Noah. "Likewise, our fellow Aeons would hate being caged in their own town."

"It would not truly be an act of mercy," said Seth. "A cage is still a cage, no matter how comfortable and spacious it is."

Rima sighed. "You're right. I just wish things could be different."

Eve again took in both Cain and Seth. "Would you allow me to help you attempt to break your prison? The power of four Aeons are woven into it. I am not one of them, but perhaps my power could nonetheless aid you all in unraveling it."

Cain hadn't expected the offer. It shocked even his creature. She might care for him and Seth, might even love them, but she wasn't a mother in the typical sense of the word. They didn't have the sort of bond that would pull at her to protect them.

Plus, Eve was something of a pacifist by nature. To help free the Ancients would also be to indirectly help them launch an attack on her old home. In that sense, she would be an accomplice. And since she had stayed out of all previous wars, preferring to remain neutral, he had thought it would take time to convince her to help them. He'd even been braced for her to refuse point-blank to do so.

"I let you down during the first war." Eve swallowed. "If I had stood up to Adam, if I had sided with you, perhaps I could have helped. Perhaps I would have instead simply died. In any case, by doing nothing I have always felt that I played a loose part in imprisoning you. The least I can do is assist you in righting that wrong."

Appreciative of that, Cain dipped his chin. "You hold no blame in this, you have nothing to atone for. That said, we would be grateful for your assistance."

He wished her words could have moved him somehow. Wished they could have punched through the wall of apathy he'd seemingly erected between them. Wished he could feel *something* as he looked upon his own mother. But still, he struggled with that.

Noah stroked a hand down the front of his shirt. "I will help as well."

Cain exchanged a stunned look with Seth.

Rima gaped at her brother. "*Noah*. I'm not siding with Adam—far from it," she hurried to assure Cain and Seth. "But I'm also not keen on the idea of Aeon and its last inhabitants suffering for his sins."

Noah thrust a hand through his hair. "Neither am I, but—"

"The place will be ravaged," Rima went on. "The people there will be killed."

"Aeon is already being ravaged—the decay is more prevalent than ever," Noah pointed out. "And if the Ancients don't take the war to Aeon, Adam will bring it here. *Where we are*. And then we could very well die. Not sure about you, but I want to live."

Rima pressed her lips tight together.

"And you know full well that the Aeons there aren't all goodness and light," Noah said to her. "They follow Adam. They always will. It was why we didn't dare ask if any wanted to leave with us. We didn't trust that they wouldn't report it to him."

Wynter took her napkin from her lap and carefully set it on the table. Her eyes soft, she said to Rima, "I get it. Aeon holds the home you shared with your mother; you hate the thought of it being destroyed."

Cain blinked, not having looked at the situation from that angle.

"I understand," his consort went on. "I do. My mom lived there too, for a time."

"You don't care for Aeon, though," Rima pointed out, her voice clipped.

"Because my mom might have spent many of her years there, but she also suffered greatly at the end," said Wynter. "She was exiled—or, more specifically, marked for death—as I was. Completely paralyzed, she was tossed over the falls where she then drowned, powerless to help herself. So no, I don't care for Aeon. But I *do* understand why you so hate the thought of the place meeting its end."

THE MONSTERS WE ARE

Detesting the pain in his consort's voice, Cain rested his hand on her thigh and gave it a comforting squeeze. He knew that part of her anguish came from not realizing until recently that her mother had never truly left Aeon; that her dead body had been so very close all along.

He also knew that there was some guilt mixed in with her hurt. Not only guilt at believing the lie that her mother was alive and in exile. Wynter also felt that some of the responsibility for her mother's suffering lay with her. Because Davina Dellavale had given her life to spare that of her daughter's; had pled guilty to bringing a ten-year-old Wynter back from the dead so that no one would know the truth.

He'd tried convincing Wynter on numerous occasions that her guilt was senseless. He'd insisted that there was no reason she *shouldn't* have bought the lies she'd been told. He'd firmly stated that the only people who had any real hand in her mother's death were the Aeons and the keeper who personally carried out the "exile".

But that's the thing about someone sacrificing their life to save yours, she'd once said to him. *They meant it as a gift, but it will always feel like a heavy, painful weight.*

Noah swallowed. "Our mother suffered there, too."

Rima let out a heavy exhale, her gaze dulling. "Yes. She wasn't happy. She spent most of her years pining for Abel."

"She spent the rest of them hating him for forbidding other men to touch her," Noah chipped in. "She despised Adam with a blinding passion."

Rima's gaze went unfocused, as if she were lost in her memories. "Unable to move on and find happiness, she grew bitter and angry until there was no softness left in her. Both men killed it."

Noah nodded. "I think she would be glad that Abel's dead. I think she would support the Ancients in seeing Adam dead. And I don't think she would care if Aeon fell. I think it might even bring her some peace."

Rima's shoulders lowered as all hostility seemed to seep from her body. "Yeah. Yeah, maybe."

*

"Well," began Wynter later that evening as they entered Cain's chambers, "that was sure the height of casual dinner conversation." She wasn't gonna lie, she was glad the meal was over. "Something good came of it, though. Your plan to settle ruffled feathers worked with Eve and Noah."

Cain flicked a hand to light the many candles. "I wasn't expecting them to volunteer to help us."

"Yeah, I was surprised too. Well, I guess you now know it's extremely improbable that Eve and Noah are here to do Adam's bidding. Sadly, we can't be too sure about Rima yet, though I'm not certain her reluctance to help stems from anything other than the grudge she's holding."

"I'm rapidly losing my patience with her."

Wynter gently laid her shawl over the armchair. "I noticed. She's full of resentment and helplessness."

"Helplessness?" Cain echoed.

Wynter nodded. "I get it. She had to watch her mother suffer for years in various ways. She couldn't do anything to make it better. I felt that same sense of powerlessness when I watched my mother be exiled and taken away. Being unable to help someone you love leaves its mark on you."

His gaze flitting over her face, Cain tipped his head to the side. "You're thinking that I should be able to empathize, given I was unable to help Eve when I was a child."

"Maybe not empathize *as such*." It wasn't something he seemed to be much good at. "But I figure you can at least intellectually understand."

He sighed long and loud. "The chip on her shoulder that Seth spoke of will hold her back. She gives her emotions so much power over her that it weakens her."

THE MONSTERS WE ARE

"Well, that chip didn't hold her back from flinging bold question after bold question at you." Recalling something, Wynter said, "You told Rima you had an uncle who gave his life to save yours. What happened? You don't have to tell me if you'd rather not talk about it, I won't be upset or anything."

"I don't mind talking about it. Though there isn't really much to tell. As it happens, you've probably heard of my uncle. His name was Baal."

"As in the Baal who humans believe to be a demon?"

"Yes. They have a habit of mistaking Leviathans for demons." Cain opened the top two buttons of his shirt. "Anyway, Baal was my father's youngest brother but much older than me. He was exceptionally powerful. Brutal in battle. Utterly fearless. Loyal to family. And when an Aeon blasted me with power, Baal leaped in front of me and took the hit."

"Then, as much as I'm sorry he died and you lost an uncle, I'm grateful to him."

"Seth said the same thing. Abaddon took his loss the hardest. He was close to Baal. Very close. It will be yet another death that haunts Abaddon when we wake him. But it must be done."

"Is the plan to still go ahead with it tomorrow night?"

"Yes, though there's no saying it won't take more than one attempt to bring him out of his Rest."

Sensing that he was eager to change the subject, she asked, "Want to do some raw and dirty stuff?"

Cain's lips bowed up. "Always, pretty witch. Always." He slowly swept his gaze around the room. "I like that you brought more of your things here."

She'd sensed that. When he'd earlier noticed the plant she'd propped on a nightstand and the books and bookends she'd set on a shelf she'd claimed, pure satisfaction had rippled across his face.

"I like seeing your possessions mixed with mine." He took a fluid step toward her, raking his gaze over the full length of her body. "I also like this dress." He put his face closer to hers. "But I want it on the floor." He scraped her lower lip with his teeth. "I want every inch of you bare."

Phantom fingertips ghosted up her spine as anticipation began to thrum through her. She licked her lips. "I can accommodate that wish." She shed her dress, underwear, and shoes.

Humming to himself, he began to slowly circle her, dancing his fingers over her tingling skin. "So very beautiful. You make me want to take a big bite." Facing her once more, he stepped back. "Don't move." He kept his gaze fixed on hers as he undressed. "Such a well-behaved toy."

She narrowed her eyes.

His brow inched up. "Oh, are we pretending you don't like it when I refer to you as my toy?" he asked, covering the small distance between them in one predatory step that sent her pulse wild.

"No. I simply didn't like the taunting note in your voice. But then, you knew I wouldn't."

His lips kicked up. "Well, of course I knew." He dipped his head and kissed her, sweeping his tongue into her mouth.

Wynter held his shoulders as he melted her with a wickedly slow kiss that quickly turned wet, deep, and dominant. His hand collared her throat as he backed her into the wall. The shock of the cool stone against her skin made her gasp.

He kept on ravishing her mouth until their breaths were ragged and she started to feel dizzy. Wynter wrenched her lips free and sucked in some much needed air. With a low growl, he took her mouth again and closed his hands over her breasts. She arched into him with a soft moan, wanting more. So much more.

"I do love these pretty breasts," he said, squeezing them. "I love them so much more when they're covered in my come." He swooped down and latched onto a nipple.

Her breath caught as he sucked hard, sending streaks of pleasure to her clit. He licked his way to her other nipple and suckled until it throbbed. Then he bit down on it.

She hissed at the sting. "Not too hard."

Cain flicked her a silencing look. "I'll bite you as hard as I please, pretty witch." He sank his teeth into the swell of one breast, and she knew he'd left a mark.

Wynter's breath snagged in her throat as carnal, spinetingling pleasure breezed over her soul, hot and drugging. *Oh, mother of God.* Her nerve-endings fired up. The fine hairs on her body lifted. Her feminine parts went crazy.

The pleasure came again, surfing along her soul in a scorching crackly wave that bit and scraped like teeth and nails. More and more sensations assaulted her—some soft and gentle as a feather, some dark and sharp like the spank of a hand.

Endorphins flooded her body and made her head swim. Every part of her felt so ultra-sensitive she didn't think she could take it. Her core was hot and wet and achy—worse, *empty.*

As yet more pleasure rolled over her very being, she became distantly aware of him dropping to his knees. Of a hand cuffing her ankle and snaking its way up her leg. Of sharp teeth nipping her inner thigh. But the soul-deep sensations made it hard for her to focus on the physical.

"Such silky smooth skin." He tossed her leg over his shoulder and nuzzled her pussy—and *that* she easily focused on. "Hmm, deliciously slick. I'm going to lick you clean."

Wynter groaned as a tongue swiped between her folds in a long, sensual lick that ended with a lash to her clit. *Oh, Jesus.* She slapped her hands onto the wall behind her, careful not to knock the nearby tapestry.

Her eyes fluttered closed as his tongue lashed and delved. The friction inside her built with every lick, flick, and stab of his blessed tongue. Then there was the wicked assault on her soul. So many sensations . . . There was heat. There was cold. There was pain. There was pleasure. It all blended together and shoved her closer to her release. God, she was gonna come *so hard.*

He stopped. It all stopped.

Her eyes snapped open as a growl of frustration scraped the back of her throat. "Motherfucking sadist."

Cain stood, not bothering to fight the urge to smile. "At your service." There was something exhilarating about seeing her caught on the knife-edge of an orgasm, desperate to come and furious with him for making her wait.

He wouldn't make her wait any longer, though. Couldn't. He needed to be inside her. His dick was so full and heavy it hurt.

He lifted her and hooked her legs over the crooks of his elbows. "Now be a good little toy and let me wreck you." He thrust upwards, slamming his cock deep, gritting his teeth as her inner walls gripped him tight.

The breath whooshed out of her, and her head fell back. "Jesus," she rasped, clutching his upper arms.

He licked his way up the lifegiving vein in her neck. His inner creature wanted to bite it. Taste her blood. Inject its venom into her so it would be part of her. "You have no idea how badly my monster wants to mark you right now. It'll do it soon, Wynter. You and I both know it."

Cain used the weight of his upper body to pin her in place as he fucked her. He took her *hard*. Aggressively. Possessed her like a feral beast caught in a frenzied mating.

Even as he pounded into her pussy, he repeatedly struck her soul with waves, whips, and featherlight flicks of electric pleasure/pain. She was with him every step of the way, verbally urging him on.

His balls tightened when her eyes lost focus and turned cloudy, as if she was floating in some in-between space. Knowing he didn't have long before his release took him, he changed his angle, ensuring he hit her clit with every bruising thrust.

She sucked in a sharp breath and dug her nails harder into his upper arms as her pussy began to spasm. "Cain, I need to come," she all but whimpered, her eyes now wet with tears.

He groaned, his cock swelling. "So do it. Come on, let go, cry for me. Yes, that's my baby." They both came together—her screaming and shaking, him snarling and ramming his cock hard into her body over and over.

As they trembled with aftershocks, Cain buried his face in her neck, utterly sated. His monster made a low hiss of complaint, acutely feeling the absence of a bond to the woman it had chosen as its own. *Soon*, Cain assured it. They'd be bound soon.

Chapter Six

Anabel groaned in delight. "Oh my God, how have I never eaten this before?"

Wynter felt her face scrunch up. "Pumpkin and pizza are two things that really shouldn't go together." She loved both foods, but she had no desire whatsoever to combine them in such a way.

All sorts of fall- or Halloween-themed food and drinks were being sold by the many street traders. The town was currently a hub of buzzing activity. When she'd seen "street party" on the schedule, she hadn't anticipated exactly how hectic it would be. It was like almost the entire underground city had made their way up to the surface.

Cain had wanted to attend the street party with Wynter, but of course he and the other Ancients needed to attempt to wake Abaddon. She sure hoped it worked, because she wasn't so certain the Ancients could truly punch a hole through their cage without Abaddon's help. She looked forward to asking him why on Earth he kept drawing her to Cain's garden in her sleep.

Anabel held out her pizza slice. "Taste it, Wyn, you'll like it, I promise."

Munching on his own slice, Xavier nodded.

Leaning back slightly, Wynter held up her half-eaten pretzel. "I'm good, thanks."

Hattie's eyes briefly darted from her book to the pizza and then back again. "What's it taste like?"

"You'd never tried it either? Oh, you haven't lived." Anabel bit off another piece. "I really need more of this in my life. Seriously, Hattie, try some."

"Maybe later, the characters are having a huge argument right now," said Hattie. Like she'd miss the whole thing and the story would go on without her if she looked away from it.

Shaking her head with a smile, Wynter turned to Delilah. "You still not hungry?"

After taking a sip of the—literally—smoking cocktail she'd bought, Delilah shook her head. "I'm good for now," she said, half-walking, half-dancing to the live music. Residents were singing on the manmade stage not far from the bonfire, and there seemed to be a battle of the bands going on. "Hey, we've gotta give that straw maze near the forest a try."

Anabel pulled her arms close to her body. "I don't know if I could handle having people leap out at me." She glanced around her, edgier than usual. To be fair, some residents were dressed up in costumes and hiding behind corners to jump-scare passersby, so . . .

"We've got to at least try the horse-drawn hay rides," said Delilah. "And stop vetoing everything just because you want to go home."

Anabel frowned. "I'm not vetoing *everything*."

The Latina winged up a brow. "Oh, really? So you didn't say no to checking out the carnival booths, the beer tent, the funhouse, the—"

"Okay, okay, so I'm eager to get home," admitted Anabel. "But can you really blame me when death stalks us every minute?"

Delilah rolled her eyes and took another sip of her drink. "There's really no helping 'chemically unbalanced,' is there?"

"You'd know all about unbalanced," snarked Anabel. "That shit runs in your family, and it all started with your precious Annis."

"She *was* precious," said Delilah with a smile, apparently deciding to play clueless.

"Twisted, Del," Anabel corrected. "She was twisted. Evil. A true plague on this planet."

"God, you're such a hater."

"What normal person wouldn't hate a child killer?"

"An *alleged* child killer."

Anabel let out a derisive snort. "You know very well that she murdered kids, just like you know very well that *she also ate them.*"

"We all do things we regret."

"But does she regret it?" Anabel perched a hand on her hip. "Be honest. You chat with her when you meditate—which, on a side note, *totally* disturbs me. Is she sorry for what she did to those children?"

Delilah opened and closed her mouth a few times. "In a manner of speaking."

"So that's a no?" Anabel smirked. "See, evil."

"As were a lot of your relatives from your past lives, so maybe you wanna crank back the whole 'let's judge people's family' thing. And weren't you Bloody Mary in a past life? Or is that belief just yet more proof that you're chemically unbalanced."

"*I* am as normal as they come." Anabel patted Xavier's chest. "Tell her, Xavier."

He chucked the last piece of pizza into his mouth. "Tell her what?"

"A barefaced lie," sassed Delilah.

His brows inched up. "I'm good at that."

"You know," Wynter cut in, wiping her hands on a napkin now that she'd finished her pretzel, "I once read that the magician Houdini died on Halloween. How freaky is that?"

"My uncle died on Halloween," said Xavier.

Delilah's face softened. "Aw, did he really?"

"No, not really," he replied.

Delilah let out a little growl. "Then why lie?"

"Maybe the truth will only confuse you more."

Anabel sighed and slapped his arm. "Xavier, you're an idiot."

He chuckled. "You adore me really."

Feeling eyes on her, Wynter looked to her right. A trio of witches swiftly averted their gazes. She recognized them. The Oasis Coven lived in the city not far from Cain's Keep. They'd also once been led by Demetria, a witch who'd not only wanted Wynter dead but died at her monster's hands.

THE MONSTERS WE ARE

The newly appointed Priestess of the trio, Kyra, cut her eyes back to Wynter. Clearing her throat, the woman nodded. "Wynter."

"Kyra," she greeted in return.

Once the Oasis witches were out of hearing range, Delilah turned to Wynter. "I'm still not sure I believe that they weren't in cahoots with Demetria."

Plenty weren't so sure, which was why many residents gave the coven the cold shoulder. Wynter kind of felt sorry for them. Paying for other people's fuckups never felt good. "They convinced Cain's aide that they weren't involved. Maxim doesn't strike me as a person who'd be easy to fool."

Delilah took another swig of her drink. "Hmm, well, I don't like that they were staring at you. *Far* too many people keep looking at you. It's pissing me off."

"It's not as bad as it was before Cain made his speech, so it seemingly had the desired effect on the majority of the town's population."

A figure dressed as the grim reaper jumped out of the nearby shadows with a maniacal laugh.

Anabel screamed in his face and threw her pizza at his feet. Wynter, Xavier, and Delilah laughed while Hattie didn't react whatsoever, absorbed in her book.

His shoulders shaking with silent laughter, the reaper backed up, melting into the shadows once more.

Standing very still with her hands balled into tight fists, Anabel ground her teeth. "That wasn't funny."

"I have to ask," began Xavier as they resumed their walk along the street, "why didn't you toss the pizza at his head or something? Why his feet?"

Anabel threw up her arms. "I don't know, I wasn't thinking. I panicked. I don't operate well when running on panic."

Delilah snorted. "You don't operate well in general. And I say that with love."

Anabel scowled. "Screw off, Del."

The Latina blew her a kiss. "You'd miss me if I wasn't here."

"Yeah, like I'd miss a punch to the tit."

Hattie looked up from her book. "What does it mean if someone figs you?"

Wynter almost tripped over thin air. Anabel let out a groan. Xavier coughed to hide a laugh while pounding a fist on Delilah's back, since she'd began to choke on her drink.

"The heroine's threatening to walk out if the hero ever again talks about figging her," Hattie elaborated. "What does it mean?"

"It's just another word for 'tickling'," lied Anabel, who'd recently proposed to all but Hattie that they should provide "innocent" bullshit answers to the old woman's awkward sexual questions.

"Bless you for explaining." Hattie patted Anabel's arm. "I'd believe you if Delilah wasn't still snickering to herself. Now someone tell me what it really means."

Xavier leaned into Wynter. "She'll only ask a perfect stranger if we blow her off."

"Come on, tell me," urged Hattie.

Wynter cringed at the mere thought of explaining. "Can we talk about this later? It's not . . . pleasant, okay? It's painful."

The old woman gave Wynter a kind smile. "Sometimes pain spices things up, dear. Did you not know that? Oh, you're so sheltered."

That was when Delilah lost it. The woman literally doubled over with laughter.

Wynter shook her head. "This kinda pain isn't merely about spice, Hattie. Figging is generally for those who really get off on pain. I personally don't see the appeal in this particular act, but to each their own."

"So you've been figged yourself?" Hattie asked.

Wynter jerked back. "What? No. Never."

"Then how do you know you won't like it?"

"Because I know I'll *never* find anything likeable about having a piece of ginger peel pushed into my ass."

Hattie's felt went slack. "Ginger peel? In your rear end? Dear Lord. That sounds like *torture*."

"It *was* a form of torture at one time," Anabel cut in. "The Romans were pretty big on it, actually."

Hattie puffed out a breath. "No wonder the heroine's so against it. Masochism is so not her thing." She tapped the book's spine, adding, "I don't like this hero much. Don't get me wrong, he's delightfully hardcore in bed. But he has no compassion or sensitivity. He's been teasing her because she has red eye."

"Ah, I used to get that when I was a kid," said Anabel. "I had super bad allergies back then."

"The heroine doesn't seem to have allergies or anything, she . . . I don't know, it's strange. There was nothing wrong with her eyes the day before. But she and the hero had sex last night, he introduced her to anal, and then she woke with red—why are you grinning, Xavier? What am I missing?"

"Nothing, Hattie," Anabel quickly said, shooting him a pointed look. "He's just happy. Right, Xavier?"

He smirked at Hattie. "It's not actually the heroine's eye that's red. It's her asshole."

"But he—*oh*." The old woman's eyes went wide.

Anabel shook her head at him. "All you had to do was lie. You do it frequently. Why, this one time, did you break the habit?"

Xavier blinked. "I gotta admit, I don't know."

Delilah knocked back the last of her cocktail. "Come on, let's try the maze."

It took a lot of convincing, but they eventually managed to talk Anabel into giving it a go, though she made it clear that she was there under protest. Her fear shot up a level when they began to wander through the labyrinth. There was fog everywhere, and the straw walls were too high for any of them to see over.

The first time someone jumped out of the fog, Anabel screamed. The second time, she almost climbed on Xavier's back. The third time, she ran. Ran like death truly was stalking her ass.

73

Losing sight of her in the fog, they jogged after her, calling out her name while also chuckling.

Wynter lagged behind, laughing so hard she could barely walk. That laughter faded as an otherworldly breeze ghosted over her face, screaming with warning. Before Wynter could react, a hand shot out of the fog, gripped her arm, and spun her around. *Kyra.* She blew dust into Wynter's face and ... oh shit, everything got real blurry and weird.

Wynter yawned, inexplicably tired all of a sudden. She blinked hard to fight the urge to sleep. But the world spun, her legs crumbled beneath her, and then everything went dark.

*

Cain led the way down the twisting path as he and the other Ancients strolled through his garden toward the temple. It could be said that it was not your typical garden. Not with its gothic tone and the many snakes that roamed it. They dangled from tree branches, slithered up the wall ruins, curled around the moss-covered statues, swam in the bog-like pond, and slinked along the ground. There were no vividly colored plants to brighten the place up. The flowers only came in shades of black, red, and burgundy.

Most people, aside from he and the other Ancients, were uncomfortable out here. Not Wynter. She often sat in the garden with him, unbothered by the snakes, since they paid her no mind.

They didn't even harm her when she walked out here in her sleep. Something he still couldn't understand. He hadn't been at her side so, by rights, they should have swarmed her for intruding. Instead, they'd followed her—curious? Protective? He wasn't sure. He was simply grateful for it, because she would otherwise have been attacked by them on multiple occasions.

Reaching the temple, the Ancients walked up the pitted steps and strode between the main stone pillars. Inside, Cain couldn't help but grimace at the scents of mildew, dust, and cold stone. He lit the wall torches with a mere wave of his hand. The whoosh of the flames whirring to life stirred the cobwebs and dust motes. Said flames danced in the air, casting shadows over the statues.

"It has been so long since I was last here," said Inanna.

And not only because, until some months ago, she'd been at Rest for a long time. The truth was that she'd never been a frequent visitor of Cain. She'd always kept a certain distance between them. No doubt to placate her sister, whose jealousy was easily whipped up.

Cain stalked through the sculpted archway, passing pretty marble pillars and the intricately carved animal totems. His eyes caught on the old, rudimentary carvings on the wall up ahead that told the story of his kind. He remembered bringing Wynter here. Remembered explaining what the various symbols meant, even as he'd feared she'd pull away from him once she learned the truth of what he was and, more, who his father was.

But she hadn't. His own personal miracle had been more bothered by the fact that cherubim blood flowed in his veins.

Coming to a spiral staircase, Cain descended it slowly, his footsteps echoing. At the bottom, he moved to the arch that featured a wrought-iron gate. A padlock kept it closed—one that could only be opened by an Ancient. So a zap of Cain's power was enough to unlock it. The gate slowly swung open. He and the other Ancients then filed into the grotto there.

The smooth rock walls and arched ceiling glimmered like they'd been dusted with gold. Cain lit the torches with a flick of his hand. The flames danced and sliced through the shadows, illuminating the natural hot spring.

Energy fairly bounced around the space, static and wild. The scents of damp rock, minerals, algae, and mildew laced the air—air so thick, moist, and hot it was uncomfortable to inhale.

It also hummed with power.

Abaddon's power.

If any nosy residents somehow managed to get this far, they wouldn't understand what was down here. Wouldn't have a clue what was so special about this grotto. Wouldn't understand that the natural hot spring protected an Ancient.

Yes, they slept in water when they went into the deep state of Rest. Not many people were aware of that. He suspected it was where tales of Leviathans being sea monsters came from.

Cain walked toward the spring, feeling the heat of the smooth stone through the soles of his shoes. The turquoise water lapped at the stone edges, burbling and steaming. White/blue flickers of power crackled along the surface like miniature whips of lightning.

"I'm not getting any sense that he's close to waking," said Ishtar.

"No, nor am I." Inanna let out a disappointed sigh.

Cain exchanged a brief look with Azazel. It might seem that Abaddon was sleeping deeply. But the fact that Wynter had been called to the garden several times suggested differently.

Cain swept his gaze along the other Ancients. "Shall we begin?"

They nodded or murmured their agreement. Then, as one, they knelt on the smooth stone ledge.

Subtle vibrations buzzed against Cain's kneecaps, and the steamy air rising from the well fanned his face. As he was deep in the shadowy depths of the spring, it wasn't possible to see or physically touch Abaddon from there. But touching him wouldn't be enough to wake him anyway.

As Cain reached down to dip his hand inside the well, the water burbled upward and closed over his hand, silky and hot; tiny air bubbles brushed over his skin. Seeing that the other Ancients were ready, he nodded. Together, they chanted in their old language, calling for their fellow Leviathan to join them, as they poured their power into the water to stir him awake.

When they had recently woken Inanna in much the same way, it had only taken one try. It usually did. But Abaddon hadn't fallen into a simple rejuvenating Rest, and he hadn't been asleep for a mere century or so. He'd been in this state for a millennia. So it didn't entirely surprise Cain when nothing happened.

"Let us try again," urged Seth.

And so they did. Still, the ritual failed to wake Abaddon.

His jaw clenched, Dantalion cricked his neck. "Once more."

Again, they chanted and flooded the water with power. Again, nothing happened.

"I say we return tomorrow evening," said Lilith as everyone rose to their feet. "The more frequently we try, the more chance we have of success."

Ishtar shook droplets of water from her hand. "*Or* we are merely wasting our time," she snarked.

Lilith gave her a cold smile. "Either way, it will do us no harm, will it?"

They made their way out of the temple and back to the Keep.

Azazel lingered when the others left and turned to Cain. "Given what we believe causes your consort to sleepwalk, I didn't think your uncle would be so hard to wake."

Cain shrugged. "The longer an Ancient has been asleep, the more difficult it can be to wake them."

Azazel inclined his head. "True." He sighed. "I really hope Ishtar's wrong and that our efforts to disturb his Rest will pay off."

"I believe they will," said Cain. "We just have to accept that this may take time."

Azazel grunted. "The problem is we don't have much of that."

*

Wynter's eyelids fluttered as sleep began to slowly lose its hold on her. Her heels scuffed the ground as someone dragged her limp form backwards, their hands tucked beneath her armpits. Her monster was pushing against her skin, furious, wanting out. It seemed to only be the cautioning preternatural breeze fluttering around Wynter that kept the monster in check.

She could hear voices whispering to each other. Female voices. Ones she recognized.

Demetria's coven.

Bitches. They'd pay for this. Dearly. Not at this exact moment, though. Because the chatter and laughter of the other townspeople was far too close. If she freed her monster here, it could go after nearby innocents—that would be bad.

Sure, Wynter could try taking on her kidnappers herself. She was pretty sure it wouldn't be hard to take them out. But she needed to make a public statement. While she couldn't allow everyone to *see* her monster, she could certainly allow them to see what it could do—it was about the only way she could prove it existed. As she'd told Cain, only fear would truly discourage assholes from trying to cash in on the bounty.

She wondered if her coven had yet realized she'd been taken. Oh, they'd notice she was missing. But, naturally, they'd initially assume they'd merely lost her in the maze or simply couldn't see her due to all the maze's fog.

"We need to move faster," whined the person dragging Wynter. *Missy.*

"For heaven's sake, lower your voice," said Kyra. "We don't want to get spotted."

Missy snorted. "People won't care. They'll be glad to see the skank go."

"Not after Cain's speech they won't," objected another voice—Vera. "Most are fully behind him, and they're too scared to cross him anyway."

"Exactly," agreed Kyra. "Everyone knows what he did to Grouch when the berserker didn't stop mages from kidnapping his consort. They won't want to meet that same fate if Cain finds out they saw her being taken and didn't do anything to help."

"Most also believe he's right that Adam won't hand over a single dime," Vera added.

Missy made a *pfft* sound. "It's obvious that Cain only said that to discourage people from going after his consort."

"No one really trusts Aeons, though," said Kyra. "So they're more willing to believe Cain than Adam. Not that I'm complaining. It means that no one got to her before we could. The bounty is now ours for the taking."

"Damn right. And it means we can also avenge Demetria. I don't condone that she freed that Saul asshole, but she didn't deserve to die for it." Missy paused walking for a moment, breathless. "We should have parked the car somewhere close."

"It would have been noticed," Vera pointed out. "It was better to park it outside the tunnel."

Grunting, Missy resumed walking. "How pissed do you think she'll be when she realizes she was rendered defenseless by a simple sleeping powder?"

"*Seriously* pissed, hopefully. This proves she ain't no revenant."

"Not necessarily," said Kyra. "Even a revenant would be knocked out by a sleeping potion."

"You can't truly think this bitch was Favored by a deity," said Missy, her voice ringing with disgust and incredulity.

"I don't," Kyra told her. "Demetria always said it was a lie, and I agree. I'm just making the point that—"

"Oh, who cares?" Missy halted again. "God, does the skank really have to be so heavy?"

"Stop complaining," said Vera. "She's only a slender thing. She can't weigh much."

"Yeah? Then *you* drag her the rest of the way." Missy unceremoniously dumped Wynter onto the ground.

Fucking ow.

Vera huffed. "Fine."

Right then, a gust of air humming with encouragement whispered over Wynter. Her monster responded instantly, shoving closer to the surface, readying itself to lunge.

Sensing someone hover over her, Wynter flipped open her eyelids, knowing black inky ribbons were wriggling over her eyes.

Vera froze, her lips parting.

Wynter smiled. "Well, hello." Her monster charged forward, and everything once more went dark.

Chapter Seven

Wynter woke with a groan and blinked hard a few times. A purple night sky streaked with thick clouds came into focus, and she became aware that she was indignantly splayed out in the grass.

The back of her head throbbed a little, which could no doubt be courtesy of her hitting the ground when she passed out. One side of her face burned in a way that told her Kali's mark was now visible—at least temporarily.

No other part of Wynter's body hurt, so she didn't think she'd been injured when her monster took over. Thankfully, that was usually the case.

She didn't always fall unconscious when the entity withdrew. Sometimes she simply "jolted" back to herself. Maybe it was dependent on how long her monster was in control, or maybe it was dependent on Wynter's physical condition at the time—she really had no clue.

Sitting upright, she took in the scene with a grimace. There was a lot of blood. It discolored the soil, dotted the blades of grass, and left slashing marks on the trees. All that was left of the witches were the occasional chewed limb, half a torso, and a severed head.

Lovely. And not an uncommon sight in such instances.

Her monster had a tendency to eat its enemies alive when it attacked. And it gave few fucks about what kind of mess it left in its wake. Which was when Anabel's special evidence-ridding brews came in handy. They were stronger and more fast-acting than any bleach.

Wynter took stock of herself as she stood. No wounds, just as she'd suspected. But there was plenty of crimson splatter on her clothes and skin. Also some bits of flesh and guts.

Her scalp was wet and itchy. She didn't need to reach up and touch her hair to know that it was streaked with blood. Awesome.

Her head whipped to the side as she sensed people bearing down on her. Her coven, she quickly realized.

"Are you okay?" asked Delilah.

Wynter grunted. "Never better."

"It took us a few minutes to realize you'd been taken," said Anabel. "We just thought we'd lost you somewhere in the maze. We tracked you this far, but then we heard your monster when we got close. We decided to stay out of the way and let it take care of business."

"Good call," said Wynter, cricking her neck.

Settling her hands on her hips, Anabel sighed. "You know, you all really need to listen to me when I say that death stalks us. It's not a difficult concept to grasp, people." She raked her gaze over Wynter. "Do you have any of my healing potions with you?"

"Yes, but none of this blood is mine." Wynter looked at what was left of the bodies. "They didn't hurt me. They knocked me out with sleeping dust."

Honestly, she was kind of insulted that they'd thought it would be enough to incapacitate her for longer than a few minutes. But then, they'd insisted on believing that she was simply a good ole regular witch. That was their mistake, and she supposed she should be glad they'd made it. Not that they would have otherwise gotten her to Aeon. Neither Wynter nor her monster would have allowed that.

Xavier circled their remains. "I recognize that head. It's the Oasis Coven, huh?"

"Yup." Wynter scratched at her sticky scalp, and a small meaty blob plopped to the ground. Nice. "Kyra grabbed me while I was in the maze. She blew powder in my face before I had the chance to react. I went out like a light. I don't think I was out for long, because I wasn't far from all the activity when I woke up to find that I was being dragged off by Missy. They had a car waiting outside the tunnel, apparently."

"So they *were* in cahoots with Demetria?" asked Delilah.

"No, it seemed that they wanted to avenge her death."

Humming to herself, Hattie began pulling fragments of bone and brain matter out of Wynter's hair as casually as if they were blades of grass. "They meant to hand you over to Adam, I'm guessing," said Hattie.

Wynter nodded. "That was their idiotic plan."

The old woman sneered at the dismembered corpses. "Then they deserved what they got."

Anabel pulled out a vial. "Here, let me clean your clothes." She splashed the vial's contents over Wynter's tee and jeans. The blood gradually faded like, well, magick. The blonde's nose wrinkled. "I can't pour it over your hair unless you want it bleached white."

"Thanks, but no," said Wynter.

"If it helps," began Xavier, "a lot of people have poured fake blood on themselves for the street party, so I don't think you'll stand out too much when we're walking home."

Wynter didn't care if she stood out, because this would be an occasion when she wouldn't hide what she'd been forced to do. But she *did* care that she hadn't been able to quite simply enjoy an evening out with her coven. It had been going so well up until that point.

Delilah blew out a breath. "Your man is gonna be *pissed* when he hears about this, Wyn."

Totally. "And no doubt disappointed that he wasn't able to administer some punishment himself." She truly hoped that Cain wouldn't start to again argue that she needed guards, because he really wouldn't like it when she refused to back down on this.

Folding his arms in a petulant manner, Xavier glanced at the corpses again and sighed. "Your monster never leaves me anything to play with. I could have had so much fun reanimating the bodies and sending 'em running after people. It probably would have been a while before anyone realized that the witches were actually dead and not just acting scary for the street party."

Anabel gaped at him. "You're really thinking about how you were deprived of *fun* right now? Wynter was almost *kidnapped*, you tool."

He shrugged. "It wasn't the first time. Probably won't be the last."

Wynter snickered. "I really wish I could say you were wrong."

Anabel huffed at him and held out another vial. "Here. Make yourself useful and clean the scene."

"No," Wynter objected, closing her hand around the vial before Xavier could take it. "People need to see what happens to anyone who fucks with a revenant. They need to understand that I *am* a revenant."

"This will definitely make that clear, so all right," said Anabel. "What do we do with your monster's leftovers? Leave them here?"

Wynter touched the edge of her incisor with her tongue. "I have a better idea than that."

*

Pausing in his pacing, Cain blinked at his consort. "You ... you all you played catch with Missy's severed head near the bonfire?"

She lifted her shoulders. "Well, it caught people's attention."

He'd bet. Bodiless heads tended to do that.

"And it delivered a message that they needed to hear loud and clear." She went to drop onto the leather desk chair but then hesitated, scrunching up her face as she looked at the blood matting her long hair. "I don't think people thought that it was a real head at first, what with the street party being a Halloween celebration and all. But then a lycan came over to mess with Xavier, who promptly tossed the head at him. The dude spat out a seriously loud curse when he caught it. Kind of squeamish, for a lycan. Don't you think?"

Cain ground his teeth. He didn't care about lycans. He cared that people—worse, *his own people*—had dared try to deliver Wynter to a man who likely meant to put her through a shitload of pain for cursing his land.

When she'd walked into his ledger room looking like she'd had her head dunked into a pool of blood, Cain had pushed out of his desk chair so fast he'd sent it skidding backwards. He'd seen her in this state enough times to conclude that she must have been forced to free her monster to save herself. And when he'd heard what exactly went down tonight, he'd almost lost his mind.

Yes, he'd known something like this might happen. But there was intellectually *knowing* that someone could target her, and there was *hearing* that people had actually attempted to take from him the one person he needed.

Until Wynter waltzed into his world, it had been a long time since Cain felt anything *deeply*. Even the strongest emotions lost some of their impact when you'd lived so many years that you'd experienced them over and over and over. It was inescapable, really.

But having Wynter in his life ... Everything seemed so much more vivid nowadays. Hence the rage pumping through his veins, hot and thick like lava. His creature was equally furious.

"Afterwards, we threw all the body parts on the bonfire." Her nose wrinkled. "We later regretted it, though, because it made quite a stench. I forgot how much I hate the smell of burning flesh."

"How exactly does one forget that?"

She shot him a sour look. "I know what I did was pretty gruesome, okay, but I had to make a statement."

"I'm not angry about what *you* did. I'm angry that the Oasis Coven dared touch you." He was also a little pissed that none of the witches were alive for him to punish. He'd owned rights to their souls, which meant he could have subjected them to an overload of pain that would have threatened to fracture their sanity. That would have gone a long way to making him feel better.

"Yeah, join the club."

Cain scrubbed a hand over his face. "I should have exiled them after you killed Demetria. I shouldn't have allowed them to stay."

"Why? They gave you every indication that they were ashamed of what she did and that they had no intention of seeking vengeance for her death." She scratched at her bloody scalp and then eyed her red fingernails with distaste. "Honestly, I don't think the coven would ever have so much as touched me if Adam hadn't offered that bounty. They considered it a risk worth taking."

"And, despite what you did tonight, there may still be others who feel the same. It would be better for you to have a few guards until—"

"No."

Feeling his nostrils flare, Cain forced his back teeth to unlock. "I won't take chances with your life."

"I wouldn't expect you to, so I suspected you'd start with this again. But everything I said last night still applies. Also, consider this: No one will try to kill me. Adam wants me alive. Besides, being immortal now, I'm not so easy to kill anyway. And it's not like I'd permanently stay dead."

"We've already covered that we can't be sure that there won't be a time when you don't come back."

"Cain, you won't get your way here. I won't agree to have guards. And be honest, you're suggesting this out of anger, not good sense."

"Of course I'm fucking angry. Did you expect anything different?"

"Nope. But you're not a stupid man. You know I have to deal with this matter on my own, just as you know you wouldn't truly trust any guard to not at some point betray me—we've been over this already. We both agreed it made sense for me to handle this my way."

Cain inwardly cursed. His monster wasn't annoyed with her. It believed she could take care of herself and it agreed that she needed to make it clear to one and all that she was not easy prey.

"I learned a few things tonight," she said. "I overheard a little conversation between Missy, Vera, and Kyra. It seems that your speech did a good job of convincing people to back you. Allegedly, most do. Just the same, most believe that Adam wouldn't truly offer any of his promised rewards and, in any case, they fear you too much to cross you."

Cain's hirelings had made that very same assessment.

"Don't let what happened tonight make you suddenly feel that there are threats to me everywhere. Yes, there will still be some people who are so tempted by the thought of becoming a millionaire that they'll take their chances. But most people won't. Most are behind you. And we both know that I can take down any who come for me."

He rubbed at his nape. He couldn't even claim she was being overconfident. Not when she was a being that could kill literally anything—including an Ancient. "You could have at least let *one* of the witches live so I could get my own message across."

Her lips twitched. "I totally knew you were gonna complain about that. If it had been me who personally dealt with them, I would have kept one of the bitches alive for you. But my monster was behind the wheel, and it pretty much does whatever it wants."

Cain grunted. "I've noticed." He let out a long sigh. Rage still held him in a tight grip, but it was no longer hot and wild. It was cold. Logical. Controlled. "You and your coven really played catch with Missy's severed head?"

"While singing 'Ding Dong the Witch is Dead'."

He felt one corner of his mouth cant up for the briefest moment. "And whose idea was it?"

"Mine, of course. The best ideas are always mine. The craziest? Usually Delilah's, though Xavier contributes his fair share of insane suggestions."

Cain gave a slow shake of the head. Wynter never did what he expected her to do, but he found that he liked that. "I'm almost sorry I missed it. Other things required my attention, as you know."

"Shit, I forgot to ask, did you have any luck waking Abaddon?"

"No, but we'll keep trying. It's all we can do."

"I truly think your efforts will eventually pay off."

"Is that so?"

"Yes." Wynter didn't see how seven beings so unbelievably powerful wouldn't manage to bring another Ancient out of their Resting state. But she understood why it might be difficult, given how long Abaddon had been under. Snapping people out of comas wasn't something that people just *did*.

"You'll wake him up, and then you'll get out of this damn cage, and then you'll kill Adam and all will be well." She cocked her head. "What will you do with your freedom?"

"Travel a little. You'll go with me, of course."

She hiked up an imperious brow. "Is that so? You know, you could try asking rather than telling." She doubted he'd do it all that often, though. He was a person used to being in charge and dishing out orders, and he'd been that way for an exceptionally long time. Someone like that didn't suddenly just *change*. He did usually make an effort to tone his highhandedness down for her, which she appreciated. It was likely the best she could hope for.

"But that would give you the chance to refuse, and I want you with me," Cain told her. "I don't want to be away from you. And you wouldn't want me to go alone in any case, so let's not pretend differently."

Rather than concede he was right, she gave him a haughty sniff. "Where is it you want to go?"

"Nowhere in particular."

He merely wanted to get a taste of freedom, she understood. He wanted to prove to himself that he wasn't imprisoned anymore; that he could go where he pleased, when he pleased, however he pleased. "But you intend to come back here?"

"Yes. This place was supposed to be strictly a cage, but myself and the other Ancients made it into a home. I'm proud of that. I don't wish to build another for myself. I'm content to live here. I simply want the walls of the prison gone."

"Good. This place is a refuge for a lot of people, including me and my coven. I like living here." She didn't want to move. Nor did she want her coven to leave here—this was likely the safest place for a bunch of insane fugitives such as them. And it would be no easy thing to get them to leave that cottage anyway. Plus, they'd likely blow it up before they'd let anyone else have it. "Do you think the other Ancients will also travel?"

"Probably, though we won't all do so at once. Devil's Cradle needs to be protected, so I suspect there will always be at least four Ancients here at one time. We don't want others thinking that it's up for the taking."

She snorted. "I doubt you have to worry about people thinking to take over the place or anything." On the way to Devil's Cradle, she'd questioned many of the people she'd come across about the Ancients. All had demonstrated a healthy dose of fear when they spoke of them.

"Probably not," said Cain. "But it's still best to take precautions."

That she could agree with. "I'm sorry you didn't manage to wake Abaddon."

He shrugged. "I wasn't expecting it to be so easy. I just hope it doesn't prove to be impossible. The other Ancients and I have had two things on our mind for an eternally long time—vengeance and freedom. We're so close to finally gaining both. If everything fell apart now, I don't think they would all mentally cope.

"I think it would be too much for some, particularly Ishtar. They'd snap, and another Ancient would have to kill them. It would be sad if, after we've managed to stick together for so long, we suddenly turned on each other as the Aeons had always meant for us to do."

It would be a sad ending for sure. And it would not only mean that the Aeons had won after all, it would mean that the Ancients had held out this long for nothing. Worse, it could even mean that Cain and Seth turned on each other. The thought made her stomach twist.

Cain had already killed one of his brothers—there was no love lost between him and Abel, no, but finding yourself in a position where you had to kill your own sibling or die was still nothing other than plain shitty. He cared for Seth, though. To lose their closeness would destroy something in Cain for certain. And as she took in his expression, she could sense that he was imagining just how hard it would be. "I'd come hug you but I'm all gross right now."

A hint of warmth slid into his eyes. He held out his hand. "Shower. Then I need to fuck you; remind myself that you're safe and well here with me."

She smiled and slipped her hand into his. "Best plan ever."

Chapter Eight

As they headed toward the plaza, Anabel sighed at Xavier. "Are you going to wear that stupid grin all evening?"

The aforementioned grin didn't shrink in the slightest as he said, "Why wouldn't I? It's been a relaxing, beautiful day from start to, well, now."

"And you're enjoying that Stewart just snubbed you again," guessed Wynter. It had been a few days since she'd had to sic her monster on the Oasis Coven, but the Beta lycan still appeared to be in a funk over how he'd found himself holding Missy's head, which delighted Xavier to no end.

He slipped his hands into the pockets of his jeans. "What can I say? I'm all about payback. The bitchier it is, the better. Who would've thought a lycan would freak out so much over such a small thing? It's not as if they ain't used to blood and violence. God, it was so cool when he retched."

"Small thing?" Snorting, Anabel cast Xavier a sideways glance. "I think most people would be weirded out if they realized they'd just caught the head of a corpse—especially the head of someone they know. It was pretty mean of you to toss it at him, if you ask me."

"*He* was mean first," Xavier pointed out. "I was merely acting as a conduit for karma. Del does it all the time. There's something very satisfying about it."

Smiling, Delilah nodded. "Right?"

"Right. It made me feel all warm inside."

Delilah gently nudged him. "You should do it more often. Make it a new habit. Let it replace the whole chronic lying thing. Reinvent yourself."

His brow creased. "But I like the 'me' I am now."

"Dear God, why?"

"Hey." Xavier slapped a hand over his chest. "That hurt, you know."

"And now you're lying again."

"It brings me joy and comfort. Don't you want me to be happy?"

"Fuck, no. You make me crazy."

Feeling her lips twitch, Wynter shook her head. As the two went on to squabble, she once more scanned her surroundings. A week had gone by since Adam called for her and Cain to surrender themselves to him. There had been no other attempts to snatch her, but she wasn't relaxing her guard. Nor were her coven, which was why they had all insisted on coming along for the shopping trip to grab essentials and work supplies.

There was no countdown-to-Halloween celebration tonight—that would come tomorrow. But there were still plenty of people out and about on the surface of Devil's Cradle. Honestly, it seemed to never sleep.

Residents still often glanced her way, just as they were doing now. But the looks they cast her tended to be quite different from before the street party incident. Some were assessing. Some were respectful. Some were fearful.

Some were even awed.

Well, it was no small thing to be Favored by a deity. And if Kali made you different from other revenants, it said something. People were probably questioning whether it meant something good or something bad.

It was a question that she knew haunted Cain.

Unfortunately, he and the other Ancients hadn't yet managed to wake Abaddon. They had tried every evening without fail. Cain didn't believe that the sleeping Ancient had so much as stirred, but he couldn't tell for sure.

A growl came from Anabel as she glanced from Xavier to Delilah. "Will you two stop bickering. I swear, you're like children sometimes."

Hattie put her fingers to her lips. "My, my, my, would you look at that derriere?"

Wynter tracked her gaze and noticed a well-built male bending over to grab bales of hay, stacking them on top of one other. "You really need to stop ogling asses."

"It can't be helped," said Hattie.

Delilah made a humming sound. "I'll admit, that *is* a fabulous behind." She let out a sigh of longing. "I wouldn't mind a good ole roll in the hay."

Hattie pulled a face. "It's not as fun as it sounds. I wouldn't recommend it."

Wynter felt her brows inch up. "You and George did some hot yoga in the field?"

"Stables," corrected Hattie. "And it wasn't George. It was my first husband."

"The one who was hung like a bull?" asked Anabel.

Hattie gave a curt nod. "He wasn't very skillful in bed. Relied on his size to do all the pleasing. He would just pound away and traumatize your cervix. If you wanted him to find your clitoris, you needed to draw the oaf a map. It was such a shame that he died," she added sadly . . . as if he'd lost his life in a freak, tragic accident.

Delilah fired her an incredulous look. "You find it a shame? Really?"

Hattie shrugged one shoulder. "I did miss him when he was gone."

"Enough that you wished you hadn't killed him?" asked Delilah.

"Not quite that much."

Delilah set one hand on her hip. "Okay, here's what I don't get. You say you're sorry you ended the lives of your husbands. Yet, you don't wish that you hadn't done it. How can you be sorry and *not* regretful?"

"I'm sorry that they put me in a position where I was forced to kill them," Hattie clarified.

"Forced? They forced you?"

"What else was I supposed to do after they betrayed me and broke their vows?"

"Spit on them? Leave them? Kick them in the balls?"

Hattie shot Delilah a snooty look. "Ladies do not spit, though I would not expect you to know that. I couldn't have left them without also divorcing them, and we've already covered that I don't believe in divorce. And I would never kick a man's testicles—that can cause real damage, you know."

"More damage than a deadly poison?"

"I don't see where you're going with this."

Halting outside the grocery store, Wynter raised her hands. "Let it go for now, okay? Go inside and grab whatever stuff you need."

"Don't forget we need to head to the bookstore after this," Hattie piped up.

"It's not exactly a 'need'," began Delilah, "but don't worry, old woman, you'll get there."

Hattie's brow furrowed. "Books are a necessity. I can't believe you'd imply differently. Or that I ever trusted you."

Delilah snorted. "Works of fiction are a form of entertainment, nothing more."

"Your negativity is not appreciated."

"I'm not being negative, I'm being real."

"You're being a tight-assed bit—"

"*Enough.*" Wynter nudged a grinning Delilah. "Stop winding up old ladies and go shop. Hattie, ease up on the insults, would you?"

"For you, Wynter," agreed Hattie, ever so benevolent.

Honest to Christ, they were a handful.

The five of them headed into the store and each grabbed a basket. They usually split up to go nab what they needed. But today the coven insisted that Wynter wasn't to be left alone. They were still pissed that they hadn't noticed she'd been snatched by Missy, Kyra, and Vera until it was almost too late.

As a group, they went from aisle to aisle, chucking items into their baskets. Xavier didn't need much, so he quickly got bored and started throwing unnecessary stuff into Delilah's basket. That led to yet another argument between the two. An argument that continued even as they bagged up their purchases and then walked out the exit. And that, in turn, led to Anabel once again ordering them to "quit it already". It was as the annoyed blonde marched off in a strop that she almost crashed into Shelia, one of Ishtar's aides.

The female vampire sneered. "Watch where you're going."

"I am watching, I'm not impressed with what I see," snarked Anabel.

Shelia blinked in surprise. The three female vamps behind her looked equally stunned. Yeah, people didn't always sense that Anabel wasn't quite as innocent or harmless as she looked. Wynter got the feeling that the witch liked that.

"Oh, is that so? Well, that makes two of us." Shelia skimmed her gaze over the rest of the coven. "Nope, nothing impressive to see here."

The other vampires shifted nervously.

Sidling up to Anabel, Wynter gave Shelia a sweet smile. "Well, you could continue to watch us not give a crumb of a fuck what you think about literally anything ... or you could walk away. Totally up to you."

Shelia scoffed. "You think you're special just because you get to ride Cain's cock. Sorry to point out what should be obvious to you, sweetie, but you're not the first. Plenty of women had him before you, and plenty will have him after he dumps your ass. Which he will. It's merely a matter of time. And when that day comes, I'll remind you of this conversation."

"And my give-a-shit-o-meter still ain't moving." Wynter gave her a "what can you do?" shrug. "*Lovely* chatting with you." She went to pass the vampires, but Shelia stupidly slipped in front of her.

The vampire snarled. "You think I'm afraid of you?"

Wynter took a step forward, pleased when the little bitch tensed. "What I think is that you believe being Ishtar's aide protects you. Maybe it does usually. But it won't protect you from me. You don't believe that? Well, consider that it didn't protect Azazel's aide. You never wondered where Bowen went?"

Shelia's eyes flickered.

One of the other vamps rested a hand on Shelia's shoulder, avoiding Wynter's gaze. "Come on, let's go."

"Yes, do go." Wynter skirted around Shelia, whose hand shot out and gripped her arm. Wynter didn't hesitate to act. She struck with magick, lashing it like a whip.

Stumbling aside, Shelia stared at her decaying hand in horror. It burned, charred, and flaked away. She screamed and screamed and screamed ... and then she stopped as her hand "returned" to normal, only then realizing it had been a mere illusion.

"I can make it happen for real, if you'd like," Wynter offered.

Shelia swallowed, looking dazed. She didn't protest as her friends led her away.

Anabel looked at Wynter as they and the rest of the coven resumed walking. "Do you think Ishtar encourages *all* her hirelings to hate you?"

"Probably," Wynter replied. "I can understand why those who are excessively loyal to her would loathe me so much. Maxim would be pissed at anyone who gave Cain problems."

"Hmm, I guess so," said Anabel. "I still don't like it."

"Me neither," Delilah fairly growled. "I'm in the mood to cut a bitch up right now."

"That'll have to wait until we've been to the bookstore," Hattie declared. "I'm not missing—" She jumped as thunder cracked the air.

Wynter looked up to see thick gray clouds gathering in the sky. More, a face flashed to life within it. *Adam's* face.

"Oh, shit," said Delilah.

"You were given time to bring me what I want," Adam began, his voice loud but crackling, "just as Cain and Wynter Dellavale were given time to hand themselves over. You were warned what would happen if my terms were not met. Now you will know what that meant."

A godawful howl of wind came whistling over the town, and the temperature dropped in an instant. No, it didn't merely drop. It took a fucking nosedive.

Her ears popped as the air pressure changed, and then Wynter spat a curse as the wind went *insane.* There was no real turning away from the onslaught, because it wasn't going in any one direction. It seemed to come from every angle.

Autumn leaves, grass, and debris were swirling around the air, swept up in the gale. Trees swayed with audible creaks. Awnings flapped like crazy. Garbage cans rattled.

Wynter's hair whipped at her face and partially obscured her vision. Her clothes fluttered against her body, the bags she carried swinging and bashing her legs.

The wind quickly went from sharp to *buffeting.* It bit at her skin, icy cold and hard as a stinging slap. Her eyes watered, and each puff of breath she let out fogged the air. Air that suddenly smelled of ozone and was so crisp it hurt to breathe it in.

Delilah staggered into a lamppost, bumping her hip hard. "The hell?"

Wynter stumbled against the gust of air rushing over the town, squinting at her coven. "The liquor store!" she yelled, her voice somewhat muffled by the horrendous noise of the wind. "Get inside!"

Ducking their heads, they pushed against the force of the wind as they tried heading to the nearest building. Which was the exact moment when a flurry of snowflakes came tumbling from the sky and all but *battered* them.

Wynter almost let out a shocked squeal. The wind whipped the snow everywhere, so it pelted her from all sides. She swore as some flakes found their way down the back of her collar.

The garbage can in front of them fell over with a clang—

And rolled toward Hattie at top speed.

It crashed into her legs, taking them out from under her.

Shit. Straining against the force of the wind, Wynter and Xavier forged forward until they reached her. He kicked the can aside and then helped Wynter lift Hattie off the ground. It was hard to tell while she was squinting against the force of the wind, but the woman *looked* okay, just furious.

"The liquor store!" Wynter repeated.

Her equilibrium a thing of the past, she pushed forward against the wind again, her clothes flapping, her hair whipping everywhere. The howling gale carried the sounds of glass breaking, voices crying out, branches snapping, and objects scraping concrete as they rolled down the street.

She hissed as some swirling debris scratched her eye just as the snow became heavier and sharp and . . . no, it wasn't snow anymore.

Hailstones.

They powered down and *pummeled* everything—pinging off the ground, leaving little cracks in windows, denting metal cans, bouncing off brick walls, assaulting her body like darts. Glass shattered as a hailstone the size of a freaking golf ball crashed through a store window. *Oh, hell.*

She and her coven tried to run, but the wind was too powerful. Her free hand clinging tight to the handles of her bag, she threw her free arm over her head to shield it from the icy pellets. They kept tumbling down, battering and scraping and stabbing her skin.

The wind abruptly began lashing out like swiping hands. It barreled into a tree, knocking it down with an ominous crack. A gust then slammed into a fleeing male, sweeping him off his feet and sending him skidding backwards on his stomach. The wind then lifted the fallen tree and batted it through the air, causing it to crash through a store window.

Jesus *Christ* this was crazy.

A ball-sized hailstone smacked down hard on her shoulder, making her hiss through her teeth.

Almost there. They were almost at the store.

A branch tore off a nearby tree and came sailing toward Wynter. She leaned to the side, but it clawed at her temple as it passed. She hissed at the sharp sting, feeling warm liquid pool to the surface.

Fuck this shit.

It was as they *finally* neared the store that a fey staggered toward the door and—

Tiles tumbled off its roof, slammed down on his head, and crashed to the sidewalk. His body hit the ground hard. Dead? Unconscious? She didn't know yet.

Xavier yanked open the shop's door as they reached it. "Inside!" he shouted, barely audible over the whistles and moans of the wind.

Wynter hurried the others into the store and then helped Xavier drag the fey inside. As Xavier slammed the door shut, she put shaking fingers to the fey's throat to feel for a pulse, but they were too numb to sense anything.

The shopkeeper hurried toward them. "He's alive, I can hear his heartbeat. What's going on out there?"

Wynter shoved her tangled hair away from her face and dropped her bags on the floor. "Adam," she replied simply, her cold lips trembling.

The woman's eyes widened. "He's here?"

"I doubt it, or he wouldn't have bothered doing one of his little cloud broadcasts, he would have shouted at us from wherever he stood." Wynter frantically brushed at the flakes of snow and hailstones that peppered her skin, hair, and clothes. It didn't help much. Plenty had already melted into her hoodie and jeans, leaving them damp and icy.

Blowing out a breath, she took stock of herself and her coven. They were all covered in scrapes, cuts, and welts. At least they'd heal pretty fast.

Anabel, her hands jammed under her armpits, shivered as she said, "He most likely sent other Aeons to do his dirty work."

Wynter gave a jerky nod. "They'll be somewhere just beyond the boundaries." And with any luck, the scouts had spotted them and already alerted the Ancients.

Shuddering, Xavier adjusted his collar and dropped his chin down to his chest. "I know Adam said he'd punish the town but, great mother of fuck, I was not expecting a blizzard."

Wynter pulled her limbs tight to her body. "Me neither." She rubbed her hands together, enjoying the brief flashes of warmth that came from the friction.

Delilah exhaled heavily over her cupped hands and then tugged down her sleeves to cover them. "I can't feel my fingers."

Her arms wrapped around her body, Hattie stamped her feet. "My toes are like ice."

Flexing her own toes inside her shoes, Wynter slung an arm around the old woman's shoulders. "At the very least, *one* of the Ancients will intervene soon."

The entire coven stood close, sharing body heat, as they turned toward the window and stared at the scene playing out outside. The wind continued to howl and drone. The force of it made the door rattle. Pebble-sized hailstones pattered the building and drummed at the windows.

She was glad that the vehicles were kept inside the warehouse, or she had the feeling that they would be flipping over and skidding along the pavement.

No one moved. No one spoke. They could only stand and watch the storm reign, a little shaken by the show of power that—

A shimmering blast clashed hard into the wind. Rolled around it. Engulfed it somehow. And, soon enough, the gust calmed as the hailstones became locusts.

Cain.

The swarm of insects gathered in a tornado-like swirl that grew and grew and grew . . . only to then zoom away and disappear over the mountains.

Wynter blew out a relieved breath. The howling wind and

99

hailstones were gone. It was over. *Thank God.* If the storm had gone on much longer, it might have damaged the utility structures and possibly knocked out the town's power.

"Come on," Wynter said to her coven before pulling open the door. She stepped outside, snow crunching beneath her shoes, and looked around. God, it was like a blanket of white covered the town, weighing down trees, layering rooftops, and carpeting the roads and sidewalks. People would need to dig out some salt and shovels for sure.

She had the fleeting thought that this same damage would have been done during the battles if the Ancients weren't so tip-fucking-top at countering the Aeons' strikes.

Now that the temperature was no longer so bitterly low, the snow and pellets would likely thaw fast. But a slight chill still lingered in the air courtesy of the white coating that fell over the town.

The clouds had cleared, and the moonlight danced over the snow. She might have found it pretty if she wasn't so pissed right now. She was no longer freezing, but she was wet and cold and wanted to peel off Adam's flesh like an orange. While he was alive. And howling in agony.

Wynter turned toward the manor, and there stood Cain on the roof with Seth and Dantalion. The other Ancients began to gather behind them, seemingly too late to be of any assistance.

Xavier scratched his temple. "That was a lot of elemental power. But Adam could have done way worse than that, right?"

Wynter nodded. "He must have sent other Aeons to issue this 'punishment' on his behalf."

"What kind of damage should we expect him to do if he does ever come here personally?"

"We should expect him to destroy every last inch of Devil's Cradle. My opinion? He'd stand for nothing less."

*

Ishtar strolled along the roof, sweeping her gaze over the sight below. "A blizzard. *Pfft*. Far from creative."

"The Aeons aren't going for 'creative'," said Cain. "They're going for 'destructive'."

She flicked her hair over her shoulder. "There was no follow-up after you retaliated. The Aeons responsible must have let loose a little power and then fled."

"One of our scouts caught sight of them before they struck." If any of the creatures here were able to take on Aeons, Cain would have ordered for them to take the bastards out or at least attempt to capture them. Instead, all he could ask of the scouts was that they report the Aeons' arrival immediately.

"I will have some of my aides assess the level of damage," said Dantalion.

"I don't see any sign of fatalities," said Lilith.

"No, nor I," added Inanna.

Ishtar fired a tight smile at Cain. "It appears that your witch and her coven are fine."

Yes, Cain had noticed. He was relieved even as he was furious that she'd been subjected to the wrath of the blizzard in the first place.

Azazel grinned at Ishtar. "I'm sure that fills you with so much delight you almost can't take it."

She shot him a droll look.

"I doubt the Aeons are still close, but we should probably have the scouts confirm it before we step down from here," hedged Seth.

So that was what they did.

By the time they'd received their confirmation that the Aeons were gone, Wynter and her coven had disappeared into the manor and, Cain assumed, to the underground city. When he returned to his Keep, he was informed by one of his aides that she was "home", and the simple word made a smile build inside him.

The moment he stepped inside his chamber, Cain heard the shower running. He padded into the attached bathroom, noting the damp clothes that were piled beside the stall. His consort stood inside it, but he couldn't see much of her due to the steam.

He stripped off his own clothes—they weren't quite as wet as hers, but they were still uncomfortably damp—and joined her in the shower.

She squealed when he cupped her hips from behind. "Christ, your hands are *freezing.*"

Chuckling, he pulled her back against him, which elicited another squeal from her.

"Let me go, asshole!"

He licked a line up her throat. "But this is far more fun."

She bitched at him right up until his hands were warm, at which point she allowed him to soap her down ... which quickly turned sexual, so it wasn't long before he was fucking her against the tiled wall.

Her body trembling from the aftershocks, she slumped against him, breathing hard, burying her face in the crook of his neck. "For an old and decrepit dude, you have a whole lot of energy when it comes to sexytimes."

Feeling his lips curve, he gave her earlobe a sharp nip. "I may be old, but I'm not decrepit."

"I'm going with you when you storm Aeon. You know that, right?"

He tensed. Where in the fuck had that come from? And why in the hell would she ever think he'd allow it? "That's not going to happen. And if you're mentioning this now because you thought that I'll be easier to convince while in post-sex throes, you were mistaken."

She lifted her head, meeting his gaze. There was no anger there, only resolve—firm, calm, and all too familiar. "That wasn't a request," she softly stated. "I know you worry about me. I worry about you just the same. But I won't stay behind."

Cain felt a muscle in his cheek flex. "More than anything, Adam wants you at Aeon. You'd give him that?"

She let out a prim little sniff. "He also wants *you* there. I don't see you offering to stay behind. Besides, it's not like I plan to hand myself over to him." She planted her hands on his shoulders. "I'll make a good distraction, Cain. You know that. He'll be caught between being desperate to eliminate you and desperate to catch me alive. He won't order any of his people to kill me, which means I'll be *way* safer than you'll be. And I'm no easy target. You remember that, right?"

He sighed, knowing she was right in all she'd said, hating to admit it even to himself. Still, he argued that she should stay behind as they dried off, returned to his chamber, and pulled on some clothes. She didn't back down. Nor did she get mad or snippy. She remained calm as she repeatedly stated her case … and he knew that he wouldn't convince her to change her mind. *Fuck.*

Wynter relented at times, even if only in the spirit of compromise so they could find a good balance in their relationship. But not when it came to something important to her. He respected that even though it drove him crazy on occasion.

Turning away from her, he stared unseeing at the wall tapestry. A ruthless voice floated to the forefront of his mind, whispering that he could force her hand. Well, yes, he could. He owned her soul, after all. But he'd never abuse that advantage he held. And there were times he genuinely lamented that there were moral lines he'd agreed—both with himself and with her—never to cross when it came to his consort.

"So you're gonna sulk, huh?"

Affronted, he faced her once more. "I'm not sulking. I'm pissed. You had to know I wouldn't want you to lay siege to Aeon along-side me."

"Considering you asked me to sit out the other two battles, it seemed inevitable that you'd do the same this time. But it isn't going to happen. And before you think about confining me somewhere, remember that Kali wouldn't stand for you holding me anywhere against my will."

"Perhaps She'd side with me on this." Cain narrowed his eyes as an otherworldly breeze fluttered over him, practically purring with an amused condescension. "Or not." He hadn't sensed the deity's presence until right then—She was very good at concealing Herself.

Wynter gave him a wan smile. "You could try convincing Her, but it's super doubtful that She'll go for it."

"You don't have to sound so smug about that."

"Come on, Cain, I'm not some terrified maiden who's inexperienced at battle. Be overprotective, be pissed, be sulky—"

"I'm not sulking."

"—but accept that it won't change anything. Admit, even if only to yourself, that I'd be an asset during the battle rather than a hindrance."

"I don't wish to be rational right now."

Her lips twitched. "All right. We can put logic aside for the moment if you'd like. The situation will remain the same, though." She bit her lip and tilted her head. "Would it make you feel better about everything if I sucked you off?"

His dick reflexively jerked. "No."

"You sure? You don't want a blowjob?"

"No."

A slow, confident smile curved her mouth. "Liar."

"That's where you're wrong." He slowly advanced on her, drilling his gaze into hers. "I don't want to fuck your mouth. I want to fuck your throat. I want to feel the muscles there contract around my cock. Want to see and hear you choke. Want to watch tears fill your eyes and trickle down your face. And then? Then I'd shove my dick somewhere it's only been a few times before now, because if you're going to be a pain in my ass, it's only fair if I'm a pain in yours."

Her pupils dilating, she licked her lips. "Bring it, old man."

He pounced.

Chapter Nine

Standing in the foyer of his Keep a few days later, Cain sighed at Azazel. "I won't get her to change her mind, no matter what I say or do. She's ten times more tenacious than I could ever be."

Azazel chuckled. "I doubt that. From what I've seen, you're both as stubborn as each other."

Cain grunted. He hadn't intended to complain to others about Wynter's insistence on being part of the upcoming battle. But the other Ancient had sensed that something was bugging him, and Cain had found himself spilling out his concerns.

Azazel slapped his arm in commiseration. "I understand why you'd rather she wasn't there, but she'll be an asset."

"That's what she said," Cain grumbled. His creature still agreed with her on that and fully supported her decision.

"And she's right. There are more Aeons than there are Ancients. It won't be easy for us to overpower them. Your consort will give us an edge. We need that."

"We'll *have* an edge." Cain gave him a meaningful look, not wanting to say Abaddon's name aloud. They hadn't yet revealed to the residents as a whole that another Ancient lived here. There weren't many people currently nearby and it didn't seem as if any were attempting to eavesdrop on the conversation, but some creatures had more sensitive hearing than others.

"Only if we manage to do what we've so far successfully failed to do," Azazel pointed out.

"If we don't succeed, we'll need to make some changes to our game plan." In other words, they likely wouldn't damage their prison without Abaddon's aid and so they wouldn't be able to storm Aeon. "Wynter doesn't believe it will come to that."

"Neither do I. And I stand by what I said before—she'll be an asset."

Cain frowned. "You couldn't have just agreed with me so I could complain?"

Azazel's mouth kicked up. "Nah, I'm not that good a friend."

Just then, Maxim hurried through the Keep's entrance and rushed over to them. "Sire, I have news from Inanna. A conduit is here from Aeon. She has shown him into the blue parlor at the manor. He says that Adam wishes to have a meeting with all seven Ancients."

"I see," said Cain, veiling his surprise. "Thank you. Let Inanna know that we'll be there shortly, and have someone pass on the message to the other Ancients."

"Yes, Sire." With that, Maxim left.

Cain looked at Azazel. "We'll take the quick way to the manor." Most people weren't aware of it, but the Ancients had other ways of arriving at the surface that didn't involve using the communal elevator.

"What do you think Adam wants?" asked Azazel as they walked down the hallway, heading for Cain's chamber.

"If he merely wished to speak to me, I'd say he wants to express his fury over Abel's death," replied Cain. "It could be that he's hoping to strike some sort of deal."

"And that he believes that the blizzard one of his people caused will spur us into agreeing?"

"Probably."

The blizzard hadn't left too much destruction in its wake. If the residents were frightened by the Aeons' display of power, it hadn't lasted long, judging by what Maxim had reported a few hours after the incident.

"Once people got over their shock and anger, they started having snowball fights, making snow angels, building skeletal snowmen, and

sliding down the hills on makeshift sleds," Maxim had told Cain. *"They seem disappointed that the snow has already started to melt."*

Although Cain found himself oddly uneasy about bringing another Ancient into the chamber he shared with Wynter, he shook off the feeling and waved Azazel inside.

"Your consort has made many touches to the space," Azazel noted as he spotted the witchy items lying around.

"She has," said Cain. He always felt a flash of pleasure each time he noticed something new she'd brought from the cottage.

Reaching his tall mirror, he placed his hand on the glass, which swiftly turned to rippling black water. He stepped through the mirror and out of an identical one that was kept in a bedroom at the manor. Azazel joined him, and then they both made their way downstairs. They halted outside the door to the blue parlor to wait for the other Ancients. It wasn't long before all seven were gathered together.

"I doubt I am the only one who suspects that Adam is about to make us some kind of offer," said Ishtar, sounding particularly disinterested.

"That would be my guess," said Inanna. "I find it odd that he does not wish to communicate his message through Cain."

Dantalion nodded, rubbing at his bristly jaw. "Requesting to speak with all of us isn't Adam's usual style."

"True," agreed Cain, "but talking with me—or even with both me and Seth—never got him what he wanted. Perhaps he thinks he will have better luck with the rest of you."

"Perhaps." Lilith pursed her lips. "It could be that, in the event that you refuse to agree to his terms, he hopes the rest of us will propose a vote and overrule you."

"It could be, yes," Cain allowed. "Also, knowing Adam, he will take this opportunity to gloat over the success of his plan. I suggest we let him believe that it is going as well as he may anticipate."

"Why?" asked Ishtar.

"Because if he believes that our residents are playing his game just as he'd hoped, he won't feel the need to change that game," Cain replied. "Right now, his moves are easy to predict. Let's not give him a reason to go off-script and take us by surprise."

"Makes sense," said Seth, and the others quickly agreed.

"Let's begin the meeting, then," proposed Azazel.

They filed into the blue parlor. Cain recognized the man sitting on the sofa as the same conduit who'd come here several times before on the Aeons' behalf. Two of Inanna's aides stood against the wall, on guard.

"Griff," Cain greeted as the slender male stood and rolled his shoulders.

"Adam waits for you alone," Griff told him, reaching out his hand, his fingers splayed.

Cain touched his own fingertips to those of Griff's and, that fast, Cain's entire surroundings altered as he projected his consciousness to the psychic space that the conduit provided. Everything was white—the walls, the floor, the eight wooden chairs. One of said chairs was occupied by Adam.

Cain's monster hissed, slamming its unblinking glare on the Aeon it loathed with every inch of its being. It had wanted to shred Adam to pieces for as far back as Cain could remember. Only the fact that Adam had been extremely well-guarded at Aeon had kept the shithead alive all the years Cain resided there.

Cain would have been outnumbered, subdued, and then contained if he had acted on his hatred for this man back then. Subjecting him to pain hadn't been worth Cain's freedom, so he'd made no move, promising himself and his creature that they would one day get their vengeance. His cage alone had prevented that.

The creature hadn't complained when Cain dealt Abel the killing blow, because it was satisfied that Cain would allow the monster the pleasure of obliterating Adam. If there was a way of causing physical harm to anyone in the psychic space, the creature would have killed him already.

Given the recent loss of Abel, Adam's insides would no doubt be churning with fury. No one would think it to look at him, though. Instead of firing a look of such hatred at Cain that it would snatch a weaker man's breath from his lungs, Adam did nothing. Said nothing. Merely sat very still, looking perfectly at ease.

After Saul lost his sister in the first recent battle, he'd looked a mess, overcome by grief. But Adam? His dark-green eyes were clear and calm. His stubborn jawline was loose and relaxed. His thick, copper-brown hair was neatly combed.

One thing could be seen in Adam's eyes. There was an element of smugness there—he believed that all was going according to plan. There was no grief or devastation to be seen.

Then again, Adam wouldn't be experiencing the gut-wrenching grief that a loving, devoted father would generally feel after losing his son. Abel had mattered to him, but Adam had treated him as more of a protégé and part of his legacy than a son. If he had loved Abel, it hadn't been with a full heart.

Still, Abel's death will have affected Adam on several levels. That he was so affected would be something he'd hate, something he'd consider a weakness. He would also despise that Cain—a person who was a living reminder of his ex-consort's betrayal, a person he had wanted dead since the moment of his birth—had been the one to end Abel's life.

The other Ancients were quick to enter the psychic space, and soon the seven vacant seats were occupied. Cain sat in the center with Seth and Azazel either side of him. None of the Ancients spoke. They simply stared at the Aeon, all looking varying degrees of bored.

"Tell me," began Adam, sweeping his gaze over each of them, "how does it feel to have a divide among your people?"

"A divide?" echoed Lilith, an edge to her voice that said she hadn't forgotten how he'd once treated her. Despite that the Aeon had no liking for her kind, he had pursued her relentlessly while also seeming to resent her for her effect on him. Viewing women as the weaker species, he'd genuinely felt that she had no right to object to his advances. He'd acted like a spiteful piece of shit right up until her brother stepped in.

Adam flicked a hand. "Oh, let us not play games. I know the type of beings you welcome to your town. Dark characters. All of them. So dark they would gladly act on generous bounties, even if it meant going against their neighbors and leaders. Such people are far too easily manipulated. Just how many times has the witch almost been brought to me?"

Cain fought a smile as he realized just how much the Aeon had overestimated what success his sneaky move would have. That was Adam all over, though. The man was so arrogant and superior that it often didn't occur to him that a plan might not pay off.

"What is it that you want?" Seth asked.

Adam notched up his chin. "I think you all now realize just how serious I am about striking at your town until I get what I want."

"Even if I had a sliver of an interest in cooperating—which I don't—I couldn't possibly give myself up to you and make my way to Aeon," said Cain. "You know that perfectly well."

"Yes, I do," said Adam. "But your people do not, do they? And so they will turn on you." He paused, his eyes scanning each Ancient but purposefully skipping over Cain. "It is the witch I want. Perhaps Cain has reported all that was said in our previous meetings. Perhaps not. It would not surprise me to learn that he held certain details back."

Inanna sighed. "If you are only here to make some sad attempt at causing trouble among us, we might as well end this meeting now. None of the Ancients will ever view one of their own as the enemy. Like it or not, you firmly united us when you dumped us here."

Ishtar nodded. "We will never see you as an ally or trust a word you say. So simply be clear about what it is you want. I do not like to have my time wasted."

Adam's jaw hardened. "I have already been clear on what I want. The witch. Wynter Dellavale. Give her to me."

Cain was expecting Adam's request. Even so, his gut went tight and his enraged inner creature coiled its muscles in preparation to lunge, however pointless it would be.

Azazel snorted. "Why would we do that?"

"I will continue to wreak havoc on Devil's Cradle if you do not," threatened Adam.

"You will have *your people* wreak havoc on your behalf, and you will continue to do it either way," said Dantalion with an unconcerned shrug.

"Let's be honest, Adam." Lilith crossed one leg over the other. "You are attacking our town and attempting to scare our population because you hope to weaken us. You want the people to run scared or betray us. You want the place to crumble—a fruitless exercise, I might add, since the land is as protected by power as that of Aeon. In short, you are not prepared to take us on right now because you quite simply don't believe that you can. Did you think we would not see that?" she scoffed, shaking her head.

A flush stained Adam's cheeks. "Why are you so certain I want a war? As I have told Cain in the past, there does not need to be one."

"Don't bother claiming you would leave us in peace if we cooperated," said Cain. "You will seek revenge for Abel's death—we're all well aware of that."

Adam's eyes briefly glittered with something dark. "Revenge is most certainly what I want. But my beef is not with the Ancients as a whole. It is with *you.*"

"Again, we're all well aware of that," said Cain.

"Here is my offer," said Adam, addressing everyone. "Yes, I will eventually come to Devil's Cradle if the witch is not brought to me. But I do not have to destroy the place. I do not have to destroy all of you. If you agree to give Cain and the witch to me, I will quite simply take them and leave. The rest of you will be left to live here in peace with your people."

Seth snarled. "You can shove that offer right up your ass, *Father.*"

Adam gave him a pitying smile. "Oh, dear boy. You may wish

to pose as a Leviathan, you may possess many of their abilities, but you are not one of them. You never truly will be. As such, I am not surprised that you believe the others here would never accept my offer. You have no real concept of how callous, disloyal, and ruthless they can be. Believe me, they are tempted. Do not be shocked if they choose to betray Cain and the witch. And if you wish to live, I would advise you not to take sides." Adam "winked" out of sight.

Cain exchanged a look with the other Ancients and then exited the psychic space. The others did the same. He dismissed the conduit, who was then escorted out of the parlor by Inanna's aides. Now that only the Ancients filled the room, Cain said, "Well, we were right to assume he'd make an offer."

Azazel folded his arms. "I don't think he truly believes that the rest of us would betray you. In fact, he has to be well aware that we would not wish to give you up if for no other reason than we would then be easier for him to take out. I think he merely wishes to cause a strain on our . . . bond, for wont of a better word."

Dantalion dipped his chin in agreement. "He hopes you will now not trust us, Cain. The Aeons really are fond of the divide-and-conquer trick."

Seth shrugged. "It's often successful. But it won't be this time."

"Definitely not," affirmed Lilith. "His offer changes nothing. We still will not propose that we surrender Wynter to him."

Ishtar nodded. "It will gain us nothing."

Everyone looked at her, eyes narrowed in suspicion.

She frowned. "What? I have no liking whatsoever for the witch. Never will. But she is what Adam most wants, and he wants her alive. The moment he has her, he will no doubt seek to destroy the entire town and everyone in it—including us—to avenge Abel. I am not afraid to die. But I have no interest whatsoever in granting Adam's wish before I do. Now if you will excuse me . . ." She strode out of the parlor.

Lilith's brows shot up. "Well, that was a surprise."

112

"Ishtar made perfect sense," said Azazel. "But I can't trust a single word she just spoke."

Neither could Cain, because ... "She has never been rational where Wynter is concerned. I don't see why that would suddenly change."

Inanna sidled up to him. "Your punishment had more of an impact on my sister than you know. Ishtar needs to own pretty things to *feel* pretty. Adorning herself with beautiful things such as clothes and jewelry was always about more than just style. Plus, each gift she is given feeds her sense of self-validation. She may not appreciate those gifts, but she loves what they represent—that another person might adore her, even if it is only her beauty that draws them.

"I do not judge you for what you did, but she does. You destroyed all her pretty things, Cain. You destroyed all her gifts and collectibles. You left her with nothing. You made her *feel* nothing for a short time. She was devastated. And she was also forced to accept that she is not as important to you as she had believed. So while she does—and will likely always—resent and loathe your consort, Ishtar will not be eager to cross you again."

Cain would love to believe that, but he wasn't sure he could.

"Oh, give it a few centuries and she will most likely be back to pushing your buttons and taking foolish chances," Inanna admitted. "But for now, she is no threat to your consort simply because it would mean she was also a threat to herself. Ishtar will always put her own wellbeing first." She then followed her sister out of the room.

Dantalion hummed. "Inanna does make a good point."

"I hope she's right in her assumption," said Seth.

"As do I," said Cain. "I would not enjoy killing one of us. But I would if I had to."

Azazel looked at him. "And if it was because that someone was a danger to your consort, the rest of us would not blame you."

*

Anabel dipped her face in her small brown paper bag, breathed deep through her nose, and then sighed happily. "I love the smell of chocolate brownies."

Wynter was more interested in the warm bag of mini sugar-dusted doughnuts she'd bought. She was a sucker for carbs. She intended to devour her bag of treats as soon as she returned to the cottage.

"These little frames would be perfect for you, Wyn." Delilah scooped up several small silverplated frames from the market table.

"They would?" asked Wynter, adjusting her grip on the slippery handles of the plastic bags she was carrying. "I'm not really seeing how." Oh sure, the frames were pretty and all, but she didn't have any pictures.

"You could put the little drawings you did of your deceased relatives and Rafe inside them," said Delilah. "Then you might feel that they're more than just doodles. And they'd look great on your ancestor altar."

Huh. Wynter hadn't thought of that. It was a very sweet idea. "You're all warm and squishy inside, Del."

The Latina frowned, offended. "I can't believe you'd say that to me."

Snorting, Wynter peeked up at the handwritten price guides on the sign. Reasonable. She paid for the frames and slipped them into one of her bags.

Many tables and booths were lined up on the grassy field of the underground park. A market was held here at least once a month, mostly selling local seasonal produce. This particular market was Halloween-themed as part of the October celebrations, hence the balloons, flags, and garlands that were only available in the colors of orange, black, and green.

There were plenty of foods for sale, such as fruit, vegetables, jams, and jellies. But there were also Halloween treats and decorations, as well as costumes, masks, and props like bloody knives.

Lots of haggling went on. Vendors weren't shy about calling

out to people, hoping to lure them closer. Some people had settled on hay bales, benches, or picnic tables to munch on food they'd purchased.

Someone had dragged the piano out of the town hall and set it near the doors. Beneath all the music, chatter, and laughter were the sounds of water boiling, meat sizzling, and the flapping of tablecloths courtesy of the artificial breeze.

So many scents laced the air—flowers, fruits, herbs, meats, soaps, lotions, and food cooking. Wynter drank them all in.

"Are you planning to move your ancestor altar to Cain's Keep?" asked Delilah.

Wynter felt her nose wrinkle. "No, I don't want to disturb it."

"That's probably the wisest decision," said Hattie, fingering a scarf. "It's important to be careful with such things."

"Ooh, I want that," proclaimed Anabel, pointing at ... nothing.

"What?" asked Xavier, nibbling on one of the fresh doughy cookies he'd bought.

"That," said Anabel, wiggling the finger she was still pointing. "The electronic clapping witch."

He sighed at her. "You're hallucinating again."

Her shoulders slumped, and her arm dropped to her side. "Ugh."

"You have no one to blame but yourself," said Delilah primly.

Anabel bristled. "I never implied differently."

Maybe there would in fact come a day when the blonde actually stopped experimenting on herself, but Wynter wasn't all that hopeful. She'd chewed a chunk out of Anabel's ass as usual, and the blonde had apologized just as she normally did. And though the apology had been genuine, it had to be remembered that her apologies were *always* genuine. She always regretted her mistake. She simply couldn't help later repeating it.

Delilah coaxed them over to a table that sold handmade jewelry, her face lighting up at all the pretty, shiny things. Classic cat. Okay, so she only had the ability to shift into a cat, but she did nonetheless have some feline qualities.

Xavier was more interested in the woman behind the table. "Well, hello there, lass," he greeted in a Scottish accent. "A pretty wee thing, so ye are. My name's Angus."

Oh, dear Lord.

The woman's lips curved. "Milly. And I'm quite sure your real name is actually Xavier."

Ha, good for her.

"Or it's Angus," he said, his accent still Scottish, "and I like telling others it's Xavier."

Wynter only shook her head. He was hopeless. Utterly. Yet the lying little shit also possessed enough charisma to lure women to him anyway.

Once Delilah had bought a few dangly bracelets, they walked off.

Xavier's grin was all smugness. "Milly agreed to go on a date with me."

Wynter patted his back. "Good for you, Angus."

His grin widened. "Awesome name, right?"

"Absolutely. But it's not yours."

A line dented his brow. "So?"

"So when you introduce yourself as someone else to a woman you like, you're starting a relationship that's based on bullshit. That's not a good thing."

He sighed. "Why, why, why have you always gotta focus on logic?"

"Well, one of our coven has to, or we'll eventually get thrown out of Devil's Cradle." Did they not get that?

Anabel bit her lower lip. "You do make a valid point."

"But again with the logic," Xavier complained.

Wynter rolled her eyes.

They went from table to table. Anabel topped up her collection of beeswax products while Hattie bought some jars of honey—all in various flavors.

Anabel smiled as the pianist began playing "Somebody's Watching Me". "I like this tune."

Delilah tossed her a look. "I'm not surprised. The lyrics speak to the paranoid."

The blonde's brows drew together. "I'm not paranoid."

Delilah snorted. "Hmm, sure."

"I'm *not*."

She totally was, but Wynter was not interested in getting into that. "No arguments, please, we're supposed to be enjoying some quality coven time."

"Ooh," began Hattie, pointing to a particular booth. "I need more rolling paper for my morning joints." She paused, humming. "And some deadly nightshade seeds."

Wynter froze, as did the others. "Why?" she asked warily.

Hattie cackled. "I'm just messing with you."

"That wasn't funny, Empress of Poison," said Xavier. "I worried you'd decided to kill poor George."

"Never," said Hattie as she grabbed some packets of bundled up herbs from a wicker basket. "The man is sweet as pie."

"Wow, that dude over there by the pond is good," said Anabel. "I can't even juggle balls, let alone knives. I mean . . . wow."

Sighing, Xavier scratched at his temple. "There is no juggler."

Anabel stamped her foot. "*Dammit.*" She rubbed at her neck. "I have to get out of here. I can't tell what's real and what's fantasy anymore. The lines are too blurred. Oh God, I can't catch my breath."

Delilah nudged her. "Tone it down, diva."

Anabel's hands fisted. "I am *not* a—"

"Hello, Wynter," greeted none other than Eve, smiling brightly.

Well, gah. Hey, Wynter's sort-of-mother-in-law was seemingly a nice woman, but they didn't know each other well enough for Wynter to be comfortable with just bumping into her in public without Cain at her side. And, if Wynter was truly honest, a part of her struggled to warm to the woman, unable to help but resent Eve for how thoroughly she'd let him down even as Wynter understood how that had come to be. She didn't judge Eve, she just hated how it had impacted Cain.

Noah and Rima stood behind their grandmother. He gave Wynter a nod while Rima just glared at her. So pleasant.

Wynter forced her lips to curve. "Hi, it's nice to see you all."

"Thank you," said Eve. "This must be your coven."

"Yes." Wynter introduced each of them to Eve and the twins before then introducing the Aeons to her coven in return. They all exchanged greetings, though Rima's were pretty stiff.

"It's a pleasure to finally meet you all," Eve told the coven. "Wynter has spoken of you many times."

Wynter held her breath, half-expecting them to say crazy shit or relay embarrassing stories about her. But they merely smiled, polite and calm. Which was weird but a relief.

"Is Cain not with you?" Noah asked, glancing around.

"He and the Ancients have a meeting." More specifically, they were making another attempt to wake Abaddon, but that wasn't something Wynter could mention in public.

"Shame," said Eve. "I would have liked to see him."

Noah's nose wrinkled. "I can't imagine him doing something as mundane as peruse a market. He would surely look out of place."

Nah, Cain had a way of fitting into whatever environment he placed himself in; of always seeming as though he *belonged*. But she understood Noah's meaning—the Ancients just seemed so set apart from "normality".

"He would probably also be bored." Noah sighed. "I can relate."

Eve tossed him an exasperated look that was tinged with affection. She then refocused on Wynter. "I'll let you continue shopping. You all take care now." She and Noah walked away, but Rima lingered. Wasn't that nice?

Rima looked Wynter up and down. "I heard about what you did to the witches who tried to kidnap you. A little harsh, wasn't it?"

Wynter blinked. "That was kind of the point."

"You could have simply dumped their bodies in a public place and then walked away," said Rima.

"What, like Aeons dump people over the falls?" Wynter cocked her head. "You know what your problem is? You think that your emotional scars give you a free pass to be bitchy—something you're not very good at, on another note; you just come across as petty and childish. *Anyway,* you really need to snap out of this mindset. You're not the only one who's suffered. Losing your mom is hard, I know. But your mom died peacefully in her sleep. We don't all have that comfort. And we don't all make others pay for our pain."

Rima's cheeks reddened. "I don't need a lecture from someone who's only lived, what, thirty years? Probably less. You're a kid compared to me."

Wynter almost laughed. "Oh, you might have walked this Earth a lot longer. But you haven't *lived* the same way I have. You've never fought in a war. You've never lost your life over and over. You've never led people into battle, hoping like hell it won't get them killed. You've never hosted a monster that doesn't belong in this world.

"Your experiences, the loss of your mom . . . you didn't let those things strengthen you, you just stewed over them. So it doesn't matter how much longer you've lived, I'm still far more mature than you. But you could change that if you only took my advice. I guess we'll see if you bother or not." Before the Aeon could say another word, Wynter strode off.

Delilah sidled up to her. "You're totally right about Rima. She's like a naïve, defiant teenager."

Wynter exhaled heavily. "I really don't want to have a bad relationship with any of Cain's relatives, but she makes it hard to like her. She feels the need to be rude toward and question everyone. There's so much bitterness inside her, and she lets it rule her." Wynter swore. "Damn her, I was having fun until then."

Delilah patted her shoulder. "The fun doesn't need to stop. All is good. Things can go back to being light-hearted."

They all halted as a male bore down on them, his eyes flaring with anger—eyes that were pinned on Delilah.

"I've been looking for you everywhere," he growled. "What in God's name did you put in that potion?"

Wynter felt her eyes drift closed. "Oh, Del."

Delilah folded her arms. "You'll have to clue me in on what potion you asked for. I get a lot of customers."

He glanced from side to side, leaned in, and lowered his voice as he said, "I wanted something that would make my boyfriend lose a few pounds."

"Oh, I remember now," said Delilah. "You felt that he'd 'let himself go,' and you didn't like it."

"Obviously," he said with a snicker. "You told me that all I had to do was put a drop of the potion in my mouth and then kiss him. Well, he hasn't lost any weight. And I . . ." He let the sentence trail off.

She made a prim noise. "I warned you there might be side effects."

His jaw clenched. "You didn't mention I could grow a curly tail on the base of my spine."

"What, like a pig?" Delilah hummed. "Interesting, since you sort of are one. You know, you're growing some pink hairs on that chinny chin—"

"*What?*"

"Del," Wynter quickly cut in, "take him back to the cottage and give him a reversal potion."

"I'm not taking anything else from *her*," he stated.

Delilah grinned. "That's fine. I think tails are cute. Pink chin hairs? Not so much. But hey, I'm sure your boyfriend will accept you exactly as you are. And I'm sure he won't ask any questions about how exactly you came to have—"

"Reversal potion it is," he ground out.

Wynter waved a hand toward the cottage. "Go." Watching the two walk off, she rubbed at her nape.

"She's never going to listen to you, you know," said Anabel. "She's going to keep ignoring your warnings and doing what she wants." The blonde shook her head sadly. "Really, she's her own worst enemy."

Hattie leaned toward Wynter. "Anabel's lack of self-awareness is worrying."

Well, Wynter could say the same regarding the old woman, so . . .

Anabel turned to Xavier, and her eyes went wide. "Ooh, spider, spider, spider!"

Wynter looked and *Jesus Christ* it was big.

Xavier peeked down at the insect on his shoulder but then frowned. "What spider?"

Anabel jabbed her finger toward it and then stilled. "Wait, I'm seeing things again?"

"Seems like it," he said.

She gingerly reached toward the moving spider, which promptly crawled onto her hand. "Wow, I swear I can *feel* little spider feet pattering over my skin. It's amazing how the imagination just fills in this stuff to make it more realistic for the hallucinator, right?" She smiled at Wynter, who pulled a face.

Realization dawned on Anabel. An almighty squeal erupted from her as she frantically shook her hand to throw off the insect. *"Xavier, I am gonna* fry *you!"*

The idiot doubled over with laughter.

Chapter Ten

Wynter was closing her bedroom window at the cottage later that day when she heard footfalls coming from behind her. She turned to find Cain slowly stalking into the space, each step smooth and predatory. Her stomach predictably went all fluttery.

"Well, hello there." She smiled, surprised to see him. Busy as he was, he didn't regularly turn up at the cottage. "What brings you here?"

He came straight to her and drew her close. "You," he said, dipping his head. "Always you." He took her mouth in a slow, lazy, deep kiss. It held an edge of dominance that made her hormones swoon. He broke the kiss with a satisfied hum. "Needed that."

Wynter slid her hands up his hard chest. "Since you don't look in the least bit triumphant, I'm guessing you again had no luck waking Abaddon."

"You guessed correctly." He sighed. "If we had, it would have gone a long way to lifting not only my mood but that of the other Ancients."

She felt her brows knit. "What's wrong with your mood?"

"It soured a few hours ago when a conduit from Aeon arrived. Adam wanted to speak to all seven Ancients this time. He offered the others a deal—if they surrender both you and me to Adam when he arrives here, he will spare their lives and leave them in peace."

Wynter felt her mouth drop open. "He's trying to turn them against you, or make you worry that they will. That motherfucker. Do you think they'll give him what he wants?"

"Absolutely not. There isn't a chance that Adam would refrain from trying to lay waste to Devil's Cradle. Not after what happened to Abel here. The other Ancients know that, just as they know that if they handed you and me over, all they will have done is made themselves more vulnerable to an attack."

Maybe so, but Wynter wasn't quite ready to trust that they wouldn't betray Cain if it came to a point where they felt that there would be no waking Abaddon or escaping their prison. One of the Ancients had betrayed Cain's trust once before without an issue. Speaking of that particular Ancient ... "I'll bet Ishtar suggested they could try to placate Adam by passing me over to him."

"I thought she might do something along those lines, but she didn't. She claimed she's quite aware that giving Adam what he wants wouldn't change the man's intentions, and she seemingly has no wish to give our last jailor anything."

That was a surprise. "Hmm." Even she heard the doubt in her tone. Wynter knew how much Ishtar hated her; knew that the female Ancient would happily see her gone.

"Yes, I'm just as skeptical. We'll see how things go." Cain trailed his finger behind her ear and down the side of her throat. "I heard from one of my hirelings that you came across my mother and the twins at the market. I also heard that you and Rima appeared to get into some sort of argument—he wasn't close enough to pick up any words that were spoken."

"I wouldn't say we argued. She was her usual snarky self, and I called her on it." Wynter briefly elaborated and then added, "Maybe she'll take my advice."

"I highly doubt it."

"I can see that you'd like to give her a bucketload of shit for what she said—"

"If you're going to ask me to let it lie, don't bother. You're my consort. She was rude to you. She knows better. I wouldn't tolerate it from others, and I certainly won't tolerate it from her." Cain nipped her lip, as if to punctuate his point.

"If you subjected her to a punishment, it wouldn't wash down well with Noah and Eve. You can't afford to alienate all three Aeons right now. You need them on side. My suggestion? Just give her a verbal warning like you initially did with Ishtar. If Rima repeats her actions, well, no one can then say she didn't have it coming—not even her own twin. Come on, you know I'm right on this."

Cain sighed. "I do. I just don't like it."

Wynter snorted. "I can see that." She drifted her fingers through his hair. "Now how about we drop annoying topics?"

"Works for me. I'd much rather discuss what items you're taking to the Keep today." He glanced around the room. "One of the reasons I came to escort you there is it occurred to me that you might need help moving more of your things."

She narrowed her eyes, very aware that he'd come here to *ensure* she transferred more of her belongings to his home. "Oh, how very thoughtful of you," she said, her voice dry.

His lips curved. "I'd say so."

She *hmph*ed. "I've already boxed up my crystals to take with me. I have no idea where I'll put them, though. They won't really fit in with the style of your chamber."

Skating one hand up her back, he brushed his mouth over hers. "They fit with you. And you fit with me."

Warmth bloomed in her chest. He might not be whatsoever romantic, but he could say the sweetest stuff—not to melt her, but because it was pure truth and he wanted to give it to her. She loved that.

His gaze slid to the side as something caught his attention. "What's this?"

Tracking his gaze, she replied, "An ancestor altar. Most witches create one around this time of year to honor those they loved and lost."

He crossed to the altar and studied it carefully, taking in each item.

Sidling up to him, she pointed at the newly framed drawings. "I don't have any photos of any of the people I lost, so I drew some pictures. They're not very good, but they're better than nothing. This is my mom, Davina. That's my grandmother, Agnes. And you met Rafe. He was like an uncle to me." The male witch had been sent by the Aeons to convince her to return, and the cruel bastards had later killed him when he went home without her.

Cain cut his gaze back to her. "Tell me about Davina and Agnes," he softly urged.

She blinked, surprised. "Why?"

His brow furrowed. "Why not?"

"I don't mind talking about them. It's just that, well, you rarely ask about my life before I came here unless it's to discuss the Aeons."

Turning to fully face her, he skimmed his hand up her arm. "Only because I know you don't have many good memories of your time at Aeon, and I'm hesitant to raise any subjects that might cause you pain. But I hear the affection in your voice as you talk about these people, especially your mother and grandmother. You seem happy to speak of them at present, so I'm asking if you'll tell me more. They were your family, they're part of you. I want every part." His lips twitched at her snicker. "Yes, as you well know, I'm greedy when it comes to you."

That was a two-way street, so Wynter didn't mind. "My mom was sweet and brave and spunky. Davina had a contagious laugh. Loved to cook and garden. I swear, flowers seemed to *lean* toward her. Like she was some kind of magnet for nature."

Wynter paused as her throat thickened, forcing her to clear it with a cough. "She taught me how to use and control my magick— which, before I died as a child, was light and comforting like hers."

"Really?"

"Yes." She felt her mouth cant up. "Hard to imagine that, huh? Given all I've done with it as an adult, I mean."

"It's not simply that." He tucked her hair behind her ear. "The darkness and chaos suits you and your personality."

"I said my magick was light and comforting back then, I didn't say it wasn't chaotic. My mom had a hard time helping me channel it, but she persevered. Davina was even more stubborn than I am. She had no quit in her . . . And it hurts like motherfucking hell that she pled guilty to bringing me back from the afterlife so that no one would know I was a revenant.

"She knew that the Aeons wouldn't want a being in their midst who could destroy them; she knew they'd kill me so, unaware that Kali would send me back, she lied to protect me. And she paid for that with her life, though she hadn't known that would be the price until it was too late." Wynter's voice broke at the end.

Curling one arm tight around her, Cain stroked a hand over her hair. "You're right, your mother was brave. And she very clearly loved you."

"She did. She made it apparent in everything she did. My grandmother, Agnes? She was more about tough love. She was brisk and curt. She led the coven with an iron fist. But Agnes was always there for those who needed her. She had a big heart, it was simply encased in steel."

"You miss them both," he sensed.

"I do."

"Did Agnes know what you are?"

"I think she guessed. There were a few things she said that hinted at it. But she never outright asked me. Maybe because she knew I'd lie and she didn't want to create a situation where she'd have to force a truth out of me that could very well condemn me."

"And Rafe? Did he know?"

She shook her head. "He sensed that I was different, but I don't believe he suspected that I was a revenant. I think he simply thought that death had warped my magick in strange ways."

"As you have him to thank for all your training, I'm glad you had him in your life. Though I'll admit I'm petty enough to not like hearing you speak of another man with such affection."

"I'm petty enough that I would have had the same reaction if our situations were reversed, so I can't judge." She licked her lips. "I didn't care for him the way I do you. He was . . . an addition to my life. You're central to mine."

Cain's chest squeezed. "As you are to mine." She probably had no idea what it did to him to hear her say such things. No one else had ever openly loved or claimed him the way she did. His mother and Seth cared for him, might even love him. But the relationships Cain had with them had always been complicated. With Wynter, it was the opposite.

Before her, he'd only existed on the periphery of the worlds of those in his life. Even surrounded by people, he'd always been alone. He hadn't really lamented it; hadn't craved more. Until Wynter.

Even at the beginning, it hadn't been enough for him to sit on the sidelines and be a mere part of her life. He'd felt driven to infiltrate it. To make a place for himself in it.

Cain hadn't only wanted for her to belong to him. That hadn't been enough for him. He'd wanted to belong to her in turn. And now that he had what he'd so badly yearned all along, he knew there was nothing he wouldn't do to keep it. To keep *her*.

Likewise, he couldn't imagine a scenario in which his creature would ever let her go. It had claimed her as its own. That wasn't something such an entity would ever do or take lightly.

Cain slipped his hand beneath the sleek curtain of her hair to palm her nape. "Have you given any thought to bonding with my monster?"

"I have. And, on a personal level, I have nothing against the idea."

Satisfaction bloomed inside him and perked up his creature, who'd been in a foul mood since having to sit across from Adam.

"But it makes sense to wait until after the present danger has passed."

Cain frowned, and his monster stilled. "How does that make sense?" There was no logic at all in delaying it; no reason she'd reach such an idiotic conclusion. Unless . . . "Wait, are you trying to protect me?" Surely not.

She straightened her shoulders. "Hey, I know you're a big, bad

Ancient—yippee for you. But you're not invincible. The last thing you need right now, with all the shit going on around us, is for anything to weaken you."

"I've already explained that the bond wouldn't weaken me even if you died."

"That's providing I come back from death. But as you so often remind me, we can't know for sure that Kali will always return me to this realm. If She didn't—"

"I'd find some way to drag you back."

"You'd *try*. But not even your hold on my soul could cheat death. At the moment, there's all kinds of danger hovering around me. It's not a good time for your creature to tie its life-force to mine. You can't afford to be stuck in a deep state of Rest recovering from the effects of a broken preternatural bond. The other Ancients need you—"

"And I need you," he all but growled.

She gently squeezed his shoulder. "I'm not going anywhere. I'm just saying it's best to wait a little while before I bind myself to your monster."

It snarled in disagreement. "We don't want to wait."

"Shocker. Like it or not, I'm making a valid point here. And as it happens, we need to be certain of something before we go through with it."

Cain unlocked his back teeth. "What?"

"A person's life-force is the energy their soul gives off, right? My soul is undead, remember? I don't know what kind of energy it gives off, but it might not be a *good* kind; it might be something that harms or weakens your creature. I could be wrong. It could be a senseless concern. But I need to know for sure before we proceed."

"Your life-force has a dark energy, yes, but nothing that would harm my creature."

"You know this for a fact?"

"Yes."

"Ooh, that was a definite lie. No, don't argue. I am in the

company of a pathological liar every day. I know a bullshit line when I hear one."

Cain let out a heavy exhale. "Fine. I'm not entirely certain. But I don't believe your worry is warranted."

"I'd rather wait until we *know* without a doubt that you're right about that. Come on, you have all kinds of ancient texts and rare books. Surely at least one of them covers subjects like life-forces."

"Some probably will, yes."

"Then flick through them. Find us a definitive answer. We can go from there. And before you object again, just consider that you'd say the same to me if the risk was *mine* to take."

Grinding his teeth, Cain glared down at her. "So stubborn." It maddened him at times. As she often pointed out, he was used to having his way. Used to people hurrying to cater to his every whim, never daring to disobey or question him. Wynter, however, had no qualms with challenging him on any subject. But he liked that, liked that she demanded to be counted and wasn't intimidated by him, so he couldn't even complain about it.

Well, he could. But, really, it would make him a hypocritical bastard. Especially in regards to this particular matter. Because, just as she'd accused, he would make the same decision in her shoes.

Nonetheless, he was self-centered enough to have pushed her to change her mind if he'd thought it would get him anywhere. But when she did that thing where she calmly stated her case in that non-negotiable tone, he knew from past experience that he was fighting a losing battle.

"All right," he said, his reluctance clear. "We'll hold off on per-forming the binding." His inner creature grumbled in annoyance at that.

"Performing," she echoed, her eyes lighting with curiosity. "So, what, it's like a ritual?"

"Not quite."

Her brows dipped. "You're not going to explain?"

No, because he wanted her to be intrigued. And, yes, it was amusing to poke at her a little—he liked to keep her on her toes. It was only fair, since she did the same to him. "Wouldn't you rather have the surprise?"

"No."

He gave her a look of mock sympathy. "Hmm, what a shame."

"Because you have no intention of telling me in advance?"

"None whatsoever."

"Asshole," she tossed out, but there was no real heat in the word. "I don't have to drink blood or anything, do I?"

Cain felt his brow crease. Her thought processes often took him off-guard, but it was another thing he liked. "Why would you even ask such a thing?"

"Well, I'd be tying my life-force to that of your creature. Blood is the elixir of life, right?"

He let out a long sigh. "You won't have to drink blood."

She put a hand to her chest, her shoulders lowering slightly. "I have to say, that is a relief."

"Going back to a question I meant to ask you before . . . Do you need help dismantling and moving the ancestor altar to my Keep?"

Her nose wrinkled. "It's best not to disturb it. That's why I set it in the corner where it wouldn't be knocked or anything. I had to perform a blessing just to add the silver frames to the drawings. I won't be dissembling the altar until after All Hallows' Eve, but thanks anyway. Don't worry, I'll take some of my other possessions to the Keep instead."

Satisfied, he dropped a soft kiss on her mouth. "Good. But next year, you'll set up the altar in what will then be officially our chamber, yes?"

"Yes," she relented.

"Good."

"My coven asked me to have dinner with them tonight. And, to be honest, it's hard to turn down Hattie's stew. Want to eat with us?"

"If you're certain there'll be enough stew to go around, yes, I'd like that." Spending an evening with the Bloodrose Coven never failed to be interesting. "How long before dinner is served?"

"Hmm, we have about fifteen minutes."

"Not long, then. We'll have to make it quick."

"What?"

"I intend to fuck you."

Her pupils dilated, and a slow smile curled her lips. "Dude, that's literally one of my favorite things to hear you say."

His mouth hiking up, he nipped her lower lip. "Strip while I close and lock the door. We don't want people barging in again, do we?"

"It only happened once, and Hattie didn't really see much."

"Not the point since, despite what she claimed, she waltzed in with full knowledge that you and I were having sex. Now, you're not stripping. Why is that?"

Rolling her eyes at his high-handed tone, Wynter totally ignored that her hormones started fanning themselves at said tone. Already a little tingly—yeah, just knowing how good he could make her feel was enough to push all her best levers—she peeled off her tee as he crossed to the door. Her bra went next, and her nipples tightened at the slight chill in the room. She shucked her panties and leggings as he prowled back to her, each step slow but purposeful like a predator on the hunt. It made the best kind of shiver race down her spine.

She didn't mind that this would be fast. Nu-uh. From what she'd observed, there seemed to be something about *knowing* he had little time to possess her that made him more intense. Like it played on his sense of ownership, driving him to claim and mark in a very . . . almost cold, detached way. Whatever. She dug it.

Hell, she dug everything he did.

As she finally stood naked before him, his dark eyes drank her in, hot and hungry. The boldly indecent look shot straight to her womb. An electric tension built between them, sending little sparks skittering over her skin, making it heat and prickle. She licked her dry lips, her pulse racing with anticipation.

He took a single step toward her, covering the tiny bit of distance between them. "It often astounds me that everything I need could be all bound up in one pretty package."

He nipped and licked at her lips but didn't sweep his tongue inside, teasing and making her wait. His hands roamed over her, greedy. Reverent. Dominant. Territorial. Like someone touching a cherished possession, smug that they alone owned it.

Wynter's breath snagged in her throat as an outpouring of electric, decadent pleasure explosively *burst* over her soul, so intense and hot and carnal she almost couldn't bear it. That quickly, her body went from tingly to one big giant ache. Like she'd already suffered through hours of foreplay.

Her nerve-endings screamed to be touched. Her pussy heated and slickened. Her heartbeat galloped like crazy. Her breathing . . . well, it was fucked.

"On the bed. Spread your thighs wide." His voice was low. Deep. Authoritative. Wicked.

Trembling, she complied without complaint, desperate for whatever he planned to give her.

"Very good," he said, moving to stand at the foot of the bed, his gaze dropping to her pussy. "One day, I want you to be waiting for me in our chamber just like this. For now . . . get yourself wet and ready for me. And be quick about it. We're short on time."

"Getting me wet is your job."

"Ordinarily, yes, it is." His hands lowered to his waistband. "It's a job I take very seriously. But right now, all I want is to sink inside you and fuck you hard and raw." He lowered his zipper, freeing his hard cock. "No foreplay, no build up. Just me playing with my favorite toy."

Her inner muscles clenched. Yeah, here came the whole cold and detached thing. She wouldn't have thought she'd get off on sexual objectification. With her past lovers, she wouldn't have liked it. But with Cain, it was different. She trusted him, trusted that he cared for her and that her pleasure mattered to him, and he toed the line in the exact way she needed. As such, it was easier to relax and let herself admit to and enjoy what she liked. "I'm already wet."

"Show me."

She dipped her fingers inside her, scooped up some of her slickness, and held out her hand.

He leaned forward. "No sense in it going to waste, is there?" He sucked her fingers clean.

Damn if her toes didn't just curl.

He gripped her thighs, yanked her closer, and lined up the broad tip of his cock to her gate. "Playthings don't need to move, so put your hands above your head and keep them there. I can't have them getting in my way."

The words shot straight to her core. If he was planning to talk her into an orgasm, it would likely work. She put her hands above her head, loosely linking her fingers.

He punched his hips forward, forcing his cock deep, stretching her without mercy. He didn't pause. He just pounded into her, letting out primitive little grunts that hit her in her core.

He didn't otherwise touch her. Didn't meet her eyes. Didn't talk to her. He quite simply took her. Possessed her. Made use of her.

She lifted her hips to meet every pitiless thrust. He drove so deep. Slammed so hard. And it felt *so fucking good.*

Even with her moans, his grunts, the smack of flesh, and the slap of his balls she could *hear* how wet she was. It would have been embarrassing if she wasn't consumed by pleasure.

His eyes lifted to hers, glittering with the same savage need that she felt in every thrust. "I swear I could live my life buried in this pussy."

Waves of pleasure rolled over her soul—some hot, some cold, some crackly, some smooth. Sensation after sensation thrashed, scraped, kneaded, and played along her very being. Soon, she was adrift with pleasure and over-sensitized from head to goddamn toe, both inside and out.

Cain rolled his thumb around her clit and *fuck, fuck, fuck.* "Come," he ordered. "I want to see my baby break for me."

He spanked her pussy just as he sent a surge of pure rapture sweeping over her soul. Oh, she broke all right. A supernova wave of euphoria caught her up and all but drowned her.

Spitting out a curse, he draped his body over hers as he hammered into her violently. His cock swelling, he licked at the corner of her eye, scooping up a tear. And then he exploded.

Chapter Eleven

Gratefully accepting cash from her customer, Wynter waited until he'd left before stuffing the bills in the locked box she kept out of sight. She doubted anybody would get the stupid idea to swipe some of her earnings, but it was better to be on the safe side. After all, many of the people here were criminals. Including her coven members, as it happened.

Taking the small empty potion bottle, she plopped it into the basket of other empties to be washed. Whenever she embedded runes into weapons, she demonstrated on her customer just what sort of enchantment she'd chosen for them—there was no other way for them to "know" its effects. Hence the need for the many reversal potions lined up on the shelf.

Said shelf also included healing potions, since demonstrating enchantments involved cutting flesh. But some preternatural beings, including those who were immortal like herself, didn't need such brews—any superficial wounds healed swiftly enough to not require any magickal interference.

Needing to ready the shed for whatever customer might come next, she reached for the cloth so she could wipe down the wooden bench. Her fingertips barely scraped it when a breeze slammed into her face vibrating with a warning, but it was too late—a hand clutched Wynter's hip from behind before she could even consider reacting. The world around her flashed white, and then suddenly she was standing in what appeared to be the middle of goddamn nowhere facing four familiar male vampires.

What in the fuck?

It all happened so goddamn fast it was almost dizzying. She snapped out of her shock quickly, but she didn't attack—not the people in front of her, and not the person behind her. In fact, Wynter didn't move at all. Because one of the vamps before her, Claud, was pointing a freaking gun at her. He happened to be one of her best customers. *Traitorous bastard.*

"Don't move," barked Claud. "This is loaded with iron bullets."

Huh. Special.

Revenants were susceptible to iron. Although the bullets wouldn't kill her unless the shot was fatal, they'd weaken her for sure. Possibly even weaken her enough to prevent her currently furious monster from surfacing. It wanted to eat these bastards alive, along with the person who'd teleported her here. Said person released her hip quickly and stepped away.

"I'd shoot her in the leg or something, if I were you," said her kidnapper. *Shelia.* "It'll be best for you to keep her weak."

Her blood boiling, Wynter looked over her shoulder and pinned the little bitch with a glacier cold glare. The otherworldly breeze brushing over Wynter's skin buzzed with the same rage she harbored—still, the deity silently cautioned her inner monster not to rise yet.

Wynter felt her nostrils flare. "You'll die for this."

Shelia laughed. "How? No one will know I had anything to do with your disappearance."

"But *I* will. And I'll come for you."

Shelia smirked. "Sure you will." She waggled her fingers in good-bye. "Do enjoy your time with Adam." In a blink, she was gone.

Oh ho, ho, ho, someone needed to cut that bitch up.

Drawing in a calming breath through her nose, Wynter let her gaze flit around as she slowly turned her head to face the front. All she could see for miles was prairie land. There were no distant noises to indicate that there were other people anywhere close.

Refocusing on the vampires, she flexed her fingers. "This was *seriously* ill advised. I really can't stress that enough."

"Don't do anything stupid," said Claud, his grip steady on the gun *still* aimed at her.

Oh, he had "stupid" covered.

"We'd rather not hurt you, but we can," he added. "We're not without gifts."

That was true. If she recalled correctly, two of the vampires were telekinetic, one could cause people to hallucinate, and Claud could drug a person with a single but very fatal touch.

Her monster rumbled a growl, eager to take the wheel. Wynter was hesitant to oblige it. She didn't know how badly the bullets would affect the monster and she didn't care to find out. So, needing it to wait, she sent it telepathic images, letting it know that she wanted to disarm the vampire first. It made a petulant grunt of complaint but didn't push.

Another vamp, Enzo, pushed a button on his key fob. The SUV's trunk softly whirred as it opened. "Get in."

Wynter snorted. If they were expecting her to cooperate, they were out of their minds. "No."

The corners of Claud's eyes tightened. "Don't make me shoot you."

"I'm not *making* you do anything," she said. "You're *choosing* the path of suicide. That's on you."

A muscle in Enzo's cheek flexed. "Get in the fucking trunk."

She flicked up a brow. "Would *you*?"

"If I didn't want to get pumped with bullets, yeah," said Enzo.

"Low pain tolerance threshold, huh?" Her monster filed that little nugget away. "Sucks for you."

"Don't think dragging this out will give your coven or the Ancients a chance to get to you. You're a *long* way from home."

"That so?" Well, that was unfortunate. "Then here's a question. Why didn't you ask Shelia to teleport you all the way to the boundaries of Aeon?"

"We did. She doesn't trust that the keepers won't kill us on sight and just take you. And since she doesn't know how far past the perimeter they patrol, this is as far as she's willing to go. We're an hour's drive from the boundaries of Aeon."

Considering the distance between Devil's Cradle and Aeon would take at least two days of driving to cover, these dudes had been on the road for a while. "You really should heed Shelia's concerns. I once lived at Aeon, so I can tell you two things—one, they patrol *far* and wide. Two, they're not very friendly toward trespassers."

"But they are expecting someone to turn up with either you, Cain, or both of you," Enzo cockily pointed out. "That'll make them a lot less hostile toward anyone who heads their way."

"Only for as long as it takes to confirm that you brought them what they want. After that, you'll be executed."

"We're done chatting," Claud cut in. "Now get in the fucking trunk."

"All right, fine." She raised her hands in a gesture of peace. And then she let out a blast of toxic magick from each palm. The dark, ultraviolet-tinted force shimmered through the air like heatwaves as it rushed at the vampires.

They tried evading the blasts but didn't move fast enough. The magick crashed into them like a wall. They hit the ground hard, sizzling deep welts appearing on their bare skin. Welts that swiftly began to heal. *Fucking vampires.*

She'd called to her sword just as Claud fired the gun. She angled her black glass blade, deflecting the bullet. And another bullet. And another.

A heavy surge of telekinetic energy slammed into her chest and knocked the breath right out of her. She skidded backwards several feet but remained standing, sending whips of crackling magick bouncing along the ground toward the vamps. They swore and yelped as the scorching hot power lashed at their bodies yet again.

Enzo blurred to her side and tried snatching the blade as he reached for her. He might well have dealt her a nightmarish hallucination before she had the chance to fight him . . . *if* the razor-sharp sword hadn't sliced into his skin. Her enchantment went to work on him, making him jerk backwards as he was overcome with the sensation of beetles scuttling over his flesh.

Taking advantage of his distraction, she thrust her blade through his heart. Vampires could heal from a lot, but not that. His eyes went wide, a croaky breath crawled out of his throat, and then he burst into ashes.

More telekinetic energy rippled through the air toward her. She jerked aside unnaturally fast, dodging it cleanly. *Thank you, immortality.*

Yet another blast came toward her. She ducked—

An impact slammed into her head as blinding pain *burst* through her skull. She staggered backwards, blinking hard. The agony snatched the strength from her body, and her sword slipped from her limp hand. She dropped to her knees, feeling like she was fading.

Claud gaped at her, his eyes wide in horror. "Oh, shit."

She slumped forward as the life left her body.

*

Cain looked up from the book in front of him as Maxim showed Seth into the ledger room. The aide left with a respectful nod toward Cain.

Seth strolled toward the desk, eyeing the many thick, heavy— and in many cases also dusty—books with curiosity. "Doing some light reading, are we?" he quipped.

"I'm trying to find specific information on the tying of life-forces." Cain had spent days scouring ancients texts. He hadn't found anything that really answered Wynter's questions or properly addressed her concerns.

Seth's brows flew up. "Your creature wants to bind itself to Wynter, I take it?"

"Yes." It had settled slightly now that it knew she wouldn't fight the binding, although it wasn't at all happy at being made to wait.

139

Letting out a low whistle, Seth took the seat opposite him, loosely clasping the armrests. "That's pretty huge."

It was, though Wynter didn't quite realize that. Leviathans rarely formed such bonds with others. As he'd told her before, the monsters they carried weren't built to love. "My monster is determined to own her, and it won't cease pushing until it gets its way."

"Have you told her?"

"Yes. She's willing. But she's also reluctant to go through with it any time soon."

"You can't exactly blame her for requesting a little time to get used to the idea and settle more firmly into your relationship. Anyone would find it unnerving to tie their life-force to that of another, let alone to a monster like yours—no offense."

Oh, there was none taken. Cain was under no illusions about the creature; he knew it was a living nightmare. "That's not why she hesitates. Her issue is two-fold. One, she knows that if she was to *permanently* die while she and my creature were bound, her death would profoundly affect both me and my monster—she doesn't want to ever be a weakness for me." It warmed him even as it exasperated him, because she could never be anything but his greatest strength.

"I can understand that," said Seth. "But she's far from easy to kill, which makes it less risky. And she's returned from the afterlife God knows how many times. Why would that one day stop?"

"It might not, but she can't be as certain of that as she wishes to be."

Seth pursed his lips, nodding in understanding. "Then I see why she's concerned."

So did Cain, though he'd probably never say as much to her. He didn't want to encourage her to think that way, he wanted her to give into him. "She would prefer to wait until the danger with the Aeons has passed, but she will only go through with the binding if I can ease another deep concern she has. Wynter worries that, given her life-force is that of an undead soul, being bound to her could be harmful for my creature and me."

"Ah, I hadn't thought of that." Seth rubbed at his jaw. "Do you believe it would be?"

"No. But that's not enough for her. Because she's fully aware that I'm not certain of it. Hence why I'm flicking through ancient texts in search of answers."

Puffing out a breath, Seth lowered his hand. "I can see that you'd prefer she ignore her concerns. But she isn't merely being difficult here, Cain. She hesitates because she cares for you. She'd never forgive herself if she later discovered that her life-force was negatively affecting you."

Cain let out a deep sigh. "I know. I simply feel that her worries are senseless. And I intend to prove it."

"I'm sure you will." Seth paused. "But if you do, I think it would be best for you both to still wait until after the upcoming battle is over before performing the binding. Yes, I can see that you are not fond of that idea. But think of her, Cain. It's easy for you to overlook, since you're incredibly difficult to kill, that you have your own vulnerabilities.

"As much as we might wish differently, you're not indestructible. More notably, you'll soon be knee-deep in a war with beings whose power is almost as great as yours. You need to know what your death would do to her before you take the step you want to take."

Cain rubbed his nape, pensive. He truly hadn't looked at the situation from that angle. Purely because, as Seth pointed out, it was easy for Cain to overlook his own weaknesses due to there being very few people who could take him on and live to tell the tale.

"It stands to reason that if I died while she and my creature were bound she'd come back just like she always does. The breaking of the bond wouldn't affect her monster—it would have no tie to me or my creature." Cain would like to have its acceptance and approval since, in a roundabout way, it was part of Wynter. But she'd made it clear that the bestial entity wanted only to kill, not to find a mate.

"Maybe she *wouldn't* come back, though," said Seth. "Think about it. If the snapping of the bond *is* something that will drain her, it might do so to the point where she's too weak to come back."

Fuck, Cain hadn't thought of that. His stomach rolled at the mere idea of it. His witch *had* to live. There was no other acceptable option.

"You could try asking Lilith. Her creature bound itself to her consort. Maybe she'll know more." Seth's brows dipped as he added, "Though I doubt it. He wasn't a revenant, and your concerns center around the fact that Wynter *is* one."

Sighing, Cain sat back in his chair. "I thought about consulting Eve. She's a far older being than any of us. Far older than even the texts in front of me. There's a chance she'll be able to answer my questions."

"I'm sensing a 'but'."

"*But* . . . I don't feel that I know her well enough to entrust her with any information that concerns Wynter or my relationship with her."

Seth's mouth quirked. "I'd do the brotherly thing and tease you for being so paranoid and distrustful, but I know that in this instance it mostly stems from how protective you are of Wynter. I like that she's so important to you. I like that you're equally important to her. She wouldn't otherwise ask you to hold off on the binding until the danger had passed if she didn't feel—"

A frantic knock was quickly followed by the reappearance of Maxim.

"I'm sorry to barge in, Sire," began the aide, breathing hard, "but a lycan rushed here with word from Wynter's coven—she's missing."

*

Fuck, it was cold. And dark. The glacial mist dampened and chilled Wynter's skin, surrounding her like a thick cloud. She shivered, righting her tee.

A spinetingling scream split the air, raising the little hairs on her body. A roar came next, deep and feral. She swallowed, a breath stuttering out of her. The sounds seemed to come from the far distance, but she couldn't be sure. And since she couldn't see a damn thing, she also couldn't be certain if any other souls were close by.

Vibes of misery and pain throbbed in the air. Fear had a smell here. Clinical and metallic and sickly.

And where was here?

The netherworld.

She wasn't a stranger to this place. Or to the haunting, bloodcurdling sounds. Or to the bitterly cold mist that went on and on and on. Or to the many entities that loved to circle, chase, and taunt the souls.

Wynter figured that the reason humans had mistaken the netherworld for hell was that, essentially, it put you through hell. Not to punish, but as part of the purification process. It used agony and terror to break you down so your soul could be cleansed and then rebuilt, free of sin and ready to be reborn.

The rustle of fabric.

Wynter spun, clenching her fists. The mist stirred and danced as a figure walked through it, small, slender snakes twined around Her arms. Long, flowing obsidian hair tumbled around Her like a soft curtain. Only a beige bralette-type top and a short skirt covered smooth dark skin. Deep brown eyes that, regardless of Her mood, always held a red glint of absolute rage were laser focused on Wynter.

Kali. Goddess of vengeance. Creator of revenants. Wrath personified.

She was sometimes present when Wynter's soul again found its way to the netherworld, but not always. And they rarely spoke to each other. The deity always seemed to have more interest in immediately returning Wynter's soul back from where it came.

Not this time, apparently. Because Wynter was *still* there. Not a good sign.

Kali stood before her, studying her closely, a faint smile touching Her lips.

Wynter swallowed. "So I'm dead for real now?" Her chest seized, and her gut sharply twisted. The thought of never seeing Cain again made her feel ill.

Kali scoffed. "It takes more than an iron bullet to the brain to permanently put down a revenant," She said, Her voice thick and deep with *so much power* that Wynter felt the vibration of it in her teeth and bones. "Any book on mythology will tell you that in order to ensure revenants do not rise from the dead, someone must behead them, incinerate every part of their body, and then scatter their ashes into the sea. Mythology does get *some* things correct. But there are so many errors that people tend to dismiss all the tales."

Wynter frowned as the implication of that sank in. "So, wait, all those times I came back to life, it wasn't that you were sending me back?"

"I did not need to. Though I would have if necessary." Kali turned a brief smile on the snake that flicked its tongue at Her cheek. "As I have told you before, you have a purpose, Wynter. That purpose is what ties your soul to that realm."

Since the deity seemed to be in the mood to answer questions—an extreme rarity—Wynter asked the one that had pricked at her for years. "And if I fulfill that purpose, will I then die?"

Kali's eyes slid back to hers. "No. Because now you have an extra tie to that realm."

"Cain."

Kali gave a slow, graceful nod. "Yes."

"He was right," Wynter realized. "You shaped me into a weapon so that I could do something for you."

Kali's smile became slightly more pronounced. "You have exceeded my expectations at every turn."

No *I'm sorry I pulled you into my personal shit.* But then, Wynter was a mere Earth-bound creature while Kali, on the other hand, was a goddamn deity—of course She wasn't sorry. They weren't anything close to equals, in the deity's opinion.

Knowing there was no sense in complaining when said objections would be dismissed as unimportant, Wynter instead asked, "What's this purpose you have for me?"

Kali's eyes sharpened with approval. She took an elegant step forward. "Let me tell you a story."

Chapter Twelve

The sounds of voices arguing *loudly* greeted Wynter as she came to. Dying seriously sucked. It was hardly ever pain-free. Worse, some of the pain was often still there when her soul returned to her body, though said pain would quickly fade. More, she always felt weak and groggy.

Her wounds were no doubt closed, since they always were when her soul came back. Her death must have also neutralized and disintegrated any traces of iron in her system, because she wasn't suffering any aftereffects.

She had no clue how long she'd been dead in this realm. Time wasn't in sync with that of the netherworld. A minute here could be an hour there, or seconds or even months.

Her monster was writhing within her, somewhat pissed and eager to savage those who'd dare harm her. She sent it some telepathic images, communicating that she needed to fake 'dead' for a few moments while her body recovered—then it could do whatever it wanted. Still, that might not have been enough to stay its hand, given how utterly furious it was, if Kali wasn't close and urging it to wait. The deity stroked Wynter's hair like a cooling breeze.

Wynter didn't need to open her eyes to sense that the vampires were stood only a few feet in front of her—and still arguing loud enough to scare any local wildlife.

She wouldn't be able to give herself *too* much time to recover. The moment they lowered their voices, they'd likely hear her heartbeat—it was a little sluggish right now, but that would soon change.

God, she needed one of Anabel's rejuvenating potions in a *major* way. A cup of Delilah's energy teas wouldn't go amiss either.

One side of her face burned in a telling way that told her Kali's mark was now visible on her skin. Thankfully, it was nonetheless currently hidden from the vamps, since that side of her face was pressed against the ground.

Claud swore long and loud. "Stop yelling at me!"

"You just cost us a million fucking dollars!" spat Enzo, who she sensed was pacing, the dry grass crunching beneath his feet.

"I didn't *mean* to shoot her in the head. She was moving so damn fast . . ."

"Maybe Adam will still want her body," suggested another voice. *Marvin.*

"Why the fuck would he?" Enzo demanded. "He needs her to undo the curse. She can't do that if she's dead. *Fuck.*"

"Maybe she'll come back to life," said Marvin. "I mean, she's a *revenant.*"

"Won't happen," said Claud. "Shelia was clear that a lethal shot from an iron bullet would be all it took to take her out for good."

"I guess we could just leave her here or bury her somewhere," said a fourth voice. *Mickey.*

"I say we take our chances and offer her up to the Aeons," stated Claud. "They might still reward us. We've come this far. All they can say is no."

Enzo growled. "Yeah, and they can also kill us for killing *her*— their one chance at undoing the curse!"

"Her death might have undone it," said Marvin.

"If it would have been that simple to fix what she did, Adam wouldn't have been so bothered about her being brought here," Enzo pointed out. "He would have just made it clear that he wanted her dead."

"Not if he was also set on torturing her for what she did to his land," Claud shot back. "I say we take her to him."

Her strength regained, Wynter signaled to her monster that it was almost time to lunge. The vampires seemed to be calming now, so they'd soon become aware of her heart beating in her chest.

"So do I," said Marvin.

Enzo stopped pacing. "Well, *I* don't."

"Yeah, me neither," said Mickey.

Her monster slinked to the surface of Wynter's skin, and she sensed more than saw black little ribbons crisscrossing over her eyeballs. Claud still held the gun, but she didn't worry about that—no bullet would take down the being she hosted.

"Then how do we settle this?" asked Marvin.

"Rock, paper, scissors?" Claud suggested.

Enzo growled again. "Are you for real?"

"Do you have a better idea?" asked Claud.

"I do," Wynter cut in, rolling onto her back.

The vampires looked down at her, their bodies tense, their mouths open wide. Before any had the chance to strike, her monster took over.

*

Wynter stumbled forward as she came back to herself. She was on her feet, so she clearly hadn't passed out this time. She wasn't injured, but her skin and clothes were streaked with blood. Oh, grand.

As for the vampires, well, going by the large scattering of ashes they were all in fact dead. There was enough blood to suggest that her monster had brutally torn into them as it killed them. Its mood was still foul, though. Mostly because the entity was too close to Aeon for its liking. The monster *loathed* that place. It wouldn't be happy to return unless it would be free to feast on its residents.

Damn, it was gonna take her a while to get back to Devil's Cradle. It sucked that she had no way of contacting anyone to give them her location and assure them that she was fine. One touch to her soul would confirm for Cain that she wasn't dead, but it

THE MONSTERS WE ARE

wouldn't tell him that she was safe. Hopefully neither he nor her coven would do anything stupid.

Had anyone even realized that she was missing yet? Maybe. Maybe not. Her coven would assume she was in the shed as usual. They might not notice she'd disappeared until they wondered why she hadn't returned to the cottage at the end of the workday.

People would eventually notice that Wynter was gone. Some would soon be looking for her. They'd assume she'd been taken and they would try to find her. The problem was that they weren't likely to come *this* far out, since they probably wouldn't suspect that she'd been teleported anywhere. And even if they did, they wouldn't manage to cover the distance in a hurry unless they used a teleporter—one who would probably aimlessly 'port from spot to spot in the hope of stumbling upon her.

One thing was for certain: she wasn't going to simply wait here for someone to appear and rescue her ass. Not Wynter's style. She'd try to make at least part of the journey home herself.

Well, she had no intention of making it on foot.

After magickly returning her sword to the wardrobe in Cain's chamber, she walked among the blanket of ashes in search of something that Enzo had earlier dropped and—*aha*—she found his key fob. Soon, she was in the SUV . . . at which point she realized that she had no clue which direction she needed to head in. Figuring that following the tire tracks the vampires left behind would likely take her home, she did exactly that.

As she drove, she thought of all the things that Kali had told her. Things that Wynter wouldn't have begun to guess at. Things that the deity had made clear that Cain and the other Ancients couldn't yet know.

Wynter hadn't reacted so well on learning just how many things had been kept from her. She'd cursed, she'd hissed, she'd even yelled. Kali thankfully hadn't gotten pissed. She'd only calmly asked, *"Can you tell me that my reasoning for withholding the information until now was not sound?"*

The bitch of it was that, no, Wynter hadn't been able to say that. Not when she could look back and see just how many decisions she might not have made if she'd known everything from the outset. A lot of things might have played out very differently.

Wynter also hadn't been able to claim that the Ancients should be immediately made aware of all that she now knew. It didn't seem fair that they were in the dark, and she hated the thought of keeping it all from Cain. But she understood why Kali had insisted on it. The deity was right to believe that the Ancients wouldn't react well to what they'd soon learn. If they learned it *too* soon ... well, the consequences wouldn't be good.

Approximately three and a half hours into Wynter's journey home, the SUV sputtered to a stop. She'd ran out of gas. *Motherfucker.* She slammed her hands on the wheel as she spat a string of curses.

Slipping out of the vehicle, she let out a heavy sigh and felt her shoulders slump. Walking the rest of the way really did *not* appeal to her. It would take her *days* to get home.

God, all she wanted was to get a hug from Cain, see her coven, shower the day away, and then see to it that Shelia paid for what she'd done. Was that really so much to ask?

Figuring she should be at least grateful that the sun was close to setting and wouldn't beat at her skin, Wynter rolled back her shoulders and began to walk. Until that moment, she'd never been more grateful for choosing immortality. It meant she could keep up a decent pace, wouldn't tire as quickly, and had good enough stamina that she wouldn't need to repeatedly stop to rest.

Still, her mood was super low. She'd been kidnapped. Attacked. Shot in the head. Learned some heavy shit. And now had no choice but to walk the fuck home.

More, she was all sticky from the blood that had matted her hair and dried on her skin. The smell of it taunted her nostrils and made her stomach lurch every now and then. To make matters even more annoying, the now-dry stains on her clothing had roughened the cotton, and it chafed uncomfortably against her flesh.

As she walked, she occasionally felt an otherworldly brush of air—an encouragement to keep moving, a reassurance that she wasn't alone. Her monster wasn't the least bit bothered by the situation. It was once more deep in slumber.

The sun soon set, and darkness gathered around Wynter. Still, she walked and walked and walked, only taking small periods of rest here and there. But eventually her posture stooped, her muscles began to weaken and cramp, and her dry throat felt so scratchy it almost hurt to drag air into her lungs.

The walk through a forested area was particularly shit. Especially when she could barely see. Branches slapped at her. Pine needles clawed at her. Rough tree bark scraped her skin. Her jeans got repeatedly snagged on thorns or the underbrush. Little rocks stabbed into the soles of her feet through her shoes.

More, her tired muscles burned like a bitch. At this point, she weaved more than she walked.

Licking at her dry lips, she was about to stop for a rest when she heard an almighty screech. Her head snapped up. And there in the evening sky was the source of the sound. It looked like a mere dot at first. But that dot grew bigger seriously fast as it flew closer.

A shaky smile splitting her chapped lips, she let out a blast of magick that would act as a flare, worried the dragon wouldn't otherwise notice her. It responded with yet another screech, and then it was flying toward her. Staggering to a halt, she almost dropped to her knees in relief.

*

Waiting near the tunnel, Cain *willed* his consort to walk through it. He loped back and forth like a tiger in a cage. That was essentially what he was. A predator trapped in a prison. Helpless. Powerless. Caught up in an animal fury.

Seven hours. It had been *seven fucking hours* since he'd received word that Wynter was missing. It was possible that she'd been gone even longer, since her coven hadn't thought to check on her until a potential customer went to the cottage asking if Wynter was inside.

The pressure to find his consort seemed to batter every cell in his body. It pushed him. Pinched him. Goaded him.

But he couldn't answer that drive to search for her. Couldn't pass the boundaries of the town. He'd sent others to search—some by foot, some in vehicles. Dragon shifters had taken to the sky, able to cover a lot of ground fast.

Most of those who went out on foot had already returned—not including her coven—reporting that they were no signs of her. The tire tracks they'd discovered were days old, too faint to follow, and were apparently left by an all-terrain vehicle. Seth had confirmed that a small nest of vampires had left Devil's Cradle a few days ago in an SUV that belonged to the leader. It couldn't have been them who'd taken her, they were long gone.

So where the fuck was she?

Cain cricked his neck, his nostrils flaring at the headache that was beginning to build in his temples. "Maxim, have people search the town and city again." He fairly barked the order, unable to temper his voice. "Anyone who took her would have needed a vehicle to get her to Aeon. If none are missing from the storage facility, I can't see how else someone got her away." It was possible, of course, that she'd been teleported away from here—various creatures possessed the ability—but it was equally possible that she'd been hidden by someone who might have the idea to smuggle her out of Devil's Cradle at a later date.

Maxim nodded and hurried away.

Azazel, Seth, Lilith, Dantalion, and Eve remained close by. Cain wasn't sure if they were there as a show of support or to be ready to take him down in the event that his rage swallowed him whole. If it was the latter, their presence was pointless. Even collectively these people stood no chance of subduing him or his monster.

Whatever the case, none dared get too close to Cain. He couldn't blame them. He was a hair's breadth away from losing it.

There was no getting his pulse to calm. No stopping adrenaline from shooting through his blood again and again. No getting rid of the burning sensation in his lungs.

Every muscle in his body seemed coiled with tension. His clothes felt tight and confining. Fuck, his own skin felt constricting. Just the same, his ribs seemed too snug, making him feel like he couldn't drag in enough air—a sensation that was worsened by the phantom weight on his chest.

Lost in its rage, his inner creature was having its own personal crisis. The monster thrashed and hissed. Its movements weren't smooth and fluid as usual, they were jerky and stiff. It wanted to kill. Torture. Destroy. And it didn't particularly care who its victim was. It simply craved the release.

"Is it possible that she decided to give herself up to Adam?" Eve softly asked, hesitant.

Grinding his teeth at the stupid question, Cain rolled his neck and shoulders. "Of fucking course not, Wynter's not suicidal," he replied, his words coming fast and hard like bullets.

"But maybe she thinks that Adam might leave you and everyone here be if he finally has her," Eve added.

Still pacing, Cain shook his head hard. "She knows that giving herself to Adam wouldn't change anything, and she's no martyr." He rubbed the side of his neck, feeling his tendons standing out.

Eve delicately lifted her shoulder. "Do you think ... I know it would hurt to consider it ... but is there a chance she's fled to seek refuge elsewhere?"

Cain felt his brows snap together. "And why the fuck would she do that?"

Eve flinched at his tone. "Adam has put a price on her head, and she knows she's in danger here. If she fears what he might do to her—"

"Wynter wouldn't run," Cain snapped out.

"She ran from Aeon."

Halting, he fired a glare at his mother. "Because she was alone.

She had no backing there. Here, that isn't the case. And I *know* she wouldn't willingly leave me or her coven."

"You can't be sure of that."

"Not everyone abandons those they care for when all goes to hell."

Eve blanched. "I deserved that."

Maybe. Maybe not. Right then, he didn't give much of a fuck. Not when she wanted him to consider that Wynter could have left him. Maybe Seth hadn't liked her suggestion much either, because he hadn't stepped in to defend Eve.

Azazel cleared his throat. "I don't believe Wynter left of her own accord. Not for a second."

"No, nor do I," said Lilith. "And if she had, she would have needed a vehicle. We have already had it confirmed by Maxim that none have been taken from storage."

Eve's lips flattened. "Perhaps she walked to the nearest town and stole a car from there."

"The nearest town is even further away than Aeon," Azazel told her, a note of impatience in his voice. "If Wynter had headed that way on foot, she'd have been spotted by now."

Cain gave a hard nod, pacing once more. "The trackers reported that they found no traces of her, so we can safely say she didn't willingly stroll out of here."

He rubbed at his tight chest. A roar seemed trapped there, and it appeared to gather in strength with every moment. He wasn't sure he could keep it contained much longer.

He kept loping back and forth, restlessness humming in his blood. He had so much pent up energy, so much barely contained fury. It left him twitchy. Jittery. On edge.

His gaze bounced around, just as restless. Each of his senses seemed heightened and oversensitive, making him feel *too* alert.

Cain knew some residents would wonder why he wasn't out looking for her himself. They might even mistake his seeming lack of personal action for him not particularly giving much of a shit about her. That could later be a problem, considering some might then think it wouldn't be such a huge deal if they tried cashing in on the bounty. That wasn't a problem he could address right then, though.

Realizing he was holding his breath again, Cain drew in a long gulp of air until his chest expanded. He took several more deep breaths even as he knew it wouldn't help calm him. Nothing could. The only thing that would end his inner torment would be having Wynter returned to him.

"Maybe she wasn't taken by vehicle," suggested Seth, shifting from foot to foot. "Maybe someone found another way to take her out of here."

Cain slammed his gaze on his brother. "Teleported her away, you mean? I considered that."

Seth shrugged. "They could have even taken her through a portal."

Azazel rocked back and forth on the balls of his feet. "Both would explain how she seems to have disappeared into thin air. It would mean she *literally* did."

A cold ache lanced Cain's chest at the very thought of it, because . . . "If that happened, she'll be at Aeon as we speak. She'd have been taken straight there." He snapped his mouth shut, panic once more threatening to shut down all rational thought.

"Only to the boundaries—that's as far as any teleporter or portal opener would have gotten, due to the preternatural security measures," Dantalion pointed out. "Besides, no one would dare go further for fear of being killed on sight for trespassing. That would give her an opportunity to get away. We know how good she is at that."

Cain's fingers contracted like claws. "But if she didn't, Adam has her."

"Don't go there, Cain," said Azazel. "Don't let yourself think about it. There's every chance that she's . . . " He paused, his eyes sliding to the sky. "One of the dragons is back."

"And he's not alone," said Seth. "He has a passenger."

155

Cain's heartbeat kicked up as he spun. Holding his breath, he eyed the beast heading their way. It was as it slowed its pace and began to descend that Cain got a decent glimpse of the person on its back. *Wynter.* A breath gusted out of his lungs.

Fuck, she was home. Alive. And *right there.*

Relief sank into him, wrapped around his bones, and acted like a balm to the jagged edges of his control. His eyes very briefly closed but he snapped them back open, needing to keep his gaze locked on her. Needing to be sure she didn't disappear again.

The dragon landed smoothly a few feet away. Cain instantly blurred to its side and snatched her from its back, holding her tight, uncaring of the sight and smell of the blood staining her skin and clothes. He exhaled heavily, feeling like he could finally breathe. He opened his mouth to speak, but the right words didn't come to him.

She hugged him back. "I'm totally gross right now," she warned, her voice scratchy.

"I don't care." He gave a nod of thanks to the dragon shifter, who Azazel then ordered to signal to the other searchers that Wynter had been found. The dragon swiftly took to the sky.

Cain and Wynter stood holding each other in silence for long moments until, without releasing her, he pulled back slightly to take her in. His stomach tightened. She was pale. Looked weak and tired—such a rarity for her. "What happened? Who took you?"

She gave him a grim smile that held a bloodthirsty edge. "Funny story. You're gonna love it."

The others gathered around as she relayed what happened.

Lilith's lips parted. "Shelia as in Ishtar's aide?"

"One and the same," Wynter confirmed.

Anger coursing through his system once more, Cain flexed his hand around her nape. "I see."

"We don't know that Ishtar had anything to do with it," Dantalion said to him.

His back teeth locked, Cain pulled in a breath through his nose. "No, we don't. But we're about to fucking find out."

Chapter Thirteen

Wynter followed behind Cain as he threw open the solar room door and barged inside, his attention slamming on Ishtar, who sat on an elaborate, almost throne-like chair. The only other person in the room was one of her aides—inconveniently, it wasn't Shelia.

The female Ancient shot to her feet, her brow furrowed in both outrage and confusion as not only Wynter and Cain but Azazel, Seth, Dantalion, and Lilith filed inside while another of Ishtar's aides flapped nervously behind them. Eve—who'd weirdly struggled to look Wynter in the eye—had chosen to head back to Seth's Keep rather than be part of the confrontation.

"What on Earth do you all think you are doing? I see that the witch has been found." She sniffed at Cain. "It's very hypocritical of *you* to march into my home without waiting for an invitation when you constantly criticize me for . . . Why do you have blood on you?"

"It isn't mine," Cain bit out. "Where is Shelia?"

Ishtar bristled at his tone. "Excuse me?"

"Where. Is. She?"

"What business is that of yours?"

He advanced on the female Ancient *fast*. "If I find out you had anything to do with what happened to Wynter, you are fucking dead."

Ishtar's back snapped straight. "What am I being accused of now?"

Wynter stepped forward. "Your aide teleported me to a spot not far from Aeon to deliver me to four vampires from Devil's

157

Cradle—they'd decided it would be a fine idea to cash in on the bounty. Which it wasn't. They're dead now. But Shelia? She teleported away before I had the chance to deal with her. So she's alive. And that's a problem for me."

"And for me," said Cain. "Where is she?"

"Shelia would not do this," stated Ishtar. "It doesn't even make sense that she would be involved. The only incentive she would have to betray you would be to enjoy the bounty. Handing the witch over to vampires for *them* to enjoy it, well, there would be nothing in it for her."

"But there would be something in it for you," Lilith cut in. "Wynter would finally be gone ... just as you have wanted from the very beginning."

Ishtar's face went crimson with anger. "I had nothing to do with whatever happened to her. And I find it difficult to believe that Shelia did."

"Then you'll have no problem calling her here to question her, will you?" asked Dantalion, his tone smooth but dangerous.

Ishtar made a haughty sound. "Fine." She cut her gaze to the aide who'd hurried after them when they barged into the solar room. "Have Shelia brought to me now. Do not tell her what this is about. I will know if you did."

Swallowing hard, the aide did an honest to God's curtsy and then left.

Ishtar stared at Wynter. "If you have falsely accused one of my aides—"

"What reason could she possibly have to do that?" asked Seth, folding his arms.

Ishtar gave him a look that questioned his intelligence. "So that Cain would suspect and turn on me, of course. She could be spurring him to kill me."

Wynter narrowed her eyes. "If there ever comes a time when I want you dead, I'll see to it myself—I don't need anyone to do it for me. You know that."

Ishtar's eyelids flickered. Yeah, she knew it.

"Did you put your aide up to this?" Azazel asked the Ancient.

Ishtar's face hardened. "Does it really make sense to you that at a time of great upheaval, when we are so close to gaining what we want and it is more necessary than ever that all the Ancients stick together, I would truly do something like that?"

Actually, no, it didn't. Cain must have doubted it also because, well, he hadn't yanked her head right off her body.

A knock came at the door, and Ishtar called for the new arrival to enter.

Shelia breezed inside with a cocky strut. "You called for me, Your Grace?" She idly let her gaze drift over the others in the room. When her eyes landed on Wynter, her face drained of color. Stark fear crossed her features and glittered in her eyes.

Wynter gave her a dark grin. "If you hadn't been so keen to teleport away quickly, you would have noticed that things didn't exactly go to plan for you or the vampires."

Squinting in suspicion, Ishtar strolled toward the aide. "The witch is telling the truth?"

Shelia's eyes widened. "No, of course not! She is Cain's consort. I would never be so stupid as to anger an Ancient."

Cain growled. "You lie."

Shelia cast him a brief sideways look, her posture submissive. "I do not, I swear to you I do not."

Cain's brow hiked up. "So you are calling my consort a liar?"

"I am making no accusations, I am simply stating my innocence."

Innocence my ass. "No one's going to buy your bullshit, Shelia. You teleported me to the vampires, you advised them to shoot me in the leg to keep me weak, and you told me to enjoy my time with Adam. You allegedly also told the vamps that an iron bullet to the heart or brain would kill me. It may interest you to know that you were wrong."

Shelia's gaze clashed with hers. "I said no such thing to anyone—"

"Stop fucking lying!" Cain shouted, the words echoing with a power that Wynter felt in her bones.

Shelia jumped. "I swear I'm not."

"Yes, you are," said Ishtar, squinting. "I see it."

Wynter blinked, shocked by the Ancient failing to take her aide's side. If the faces of the other Ancients were anything to go by, they were equally surprised.

Shelia shook her head in denial.

"Why would you assist those vampires?" Ishtar demanded. "What did they offer you that convinced you to betray me in such a way?"

"I would never betray you," Shelia swore.

Ishtar's nostrils flared. "I will never understand why, but Cain took the witch as his consort. By delivering her to those vampires, you betrayed him. And to betray one Ancient is to betray them all."

"I thought you'd want her gone!"

"If I wanted her gone, she would be gone."

Wynter snorted. The Ancient really shouldn't be so sure of that.

Shelia began to sob. "I'm sorry."

"Your apologies are wasted," Cain snarled. He sliced his gaze to Ishtar. "I won't allow her to live."

Ishtar jutted out her chin. "She is *my* aide. It is *my* right to punish her."

Cain prowled toward her like a predator eager to battle another. "Do not test me. My consort could have died because of what she did. The right to end the bitch's life is *mine.*"

"I cannot permit such an act to go unaddressed by me, or it would encourage others to believe they can take similar risks," said Ishtar.

"Then you may punish her," began Cain, "but the killing blow will be mine."

Wynter would much rather that the killing blow was *hers*, but she knew he needed this; knew that he needed to avenge her in some way. And since she'd already taken care of the vampires, there was only the aide left to punish.

"I can agree to that," Ishtar told him, surprising Wynter—the female Ancient wasn't the most reasonable of people. "It will be a public execution. An example needs to be made of her."

"Agreed," said Cain.

Ishtar took a step toward him. "But let me be clear on this. I will not pay for Shelia's betrayal. No matter what you might wish to believe, I did not put her up to this."

Cain cocked his head in an almost wolf-like way. "Ishtar . . . if I'd thought you were behind this, you'd already be dead."

They all knew that was true.

It was Dantalion and Azazel who dragged Shelia out of the Keep and into the courtyard of the bailey. The two males then backed away, joining Wynter and the other Ancients who were forming a circle around the sobbing aide.

The people in the bailey poured out of the workshops, barn, and other buildings to gather around, curious. Seeing the gory state of Wynter, many cast her odd looks. They really should be used to this by now.

Trembling, Shelia hugged herself, her gaze finding Wynter. There was no remorse or apology in those eyes. Only resentment and fear. A bone-chilling fear.

Wynter gave an unconcerned shrug. "I told you that you'd die for this."

Ishtar stepped into the circle. "One of my very own aides betrayed me," she called out, ensuring her voice carried to the large crowd. "How exactly? By betraying my fellow Ancient. She was party to a plan to take his consort to Aeon. Treachery is not something that I take lightly. It will *never* go unpunished. It will *never* earn a traitor anything other than an excruciating death. Apparently, some people have forgotten that. Well, let me refresh your memories."

And then Shelia dropped to her knees, screaming like someone was ripping apart her entire being. It reminded Wynter of the time that Cain had tortured a berserker by lashing out at his soul. That was the thing . . . When an Ancient had rights to your soul, they

161

couldn't only cause you pleasure on an almost unbearable scale; they could also cause you the same scale of pain.

Still screaming, Shelia fell forward, bracing herself on her hands and knees. Vessels in her eyes burst. Sweat broke out on her flushed skin. Veins stood out on her face and neck.

Ishtar gave her no mercy or reprieve. Each time it looked like Shelia might pass out, the Ancient eased off for a few moments. But then the torture would begin again. It went on and on and on.

Shelia coughed up blood, making Wynter wonder if the screaming had burst blood vessels in the aide's throat or lungs. She crumpled to the ground, curling up in a ball as if it would protect her from the onslaught of pain. But nothing could.

Wynter noticed that the crowd—which kept on growing, as though people were drawn by the cries—weren't finding it easy to watch. Some flinched or glanced away. Others looked nauseous and were clamping their lips tightly shut. But none appeared eager to speak up on the screaming woman's behalf.

Wynter's coven would be so sorry they'd missed this. They hadn't yet returned from searching for her, so she wasn't able to check in with them.

On the ground, Shelia arched and kicked her legs as the agony continued. Her wails became hoarse, strangled cries. And Wynter knew that the woman would mentally break if Ishtar didn't pull back sometime soon.

Maybe Cain had that same thought, because he stepped into the circle and held up his hand, indicating for the female Ancient to stop. Ishtar narrowed her eyes, so affronted by the authoritative gesture that she defiantly kept up the torture for a few more moments. But then, finally, she stopped.

Cain circled the aide as she shivered and whimpered. Her muscles occasionally spasmed, and she mumbled indecipherable words here and there.

Unlike Ishtar, he didn't look at or address the crowd. And Wynter knew it was because, as much as the idea of a public execution might

THE MONSTERS WE ARE

suit him, he wasn't really doing this for them. He didn't care to make a production out of this. His focus was on Shelia, on making the woman suffer purely because, after what she'd done, it would fucking please him.

Knowing what he did next would be bad, Wynter braced herself—or, more specifically, her stomach. She wouldn't look away. She wouldn't show any disgust, no matter what he did. He'd already returned that favor by never backing away whenever she came to him looking exactly as she did right then.

He lifted his hand, palm up, and a shimmering wave of power gathered in a cloud-like form. The "cloud" twisted, swirled, and pulsed. Faster and faster and faster. Until it shifted, changing color and form, becoming something else.

Becoming a swarm of bees.

Big-ass bees that buzzed almost ... frantically. Angrily, even. *Oh hell.*

The insects descended on Shelia, covering her from head to toe. She bucked and spasmed, flapping her hands and weakly kicking her legs. The bees didn't fly away, undeterred. Some crawled into her ears and mouth—possibly even into other orifices.

Crack.

Wynter almost jolted at the sound. There was another crack. And another. It was only then she realized that one of Shelia's arms was now twisted awkwardly. *Jesus.*

Cold fingers danced over Wynter's nape. It was sometimes easy for her to forget how powerful Cain was; how effortlessly he could inflict pain; how very little mercy ran through his veins.

More bones cracked. More body parts twisted at unnatural angles. Until the woman looked like a damn contortionist. It was cruel and sadistic—there were no two ways about it. Shelia's weak cries of pain were lost beneath the buzzing.

It was just as Shelia looked like she didn't have much life left in her that there was one final crack. Her neck had been broken. The bees gradually faded, eventually disintegrating into nothing. As

Leviathans were literal gateways to hell, there was only one place Shelia's soul would go, no matter how many good deeds she might have done in her life—the very depths of hell.

Bon voyage.

No one spoke. Or moved. Or even breathed too loud. Including the other Ancients. The last thing anyone appeared to want was Cain's attention.

His gaze sought Wynter. Darkened. Intensified. Gleamed. An array of emotions flickered fast in those eyes—too fast for her to discern them—as if each was fighting for dominance.

Despite that her insides were still doing sickly little flips, she held out her hand, letting him know that she wouldn't turn away from him; that she wasn't disgusted by what he'd done or who he was.

Oh, the torture had been hard to watch for sure. And it could be said that he'd taken it further than he'd needed to. But she wasn't sure she'd have been any less merciful in his position, if she was honest. And considering Adam would have done *far* worse to Wynter—something that had probably driven Cain to make Shelia's death so agonizing—it was seriously difficult to feel any sympathy for her.

Cain stalked straight to Wynter and slipped his hand into hers. "Home," he said. It wasn't an invitation. It was a warning. A message that he wasn't prepared to part from her any time soon.

Since she wasn't feeling the need to have any space or time away from him, she agreed, "Home."

*

Dragging a brush through her wet hair, Wynter sighed at the closed bathroom door. How long had he been in there? Twenty minutes? Maybe more? She had no idea. But he was definitely still showering, because she could hear water splattering tile.

She was really gonna have to do something to snap Cain out of whatever zone he was in. The moment they'd entered the bedchamber, he'd released her hand and hadn't touched her since. Not even to help her wash off the blood. Hell, he hadn't even *joined* her in the shower stall. Unless they were in a rush to be somewhere, it was very rare that they showered separately.

It didn't seem like he needed space from her at the moment. In fact, each time he looked at her, it seemed like he wanted nothing more than to drag her to him and hold her close. But he'd determinedly put some physical distance between them, and she couldn't understand why.

One thing Wynter could be certain of was that it wasn't a case of him not wanting to touch her while metaphorical blood was on his hands. He'd touched her in the past when *actual* blood stained his hands. They'd cleaned each other off after battles, big and small.

Wynter might have thought that he was simply so pissed he worried he'd hurt her if he touched her, but that didn't ring true. Cain had more control over his emotions than most people. Sure, rage could ride him hard in the right circumstances, but he never *outwardly* lost his shit. He never violently vented on those who didn't deserve it.

Even the way he'd handled Shelia had been very controlled and methodical. Cain was a damn expert at sucking in his emotions and maintaining his composure. It would take super extreme occurrences to make it evaporate.

She heard the shower shut off. *About time.* Wynter set her brush on the top of the dresser.

It was a few moments before he strode out of the bathroom, a towel looped around his hips. *Hot damn.* All that hard, tattooed muscle glistening with tiny droplets of water . . . She wanted to lick them all up. Lick him all up.

His gaze immediately sought her out, as if he simply needed to know she was still there. He drank in the sight of her in his shirt. She'd slipped it on, knowing he liked seeing her wearing his tees or shirts. He didn't react, though. Didn't speak at all about any damn thing. Instead, he silently dried himself off and then pulled on sweatpants and a tee.

She was about to ask if he was ready to talk, but then knuckles rapped on the door. He opened it, took a tray of food from whoever stood on the other side of the door, and then closed it.

The scents of cooked vegetables and grilled meat wafted her way, making her stomach rumble. She hadn't eaten dinner yet, and she was famished.

He set the tray on the table and gestured at the seat she usually claimed. As Wynter sat, he took the one opposite her.

Although she was starved, she reached for the bottle of water first. She'd downed a full bottle on the way to Ishtar's Keep, but the thirst was still a tickle in her throat. She really did need one of Anabel's rejuvenating potions. But her coven clearly hadn't yet arrived back at Devil's Cradle or they'd have come here looking for her by now.

She and Cain ate in relative silence. It wasn't uncomfortable, but it was weighted. That didn't stop her from scoffing down her food. Once they were done, he set the tray on the floor outside the chamber.

Rising from her chair, she walked toward him, not whatsoever impressed when he backed away. She folded her arms. "Okay, what gives?"

His jaw tightened. "I can't put my hands on you right now."

"Of course you can."

"No, I can't. Won't."

"And why not?"

His fingers flexed. "It's simply better this way."

"If you're going to ask for space or some shit—"

"Not space. I want you here. I want you where I can see you. But I can't touch you yet."

"You're going to need to explain that, because I don't get it."

His eyes flaring, he stalked toward her, all smolder and sexual aggression. "If I put my hands on you, I won't be able to merely hold you. There'll be no soft, lazy kiss. I'll fucking consume you.

No lie, baby, I will take and take and take. Feast and mark and fuck. I'll make you come as many times as I want. I won't stop until *I've* had enough. You'll feel utterly wrecked by the time I'm done. There won't be a single thought left in your head, because I'll have thoroughly fucked every corner of it."

Chapter Fourteen

Well, *that* promise sure pushed all sorts of sexual levers. She felt an aroused flush sweep up her neck and face. Unsurprising. Her hormones were having a meltdown.

If any other male had given her those words, Wynter would have thought he was *all* talk. But Cain could be super intense at times. Which didn't translate into her getting a rough fuck. No, he subjected her to what could only be described as pure sexual torment. He *did* take and take. He would tease and rut and draw it all out. He'd alternate between denying her orgasms and *forcing* her into orgasms, essentially taking full control of her pleasure.

Although there were moments when it felt like sheer hell, there were also moments when she came so hard that the orgasms all but flattened her; they felt as much of a mental release as a physical one. She was rather fond of those orgasms. Hence the anticipation now swirling in her belly.

"It's not as if you haven't used me like that before. I'm not seeing the problem." Damn if her voice didn't break.

No satisfaction rippled across his face. Only an irritation that made his nostrils flare. "The *problem* is that I won't be the only one who fucks you. My creature will rise. It will bite you. That's all it can think about."

Wynter tensed.

"Seven hours we were without you. We had no clue where you were. We only knew you were alive because we can touch your soul. But we had no way of getting to you. We were fucking stuck *here*."

Her chest ached at the torture and helplessness that gleamed in his eyes and left a jagged edge to his voice.

"My monster was a mess the whole time. I was no better. And though you're back and it can see that you're fine, it mentally still isn't in a good place. Neither am I, so I don't have enough control to firmly subdue it right now. It knows that; it would take advantage. It wants to lay claim to you in the only way that it can. You need to give me some physical space."

Maybe. But she didn't want to. Not simply because his sexual warning sounded rather intriguing, but because he needed a little comfort. She had no way to give it to him unless she touched him. "Would it hurt? The bite?"

His pupils dilated, and he took in a long breath ... as if just having the conversation was too much for his libido at present. "Wynter." It was a warning, pure and simple.

"You can at least tell me if I need to brace myself for pain."

He studied her expression. "You'd let my monster bite you?"

Well, it would take three bites to perform the binding, so one little bite here and now wouldn't do any harm. Although ... "Not if it's gonna take a chunk out of me. Is that what it would do?"

"No. It wouldn't purposely hurt you, but it wouldn't be careful with you. There wouldn't be anything gentle about how it touched or fucked you."

She swallowed. "And its venom?"

"It supposedly burns a little, though only for a few moments."

She wasn't exactly comforted by that, since Cain had a way of downplaying just how much his little brands hurt. "I don't need you or your monster to be careful with me. I can handle whatever you've both got."

Cain stared at her, his heart pounding, his dick excruciatingly hard. He wanted so badly to take her at her word. He needed the feel of her skin under his hands, the taste of her in his mouth, the hot slick grip of her inner muscles quaking around his cock. He needed to reclaim every part of her as his own. But his control would inevitably crumble at some point, his monster would then lay its own claim, and Cain worried it would frighten her. Possibly even frighten her away. More, he feared she'd later regret allowing it to bite her.

"Why are you still hesitating?" Her lips thinned. "You'd better not have it in your head that your creature might scare me off."

His little witch read him too well at times.

"After all the things you've told me, I'm still here. I think I've proven that I'm not easily spooked. Plus, I've met your monster before."

"It was calm, then. It isn't now. And make no mistake about it, baby, it will fuck you like an animal."

"I'm still not seeing the problem."

He inwardly swore as his cock jerked and his creature pushed urgently against his skin. Cain gripped her jaw. "Be sure, Wynter. Be very, very sure."

She winged up a brow. "Does it look like I'm not?"

"No. It looks like you're raring to fuck." Which only made his balls ache. He dropped his hand and took a step back. "Take the shirt off."

She complied, letting it slip off her shoulders and fall to the floor. The sight of her naked was always the best kind of punch to his gut. When she was naked *and* aroused, the view was even better. Her pupils were blown. Her skin was flushed. Her nipples were tight little points. Her thigh muscles bunched and flexed . . . like she was squeezing them to get some much-needed friction.

Pure male satisfaction filled him. This beautiful creature belonged to him, all the way down to her soul. "Remember you were warned," he said, his tone clipped. "Turn around. Grab the bedpost."

Again, she complied without complaint.

"Good girl." Admiring the sleek line of her back and her perfect little ass, Cain shed his own clothes. Naked, he swept his palm up her spine and then pressed his front to her back. He dragged his teeth over her nape hard enough to mark, wondering if she could sense the feral energy that hummed beneath his skin and urged him to violently ram his dick inside her with no thought to whether or not she'd like it.

He delivered a stinging smack to her soul. She jolted with a gasp, her back arching. He did it again. And again. And again. Increasing the "weight" of the smacks each time.

Knowing the combination of gentle and rough would muddle with her mental equilibrium, he also softly stroked her back and trailed light kisses along her neck and shoulders. He loved the taste of her skin. Loved the spice of magick that flavored it.

She pushed her ass against his cock in invitation. He didn't take it. Instead, he flayed her soul with light taps, hard spanks, and full on thwacks.

He crouched behind her so he could lick and nip the globes of her ass, intent on leaving plenty of his own marks before his creature took over. It currently pressed against Cain's skin, wanting at her. The only thing that kept it from pushing him too hard was the knowledge that it *would* get to have her soon; get to bite and claim her.

He'd pointed out to it several times that if the creature wasn't careful with her, she wouldn't want a repeat. He hoped that would be enough to encourage it to go easy on her—or as easy as it was capable of being.

Cain breathed deep, drawing in the drugging scent of her need. He swiped his knuckles over her slit. Yeah, she was wet all right.

Kissing his way up her spine, he dragged his nails up the backs of her thighs and over her luscious ass. She arched into the stinging caress with a hiss, her head falling back as he layered the sensation with a soul-deep wave of pure pleasure.

"Cain, I need you in me."

He lined up the head of his dick to her entrance. "Don't worry, little witch, I'll give you my cock." He slammed home as he spanked her clit. She came with a choked scream, her pussy squeezing him so fucking tight.

171

Grinding his teeth, he waited until her orgasm subsided. Then he withdrew his cock and stepped back.

She threw him a glare over her shoulder. "What the hell?"

He lifted a brow. "I said I'd give you my cock. I didn't say I'd fuck you with it."

Her eyes blazed fire at him.

"You knew what you were getting yourself into. Now turn to fully face me. Lean back against the post." He hummed when she followed his instructions. "Very good."

Her flesh so over-sensitized it prickled hotly like it was on fire, Wynter licked at her lips. Her inner muscles kept spasming, as if in search of the cock that had been cruelly pulled out of her. "Kiss me."

"Oh, I intend to." He dropped to his knees in front of her and nuzzled her pussy, his hot breath washing across her wet flesh.

She gasped, reaching above her head to grip the bedpost behind her. Cain always looked firmly in charge, even when on his back or knees. Right now, he was as cool and dominant as always. But she felt the difference in him tonight. She sensed the tiny fractures in his restraint. Dangerous as those fractures were, there was no escaping that they added a spice of excitement for her. Well, she was weird like that.

Precarious though his control might presently be, he hadn't seriously let loose on her. Hadn't dished out too much pain or flooded her with too much sensation. As if worried that to allow himself that dark pleasure would lead his control to officially go to shit.

He propped her foot on his shoulder and leaned in to lap at her slit. "I would know this taste anywhere. Like its imprinted on my system." He parted her folds with his thumbs and gave her a long lick.

Moaning, Wynter scratched at the wooden post, melting as velvet strokes of his tongue swiped through her slit. They were never mindless strokes, no, he was careful to hit every erogenous spot she had. Her inner muscles quaked again, needing more than licks and—

Her entire body jolted hard as a chilled, prickly wave of sensation thrashed and abraded her soul. Like someone had whacked her with an ice-cold, jagged-edged flogger and then dragged it over her flesh. It hurt, yet the discomfort morphed into a liquid pleasure that frazzled her nerve-endings.

A hot surge of sensation came next, sizzling its way along her soul like burning hot water had been poured over her. Again it hurt, but again the pain quickly became pleasure.

He'd been lulling her into a false sense of security earlier, she realized. He'd let her think he was keeping a tight hold on himself; that things might not get so intense.

Featherlight tingles then flicked her soul like silk ribbons. Gentle. Cool. Decadent. The abrupt switch from harsh to soft threw her off-balance.

They came again, just as soft. And the far-too-gentle sensations were nothing but a pure tease. They made her want, crave, *need* a harder touch. Her nipples became so painfully tight she hissed through her clenched teeth.

Cain's tongue drove inside her and did a little swirl, fluttering against her hypersensitive walls. She sucked in a breath and then groaned. He began pumping his tongue inside her and, sweet Jesus, that felt good.

More torturously soft touches brushed over her soul that felt like hot breaths, trickles of icy water, and washes of static. Every ultra-light sensation amped up her frustration, causing a scream to build in her chest. She got so swept up in it all that she didn't realize she was bearing down on Cain's tongue, riding it shamelessly, until a growl of approval rumbled up her core.

Gasping, she scratched at his scalp and bucked against his mouth. He licked his way to her clit and then wrapped his lips around it. Oh God, the sucking little pulses on her clit were sheer heaven. Two fingers jammed inside her, shoving her into an orgasm that let loose the scream that had been trapped in her chest.

Cain withdrew his fingers but softly licked at her pussy as if gentling her, only stopping when she recovered from her orgasm.

He stood and then took her mouth, sinking his tongue inside. She tasted herself. Tasted his hunger. Tasted the barely contained untamed energy that pricked at his control.

A surge of hot pleasure snapped and popped as it crackled its way along her soul. She cried out, stabbing her nails into his shoulders. Yet more carnal sensations bombarded her very being. They scraped like blunt nails, bit like sharp teeth, licked like hot tongues. And they dragged her into a mental place where little else existed—hell, she didn't even realize he'd lifted her and set her on the bed until she distantly became aware of the soft cotton beneath her.

Her soul endured an all-out assault. Sensations grazed, burned, pinched, and forcefully smacked her very being again and again. At sporadic moments, their pain level would dial back, or a few soft-as-satin "swipes" would come along. But then dark, wicked sensations would return, harden, intensify, overwhelm.

She drowned in it all, mindless to do anything but take more and more, so desperate to come again she could scream. Her skin was covered in a fine sheen of sweat, and she trembled so hard she was surprised her teeth didn't chatter.

Wynter opened her eyes as rough palms skated up her inner thighs. Cain yanked her to the edge of the mattress and swiped the head of his dick between her folds. *Thank you, oh merciful God.*

Electric sparks of pleasure/pain drummed their way along her soul. Her muscles jumped, and her back bowed. More sparks all but paddled her very being again and again, pulling her back to that place where she floated.

Her eyelids snapped open as Cain sank an inch of his dick inside her. He paused, and forceful smacks of dark sensation flayed her soul. Another inch of his cock slid into her pussy. Again, he paused, and a static wave of pleasure rushed its way over her being.

Another inch of his dick. More pleasure to her soul. Another inch. More soul-deep sensations.

The pattern continued, repeatedly snatching her from the

physical plane to the "floaty" plane and back again. It sent her off-balance, screwed with her mental processes, and kept her body on edge as it yearned for yet another release.

The torment paused for a long moment, and she realized why the ache in her pussy was so damn pronounced—he hadn't buried the full length of his shaft inside her yet. Her inner muscles were clutching him tight and sucking at his cock as if to drag him deeper into her body.

She whimpered as she felt him pull back. "No." It was a sob, and it made his dark gaze glitter with a predatory indecency.

Leaving the tip of his cock inside her, Cain draped himself over her. "I love fucking with your head." He tapped her temple. "Love being up here. Ruling your thoughts. Making it so that you can't even think straight." Then he was hammering into her.

She clung to him, her only anchor in the sexual storm. He plundered and possessed, his pace urgent and primal. The tip of his tongue swirled around her nipple, and then he captured the taut bud with his mouth. He thrust and suckled and bit even as he thrashed her soul with sensations yet again, overloading her on every level with so much pleasure she wanted to cry.

But no matter how much she cursed, no matter how much she bitched, no matter how much she *begged*, he didn't make her come. He just kept on brutally fucking in and out of her while again devastating her soul with sensation after sensation.

It went on and on. And on and on and on. Until she began to think it might never stop.

A thumb rolled her clit, and she imploded in an instant—screaming, arching, shaking, tears dripping down her face. She was utterly wrecked just as he'd warned her she'd be.

Cain's cock throbbed inside her, but he hadn't come.

She blinked up at him, tensing as a strange, transparent film coated his eyes. Her pulse skittered. "Cain?"

He gave her a soft kiss. "Shh, it's okay. Let it have you." He did a slow blink, and then a green, serpent gaze locked with hers.

175

She subtly drew in a breath, meeting its eyes steadily. It let out a rumbling sound of satisfaction, seemingly pleased. Maybe it had expected her to recoil or—

The monster abruptly pulled out of her, flipped her onto her stomach, and propped her on her hands and knees. *Well.* It slammed home, forcing its way past her swollen inner muscles and—*oh shit*—the shaft inside her felt so much thicker than before.

The monster pounded into her, its grip on her hips hard enough to hurt. There was no technique in the way that it took her. No finesse. Its thrusts were vicious and feral and animalistic.

Cain had consumed her, just as he'd promised. His creature *subjugated* her. Conquered her. Exploited her body. Claimed it for its own personal use. But not cruelly, not dispassionately. Just ... self-centeredly. And with so much territorialism that it made Cain's level of possessiveness seem easygoing.

She couldn't lie, the whole thing pushed some majorly hot buttons that she hadn't known she had until then. It took everything she had not to rear back to meet the hard drives of its cock. She figured it would be better to let the monster have full control. So she simply took what it gave her.

A hand fisted her hair and yanked her head aside. Her heart jumped as teeth grazed the crook of her neck. The move felt like a threat. A promise. A—

The teeth sank deep.

Oh Jesus, the venom *did* burn. Burned like a goddamn mother. But the pain spiced up the pleasure, throwing her into an orgasm that seemed to come out of nowhere. The release whipped through her like a lightning bolt, violent and *so damn good.* It drained her, leaving her feeling all-hollowed out, and she barely registered as the monster exploded inside her.

She collapsed onto her elbows, breathing hard, shaking like a leaf. A hot tongue lapped at her bite, and a pleased rumble vibrated against her back. Then the tight hold on her hips gentled, and a kiss was pressed to the spot between her shoulder blades.

"Cain?"

"I'm here." He slipped his arms beneath her, holding her to him. "My monster was content to retreat, now that you're marked." He nuzzled her. "You okay?"

"Yeah. Your creature was rough but not too rough."

"I reminded it that you likely wouldn't let it have you again if it wasn't mindful of its strength. I didn't expect it to listen to me, but it did." He kissed the hollow beneath her ear. "Are you sure you're okay?"

"If what you're really asking is if I'm freaking out about getting fucked by your monster and having its venom inside me, no, I'm not. Does that make me weird?"

"No." He pressed a lingering kiss to her neck. "It makes you a fucking miracle. My miracle."

She felt a smile tug at her mouth, adding that comment to her mental "best stuff Cain says" file. "Dude, I am *totally* sucking your dick later." Even deflating, said dick twitched inside her.

"I'll hold you to that."

"I figured you would."

Cain carefully pulled out of her and then flipped her onto her back. His gaze went straight to her throbbing bite, satisfaction glimmering in those dark orbs. "My creature is feeling rather smug right now."

"*Just* your creature?"

"Fine, maybe we both very much like that its venom will forever live in your blood, just as we like that you wear your acceptance of my monster's claim to you on your skin."

"By the way, that whole 'the venom burns a little' was a bunch of bullshit. My neck felt like it was on fire. You know, it doesn't surprise me that you'd smile right now."

He shrugged. "I like it when you hurt for me. You know that."

"You like seeing me all frustrated."

"That too," he admitted. "I didn't lie when I said that the burning sensation would fade quickly, though, did I?"

"Actually, no, you didn't. But I would bet my life that you wished it hadn't dimmed so fast."

"That is a bet you would win. I like seeing my gorgeous witch cry."

Having absolutely no idea how to respond to that, she looked away from him, shaking her head. *Goddamn sadist.*

Chapter Fifteen

S tanding in her backyard a week later, Wynter sighed. "Really, you don't have to come with me."

Looking up from the flower bed, Delilah pointed her spade at her. "We're all going, and that's that."

"There's no need."

"Thanks to the price on your head, there's *every* need," Anabel insisted, leaning back against an old oak. "You shouldn't be going anywhere alone."

Wynter didn't fear that anyone would try kidnapping her again anytime soon. People were still a little cowed after what the Ancients did to Shelia. Her screams had apparently been heard far and wide throughout the city, and the story of how she met her end had circulated wildly. No one had even so much as looked at Wynter wrong since then.

She wasn't worried that Adam would strike again soon either, considering he'd caused a thunderstorm just two nights ago. There'd been some damage to the town but not a lot, thanks to the quick intervention of the Ancients. Wynter hadn't witnessed any of it, since she'd been at the cottage when it all kicked off.

"You can't afford to get complacent, Wyn," said Xavier, lounging in the gently swaying hammock.

She frowned. "I'm not. I just figured you might all want to stay home rather than wait for me in what I noticed through the salon window was a very small reception area. Plus, you all planned to spend your day off work relaxing."

Sat at the patio table, Hattie briefly peeked up from her book.

"And we'll get back to that once your trip to the salon is over and done with."

In truth, Wynter hadn't thought they'd choose to stay behind. But, thanks to the latest attempt to hand her over to Adam, it had been days since her coven had looked this relaxed. Though they weren't wound quite as tight, they still hadn't gotten over the incident. Mostly because she'd been missing for several hours and they'd failed to find her themselves—that failure seemed to sit heavy on their chests, despite her assurances that it shouldn't.

It was no doubt why they'd insisted on a few precautions. Delilah had magickly boobytrapped the cottage. Anabel was creating—and hopefully not testing on herself—all kinds of offensive potions. Hattie had whipped up some of her special deadly teas to force-drink to intruders. And Xavier stood guard inside the shed while Wynter worked—something she'd allowed, since Cain had threatened to otherwise post Maxim inside, and she didn't want Cain to be short of an aide.

Much like when the threat of Saul had hung over her head, Cain now checked on her a few times a day. Which she might have protested to if she didn't know he needed to reassure himself that she hadn't been taken again. He still hadn't quite moved past that yet.

But then, that was no surprise, was it? Cain was an extremely powerful being. He wasn't used to being helpless or thwarted. More, he wasn't used to things being out of his control.

Waking Abaddon might have done a fantastic job of easing his tension and anger, but the Ancients were still struggling to wake him. According to Cain, some were losing hope that they'd ever have any success with it—mostly Ishtar and Inanna.

"Personally, I don't know why you want to go to a salon." Delilah sliced her shovel through the soil. "Your hair looks fine."

"There are too many split ends for my liking." Wynter stretched out a few strands. "It needs a trim."

"I can do it for you," Delilah offered.

Wynter snorted. "Are you forgetting what happened the last time

I let you near my hair with scissors?" They'd been on the run back then, so Wynter had been content to skip a trip to the salon. She'd only wanted Delilah to take an inch off the length, but the woman had cocked it up like a boss. In the end, a professional hairdresser had had to cut off four inches just to even it all out.

Delilah's back straightened. "Excuse me, I did a very good job."

"You did a *hack* job."

A huff. "It wasn't that bad."

"It looked like someone went at my hair with hedge cutters. In a panic. While blindfolded. And shaking like a shitting dog."

"You're exaggerating. Xavier, tell her she's exaggerating."

Wynter folded her arms. "You think the word of a habitual liar will honestly add weight to your claim?"

"Anabel, *you* back me up on this."

The blonde frowned. "But then I'd have to lie."

"And doing that doesn't make you feel all warm and giddy?" Xavier asked her.

"No," Anabel told him. "No, you're alone on that one."

Snickering, Wynter idly rubbed at her neck. The bite there tingled as her fingers skated over it. She wasn't sure what the tingling was about, but it appeared to be a permanent thing. As did the bite mark itself. It no longer bled, but it hadn't healed. It was still as prominent as it had been on the night Cain's monster bit her. So she hadn't been able to escape questions from her coven.

Wynter had talked *around* the subject, telling them only that it had bitten her during sex because it was all wound up after she'd been kidnapped. She didn't mention the whole "binding" thing. Cain had asked her not to reveal to anyone that his kind could tie their life-force to that of another. For him, the less people knew about the Ancients, the better.

His creature hadn't again surfaced in the bedroom, but she'd occasionally noticed something move behind Cain's eyes while he took her; she knew it was his monster. Knew it wanted to make its presence known to her.

181

"Right, I'm done." Delilah removed her gloves and tossed all her gardening tools into her basket, adding the rolled-up kneeling mat just before she stood. "Let me wash my hands and then we can go."

"You might also want to wash your nose." Wynter pointed at it. "You got some soil there."

"Why would someone want to eat hair pie?" Hattie asked no one in particular.

Delilah made a choking sound. "What?"

Hattie tipped her chin toward her book. "A man here said he's going to go home, find his wife, and eat some hair pie. I've never heard of it before." She tapped her chin. "I wonder if it's some sort of strange exotic delicacy."

Oh, dear God.

"It could be," said Anabel, tipping over the hammock when a silently laughing Xavier seemed about to answer the old woman's question.

He hit the ground with a thud. "Ow."

"I fail to see the appeal in a lot of those delicacies," Hattie went on, prim. "Especially fried tarantulas and bird's nest soup. Very not my thing."

Anabel sidled up to Wynter. "Just this one time, let her believe her own assumption," she said, her voice low.

Having absolutely no desire to explain to an old woman that eating hair pie was slang for oral sex, Wynter shrugged at the blonde and whispered, "Fine."

Shortly afterwards, they made their way to one of the city towers and used its elevator to ascend to the town's manor. Outside, they walked along the streets en route to the only hair salon at Devil's Cradle, which was run by lion shifters.

It was cooler up here than in the city. The hue of the sun was now a deep gold as it began to set. The sky was a swirl of pretty colors— mostly purples, oranges, and pinks. Silhouette shadows stretched along the ground like dark fingers.

"It might not be so easy to get an appointment," Delilah warned her.

Wynter gave a slight shrug. "I don't mind pre-booking one."

"I don't mean I think they'll be too busy to fit you in, I mean that there's a chance they won't want to."

Dodging one of the many sapling trees on the sidewalk, Wynter frowned. "And why wouldn't they want to?"

Delilah fired an incredulous look her way. "You can't *not* have noticed how many people won't *dare* meet your eyes these days. They're afraid they might accidentally offend you and earn Cain's wrath."

"That's dumb."

"That's fear," Xavier cut in. "Most had never seen the Ancients indulge in a little torture. They'd heard stories, of course, but stories can be twisted, exaggerated, or incomplete—as I often demonstrate. So there was a lot of 'oh, the Ancients probably aren't really *that* pitiless.' Until Shelia."

Anabel nodded. "The woman died *hard*."

Wynter halted. "Are you saying that people think she should have been given mercy?"

"No," Anabel quickly replied. "Far from it."

"No one's judging Cain or Ishtar for what they did," said Xavier. "Least of all us. It's not like the Ancients didn't warn people what would happen if they chose to do favors for Adam. But although people don't blame Cain for how far he went in avenging you, they do worry that he'll react just as badly to the merest slight on you."

"Not that that makes you completely safe," Hattie chimed in. "There are some who are too stupid to heed fear."

"*And* some who get off so much on taking risks that it trumps their sense of self-preservation," Delilah added.

Wynter eyed the Latina. "Kind of like you, really."

Delilah gave a slow nod. "Kind of like me."

Xavier frowned at something behind Wynter. "Hey, what's that?"

She turned. Stilled. Felt her stomach roll and her jaw drop.

A thick, orange-tinged, smoky mass stretched way up into the sky . . . like a humungous cloudy wall. Only it wasn't a cloud. Or smoke. It was a huge-as-fuck force of sand.

And it was heading right for the town.

Wynter's heart slammed against her ribcage. *Oh, no.*

"There's more of them!" shouted Anabel.

It was only then Wynter realized that stormy walls of sand were coming at the town from *all* sides. And they were coming supernaturally fast. Flumes of whirling dirt zipped in and out of them, all but hoovering off the ground whatever they touched. *Dust devils.*

Oh, this wasn't good. Like, *at all.*

"Move!" she yelled at her coven, urging them toward the ice-cream parlor way up ahead of them.

Sounds of alarm went up as others spotted the walls of brown air. People scrambled for shelter, but it was too late. There was no escape. Not when the looming gusts rushed at them like a tidal wave from every angle. They swept across the town, all but engulfing it. And it was like the day turned to an orange-hued night.

Grains of dust pelted Wynter's skin, feeling like tiny little bites. She staggered as the various winds slapped her hard enough to sting, taking her breath away; whipping her hair one way and then another so that it lashed her cheeks.

She ducked her head and threw up her arm to shield her face, but there was no way to avoid the swirls of dust. No way to stop it from slipping into her ears, entering her mouth, or shooting up her nose.

Coughing, Wynter looked around for her coven. There was no sign of them. Because they'd ran? Because she'd been turned around by her wind too much? Or because visibility was plain shit? She didn't know. She couldn't see anything through the orange-tinged haze.

She stooped over to get some reprieve from the rougher blasts. "Get low to the ground!" she shouted, only able to hope that her coven heard her. She then clamped her lips shut and tugged up the collar of her crazily flapping tee to cover her nose and mouth.

While she saw virtually nothing, she *heard* everything. Panicked voices yelling. Tree branches snapping. Hanging signs creaking. Objects crashing to the ground. The wild winds whistling and howling as they beat against hard surfaces.

Wynter flinched as something brushed by her at top speed. Something fast and almost ghostly. *Dust devil.*

"Where are you, Darla?" a male voice demanded. "Where are you? I can't—" He let out a cry that gradually faded, as if he'd been swooped away by one of the mini tornadoes.

Wynter's stomach bottomed out. Fuck, they needed to get off the damn street.

Easier said than done when her sense of direction was non-existent. There was just so much sand and noise and wind—she couldn't get her bearings. Trying to look around would only lead to her getting more sand in her eyes.

Even if she knew where to go, she wasn't sure she could fight against the power of the gale-force winds. This storm was *so* much more powerful than the blizzard.

Muffled cries of alarm came from Anabel, but Wynter couldn't pinpoint the blonde's exact location—the gale seemed to be sweeping the sounds around.

She jumped as another ghostly force whispered over her body as it zipped by at top speed. If the subsequent distinct *crack* was anything to go by, it had taken a damn tree with it.

A powerful blast of sand whacked her face and—

She hissed in pain because, fuck, that wasn't just sand. There'd been a rock or something. It had hit her smack on the cheek, leaving it throbbing and stinging in a way that told her she was bleeding.

Fabulous.

There might have been something awing about the power of the storm if it wasn't created by annoying elemental beings rather than nature.

Her heart beating hard with panic and adrenaline, she turned again and again, hoping to see or hear *something* that pointed her

185

toward her coven. But with the wind roaring down her ears and bits of grit pelting her eyeballs, she was far too disoriented.

Wynter tensed as something mostly transparent shimmered in the hazy air. The force clashed with the winds. *Pure power*, she sensed. Old and very potent power.

Her pulse jumped. One or more of the Ancients had appeared.

The gusts gradually calmed and . . . it was weird, but it was like something was sucking the grains of sand *upwards*. She felt them leaving her hair, skin, clothes, nose, ears, *everything*. The grit went up and up and up, high above all the buildings, leaving the air clear once again.

Then all that grit turned to a fast-moving funnel that soon began to hum with the buzzing and droning of insects. Cain had clearly done what appeared to be his favorite thing and twisted the elemental power in a *fuck you* to the Aeons.

She turned to look at the manor. Several of the Ancients stood on the roof, including him. She couldn't see his expression properly from so far away, but she *knew* his gaze was locked on her. Felt it drumming into her skin.

"Well, that went to hell fast," a familiar voice croaked.

Wynter spun to see Hattie cupping her neck while coughing like a chain smoker. The rest of her coven were spread out a little, so they too had clearly gotten tossed everywhere by the storm.

As they all made their way to each other, Wynter coughed and blinked hard. Her eyes stung like a bitch.

She took a moment to glance around. Thanks to Cain, there was no blanket of dust over the town. Hell, there wasn't even a faint haze of it lingering in the air. Every tiny little bit of grit was gone. Hence why she could quite easily see that, fuck, the storm had left some serious damage in its wake.

Everywhere she looked, things were flipped, torn, broken, and crushed. One of the power lines was down. A sapling tree lay in the middle of the road. Debris was scattered all around, along with tree branches, flower pots, and business signs.

Worse than all of that, bodies were sprawled on the ground further up the street. At least five. *Please just be unconscious.*

Anabel stretched out her tongue. "Ugh, I can feel little bits of grit in my mouth."

Xavier pulled a face. "Pretty sure I've got some stuck between my teeth."

"Fucking Adam needs to die," said Delilah between coughs.

"I couldn't agree more." Wynter took a long, ragged breath. She doubted the Aeons responsible for the almighty storm had stuck around long. They never did when sent to do Adam's dirty work. Which was a shame, because capturing one would be fantastic.

Glancing toward the manor, Anabel rubbed at her arm. "I have to be honest, knowing just how powerful the Ancients are makes me nervous."

Delilah snickered. "What doesn't?"

Anabel shot her a narrow-eyed look.

Wynter quickly cut in, "I say we go back to the cottage and down some tea that'll ease the pain in our throats."

"Cain will want to see you," said Xavier.

"He *can* see me," Wynter pointed out. "He knows I'm fine. Besides, he and the Ancients will be busy ordering their aides to fix the damage." They'd also probably have a little meeting about the storm, even if only to moan about Adam—it was what they usually did after his stunts.

Xavier gave her a 'fair enough' look and waved a hand toward the manor. "Then let's go."

*

Standing under the hot spray, Wynter looked down at the dust sliding toward the drain. Yeah, it turned out that not *all* the sand had been plucked from her hair. Washing it away was proving to be a bitch. It clung to her worse than any beach sand. She'd had to shampoo her hair three times and condition it twice before she could be sure it was free of grit.

At least the grains were no longer in her mouth or eyes. Also, her throat felt better, thanks to the herbal tea Delilah had made the moment they returned home. It tasted like ass, but it also did its job well.

Once out of the shower, Wynter dried herself off, pulled on some clothes, and then tackled the wet mop on her head with a brush and hairdryer. Done, she headed down to the kitchen.

The coven sat at the table, all now clean and chatting amongst themselves. Wynter only distantly noted them, though. Her attention was snagged by the tall, lean figure standing off to the side. *Cain.*

Azazel was also present, and he was focused on Anabel, who was currently demonstrating that it wasn't possible for a person to lick their own elbow. The Ancient didn't appear to know what to make of her. But then, most didn't.

Wynter walked straight into Cain's arms, humming in satisfaction when he curled them tight around her. "You're here."

"Just this moment arrived. I expected to find you in our chamber." And he seemed so very confused that things hadn't gone his way.

She felt her lips twitch. "What can I say? I like keeping you on your toes. I also badly needed one of Delilah's nifty teas. My throat was raw from the storm. How's yours?"

He gave her neck a soothing rub. "Fine. I wasn't caught in the storm long, and I dealt with it quickly."

Wynter licked her lips and then asked the question that had been gnawing at her. "Those people who were lying on the ground ... were they dead?"

Cain's expression turned dark. "Three were. The others were out cold."

She closed her eyes. "Fuck. I really, really, really, *really* hate the Aeons. I'm guessing none were caught."

"They fled too quickly," he confirmed. "Adam would have ordered them to retreat once any Ancients intervened—he won't want us eating into more of his numbers."

Tough, because they'd be "eating" all of his people very soon. She refused to believe that the Ancients' attempts to pierce the prison wouldn't be successful.

Twisting in her chair, Hattie eyed Azazel from head to toe. "You strike me as a worldly man. Have you ever eaten hair pie? Apparently it's an exotic delicacy of some kind."

Oh, for the love of all that's holy.

Azazel fought a smile and looked over at Cain, who was doing the same.

Wynter gave both Ancients a narrow-eyed "It's not funny" look.

Delilah seemed to agree, since she'd ducked her head with a groan. Similarly, Anabel had shoved her face in her hands while cursing softly.

Xavier, on the other hand, chuckled like an idiot and then turned to Wynter. "See, this is what happens when we neglect to share important details with her."

Sighing, Wynter tipped her chin toward the old woman and then told Xavier, "Take her aside and quietly explain before she presses Azazel for more info."

Grinning, Xavier nodded, urged Hattie out of her seat, and then pulled her to the corner of the room.

Cain squeezed Wynter's nape. "She's an . . . interesting woman."

Delilah snorted. "She's a menace."

"And completely shameless," added Anabel. "Which I think is why she and Xavier are so in tune with each other—he's no better."

"I heard that," he said as he and Hattie broke apart.

The old woman shuffled over to the table. "I can't believe none of you told me the truth. I need to know about such slang. You know I don't want to embarrass myself in front of George by looking clueless."

Anabel's nose wrinkled. "I hardly think he's going to use that term, like, *ever.*"

"Perhaps not, but you still should've explained," said Hattie. "It's not like I would have fainted like some unworldly maiden. Though, yes, it's disgusting that some people put pubic hairs in their pies."

Anabel jerked. "That's not what—*Xavier!*" She crossed to where he was bent over laughing and then tapped his forehead hard three times, ignoring his "ouch". "Nothing up here but empty space I'll swear it."

He rubbed at the spot she'd poked. "That hurt."

Azazel looked at Wynter. "No one can ever say that your coven isn't entertaining."

If one found "crazy" entertaining then, no, it could not be said.

Chapter Sixteen

Anabel clung to Wynter as they strode through the underground city's forests. "I hate whatever that music is. It's like the kind you hear in a horror movie when there's a jump-scare coming up."

Wynter had to admit, if only to herself, it *was* seriously creepy. As were the Halloween sound effects that could occasionally be heard. She patted Anabel's hand. "We're almost at the arena."

"Whoever decorated this part of the woods went *all* out," said a smiling Xavier.

Indeed they had. Lanterns and carved pumpkins lit the way to the arena, where the evening's upcoming Halloween celebration was being held. Rubber bats hung from tree branches. Tombstones were positioned here and there. Stray bones were scattered around. Fake blood had been smeared on logs. Ghosts hung from bushes, fluttering with the breeze. Spiders were stuck to the large webs that stretched between tree branches. More, a haze fogged the air, courtesy of smoke machines.

Anabel jumped at the fake sound of an owl hooting. "My heart is not handling this well."

Delilah cast her a look of annoyance. "Nothing is happening."

Anabel's brow furrowed. "But the *music*, the atmosphere, the—"

"Drama," Delilah finished. "Tone it down. We're fine. There's no need to be nervous."

"Does nothing scare you?"

The Latina pursed her lips. "Nah, not really."

"That's not actually something to be proud of, you know. It's a sign of low intelligence."

"It's also a lie." Xavier pointed an accusatory finger at Delilah. "You're scared of Wynter's monster."

"So are you," Delilah sassed.

Wynter sighed. "Sometimes, so am I."

The entity was presently deep in slumber, its interest not whatsoever piqued by the current goings-on. Tonight's celebration was to be a culmination of things, mostly contests. Dance groups would "battle". Daredevils would perform stunts. Comedians would entertain. Vocal artists would sing. And then there was the annual zombie gauntlet, which residents had to sign up for in advance.

Everyone was dressed in costumes—apparently the best would earn its wearer a prize.

Hattie was a scary nun tonight. Anabel had gone for the Egyptian Goddess look. Delilah had chosen a voodoo doll outfit. Xavier was dressed as a rather hunky-looking devil, but without the face paint. Wynter had picked a Miss Hatter costume that wasn't exactly skimpy but definitely had a sultry vibe.

Hattie sniffed. "This shindig had better be good."

Xavier smiled at her. "You're not still sulking that you had to come away from your book, are you?"

"I was at a pivotal part," Hattie snottily claimed.

"You mean a sex scene," he said.

"How is that not pivotal?"

Delilah gave her a playful nudge. "So tell us, is the hero good in the sack?"

Hattie's face lit up. "Oh yes. He's a rigger."

"A what?" asked Anabel.

"He likes rope bondage," Hattie elaborated. "He ties women up in all these fancy, artistic knots. The heroine in my book likes it just fine." She smoothed a hand down her nun's habit. "I'm partial to a little bondage myself."

A grin curved Delilah's lips. "Getting tied up can make things a *lot* more interesting."

"I never tried it," said Anabel. "I prefer having my hands free."

The Latina exhaled heavily. "Let me guess, you didn't trust that any of your partners wouldn't try to kill you while you were help-less." She rolled her eyes.

Anabel bristled. "One, I am *never* completely helpless—I resent that you would imply differently. Two, killers *do* like to tie up their victims."

"Victims they usually kidnap, not date. I assume you *were* dating these guys who wanted to pull out some rope."

"Most wanted to use handcuffs. And yes, I was dating them."

"Then maybe you shouldn't have been so inclined to believe that they wanted you dead."

"Just because someone's your partner doesn't mean that you're completely safe with them. Just ask Hattie."

The old woman frowned. "Ask me what?"

"We're here," announced Xavier.

Wynter looked up at the huge open-air arena that made her think of Rome's Colosseum. It was currently adorned with garlands and strings of ghost lights. Inside, the song "Thriller" played in the background, not overriding the large cacophony of muffled voices.

Ushers were guiding people to spectator rows. In the past, Wynter and her coven sat apart from the Ancients. But as Wynter was now officially Cain's consort, he'd insisted that she and her coven sit with him. She had no issue with that, so she hadn't argued. As such, they turned toward the VIP area.

Wynter spotted him instantly. She usually did, no matter where they were. It was as if he was her own personal homing beacon.

Maybe he felt the weight of her stare, because he turned his head, slamming his gaze on hers. His lips curved into a sexy as shit smile that made her body perk up.

"Damn," breathed Delilah, leaning into her. "I don't know how your hormones cope with having that much raw sexuality aimed right at you."

Wynter smiled. "You know, sometimes, neither do I."

Reaching the VIP level, Wynter and her coven headed along one of the rows toward Cain. All the Ancients were seated, dressed in normal clothing.

Eve, Rima, and Noah were also there. The three Aeons seemed tense and uncomfortable. But then, they hadn't been properly accepted by all the residents yet. It wasn't simply because they were Aeons. It made it worse that Eve was once Adam's consort, just as it exacerbated things that the twins were his grandchildren. No one trusted them as far as they could throw them.

The spot between Wynter's shoulder blades itched and heated. Someone was glaring at her *hard*. And she didn't need to look to know that it was Ishtar. The female Ancient might have ceased playing mind games with her, but Wynter wasn't taking that as a sign of acceptance.

As she reached Cain, his gaze dropped down her body and darkened. "Should I assume you want to get fucked right here and now in front of all these people?" he asked, his voice low. "Because that's exactly what I'm tempted to do."

Wynter smiled. "You're easy that way. No Halloween outfit? Lame." But she got it. A huge reason the Ancients wielded so much personal control over Devil's Cradle was that people feared them; found them so very *other* and unrelatable. That worked for the Ancients, and so they never tried to come across as fun or personable.

She and her coven quickly settled in the five vacant seats near Cain. Anabel instantly pulled down her tray table and cleaned it with one of her antibacterial potions. All seats had such trays attached to their backs, much like on airplanes.

Glancing down at the performance space below, Wynter felt her brows lift at the Halloween "touches". Hay bales were pressed against the walls. Cobwebs and streamers dangled from wall lanterns. What seemed to be *hundreds* of intricately decorated pumpkins were piled up around the perimeter. Strobe lights in colors of black, orange, and green shone down on the large space.

Resting his hand on her thigh, Cain leaned into her. "I like having you sitting here with me. The last few times we were at the arena, I had to be content with staring at you from afar. And you spent every moment trying to seem unaffected."

Wynter hiked up a brow. "Who says I *wasn't* unaffected?"

His mouth curved. "I do. You wanted me from the very beginning, sweet witch. You just weren't comfortable with it."

At first, no, she hadn't been. "Well, you're sort of scary."

Humor lit his eyes. "You were never afraid of me."

"I was wary, though."

"Only to a small extent."

True again. Because there'd always been something exciting for her about being the focus of someone so very powerful that he could probably end even a revenant. Well, she'd never claimed to be normal.

"The doors have been closed," Seth interjected. "Everyone's seated."

Cain gave a curt nod and then stood. A hush soon fell over the crowd. Using pure power to amplify his voice, he thanked the event organizers, the caterers, etc., etc.

Feeling the spot between her shoulder blades itch once more, Wynter glanced over her shoulder. Her eyes instantly clashed with those of Ishtar. The Ancient's baby blues were narrowed but disturbingly blank.

Wynter flicked up a daring brow—unwise, sure, but she was getting seriously tired of this bitch thinking she could stare at her whenever she pleased. Ishtar's lips flattened, but she did nothing.

Hearing Cain call for the celebration to begin, Wynter faced front just as he sat. People flooded the performance space, where contest after contest then occurred. Each time, two competing artists—or groups of artists—would have a "battle" of sorts. The crowd was then asked to cheer for their favorite, and whoever received the loudest applause would be declared the winner.

When there were only semi-finalists left, the event presenter announced, "The finals will be held after our break."

Food and drinks were then promptly dished out. Wynter heard

Xavier trying to charm a female server, introducing himself as Mattia Vivaldi while adopting an Italian accent.

Once the server left, Wynter frowned at him. "Did you just introduce yourself as a type font?"

His brow creased. "What?"

"You said 'Vivaldi.'"

"It's an Italian surname."

"Pretty sure it's also a font," said Delilah, forking some pasta. "More, it isn't *your* surname."

"Does that really have to be relevant to the conversation?" he asked.

Wynter exchanged a quick glance with Cain, who wasn't bothering to hide his amusement.

Delilah gave Xavier a droll look. "God, you're annoying. If *my* surname was Gamble—which is a super cool surname, in my opinion—I wouldn't be giving people false ones."

His nose wrinkled. "I don't like it. Don't like my first name either."

"Why not?" asked Delilah. "It's a perfectly nice name."

He sighed, digging into his food. "It was also my grandfather's. He was an absolute bastard. I never liked him. So I guess I resent having the same name as him."

Delilah narrowed her eyes. "That was all true? Really?"

"No, not really."

"Oh my God, *then why say it?*"

"Maybe the voices in my head tell me I should."

"You hear voices?" interrupted Hattie, slicing into her steak. "That's not good. One of my husbands, Keith—bless his dark soul—heard 'em often. He claimed they told him he should strangle me to death or I'd one day kill him."

Lifting her glass of water, Anabel twisted her mouth. "Hmm. Seems that the voices weren't wrong, huh?"

"It would have done him good to heed them, yes," said Hattie with an incline of her head.

His shoulders shaking, Cain put his mouth to Wynter's ear. "Having your coven here livens the atmosphere a little."

That couldn't be denied. The Ancients didn't really chat to one another while in the arena. They simply sat and observed, sober as judges.

"On another note," began Xavier, "it might interest you all to know that I signed our coven up for the gauntlet."

Pausing with a forkful of food halfway to her mouth, Wynter felt her brows knit. "You did *what*?"

"I signed us up," he replied, grinning.

"And you didn't think to mention it until now?"

"I wanted to surprise you. *Ta daa.*"

Wynter clenched her fork, tempted to throw it at him. "We agreed that you wouldn't try to surprise me anymore."

"You're not still upset about my last one, are you?"

She arched her brows. "Why would I be upset that you summoned Asmodeus and let him possess you *again*? Especially when you promised that you wouldn't do it anymore?"

"I just wanted you to meet him so that you'd realize he isn't so bad."

"He's a hell-dwelling demon, Xavier."

"You're really going to hold that he's evil incarnate against him? Your monster is no innocent either. *I* don't hold that against *it*." Xavier gave her a beseeching look. "Now come on, lighten up, the gauntlet was fun last time. And considering we have a battle coming up, it might not be so bad to have a practice run." He looked at Hattie. "You're up for it, right?"

The old woman shrugged. "I don't see why not."

"What about you?" he asked Anabel.

"I'm fine with anything that will remind these people just how good Wynter is with a sword," replied the blonde. "You know ... just in case any think to get the none-too-wise idea to repeat Shelia's mistake."

Delilah nodded. "Yeah, I'm thinking it would be worth

reminding them what they'd be dealing with. What about you, Wyn? If nothing else, it will get Cain all hot and bothered. That's gotta make running the gauntlet worth it."

Cain smiled, firing a heated look Wynter's way. "She's right. It will."

No surprise there. "There's no point in you all getting excited, we might not get chosen. They can't possibly include *everyone* who signed up."

"You'll be chosen," said Cain. "The organizers will worry that I'll otherwise be offended." Which he seemed to find amusing.

Wynter sighed. Oh, she didn't mind the gauntlet. As Xavier said, it was fun. And there was never anything boring about indulging in a harmless battle. But she'd really hoped to just sit and snuggle with her guy while they watched a show. You know, like a normal couple. They didn't get to do much "normal".

Soon after, servers returned to collect the dirty dishware. Returning to the performance space, the presenter announced that the second half of the celebration would commence. The semi-finalists entertained the crowd—singers, dancers, stunts people, etc. After the winners were chosen and awarded a prize, the presenter added, "And now we reach the most popular contest by far."

A rumble of power filled the air, raising the hairs on her nape. A long-ass ditch appeared in the ground that spanned the entire length of the performance space.

"And here we have the gauntlet," said the presenter. "A ditch that will soon be filled with zombies. They will not be real, of course, but they will seem it—and they will attack. Do not worry, though. The gauntlet is spelled so that any injuries a fighter receives will immediately heal. The trouble is ... such injuries will not feel or look healed, which can play tricks on a person's mind to the point where they may even believe they are dying. This contest is not for the faint-hearted, in other words."

Wynter could clearly recall her last encounter with the gauntlet. She'd known that her wounds were healed, but she'd nonetheless felt the pain and experienced the weakness that came with blood loss—none of it had disappeared until she exited the ditch.

"Many groups of five have signed up to partake in the competition," the presenter continued. "Ten of said groups will be chosen. Whichever one completes the gauntlet in the fastest time will be declared the winning team.

"The objective is to battle your way through the gauntlet, killing whatever zombie lies in your path. If a participant 'dies,' they will be spat out of the gauntlet, but the rest of their group may continue to fight. As to what you may fight with . . . there are no limits. Magick, weapons, hellfire, shapeshifting—anything and everything is permitted. For the safety of the crowd, the spelled ropes surrounding the gauntlet ensure that any magick used within it is contained."

The presenter began listing various groups who'd been chosen to participate—fey courts, lycan packs, demon lairs. And, as Cain predicted, her own fucking coven.

Wynter glanced at Cain, whose eyes glittered with eagerness. He really did love to watch her fight. It got his blood pumping every time.

She grunted, stood, and gestured for her coven to follow her. They left the VIP area and headed down to the performance space. There, the presenter directed them where to stand. It was only when all the chosen groups were gathered in the space that he then declared who would tackle the gauntlet first.

And, of course, he announced, "The Bloodrose Coven."

Oh, novel.

They crossed to the presenter, who gestured at the rack of blades he'd conjured. "Any weapons you would like to use?"

"Not necessary." Wynter called to her sword, just as Xavier and Anabel each called to their own.

Delilah took on her monstrous feline form and flexed her iron claws. Thanks to her bespelled cosmetics, she still wore pink lip gloss and peach nail polish.

Hattie shifted into a crow and quickly settled on Xavier's

shoulder. She didn't only choose to battle as an avian because she'd then be faster and have better reflexes, she did it because her crow form negated magick—any blasts bounded right off her.

Wynter turned to Xavier. "You know, reanimating corpses is going to be a useless endeavor here. The zombies are already revived corpses."

His lips parted. "Shit, never thought of that." After a moment, he shrugged off his disappointment. "They won't stand a chance against my sword."

No, they wouldn't, since the rapier weapon was actually made of angel bone.

Wynter turned to Anabel. "You ready for this?"

Adjusting her grip on her broadsword, the blonde gave a serious nod. "Absolutely. Now call her."

Wynter quietly sang into her ear, "Mary, Mary, please come out."

The blonde did a very slow blink and then, well, her eyes remained their usual pale blue shade, but they were different. Held a flickering flame of madness that often made Wynter wonder if Anabel truly was the reincarnation of Bloody Mary after all.

"Stab to kill," Wynter told her.

Anabel/Mary smiled, looking as bloodthirsty as always. "There's no other way to stab."

Whatever.

"The gauntlet awaits you," said the presenter, all dramatic.

Wynter and her coven slid beneath the ropes and jumped down into the ditch. Her blood buzzing with adrenaline, she rolled back her shoulders. There was a slight purr against her feet. *Pure power.*

Her monster woke in response to the alien power and went very still. Using telepathic images, she made it clear that this was only a game. Recognizing the gauntlet, the entity lost its tension.

"And now we begin!" shouted the presenter.

The crowd cheered and stomped their feet.

Dozens of softly swaying zombies blinked into view on the opposite end of the ditch. They were hideous. Bloody. Filthy.

And then they charged. *Charged.* Like superfast ninjas.

Wynter swiped out with her sword, beheading the first zombie that came at her. And the next. And the next. God, these things *reeked.* Like dried blood and rancid meat.

Xavier struck with his own sword, hacking through one zombie after another. Anabel/Mary did the same, singing and humming and laughing to herself.

Delilah hissed and roared as she took down the undead creatures. Hattie provided backup, raking and biting and flapping her wings at faces.

Even as Wynter thrust and sliced, she also whipped and blasted the creatures with her magick. The burns didn't bother them, nor did the decaying of their body parts. But the force of the blasts knocked them down or held them back—as did the magickal attacks from Xavier and Anabel/Mary, making it easier for the entire coven to battle their way through the zombies.

Wynter bit out a curse as one sank its teeth into her arm. "Son of a bitch." She punched it in the face once, twice. It released her arm, staggering backwards. She impaled the fucker on her sword and, ignoring the throbbing in her arm, fought on.

Not unscathed, though.

Nails dragged at her flesh. Teeth stabbed into her arms, hands, and—worse—the shoulder of her sword arm. The wounds burned in an unnatural way, and her skin began to sweat profusely . . . as if she was suffering the effects of an *actual* injury from a zombie.

Judging by the pained growls and curses, she wasn't the only one injured. Still, the entire coven kept moving, kept fighting, kept *killing.*

Heads and body parts thumped to the floor. Blood spattered the coven and ground. All the while, the crowd loudly urged them on, almost drowning out the sounds of battle. Almost. The fight was *loud.* Blades whistled through the air. The creatures groaned and snarled. The huge feline roared while the crow squawked. Anabel/Mary sang fucking "Cotton Eye Joe".

Nearing the finish line, Wynter felt another spike of adrenaline surge through her bloodstream. At this point, her hand was so sweaty she was surprised she hadn't dropped her sword. Tremors ran through her limbs, and her temperature had hit the roof. She ignored it all, pinning her focus on that finish line.

She slit throats, chopped off heads, gutted stomachs, sliced off body parts. Just the same, her coven fought harder and faster—either responding to her urgency or spurred on by the knowledge that they were almost done.

Soon, only five zombies were left. Wynter and Xavier took out four, only managing to knock the fifth to the ground since it dodged out of range.

"And then there was one," sang Anabel/Mary. She swung out her sword, beheading it in one smooth, brutal move.

Cheers went up as the crowd surged to their feet.

Anabel/Mary's shoulders slumped as she eyed the fallen zombies. "It's not the same when your victims don't cry out in pain."

Xavier wiped at his sweaty forehead with his arm. "I can agree with that."

"We need to get out of this ditch so we heal," said Wynter, panting.

Nodding, Anabel/Mary grabbed a severed head by its hair.

"No, that ain't coming with us," Wynter declared.

Anabel/Mary frowned. "But it is harmless."

"And bodiless. And gross. And *no*, it stays."

But the weirdo tried arguing, so Xavier rolled his eyes and whispered, "Night, night, Mary."

The key phrase made Anabel/Mary pout, but then the manic glint in her eyes was gone.

Back to her normal self, Anabel realized what she was holding and dropped it with a little squeal. Wiping her hand on her thigh, she whimpered. "Are we done?"

"We're done." Wynter led the way as they left the ditch. Instantly, her injuries healed, the blood disappeared from her skin and clothes, and the effects of the zombie bites faded away.

Switching back to her human form, Hattie grinned. "Well, now we know we'd survive a zombie apocalypse."

Delilah frowned. "Yeah, we'd survive it *infected*. Every one of us got bitten."

"But we faced the army and lived—none of us got kicked out of the gauntlet," said Hattie.

"We were fast," said Xavier, sending his sword back to the cottage much in the same way that he conjured it. "There's a good chance our time won't be beat."

Returning her sword to her chamber, Wynter nodded. Either way, she was a winner. Because going by the banked heat in Cain's eyes, he was as hot and bothered as Delilah predicted. A ruthless fuck was the best kind of prize.

And a ruthless fuck was what she later got. Twice.

Chapter Seventeen

A whispered voice pierced the fog of Wynter's sleep, playing into her dream. A voice that wanted her to wake. To move. To follow. She ignored it, busy cleaning the blood from her boat.

Icy fingertips fluttered over her face as the voice patiently persisted.

Ugh. Couldn't it see she was busy here?

She let out an annoyed sniff, scrubbing the fiberglass boat harder. The voice didn't give up. It kept on whispering, telling her that it wanted to show her something; something she needed to see.

Little by little, Wynter's dream broke apart around her as sleep gradually lost its grip on her. Awake, she tiredly opened her eyes. And froze. Her heart slammed hard against her ribcage.

What the hell?

She was no longer in the bedchamber. She wasn't even sure if she was still in the Keep. This place . . . it was some kind of grotto. The rock walls looked like they'd been adorned with splatters of gold glitter, much like the vaulted ceiling above her. The light from the flaming torches slashed through the darkness. The stone floor was smooth and warm beneath her bare feet.

Her monster stirred, tense but intrigued—there was *so much energy* here. An energy that was foreign and intense. It rolled over her skin, causing her flesh to prickle and making every tiny hair on her body lift.

The ethos . . . It was hard to put it into words. It was electric. Magnetic. Disquieting. Charged. Like the buzz of energy before a storm, or the unnatural quiet before an earthquake.

And fuck the grotto was *hot*. Really hot. The humid air was so thick it felt heavy. It carried many scents, such as mildew and algae.

It seemed safe to conclude that she'd gone walkies in her sleep again. But to *where*, exactly? What was this place?

Swiping her hands down the long shirt she wore, Wynter looked around her. An arched wrought-iron gate was wide open. The rudimentary carvings on one wall made her think of those that Cain showed her in his temple. Was that where—

Wynter jumped as muted male whispers floated through the air. Whispers from something sentient. Aware. Older than old. Powerful in a way she couldn't describe. And it was urging her forward.

It was the same voice from her dream, she realized. And it had led her here.

Some of the things that Kali had told her during Wynter's recent trip to the netherworld leaped to the forefront of her mind. They explained *some* of what was happening here, but not all.

Swallowing hard, Wynter glanced back at the gate. She could head back to the Keep and wake Cain. She *should*. Because this whole thing was goddamn weird. It was weirder still that he hadn't already caught up with her and ushered her back to bed the way he usually did.

Yes, she should go back and ask him to—

An otherworldly breeze nudged her back, urging her forwards.

Crap.

Wynter nervously licked her mouth, able to taste the sweat beading her upper lip and the tang of minerals in the air. Pulling up her big girl panties, she took a few steps further into the grotto. The source of the humidity soon came into view. It appeared to be a natural hot spring, but it wasn't like any she'd seen before. Whips of power bounced along the surface of the burbling turquoise water— crackly, sparkly, and beautiful.

The high concentration of power was like a beacon. She edged closer, careful not to lose her footing and slip on the wet stone.

Her pulse jumped as water briefly shot upward out of the well like a geyser. Cursing her raw nerves, she walked a little faster toward the spring.

The muted whispers grew louder, clearer, more frantic. And they urged her to put her hand in the water.

No, thank you.

She had the feeling that the little sparks of power skipping along the surface would pack a real punch if they zapped her. But the voice persisted, reassuring her that there was no danger to her here. Which didn't actually succeed in putting her mind at ease.

Only one thing made Wynter consider granting the voice its request—although Kali was brushing against her, She gave off no cautioning vibes. The deity was all calmness and encouragement, seemingly relaxed about the whole thing.

"Fine, fine. Just so you know, Kali, I'll be totally pissed if I get zapped or some shit." Wynter knelt beside the steaming well. The insane heat it gave off rose up and flushed her cheeks. "Awesome."

Steeling herself, Wynter pushed aside her doubts and reached inside the spring. She didn't need to plunge her hand into the well. The water weirdly splashed upward and swallowed her hand.

A gust of otherworldly air washed over her face, communicating ... something. Something she didn't understand. Inside Wynter, her monster abruptly rose to the surface, but it didn't take over. It *melded* with her.

She sucked in a breath as power punched into her, surging through her body so violently it bowed her back. Oh God, it was too much. It rattled her teeth. Stung her eyes. Bubbled in her blood. Buzzed against her bones. Made her heart gallop and her head spin.

She couldn't move; could only stay still as the alien power arched through her like forks of lightning—flooding her with warmth, jumpstarting her senses, waking up her nerve cells, and electrifying her body.

And then it was over.

Her eyes snapped open as her monster slinked backwards in

withdrawal. Once more herself, she shook her head hard to clear it. What the fuck was that?

Quivering, she brushed her dry palm down her face. God, she'd never felt so . . . awake. Present. Energized. *Wired.*

Swallowing around her dry throat, she pulled her other hand out of the water and stood. Which was when the spring began to ripple and splash like a goddamn Jacuzzi. She promptly backed up, only able to watch as lights began to flash like crazy beneath the water. The whips of power dancing along the surface began to wildly hiss and pop and crackle.

Wynter's breath snagged in her throat, and her heart began to pound hard and fast in her chest. Oh, hell, what had she done?

*

Rubbing at his nape, Cain walked down the stone passageway en route to the chamber he shared with Wynter. Sleep had eluded him. His mind—currently a chaotic place of messy thoughts and relentless questions—simply wouldn't rest. As such, he'd headed to his ledger room to get some work done.

He'd considered instead waking his consort and then fucking them both raw—that would have helped his brain power down for certain. But the last thing he wanted was for her to be sleep-deprived. With all that was going on around them, she needed to be sharp and alert at all times.

He'd left her a note just in case she woke before he returned. He hadn't realized he'd been in his ledger room for over three hours until he'd glanced at the wall clock and saw that it was 3:45am.

Now, Cain pushed open the door to his chamber. He frowned as his gaze landed on the bed. Ruffled sheets. No Wynter.

Calling out her name, he crossed to the en suite bathroom. *Empty.* Unease crawled through his gut, and his mouth tightened. Sleepwalking. She had to be sleepwalking again. "Fuck."

Since there was only one place she ever went during such times, he hurried out of the Keep and headed straight for his garden, never willing to take for granted that—despite how often he'd found her unharmed—she'd be safe from the many serpents that roamed in it.

The gates were wide open, and the padlock was on the ground. Yes, she was out here. And *something* had unlocked the gates for her yet again.

His pulse thudding hard, Cain rushed along the winding, twisting path. He expected to come upon her at any moment, but there was no sign of her. How long had she been out here?

His creature writhed inside him, agitated that she was missing and furious that another male could call her to them like this. Furious that they would even *dare*.

Nearing the temple, Cain frowned. *The fuck?* Mounds of snakes were piled outside, writhing on top of each other. He knew they usually followed her when she came to the garden during her sleep. Could they have followed her here?

Cursing, he took the pitted steps two at a time and rushed into the temple. "Wynter!" he shouted, lighting the wall torches even as he stalked through the eternally long sculpted archway. "Wynter!"

A ruthless little voice inside him spoke up, saying it would be better not to wake her; better not to sever the current connection between her and Abaddon—no one else could be calling her here, could they? And if the Ancient was close to waking, that could only be a good thing.

Cain quashed the voice fast. If the woman in question had been anyone other than Wynter, he would have been prepared to sit back and observe. But this was his consort.

His pace faltered as he sensed vibrations coming from somewhere below him.

Coming from the grotto.

Cursing again, Cain bolted for the spiral staircase he'd descended almost every night for weeks on end. He swiftly jogged down it and hurried through the open iron gate. His pulse leaped as he took in the scene.

Wynter stood against the wall opposite the spring, her eyes wide, her lips parted, her focus centered on it. Water splashed over the edges of the stone well as it bubbled and gushed and lit up with pure power.

He'd witnessed such a spectacle before. Many times, in fact. It meant only one thing.

A Leviathan was rising.

Cain rushed to Wynter's side and curled a hand around her upper arm. She jerked in surprise, only then noticing him. "Are you all right?" he asked her.

Looking somewhat dazed, she nodded.

"He called you here again?"

A line dented her brow. "He?"

"My uncle." Cain curled an arm around her shoulders and held her close. "He's waking." And for some reason, Abaddon wanted Wynter to be present when he did. The man had some explaining to do.

"Wait, he's in the *water*?"

"Ancients always Rest in water." Cain cast a quick look at the well. "You should go back to the Keep."

Her brows snapped together. "What? Why?"

"Because I don't know what mental state he'll be in when he rises. Like I told you once before, I don't know of an Ancient who's been at Rest for so long and I have no clue what kind of impact it might have had on his psyche." And sanity, for that matter. His uncle had always been reasonably calm and collected, but these were unusual circumstances. "That unsurety bothers me."

"It bothers me as well. Which is why I'm not leaving."

Cain sighed at the determined set to her jaw. "You're a stubborn woman. I like that about you, even as I find it an inconvenience at times." Since he highly doubted that his uncle would have any wish to harm her, Cain didn't push for her to leave. "At least let me do the talking."

"That I can easily agree to. Um, the lights beneath the water are beginning to fade. That doesn't mean he's slipping back into Rest, does it?"

"No. It means he's close to surfacing." Cain's chest tightened as he recalled the last time he'd seen Abaddon. The man had been deathly pale, so weak his heart barely beat, his face lined with grief and pain even in sleep.

They hadn't expected him to survive more than a few nights, if that. Still, they'd placed him in the water. Instead of slipping away peacefully while at Rest, he'd gradually healed. More, he'd strengthened—something they'd sensed as the level of power in the grotto slowly but surely intensified over time.

When they'd been sure he was strong enough to wake, Cain and the other Ancients had contemplated it. But they had all agreed that Abaddon wouldn't thank them for it. At least at Rest he could dream of being with his deceased family members, of having a life that didn't involve being imprisoned. Awake, he would have to accept so many deaths, process so much grief, and learn to cope with being in a cage where he'd be unable to avenge those he'd lost in—

The lights flicked off, and the bounding whips of power disintegrated.

Cain released Wynter and moved to stand in front of her, earning himself a little huff.

Head first, a man slowly rose out of the spring, water sluicing down his half-naked body. Abaddon looked so much like both his brothers, Satan and Baal. Tall, broad, dark, hard. And, at this moment, thoroughly disoriented.

He blinked, his gaze sharpening. "Cain?" he asked, his voice croaky with lack of use.

Cain nodded. "Yes."

Abaddon looked around. "Where am I?"

"A temple near my home. You've been here for some time now."

As Abaddon continued to examine his surroundings, Cain took a moment to really study his uncle. The Ancient appeared weak but not frail, and there was no glint of insanity in his gaze, merely confusion. He had the look of someone who'd overslept and was now suffering the adverse effects of it. Which, really, probably wasn't far from the truth.

Finally spotting Wynter, Abaddon squinted. "Who are you?" he asked, imperious.

Cain felt his brow furrow. He had not expected that question. He shifted aside slightly, giving his uncle a clear view of her, but the Ancient still appeared nonplussed. "You don't recognize her?"

"Should I?" Abaddon frowned, rubbing at his temple. "Everything is . . . cloudy."

Cain knew that feeling. He'd experienced it each time he woke from a long Rest. It was as if the brain struggled to make the full transition from "sleep" to "conscious". Like parts of it needed a few moments to "warm up" in order to properly function.

He watched as his uncle awkwardly stepped out of the well, his movements stiff and uncoordinated. While Ancients didn't struggle to walk after years of Rest, they weren't at their most graceful upon waking. "What is the last thing you remember?"

Abaddon's eyes lost focus. "I . . . It is difficult to get my thoughts in order."

That was another annoying thing about first rising. Until the brain caught up with reality, it wasn't always easy to tell what were memories and what were images from the dreams you'd had while Resting.

"I recall the guardians dumping us on barren land after—" He cut himself off, his teeth snapping together as an unholy rage flamed to life in his eyes. The air began to buzz and tauten with a power that hummed with sheer fury.

Cain's creature tensed, a hiss rattling in its throat at the potential danger to their consort. "If you lose your control here, you will bring this temple down upon us."

"My children," Abaddon croaked out, his voice thick with grief. "My brothers."

"I know."

The Ancient's eyelids slammed shut as he breathed deep, his face lined with pain. Long minutes went by as Abaddon took one centering breath after another. Finally, he opened his eyes. The rage was still there, but it was now cold and controlled rather than hot and wild. That he could regulate his emotions so well was a very good thing.

"Revenge *will* be yours," Cain told him, remaining calm. "Will be *ours*. First, you need to get stronger. You've been in a coma-like Rest for much longer than you can imagine." The truth of how much the Ancient had missed would likely come as something of a shock to him.

Abaddon's face tightened. "Revenge has not already been wreaked?" His voice was jagged with a growl. "The ones who massacred our people and left us to die still live?"

"Some. But perhaps not for much longer. We plan to invade Aeon soon. Very soon."

The anger in the air began to recede, but Abaddon's gaze still gleamed with it. "We are not back there, then?"

"No. We were all cursed to be trapped where the guardians dumped us. The story of how we reached this very moment is a long one. I will soon explain it all to you, just as I will explain why the other Ancients and I recently worked so hard to wake you."

"I vaguely remember hearing voices chant while I Rested. It occurred several times. The words were indecipherable to me. I heard them, recognized the rhythm of them, but they didn't reach inside me as they should have." He tilted his head. "It was you who woke me just now? It did not feel like you."

Cain felt his brows dip. "Feel like me?"

"Something disturbed my rest. *Pulled* at me. Something . . . alien. It was powerful. Too powerful. Unnerving, even."

His skin prickling with unease, Cain resisted the urge to turn and look at his consort. She was powerful, yes, but not to an extent that would daunt an Ancient. Cain could only think that it was Kali who his uncle had sensed.

"My creature didn't like it at all. It fought to surface and protect me. It was then that I woke." Abaddon took a step closer, eyeing Wynter again, still no recognition on his face. "I doubt it was you either."

Cain frowned. "You really don't recognize her? You should, considering you've called Wynter—who, I will add, is my consort—here to the temple several times."

His head drew back slightly. "Called her?"

"Yes, in her dreams. It caused her to sleepwalk, though she never got this far until tonight."

Abaddon's frown deepened. "I do not remember ever reaching out to her or anyone else while I Rested, but my thoughts and memories are still jumbled." His eyes sharpened. "You said a moment ago that we will invade Aeon very soon. Exactly how soon?"

"As I promised before, I will explain everything to you. For now, let us get you settled in my home. You may wish to freshen up and change. Then I will tell you all you wish to know."

*

Sipping his coffee, Cain looked up as Maxim escorted Abaddon into the dining room a short time later. To say that his uncle's presence had shocked the aide was an understatement, but Maxim had recovered quickly and summoned the household staff to ensure that Abaddon had a clean bedchamber and fresh clothing. The hirelings were sworn to secrecy, so Cain didn't worry that news of Abaddon's mysterious appearance would leak.

As the Ancient appeared to be stable, Wynter hadn't protested to Cain spending time alone with him. She understood that Abaddon wouldn't want an audience to his emotions—he'd for sure experience a whole array of them while he was brought up to speed on everything—so she'd headed to the cottage. Cain hoped she managed to catch up on her sleep.

Before she left, he'd asked her if Kali had woken Abaddon.

She'd only replied, "The deity had a hand in it, yes." Wynter hadn't elaborated, giving him one of her maddening "that's all I can tell you" looks.

After his aide left the dining room, Cain looked at Abaddon and blindly gestured at the table on which a selection of foods were laid out. "Sit. Eat." Being only 5am, it was a little early for breakfast—at least for Cain—but he knew the other Ancient would be feeling famished. It was always that way shortly after rising.

He again sipped at his coffee while his uncle took the seat opposite. "How are you doing?"

"Annoyed," replied Abaddon, sniffing almost suspiciously at the foods in front of him, as if he hadn't seen some of them before ... which might well be the case. "It took me ten minutes to learn how to operate that thing you called a shower."

Cain felt his mouth curve. "I offered to show you. But your pride wouldn't allow you to admit to needing help. Not my issue."

"You're still as blunt and pitiless as ever, nephew." After piling food on his plate and pouring himself a glass of water, Abaddon met his gaze. "Tell me what I have missed while at Rest. Leave nothing out."

Cain set down his cup with a sigh, regretting that there was no way to avoid overloading the Ancient with information. He didn't want to overwhelm his uncle, but there was no way around it. So many eras had come and gone since the last time Abaddon walked the Earth. There was much that he'd need to learn, adjust to, and decide—and that was without even including the recent goings-on with the Aeons.

"First of all," began Cain, "time is measured a little differently now." He quickly explained and then added, "By this estimation of time, you have been asleep for several hundred thousand years."

Abaddon went exceptionally still, pausing midchew. Long moments ticked by before he stiffly went on to chomp on his food, his movements almost mechanical. He very slowly sank back into his chair, looking like the wind had been knocked out of him. "Several hundred thousand years," he echoed, his voice rough.

Cain gave a slow nod. "We would have tried to wake you sooner, but we didn't believe you would have thanked us for it, given our current situation. We chose to instead let you wake in your own time. You simply never did."

Abaddon swallowed. "There is much for me to hear, then." Visibly gathering himself, he straightened in his seat. "Tell me everything."

Hour after hour went by as Cain updated him. He suggested multiple times that they take a break, but Abaddon waved it away, intent on hearing all he needed to learn in one swoop. Cain understood. Whenever he woke from a Rest, he liked to catch up fast on all he'd missed.

His uncle listened carefully, posing questions here and there. He mostly responded with grunts, sighs, curses, or strained chuckles that told Cain his uncle might have a tight hold on his anger but it remained close to the surface. So he wasn't the least bit surprised when his revelation that three Aeons now lived at Devil's Cradle had Abaddon shooting out of his seat, sending it skidding backwards.

"They *live* here?" Abaddon demanded, as mystified as he was furious. "As residents, not captives?"

"They came seeking sanctuary—"

"And you *gave* it to them?"

"None were part of the war," Cain calmly reminded him.

The Ancient's eyes darkened to flint. "But they are guardians! Two are the offspring of one of our jailors!"

"And if we kill people simply because of what they are or who their parents are, we are no better than Adam and those of his ilk."

Abaddon snapped his mouth shut and ground his teeth. After a few moments, he cursed. "You just *had* to word it like that, didn't you?" he grumbled. "I know that you are right. I do. But I do not care to be rational."

"For you, the war happened only yesterday. Your anger and grief are still fresh—I understand. But you've never been a slave to your emotions before, Abaddon. Will you change that now?"

215

A long sigh slipped out of the Ancient, who then grabbed his seat and retook it. "Continue," he bit out.

So Cain picked up where he left off. His uncle didn't interrupt again except to ask for elaboration on this or that. Finally done relaying everything, Cain leaned back in his seat. "I know I've given you a lot to process in a very short time—"

"It is best that you did. I would prefer not to be ignorant to the facts." Abaddon exhaled heavily. "It did not occur to me that I might have slept this long. I suspect it will take time for me to become fully accustomed to the world as it now is."

"The other Ancients and I will help you with that."

"At present, I am more interested in dealing with Adam. While I am glad to hear that Abel, Lailah, and Saul are long gone, I regret that I was not able to witness their demise." Abaddon tipped his head to the side. "How did it feel? Killing Abel?"

"In all honesty, I felt no great triumph. Not on a personal level. More satisfaction crept in as the days went by, though. But that was more due to the fact that another of our jailors were dead. Really, imagining the rage Adam would have felt when I sent Abel back to him in pieces made me feel far more victorious than the kill itself."

Abaddon's lips twitched. "I suspect his reaction to your package was a sight to behold." He paused. "You truly believe we can destroy this cage?"

"Now that you are awake, yes, I do. And then we will storm Aeon."

Abaddon gravely nodded, bloodthirst glittering in the depths of his eyes. "They must all die, Cain. They took much from me. From all of us. As for Abel's brats and your mother . . . I will leave them be. *Unless* they betray us. If that happens, I will end them."

"You won't get the chance. They'd be dead before you got near them."

Abaddon's brow pinched. "You would wish to kill them yourself? Even your mother?"

216

"My consort would get there first. She is ... protective. Not to mention vengeful—but then, revenants always are."

Abaddon nodded. "Very true. And I will be forever grateful for how she cursed Aeon just as its rulers cursed us to remain in this godforsaken place. I truly do not recollect ever reaching out to her while Resting."

"It's highly possible that you didn't. I'm more inclined to think that it was Kali who repeatedly tried leading her to the temple. After all, it was Her who woke you."

"Really?"

"Wynter confirmed it."

"Hmm. The deity did say that you and Her had similar goals. Waking me might have been one of them. Though I am unsure why She would want that. Perhaps She wishes to help us escape our cage. She may hope to right wrongs in some gesture that God would so approve of that he'd end Her punishment."

"Maybe. I wouldn't have thought that She could have unlocked the grotto gate. That came as a surprise. It was secured closed using the sacred chant. Only another of our kind should have been able to break its hold on the lock. Kali is evidently more powerful than I thought. At least I can be sure that, immensely powerful as She may in fact be, the deity won't abruptly snatch Wynter's soul from me."

Abaddon rubbed at his jaw. "You really told your consort every one of our secrets?"

"Yes. You cannot imagine how difficult it must have been for her to accept everything. Given that people of all species have been raised to believe that the Antichrist will day one come and seek to destroy the world, there is a lot of fear based around who and what I am."

"Perhaps the guardians saw to that."

"Perhaps." Cain gave him a pointed look. "Don't forget that we do not call them guardians anymore. We call them Aeons, as they call us Ancients."

Abaddon sniffed. "Back to what we were saying, the matter of your parentage means nothing to your consort?"

"No. She is more bothered by the fact that I have cherubim blood. She somewhat detests them."

A chuckle rumbled out of Abaddon. "Then I suspect I might rather like her. Though I am already inclined to like her, given that not only did she kill Saul but Aeon will soon be a wasteland thanks to her." He crossed his arms over his chest. "You know, despite all you have told me, I find it hard to truly grasp that Wynter is a revenant. Not that I *dis*believe you. Only that it is difficult to imagine a situation in which a revenant could be so singular."

"I initially had the same struggle."

He shook his head in wonder. "I can understand now why she did not look nervous around me earlier. She quite simply has no real reason to be wary. She could destroy me in a heartbeat."

Cain couldn't help but smile. "Yes, she could."

"That pleases you?" Abaddon snorted. "Your father enjoyed flirting with death just the same. It did not end well for him, but none of us could lament that he impregnated Eve, because then there would be no you." His smile faltered. "How is she? Still fragile as porcelain?"

Hearing the mocking note in his uncle's voice, Cain remembered, "You never liked Eve."

"I didn't like that she failed to protect you. That she abandoned you by falling into a state of Rest to escape her own reality." He sighed, shaking his head. "You do not know what it was like for your father to be prohibited from taking you into his care when he knew you needed him. He agonized over it.

"So many times he came close to storming Adam's home. Baal and I would have gone with him, of course. What stopped the three of us from invading the place was the knowledge that Adam *hoped* we would do exactly that. He wanted an excuse to kill your father, and we knew he would likely also kill you in front of Satan to punish him. We had to trust that you would one day come to us, and you did."

Cain hadn't been sure of what reception he'd receive, but all the

Leviathans had welcomed him with open arms, regardless of his cherubim blood. It was strange how the dark could sometimes be more accepting than the light.

"Don't trust her, Cain. Your mother, I mean. I am not saying that she would deviously set out to betray you, but ..." Abaddon let his sentence trail off, as if taking a moment to choose his words carefully. "Fragility by itself is not something I look down upon. But when fragile people are also cowards, I am wary of them.

"I have known many such characters. They never reach for inner strength when it counts. They are prepared to sacrifice anything in the name of self-preservation—their integrity, their pride, their freedom, even the lives and wellbeing of others. That is not to say that they are bad people, only that they are easily compromised and cannot necessarily be trusted to do the right thing. Eve is like that."

The sad thing was ... Cain couldn't even dispute that. "You don't need to worry that her being my mother blinds me to the truth of who she is." He tapped his fingers on the table. "Especially when she very recently demonstrated that she hasn't changed."

"Oh?"

"When my consort was teleported out of Devil's Cradle, Eve repeatedly suggested that Wynter might have abandoned us to escape Adam's wrath. And I know that that is because Eve would feel such a temptation in Wynter's shoes."

Abaddon dipped his chin. "That she would. Your mother might not have ran from Adam until recently, but she still sought an escape—she Rested for many years, even though it meant emotionally abandoning her own children. I would imagine she struggles to understand your consort."

"Many do. Myself included."

Abaddon's lips quirked. "Tell me more about her."

So Cain did.

Chapter Eighteen

"Dammit, Hattie, stop eating all the Danish." Delilah scooped up another spoonful of cereal. "The plan is to sell those, remember?"

"I'm hungry," Hattie defended.

"You're stoned and have a case of the munchies."

"So mind your business and let me munch."

Biting back a smile, Wynter sipped at her tea. It had been a while since she'd eaten breakfast with her coven. She kind of missed it, though she wouldn't wish to not spend her mornings with Cain.

Delilah's eyelid twitched as she glared at the old woman. "Eat something that *isn't* part of our shop's stock."

"Fine." Hattie snatched a pack of salt and vinegar chips out of a cupboard. "You know how to stomp on an old lady's buzz."

A snore fairly erupted out of Anabel, who'd fallen asleep at the table. The blonde could sleep through pretty much anything. Hell, two of their lycan neighbors had once had a full-on dual in the backyard while Anabel napped in the hammock of the coven's yard—she hadn't so much as stirred at any point. Well, not until Delilah poured water over her crotch, but that was a whole other story.

Eating what was left of his bagel, Xavier shook his head as he stared down at Anabel. "She needs to stop working on potions until the early hours of the morning. It ain't good for her."

"Well, at least she wasn't using herself as a potion-crash test dummy again," said Delilah. "That's something."

"You'd think she'd be more cautious." Hattie popped a chip into her mouth as she returned to her seat at the table. "She prattles on and on about how death will come for her, not seeing that she'll shorten her life span all on her own if she's not careful."

Wynter took another sip of her tea. "Her crazy scientist streak overrides her common sense at times and—Oh come on, Xavier, really?" The dude was drawing thick, diagonal eyebrows on Anabel's face with a black marker.

"I warned her I'd get her back for drawing a dick on my face when I passed out," he said.

Wynter frowned. "Wasn't that, like, seven months ago?"

"A Gamble never forgets."

She could only cross her eyes. Being a highly vengeful creature herself, she wasn't in a position to judge.

"There are many—and much safer—ways to test potions," said Delilah a little snottily. "I often used my boyfriends as trial subjects."

Wynter paused with her cup halfway to her mouth. "Did they know about it?"

Delilah hesitated. "Well, no. But they wouldn't have minded."

"Then why did you keep it from them?" Wynter challenged.

"I didn't keep it from them, I just didn't mention it. A girl doesn't need to tell her boyfriends *every* little thing, Wyn."

"I hardly think your using them as guinea pigs was a little thing."

"I hardly think that their sleeping with other women was a little thing. As Xavier says, you reap what you sow in this world."

"Cheaters should always get what they deserve." Eating another chip, Hattie looked off into the distance. "If only I'd met my George years ago. He would have been my one and only."

"I have to say, you two do seem made for each other," said Wynter . . . which was when she realized that Xavier was *still* doodling on Anabel's face. "An eye patch? Really?"

"She's gotta pay for her sins." Xavier slid his gaze back to Hattie. "So you trust George, then?"

The old woman smiled. "Oh, one hundred percent. George doesn't have a philandering bone in his body."

Delilah picked up her mug of tea. "Does he know you've been married?"

"Yes, of course," replied Hattie with a flap of her hand.

"Does he know how many times you've been married?" asked Delilah.

Hattie pursed her lips. "Well . . ."

"Then I suppose he also doesn't know that you made yourself a widow each time."

"Why would I bore him with such a long story?"

"I would think of it as more of a cautionary tale."

Hattie *hmph*ed. "I already promised you all that I wouldn't hurt him."

Wynter snickered. "You also made pretty promises to your husbands. Look how that turned out. I think they—*Seriously*, Xavier, you're giving her a mustache now? What are you, twelve?"

"She's gotta learn her lesson." He added a little goatee with his marker, as if for good measure. "I don't know why you're making a big deal out of what I'm doing."

"Try to look at the bigger picture." Wynter drank the last of her tea. "She'll make you pay for that. Then you'll retaliate again. So a cycle of vengeance will begin."

"And what is wrong with that?"

Wynter rolled her eyes. "Someone needs to wake her up." She set down her cup. "I need to talk to you guys about something."

"Hmm, sounds ominous." He put his mouth to Anabel's ear and whistled loud.

Her head shot up. "What in the—" She blinked hard and then scrubbed a hand down her face. "God, was it really necessary to whistle *right down my ear*?"

"Yeah," replied Xavier. "For three reasons. One, you're a freakily deep sleeper. Two, it would irritate you. Three, Wynter has something to tell us."

Anabel frowned. "Reason number two doesn't count as 'necessary,' asshole."

"Depends on your definition of necessary, I guess."

"There's only one definition of that word." Anabel threw up a hand when he would have spoken again. "I'm done. Stop talking." She cut her gaze to Wynter. "What is it you want to tell us?"

Wynter shifted slightly in her seat. "Okay, so you're going to hear some news today. Cain will be making a speech about it. But I want you to hear it from me first. Now, let me just preface this by saying that I'll understand if you feel let down that I said nothing about this before. I truly will. But Cain only told me because he trusted me not to speak of it to others. I couldn't betray that trust."

Delilah flicked a hand. "Of course you couldn't. Now spit it out, the suspense is killing me."

Wynter took a preparatory breath. "There's an eighth Ancient here."

"An eighth?" echoed Anabel, sitting straighter.

"Yes," replied Wynter. "He came to Devil's Cradle long ago with the other seven, but he was so deeply injured that he went to sleep in that way that the Ancients do. It wasn't a standard Rest, though. It was similar to a coma. The others expected him to slip away in his sleep at some point, but he didn't. He healed. He simply didn't wake."

"Until now," added Anabel.

Wynter nodded. "Until now. The Ancients woke him so that he can partake in the upcoming battle."

"Well," began Delilah, leaning back in her seat, "that was, like, the *last* thing I expected you to say."

"Have you met him yet?" Hattie asked Wynter.

"Yes. I met him last night." In a manner of speaking. Cain had introduced her to the other Ancient, but she hadn't spoken to him. Since Cain had asked her to keep the detail of Abaddon being his uncle private, she kept that part to herself, only adding, "His name is Abaddon."

Anabel's brows flew up. "As in *the* Abaddon? A demon who some believe might actually be the devil?"

"Yeah, him. Except he's neither of those things. Humans have a habit of mistaking Ancients for demons," Wynter reminded her. "Probably because of how darkly powerful they are. Or maybe the Aeons embarked on a sort of hate campaign to ensure people feared and loathed them, I don't know."

"I think there are some here who do believe that the Ancients are demons of some kind," said Delilah.

Wynter frowned. "Well, they're not."

"*We* know that," said Xavier. "We saw a glimpse of Cain's monster, remember? Well, we saw its eyes—they were serpentine. Demon eyes are pure black."

Rubbing at her arm, Wynter blew out a breath. "I just hope the residents here don't respond negatively to hearing that there's another Ancient in Devil's Cradle."

"It will come as a surprise to them for sure," said Anabel. "And given how many dark rumors are attached to Abaddon's name, there's a good chance that people will be wary of him. But I don't think they'll find this a *bad* thing. Especially when having an additional Ancient fighting on their side in the upcoming battle will make all the difference."

Xavier nodded. "I doubt people will line up to shake his hand, but I think they'll accept his presence."

Maybe, but . . . "They haven't accepted Eve or the twins."

"That's different, they're Aeons," said Hattie.

Well, true.

"Where do you think Abaddon will live?" asked Delilah.

"No idea. He'll probably build his own Keep after the battle is over." Wynter suspected he'd stay with Cain in the interim, given that they were blood relatives, but it could be that he was close to another of the Ancients and would prefer to stay with them—she wasn't yet sure. "Thank you all for not being upset that I didn't tell you about Abaddon before today."

Anabel waved that away. "Hey, I get it. The Ancients are a secretive bunch, so I'm sure there's lots of things they don't share. It was a no-brainer that Cain would trust you with some of that stuff but ask you to keep it to yourself."

"I might like to know everything, being incredibly nosy and all, but I don't *expect* you to tell us everything," said Delilah.

Xavier leaned back in his seat, nodding. "Everyone has their secrets."

"Especially couples," added Hattie. "It's a natural thing."

A relieved breath slipped out of Wynter. Although she hadn't expected her coven to bitchily vilify her for keeping secrets, she'd worried that they'd be hurt by it. She adored them for being so understanding.

Hiding things from people was something she'd been doing for so long that it was a little *too* easy for her these days. But when it came to her coven, Wynter didn't like holding back important things from them. She didn't like that she couldn't be fully open with them about everything.

Just the same, she didn't like withholding things from Cain. She hadn't told him exactly what happened in the run-up to Abaddon rising from the hot spring. She'd let him believe that it was *all* Kali. Wynter really didn't know how to tell Cain about her part in it. Or even if she *should* tell him.

Back in that grotto, she hadn't expected that her actions would cause the sleeping Ancient to wake. Yes, she knew more of Kali's plans now, but the deity had left *some* gaps; promising to fill them in "eventually". Kali certainly hadn't revealed Abaddon's Resting place. Wynter hadn't even so much as suspected that he would be Resting in the water. She'd thought he'd be in some kind of tomb somewhere.

"What's wrong?" asked Delilah, snapping her out of her thoughts. "Something's bothering you."

Wynter felt her nose wrinkle. "I need to work through it in my head."

"You don't need to do it alone at all," Delilah protested. "We're your coven. We're here for you. And nosy as hell, so please share."

"Yeah," said Xavier. "Also, it'll make you a total hypocrite if you do that thing you used to do where you pull inward. *You* chew a chunk out of our asses when *we* do it."

That was more because their idea of secrets tended to be things that could lead to issues for the coven, like selling dodgy potions for instance.

Anabel reached toward Wynter, setting her hand down on the table near hers. "Let us help you sort through whatever's firing through your brain. We might be able to help."

Wynter sighed. "What I tell you can't leave this cottage."

"You know better than to think we'd betray your confidence," said Delilah.

Xavier leaned forward, planting his folded arms on the table. "Tell us."

"Okay." Wynter straightened her shoulders. "So, about Abaddon . . . I think I woke him. Or my monster did. Or we both did."

Xavier cocked his head. "What do you mean?"

"The Ancients have been working at it for weeks, but they couldn't manage to wake him," Wynter explained. "Last night, I went sleepwalking again. As you know, Cain usually pulls me out of it. This time, he didn't. I just snapped awake." She licked her lips. "I was in Abaddon's Resting place. Though I didn't *know* it was his Resting place. Not at first."

"The voice that comes to you in your sleep led you there?" asked Delilah.

"Yes," replied Wynter. "And it also spoke to me while I was awake this time, telling me to touch what I later realized was Abaddon's . . . bed, shall we say." She didn't want to say *too* much about how Ancients Rested. "Next thing I knew, my monster surged forward and joined with me somehow."

"Joined?" echoed Delilah, concerned. "What do you mean by 'joined'?"

"I don't know exactly. But it was like our souls melded for a moment."

226

"Whoa," said Anabel with a jerk of her head.

"I know, right?" Wynter bit her lip. "It's *never* done anything like that before. I felt its power pour into me as I touched Abaddon's bed. And then he rose."

"In short, your monster used you to wake Abaddon," Xavier concluded.

"Seems like it." Wynter licked her lower lip. "And I think Kali told it to. She relayed some kind of message, but I didn't understand Her words—it's not always easy to make out what She's saying when She's in this realm; it's like Her voice has a thousand echoes and they all mingle crazily. Looking at the situation now, I don't think I was supposed to understand what She said. I don't believe She was talking to me. I believe She was addressing my monster."

Anabel frowned. "So, what, She wants to help the Ancients?"

"Kind of," replied Wynter. "I spoke to Her when I died after being shot by those vampires. But it wasn't just a quick hi. She told me a few things; things She insisted I didn't share with anyone, not even Cain or any of you. But She didn't mention anything about wanting me to wake Abaddon."

"She hasn't made you privy to all Her plans, then," mused Hattie.

"It seems that way." Wynter was sort of used to it at this point. "I don't know whether I should tell Cain about what part I think I might have played in waking Abaddon."

Delilah's brows drew together. "Why? You think he'd be pissed at you?"

"No. It's just ... He's uber protective of me." Understatement, but whatever. "He doesn't like anything happening around me that he doesn't understand."

"And he's not going to understand how your monster joined its soul with yours," Delilah understood.

"*I* don't even understand how it did that."

"It's not an impossible feat, but it ain't easy," Xavier cut in. "I've known witches to temporarily do it with deceased souls. Your soul is undead, and that leaves it vulnerable in many ways. I don't know what exactly you host, but it's powerful. I think it could manage something like this."

"Maybe. There's also a chance that Kali either helped or made it happen." Wynter shoved a hand through her hair. "Whatever the case, Cain is not gonna like that the entity melded its soul with mine, even though it was only for a few moments. Because that would mean two things—not only am I supremely vulnerable to my monster, but by joining its soul with mine that way . . . well, it might actually be able to pull me back to the netherworld regardless of his rights to me."

Hattie cursed. "Girl, this ain't good."

No, it wasn't. "He won't handle either of those things well, particularly the latter. I worry he'll do something rash."

"Like?" prompted Xavier.

"Like challenge Kali in some way," replied Wynter. "Like insist that She drop whatever plans She has for me. Which She wouldn't agree to do. And if She thought he'd interfere with them, She'd take me from him somehow—even if only temporarily. I don't think even Cain could take on a deity, but he'd be enraged enough to try."

Delilah winced. "Yeah, I can see that happening."

Xavier puffed out a breath. "I get why you're hesitant to tell him, but I think you should—you'll just have to be careful how you go about it. There might be something he can do to ensure that your monster isn't able to merge with you like that again. I mean, Cain owns your soul. He'd surely have some way to protect it." He frowned when she only stared at him. "What?"

"You're just the last person I expected would encourage me to be honest," said Wynter.

"Hey, the truth is overrated—I fully believe that," he stated. "But there are occasions when truths simply need to be shared. In my opinion, this is something that Cain needs to know."

"I agree," said Anabel. "As Xavier said, there might be something Cain can do to protect your soul. But he won't know he needs to if you're not upfront about what happened."

Hattie nodded. "And you can always wrangle a promise out of him in advance."

Wynter tilted her head. "A promise to do what?"

"Not challenge Kali, of course," replied Hattie.

Wynter pulled a face. "I'm not so certain he'd be able to keep that promise."

"But if you use magick to bind the verbal contract, he'd be unable to break his word."

Wynter felt her brows hike up. "That's true." And a very good idea.

"I have one question," said Anabel. "Whose was the voice that led you to Abaddon?"

Wynter gave a clueless shrug. "I know that, having heard Abaddon speak, it definitely wasn't him."

A knock sounded at the front door.

"I'll get it." Wynter pushed out of her seat, crossed the living room, and opened the front door. She blinked at the sight of Maxim. "Oh, hi." Wynter stepped aside to let him enter.

"Thank you," he said. "I came to pass on a message from Cain. He asked that you have dinner with him this evening. He'd like you to more officially meet Abaddon and . . ." Maxim trailed off, his eyes drifting to something behind her.

Wynter twisted to see Anabel lighting the candles on the living room altar.

The blonde must have felt their attention settle on her, because her gaze flew to them. "What?" she asked, frowning . . . which only served to pull down those thick, drawn eyebrows even more.

Maxim cleared his throat. "I'm just wondering why you look like a pirate."

Her muscles stiffening, she swiftly turned to glance at her reflection in the triple moon mirror. Her hands balled up into fists. "Xavier, you shit!"

"Karma spares no one!" he yelled from the kitchen.

"Amen to that," said Delilah . . . at which point Anabel began to rip them both a new asshole while Hattie cackled.

Sighing, Wynter turned back to Maxim. "Would you believe me if I told you that this kind of thing is unusual?"

He gave her a long look. "No. No, I would not."

She'd figured as much.

*

It was shortly after Cain had finished giving his uncle a tour of the Keep that he called the other Ancients there. All were pleasantly surprised to see Abaddon awake, particularly Dantalion, whose deceased brother was a close friend of his.

Ishtar made a point of flirting with him, possibly hoping it would annoy Cain to see her dreamily sighing over his own uncle, but the newly woken Ancient wasn't responsive. He seemed more interested in Lilith—each eyed the other closely as they sat across from each other in the solar room, their expressions giving nothing away. If Cain remembered rightly, the two had . . . interesting history.

Elegantly perched on one of the plush sofas beside Lilith, Inanna looked at Abaddon and said, "For you to wake without us chanting over your place of Rest . . . All I can think is that our efforts to wake you did in fact work but simply took their time to come into effect."

Lounging on the opposite sofa, Abaddon said, "Your efforts may have helped, but I do not believe they were solely responsible for my waking. I was disturbed by a foreign power. Kali, to be exact."

Ishtar's shoulders tensed. "Kali?"

"It seems that the deity has been trying to lead Cain's consort to the grotto in her sleep for some time," said Abaddon. "He always woke her and then led her back to their chamber. Last night, he didn't. I suspect Kali needed to use her to wake me, since there are only certain things that She and some of the other deities can do in this realm—hence why they Favor and use people to achieve their own ends."

Cain suspected the same. He intended to get the full story from her later.

"Why did Kali wake you?" asked Dantalion, standing in front of the elaborate fireplace.

"I do not yet know," replied Abaddon. "I'm sure that Cain's consort will explain if she has answers. As I understand it, having spoken to Cain in depth about her, she doesn't always have answers or Kali's permission to share them."

"Whatever the deity's reason, I am grateful for Her assistance," said Seth, who sat in the chair beside which Cain stood.

The others nodded, other than Ishtar, who studied Cain hard and then said, "You never mentioned her habit of sleepwalking to us."

Actually, he'd mentioned it to Azazel, sure that the other male wouldn't repeat it. Cain would have similarly trusted his brother with the information but had felt that the less people who knew the better. Cain had said nothing about it to the others because he'd known that—given Wynter only ever went to the garden during such times—they might be suspicious of it and, as such, be distrustful of Wynter. Such distrust might have given Ishtar the fuel she needed to convince the others to give his consort up to the Aeons.

Cain gave an aloof shrug and said, "It bore no relevance to anyone here. Many people sleepwalk. What Wynter does or doesn't do is the business of no one in this room but me."

Ishtar's lips flattened. "She was sleepwalking in your *garden*."

"From what I've heard, sleepwalkers often head to places they feel comfortable," said Cain. "The garden relaxes her."

Ishtar looked as though she might push the matter further, but then she made it clear with a flap of her hand that she was done discussing it. She turned her attention back to Abaddon, flashing him yet another sultry smile.

"I was beginning to think that you might never wake." Ishtar said it as if she'd nonetheless not given up hope. Quite the opposite. She'd suggested a number of times that they cease trying to pull Abaddon out of his coma.

"I am thankful that I did," said Abaddon. "I would never wish to miss the upcoming battle. It will take a few days before I am at top strength, but no longer than that. I will be ready to attempt to take down the cage on All Hallows' Eve."

Leaning back against the wall near the window, Azazel scrubbed a hand over his jaw. "I doubt we will be able to take it down, but we have a chance of forming a hole in it. That will not be easy, though. The prison is designed to hold Leviathans, and it was created by a race whose power almost equals ours."

"Having the help of Eve and Noah will make a difference." Lilith lifted a brow at Seth. "I assume they are still prepared to aid us."

"They haven't withdrawn their offer," he said.

"And Rima?" asked Inanna, sitting beside her sister. "Has she made the same offer?"

"No," replied Seth. "But it wouldn't surprise me if she did volunteer to help. She has been less dramatic of late. Less bitter. As if the chip on her shoulder is shrinking."

"We can hope that's true. Any help would be appreciated." Lilith crossed one leg over the other. "If it were not for how many secrets we harbor, we could have invited all of our residents to aid us."

"Not even their combined strength would be enough to puncture a curse created by Aeons, though," said Abaddon.

Lilith allowed that with an incline of her head.

Azazel met Cain's gaze and said, "I think we should invite Wynter to come along with us."

Ishtar stiffened. "Wynter? Why?"

"Because she is no normal witch," said Azazel. "She is a revenant. A powerful one. Powerful enough to inflict a curse on Aeon that is so strong its inhabitants can't fight it."

Ishtar's upper lip curled. "Revenants are good at cursing things, not *un*doing curses."

"You don't know that. And, in any case, she isn't a typical revenant." Azazel draped one arm over the back of the sofa. "It's possible that her presence won't make a difference. But it definitely wouldn't do any harm. Especially since Kali might help via Wynter."

"I doubt that She will, since She will count waking Abaddon

as 'help' and is likely to think that the rest should be up to us," predicted Lilith. "There is only so much deities can interfere with, even with the assistance of their Favored. Still, I am not opposed to Wynter being present. Any help would be appreciated. Would she be prepared to offer us such aid, Cain?"

"I can't imagine her refusing," he said. "She wants to invade Aeon almost as much as we do." Unfortunately.

"Are you sure that the people who reside here will also be eager to join the battle?" asked Abaddon.

"After the damage the Aeons have caused our home? Definitely," said Seth.

Abaddon accepted that with a nod. "Do your people know about me?"

"No," Seth told him. "We did not want to risk that some might attempt to find you while you Rested, even if only out of curiosity."

"It wouldn't have been the first time people sought the Resting place of an Ancient," said Abaddon. "What will you tell them?"

"The truth, for the most part," replied Cain. "I intend to make a speech shortly. I will publicly introduce you and explain that you have been at Rest for a long time, but I will claim it was by choice. Revealing that you were in what was effectively a coma might also give people the impression that you are currently weak."

"And the Ancients can never be seen to be weak, I understand. I would imagine that you will not be introducing me as your uncle," Abaddon guessed, unoffended.

"Not as my uncle, no. People believe that Adam is my father, and there are some here who have been to Aeon and so are aware that he only has two brothers. Just the same, they know that Eve is an only child."

"After the speech, I will show you around the city, let people get a closer look at you," Dantalion told Abaddon. "You can pick a spot for where you would one day like to build your own home. I am guessing that you intend to stay with Cain in the meantime?"

"That is my plan, yes," Abaddon confirmed.

Ishtar shot him another sexually suggestive smile. "If you decide you would like a change of company, I have many spare bedchambers you can use." She cast a quick look at Cain, clearly wanting to see his reaction to her offer; not looking too happy when he only looked at her blankly.

Abaddon sighed at her. "So you still like to play games."

Widening her eyes in innocence, she put a hand to her chest. "I am simply being friendly."

Abaddon snorted. "You're not friendly."

"On the contrary, I can be *very*—"

"Sister," Inanna cut in, a soft note of warning in her voice.

Ishtar gave a fake pout. "None of you are any fun."

A short while later, Cain declared it was time to make the speech. The Ancients began to file out of the solar room one by one.

Lagging behind to fall into step beside Cain, Azazel asked him, "Do you think that Kali possessed Wynter last night?"

"It's a possibility," Cain told him. "She has no recollection of the last time the deity possessed her. If it happened again, she likely wouldn't remember."

Azazel twisted his mouth. "So Kali *could* have taken over her body last night."

"Yes. There's a chance She wants to help us escape our cage, and having Abaddon certainly improves our odds. She might have used Wynter's body to achieve that goal."

It pissed Cain off that the deity used her over and over in such a way, but there was little he could do about it. That only made it worse for him. It caused him to feel that he was failing his consort; failing to protect her.

He looked forward to the day when Kali no longer needed Wynter. It would not only mean she would be both free and safer but that he would have her all to himself. For now, well, he had one comfort: Kali might have some hold over Wynter, but She would *never* be able to take his consort from him.

Chapter Nineteen

Lifting his glass tumbler later that evening, Cain tipped it back and swallowed some of his brandy. Beside him, Wynter sank back into the dining room chair, clearly full. They were alone now, since Abaddon had headed to his bedchamber to rest, determined to be at full strength fast.

The meal had gone well. Cain had watched as his consort and uncle got to know each other, and he hadn't been surprised by how easy Abaddon had taken to her. Wynter was like a Leviathan in many ways—merciless, vengeful, cunning, elusive.

She'd intrigued Abaddon without even trying. It had been amusing to watch his uncle try to pluck secrets out of her. Amusing to witness her skillfully dodge the Ancient's questions, never falling for any of his traps.

Abaddon had later given Cain a subtle nod of approval, clearly supportive of his choice of consort. Cain couldn't claim he'd craved or even wanted such approval, but it was still nice to have it.

He suspected that one of the things about her which most impressed Abaddon was that she wasn't intimidated by him. People always found Abaddon daunting—the residents of Devil's Cradle were no exception; they'd given him plenty of space when Dantalion earlier gave him a tour of both the underground city and the town above them.

The people had been shocked when Cain gave his speech, informing them of Abaddon's existence. But they'd otherwise taken the news well, according to his aides. After all, the presence of an additional Ancient meant that Devil's Cradle was now even safer.

Cain knocked back the last of his brandy, set down his glass, and looked at his consort. "Are you going to tell me what's playing on your mind? You hid it well from Abaddon, but you're distracted by something."

She bit the inside of her cheek. "You won't like it."

His scalp prickled at her grave expression, and his creature's head snapped up. "Maybe not. But that doesn't mean you should have to hold it inside." He gently cupped her chin. "Don't ever feel the need to dance around my feelings or moods or beliefs, Wynter. I would much rather you always shared your burdens with me, even if I won't like them, than for you to choose another person to confide in."

Letting out a heavy breath, she twisted in her chair. "Okay, I'll tell you. But I need you to make me a promise first."

He narrowed his eyes. "What sort of promise?"

"That you won't contact Kali about this."

He ran his tongue along the inside of his lower lip. "All right."

She let out a soft snort. "That's not enough, Cain. Nor was it very convincing." She held out her hand, which currently crackled with magick. "Promise you won't contact Kali after you hear what I have to say."

His hackles rose. He didn't like this. Not at all. "You intend to *literally* hold me to my vow? You don't trust me to keep it?"

"It's not a matter of trust. It's a matter of my knowing that you won't react well to what I tell you, and I need to be sure you won't do something rash."

He searched her eyes, seeing no room for negotiation there. "This news you have is truly that awful?"

"More like 'concerning'."

His inner alarms were blaring, warning him that her revelation would be far more than concerning, despite what she claimed. His consort had a tendency to downplay certain things.

He did not whatsoever like that he'd be magickly bound to not react freely to what he would learn, but there was no way he could turn her down. He needed to know what had put that grave look on her face, and his presently uneasy creature wouldn't rest until it knew.

Shifting in his seat so that he better faced her, Cain clasped her hand and vowed, "I promise not to contact Kali after hearing what you tell me." Black flecks of magick swirled around their joined palms, and he *felt* the restriction click into place. His creature didn't much like it, but it only grumbled its disapproval.

Cain didn't release her hand. He instead gave it a supportive squeeze and urged, "Tell me."

Both surprised and pleased that he hadn't put up a struggle to back his promise with magick, Wynter rubbed nervously at her thigh. "First, I want to explain why I didn't say anything about this last night. It was a threefold thing."

"Threefold?"

"Yes. One, I was spooked and struggling to take it all in. Two, I knew it was going to piss you off—I wasn't ready for that conversation; wasn't able to fully explain to you what I hadn't yet managed to process. Three, you hadn't seen your uncle in eons, I wanted the reunion to be something *good*. You didn't have that when Eve came here, your relationship with her is too complicated. But I could see that it was different with you and Abaddon. I didn't want to spoil it."

His face went all warm and lazy. "My sweet witch." He leaned forward and pressed a soft kiss to her mouth. "How about I make this easier for you? I suspect that what you're going to tell me is that Kali has been leading you to the grotto all along and She possessed you last night to wake Abaddon. Am I right?"

She dragged in a deep breath, wishing it were that simple. "Uh, no. She wanted to wake him. She played a part in it. But so did I. Sort of."

He squinted. "Sort of?"

"I didn't do it alone. The voice that led me to the grotto and spoke to me when I woke from my sleepwalking escapade was the male voice from my dreams. It coaxed me to put my hand into the spring.

I wasn't keen on the idea. I thought about going back to the Keep and telling you I'd been led there. But I wanted to know what the voice was so damn interested in showing me."

"So you did as it asked."

She nodded. "And then something weird happened. Like *seriously* weird. There was a brief interaction between Kali and my monster—I couldn't make out what message She gave it. But mere moments later, my entity rose up and . . . well, it joined its soul with mine."

Every muscle in his body locked tight, Cain blinked. "Say that latter part again."

"Our souls joined. Only for a few moments but—"

"When you say 'joined'," he began, dread building in his gut, "you don't mean it merely pressed its soul tightly against yours?"

She slowly shook her head. "The two merged. Fused into one."

Cain's insides seized and twisted. He wanted to say it wasn't possible. Wanted to believe she must have been mistaken. But he'd never been one to blind himself to something simply because he didn't like what he'd heard. "Then what?" he bit out.

"The entity's power poured into me, reacted *with* mine like two chemicals crazily clashing . . . and I guess that then caused Abaddon to wake."

Unable to sit still, Cain abruptly pushed out of his chair and stalked away from the table. Pain pulsed through his jaw at how tightly he clenched it. His creature predictably lost its mind, not a rational thought in its head. "You should have told me this before."

"I already explained why I waited."

He shot her a hard look. "None of your reasons fully justify keeping something as serious as this from me. Especially your claim to have been spooked. Nothing spooks you—an assertion you yourself made several times."

"No, I said I'm not *easily* spooked. And I'm not. But last night, I was a little freaked. My monster has always been separate from me. It's never done anything like that before. I felt a whole bunch of things—confused, violated, weirded out, even betrayed. I wanted a little time to process it all."

His blood hot, his body tight, Cain paced up and down. He tasted anger with every breath. Felt it course through his system with every beat of his heart. "You know what this means, don't you? It means Kali can still take you from me. All She'd need to do is instruct the entity to merge its soul with yours, and then She could drag you both to the netherworld."

Wynter stood. "But you could do something to stop that from happening, right? You could protect my soul somehow. I mean, you *own* it."

If there was room in his system for any emotion other than deadly rage, he would have been touched at her faith in him and his ability to protect her. "Having full ownership of your soul won't be enough in this instance," said Cain, still pacing.

"But—"

"Kali owns the soul of whatever monster you host or, if nothing else, has full control of it. If that entity merged with you, yanked you to the netherworld, and then didn't break that merge, I could of course pull on your soul to drag you back. But, just the same, Kali could keep pulling on the monster's soul and, thus, yours. Between the two of us, we'd be fighting over who gets to keep you. I don't know for sure that I could beat Her at a push-and-pull contest."

Wynter bit down on her lower lip hard enough he wouldn't have been surprised if she'd drawn blood.

Bringing himself to an abrupt halt, Cain raked a hand through his hair. "We need to speak with Her. Now."

Wynter gave him a pointed look. "You promised."

Cain advanced on her fast. "Why the fuck would you have *wanted* me to promise not to contact Kali about this? You don't care if She takes you?"

"You know I do. Don't be a dick. The problem is that what you most want right now is for Her to drop what plans She has for me. We both know you'll insist on it if you speak with Her. Just as we both know She isn't going to dance to your tune." Wynter lifted a brow. "Remember what She once said to you? She warned you that She'd tolerate your presence in my life unless you tried interfering with Her plans."

Cain bared his teeth, and his creature hissed long and loud. "I don't give a *shit* what She's prepared to tolerate."

"That's my point."

His monster lunged quickly, fighting for supremacy with such vigor Cain almost flinched. Struggling to maintain control of it, Cain backed away from Wynter. "Give me a minute," he said through gritted teeth.

She didn't argue or approach him, so maybe she sensed the current danger. Not that his creature would hurt her. But it *would* bite her. Would take another step toward binding with her, determined to somehow ensure that she remained locked to its side. Not that tying her life-force with that of his monster would be enough, but the creature didn't much care to think rationally right then.

Once it threw up its metaphorical hands and stopped fighting, Cain took a deep, steadying breath.

"You okay?" Wynter asked, her voice soft.

"Yes." Cain cricked his neck. "My creature isn't quite stable right now. It doesn't react well at the best of times to the emotions you make it feel. It's never been so attached to another person, and it's not very good at handling any situation where it feels it could lose you." Not that Cain was much better. "What your monster did to you last night ... we can't ignore that, Wynter. We can't ignore what it means."

"We also can't confront Kali the way you want to."

Cain felt his nostrils flare. "Regardless of what She might want to believe, my claim to you runs deeper than Hers ever could."

"But that's not how She sees it. And it doesn't change that She has a way to still take me from you. So let's not tempt Her to do that."

Cursing beneath his breath, he scrubbed a hand down his face.

"Before last night, I might have thought She'd never truly take me away from you; might have believed that She wouldn't want to hurt me that way. But when She urged my monster to merge with me, She didn't bother to warn me, She clearly wasn't concerned for how I might freak the fuck out. She just did it." Wynter swallowed. "It was the first time I've ever really felt like I was just a tool to Her."

The note of pain in her voice pierced the rage fogging his mind like nothing else could have. Struggling to be gentle, Cain drew her to him, curling his arms around her. "I don't believe you're merely a tool to Her. She's too invested in you for that to be the case. But that doesn't change who or what She is. A deity. A being that will never consider us Her equals. I doubt She'd even *think* to consider your feelings before acting on Her own."

"Is there something you can do to protect my soul from it ever again merging with my monster like that?"

"I can protect it from souls who exist *outside* your body—I already do purely by owning it so completely. But a soul that your body acts as a vessel for? No. You might be two separate beings, but you are connected in a fashion."

Her brow creased. "I don't know if I'd say we were connected."

"You once told me that you feel its emotions. You know when it wants something. You can sense if it's sleeping. You feel it when the monster wakes. It's an independent entity, but you both share something that is a similar yet preternaturally advanced version of a twin bond."

Wynter inwardly cursed. She hadn't looked at the situation that way before. She didn't like the implications. "Back onto the subject of your creature . . . You read up a lot on the tying of life-forces, but you never brought it up. I'm guessing none of the books held the answers we're looking for."

"They didn't, no," he confirmed. "But I'll keep searching."

"You discovered something you don't like," she sensed. "Something that has stopped you from pushing me on this."

Irritation flared in his eyes in that telling way that said he didn't like how well she'd read him. "It's not something I discovered, it's something that Seth said. He pointed out that if I was to die while your life-force was tied to that of my monster, it could possibly drain you to the extent that you die and are too weak to come back."

Huh. She hadn't considered that. "Do you think he's right?"

"I have no idea. My creature doesn't think so, but it's not a source I trust on this matter—it wants to bind with you so badly there's a chance it won't apply logic to the situation."

Sighing, she slipped her arms around his waist and held tight; needing comfort, giving it. "I can promise you one thing: if my monster does try to pull me back to the netherworld, I won't make it easy. I will have to be dragged there kicking and screaming and cursing. I will do everything I can to fight it."

Cain's arms contracted around her. "I will hold you to that promise." He looked toward the door at the sound of knuckles rapping on it. "Come in," he called out without first releasing her—not something she'd expected, since PDAs weren't generally his thing.

Maxim breezed inside the room, his expression odd.

Cain exhaled heavily. "What now?"

"Sorry to disturb you, Sire, but the conduit is back." Maxim hesitated. "He says that Adam wishes to speak to both you and Wynter."

Cain stilled. "Is that so?" he drawled, so much menace in his voice it sent a shiver down her spine.

"The blue parlor is occupied, so I placed him in the parlor beside it," said Maxim.

"I'll be there shortly."

Once the aide was gone, Wynter looked up at Cain and corrected, "*We'll* be there shortly. No, don't argue. I won't be unsafe. Adam can't hurt me in a psychic space."

Cain's jaw tightened. "He'll try to convince you to give yourself up."

"You don't think that would actually work, do you? I'm not like those idiots you see in movies who give themselves up to the bad guy to save everyone else. I know for an absolute fact that handing myself over to Adam would achieve nothing. I know it wouldn't keep you or anyone here safe. And I'm not noble enough to do that anyway."

Cain's expression gentled. "Yes, you are." He stroked a hand over her hair. "But in this case, you wouldn't do such a thing—I know that. It's simply instinct for me to not want Adam anywhere near you."

"Physically, he won't be. And like I pointed out before, he can't harm me in a psychic space. So let's get this over with so we can go to bed and fuck each other's brains out."

His lips quirked. "I like how you think." He took her hand in his. "Here's where you find out how I get to the manor so quickly without using the elevator."

She smiled. "About damn time." The last thing she'd expected was that she'd have to walk through a mirror. As he followed behind her, stepping into a bedroom at the manor, she blew out a breath and said, "I had *not* seen that coming."

Humor lit his eyes. "Good. You surprise me often. It's only right that it's a two-way street."

"I'm not sure I agree with that."

Downstairs, Cain led her straight to the parlor but didn't enter. "Remember," he began, "Adam has no idea that you're my consort. Let's keep it that way. I don't want him more focused on you than he already is."

She gave a short nod and tugged on her sleeve, ensuring that Cain's seal was well-hidden.

Inside the room, Wynter greeted the conduit, vaguely recognizing him from her years at Aeon. He was an okay dude. A little spineless, though.

The moment she pressed her fingertips to his and entered the all-white psychic space, Wynter fixed her gaze on Adam. It was hard not to sneer. She *loathed* this motherfucker. Loathed him with a glorious passion.

He was responsible for so much, including her mother's death in an indirect way. But what Wynter most hated him for was the torment he'd caused Cain over the years. She truly couldn't wait to see this asshole breathe his last.

As she and Cain took the two seats that faced him, Adam continued to stare at her, pointedly ignoring her consort. She inwardly snorted. Did the Aeon honestly believe that Cain would be bothered by the petty snub? If so, he truly did not know her guy at all.

"Wynter Dellavale," Adam drawled. "I would say 'we meet at last,' but I do recall seeing you at Aeon from time to time. I don't believe we have ever before spoken to each other, though, have we?"

"No, we haven't," she replied. "To what do I owe this not-so-great honor?"

His lips slightly thinned, but he quickly blanked his expression. "You have caused me many problems. In cursing your homeland, you essentially betrayed it. Betrayed your people."

"They betrayed me first."

"Your old coven is now dead, though. It was in fact you who killed them."

Actually, she'd killed *most* of them. She'd then trapped her old Priestess in the netherworld. Wynter wasn't sure what had happened to the bitch in that place. Hopefully lots of dark and scary things. *Fingers crossed.*

"Likewise, the boys who hurt you long ago are dead. Those at Aeon who wronged you have paid the price," Adam went on. "You could easily undo the curse rather than punish everyone else there."

"But it wasn't only my coven who made my life difficult. The mages did their fair share of that, and they were worse. You or any of the other Aeons could have put an end to it. You didn't. Instead, *I* was the one who was exiled. Only an exile isn't truly a banishment. It's a straight-up execution. An execution I'd done nothing to deserve.

"Yet, Lailah ordered it anyway. And she couldn't have done that without your say-so. Which means *you're* also responsible for my near death. You had God only knows how many people unjustly 'exiled' over the eras. In truth, Aeon lost its true beauty a millennia ago, after it slowly became infected by the godly arrogance you Aeons have."

Beside her, Cain chuckled.

Adam's face hardened, but he still made a point of not looking at the Ancient. "Well, you certainly made the land and its people pay, Miss Dellavale. Is it really necessary to drag out this 'lesson' you wish to teach us?"

She cocked her head. "Necessary? No. Satisfying? Oh, yes."

His green eyes briefly blazed at her. "You have no idea what you have done. None. If Aeon falls, we will all suffer for it."

"I don't see how."

He opened his mouth but then quickly snapped it shut.

"It seems to me that if there was *really* some great big reason why Aeon shouldn't fall, you'd have told everyone about it by now. Yet, you haven't elaborated. So I'm pretty inclined to think that you're talking out of your ass. But if I'm wrong, please do enlighten me."

His fingers flexed. "Would you really die for the Ancients, Miss Dellavale? That is what will happen if you are still at Devil's Cradle when the war begins. No one there will be left alive. But if you come to me and undo the curse, I will spare you. You will be free to leave Aeon and continue with your life."

She shot him a look of pure disbelief. "You don't honestly think I'll believe that, do you?" He couldn't. Surely not.

"I can draw up a binding contract, if you wish."

"Yeah, and there'll be loopholes galore. Sorry, I'm going to have to turn down your offer."

"Then you are foolish."

"Funny. I was thinking the same thing about you. But although you're many things, Adam, you're not foolish." Which was a shame, really, because defeating the Aeons would otherwise have been so much easier. "You knew I wouldn't accept your offer. Even if I had, the Ancients wouldn't have let me leave Devil's Cradle—you're well aware of that, too. So why did you really call me here?"

He didn't respond. Merely stared at her.

She tilted her head. "Let me guess . . . you wanted to get a good look at me; to get a sense of whether or not I truly am Favored by Kali. It doesn't seem possible to you. You can't see how you wouldn't have sensed it long ago or how I'd be different from other revenants. But you can't think why else the curse would be something you simply can't beat."

He flapped a dismissive hand. "You are not a revenant. I know that much for certain. I had hoped to here and now detect just what it is you *really* are." He folded his arms and lifted his chin, all pompous. "I had some of my people look into your background. You have never met your father, have you? Your mother refused to speak of him to anyone who asked, but my people were able to find out who and where he is."

"So?"

Adam's brows dipped. "So wouldn't you like to know the identity of your father?"

"Can't say that I do, no." It was pure truth. "After all, he was never a father to me. Just a sperm donor, really."

She didn't believe for a single moment that Adam had any clue who her father was anyway. And if the Aeon thought it would be this easy to manipulate her into doing his bidding, she was seriously insulted.

"I suppose it is good for you that you feel that way," said Adam. "Not so much for him, however. I had him brought here. He is not very . . . comfortable at the moment. But you can change that. Give yourself up, and I will free him."

"Nah."

Adam's arms unfolded. "You cannot expect me to believe that his life means nothing to you."

"Why? I got the impression that the lives of *your* blood relatives don't always mean much to *you*. Besides, I don't think you really are keeping the sperm donor captive."

"I assure you, witch, I am not calling your bluff. I have him in my dungeon."

"Right," she said, all skepticism. The Aeon would have been the epitome of smug if that were genuinely the case.

"I rather think he'll be most disappointed to learn that his daughter cares so little for him."

"There are few people in this world I care about. My father has never been one of them. The only parent who mattered to me was my mother. She was the only person throughout my childhood who I was truly able to count on. Your son, Abel, sentenced her to death. Which means *you* initially cast down that sentence. *You* took her from me. So no amount of bribes, threats, or attempts at emotional blackmail would make me give you a single fucking thing that you want."

Cain smiled. "Really, Adam, you cause these messes for yourself. I do thank you for pissing her off so spectacularly and then pretty much driving her to seek sanctuary here. Your help in this matter has not gone unrecognized or unappreciated, I assure you." He glanced at Wynter. "I think we're done here."

"I agree," she said.

As one, they both withdrew from the psychic space.

Cain dismissed everyone in the parlor, including the conduit, before then turning to her. "Are you all right?"

"Yes. It's just, ugh, I *hate* that fucker."

Cain felt his lips twitch. "You're not alone in that. I wanted to intervene a few times, but I didn't want to chance that he'd sense you mean something to me."

"I don't believe he really has my father in his custody."

"Neither do I. Adam can be a smug bastard. He likes to gloat. Back there, he wasn't gloating. It was more like he was fishing, testing to see if you'd care to save a father you've never met—Adam would have interpreted that as a weakness."

"That was the feeling I got."

"If it had seemed that you *would* care, he'd have searched high and low for your father in order to use him against you. You made it clear he'd be wasting his time." Cain tipped his head to the side.

"But you and I both know that you wouldn't truly have been so indifferent in such a situation, don't we?"

"I wouldn't have been indifferent, no. But I wouldn't have given Adam what he wanted. *No way* would I have traded the lives of you, my coven, and everyone here for the freedom of a man who never gave a single shit about me or my mother. I'm really not as honorable as you seem to think."

Oh, she was. She merely didn't like to acknowledge that soft underbelly she possessed. She was also used to hiding her true self—she'd been doing it for most of her life to stay under the radar.

Setting her hands on her hips, she shook her head in wonder. "After all that's happened, Adam still won't accept that I'm a revenant."

"To do that would be to accept that he had no idea, despite that you'd lived at Aeon at one time. It would also be to accept that he'd been foolish to doubt your word and your connection to Kali. Adam is far too egotistical to face that he was wrong about anything without solid proof."

"The way I see it, that's a good thing. If he doesn't believe I'm a revenant, he won't be ready to *deal* with a revenant. That gives me an edge where he's concerned. I like having an edge."

Cain flicked up a brow. "You envision you and Adam going head to head? That won't happen, baby. I plan to take up *all* of his attention. Besides, he won't want to battle with you, he'll want to capture you so he can force you to do his bidding."

"And that will be his mistake."

"Yes. Yes, it will." Cain frowned as a crack of thunder came from outside. A thunder that was unnatural. Familiar. "Adam." *For fuck's sake.*

Cain stormed out of the parlor with Wynter hot on his heels. They rushed down the long hallway and out of the manor's front door.

"... understand it is not easy to betray one of your own people," said Adam, his face a flashing image in the storm cloud high above the town. "I understand why you would all hesitate to accept my offer. But Wynter Dellavale is not worth your sacrifice. She is, how-ever, worth two million dollars as of now. That is right. I am upping the bounty. Cash in on it if you dare." With that, he was gone.

Wynter gaped. "That son of a bitch. I'll kill him. I will mother-fucking kill him."

No, she wouldn't. Cain's monster would get there first.

Chapter Twenty

"Why are you looking at me like that?"

Chewing the last of her bagel a few days later, Wynter shrugged at Cain. "I'm just surprised by your request, I guess." Well, it had been more of a declaration of intent, but still. "Very surprised, in all honesty."

He set his mug down on the bedchamber's table. "Why?"

"You got to know my coven a little but, for the most part, you've stayed separate from the witch-side of my life."

"Not out of disinterest. It's like how you haven't asked to be part of my day-to-day business. It's not a slight, is it? You simply have other responsibilities. A coven to lead. A shop to run. A position you can never neglect. You wouldn't wish to push any of that aside to attend meetings with me, deal with complaints from or issues among those in my service, interview potential new residents, or go through my heaps of paperwork."

She definitely wouldn't. Not merely because it sounded boring as fuck and she was a busy girl, or even because to not keep a close eye on her coven could possibly be disastrous. But because it would be pointless—it was all quite simply *Ancient business*. She was no Ancient.

"Just the same, I can't neglect my own duties," he continued. "But I will when it counts. And I know the Samhain Feast is important to you, so I'd like to attend it with you and your coven."

Touched that he not only acknowledged its importance to her but wanted to share in that with her, Wynter said, "I'll be happy to have you there."

Warmth filled his eyes. "Good."

The Samhain ball, which would begin tomorrow on All Hallows' Eve in the city's hall, was exclusively for magick users and their partners. A separate gala would occur in the town up above for the rest of the residents. Both events would mark the end of the Halloween celebrations. Sadly.

"The ball won't be over until after sunset November first," she told him. "What time will you have to leave?"

"The other Ancients and I decided we'd try at midnight."

Wise choice, since both magick and power were more potent then.

"I'd like you to be there when we attempt to fracture the cage."

Her brows lifted. "You would?"

"Yes. I know it's not fair to ask that you leave the ball early, but I believe that your assistance could make a difference. Your magick is dark. It causes things to burn and rot and decay. If we add it to the power of the Ancients and the Aeons, it could truly help damage the cage."

"Then of course I'll be there." Maybe it would make a difference just as he thought, maybe it wouldn't, but she'd give it her best shot. She glanced at the clock on the shelf and then gulped down the last of her coffee. "Time for me to get dressed."

Standing, he helped her place their dishware and napkins back on the tray, which he then set on top of the dresser. "I haven't finished my breakfast yet," he said.

Wynter felt her brow wrinkle. "Huh?"

He fisted her shirt and yanked her close, his gaze darkening with need and intent. Then his mouth was on hers. He didn't roughly devour her as she'd expected. He sipped, licked, nibbled, savored. Like she was a dessert he wanted to take his time enjoying. They didn't *have* time.

Still, she felt herself melting, lured into that warm, sensuous, exquisitely languid place where nothing but pleasure existed ... only realizing he'd lifted her when she felt her bare ass meet the wooden table. "Dammit, Cain, you'll make me late."

"Not this morning, little witch. This is going to be fast. I just need to get you nice and wet first." He gripped the hand he'd marked and pressed his thumb into the center of the brand.

She jolted with a gasp, feeling like the digit was now buried in her body. He kissed her hard and deep as he played with her pussy using her mark. His mouth wasn't soft and tentative this time. It was hungry. Urgent. Demanding.

She braced her hands on the table, unconsciously lifting her hips to meet the phantom thumb—she couldn't help it. That thumb swiped, stroked, flicked, swirled, and probed. God, she was so damn wet, and she needed more.

Cain crouched in front of her and licked at her slit. "I can see your pussy spasm and clench as it tries gripping a cock that isn't there." He rolled his tongue around her clit. "Let's fix that, shall we?"

Yes, let's.

He stood, released her hand, and freed his cock from his pants. "Lay back. Good girl." He lodged the head of his cock inside her, his eyes two pools of heat and menace. "You're going to hurt for me this morning. You're gonna hurt so hard." He slammed home, ruthlessly stretching her to bursting. "And you'll come just as hard."

His jaw tight, he gripped her shoulders and pounded that long, thick cock into her pussy again and again. Fast and aggressive, he plundered and ruled her as blatantly as always. The message was never anything but abundantly clear—he owned her, and he could take and do what he wanted. Which she'd have totally slapped him for if she hadn't gotten off on it.

Her breath caught as a ripple of pleasure/pain scraped along her soul like blunt nails—they stung. Burned. Set her nerve-endings on fire.

She hissed as more "nails" scored her soul—harder this time. "Fuck, Cain."

"You like it. You want more. Don't you?"

"Yes," she bit out.

A decadent assault on her soul began. There were no waves of pure pleasure. He struck her with outpourings of dark, electric sensation. Hot smacks. Cold bites. Prickly thrashes. Fiery scrapes.

It was raw and wicked and intoxicating. It pushed her into that oh so familiar hazy place where she felt like she was soaring. Drunk. Bodiless.

Cain felt his balls begin to ache as her eyes completely glazed over. Tightening his hold on her shoulders, he upped his pace, fucking in and out of her so savagely it was nothing short of animalistic.

She bucked and arched beneath him, moaning and whimpering, scratching at the table. The slapping sounds of her breasts bouncing, his cock hitting her slick core, and his balls tapping her ass filled the room.

His pace now close to feverish, he tunneled deep into her pussy with every thrust, all the while still pleasuring her soul and dazing her mind. He overloaded her with sensation on every level—mental, physical, soul-deep—wanting her to feel like there was no part of her he couldn't touch. No part he couldn't possess. No part that didn't belong to him.

His creature urged him on, just as possessive, wanting to see her explode beneath them. It also wanted to sink its teeth into her skin but, unscrupulous though it might be, it would never force its mark on her—not while in full control of itself anyway.

Feeling her pussy blaze and clasp his dick tighter, Cain plunged faster and inundated her soul with more pleasure that was edged with pain. Her breaths came quicker. Her skin flushed deeper. Tears gathered in her eyes, making his balls draw up tight. He groaned, slamming harder.

"I can't take any more," she sobbed. "I'm gonna come."

He grunted. "Then come."

She imploded, her head falling back, her spine arching, a broken scream clawing its way out of her throat. Her pussy clamped down on his cock with a scorching, tight, rippling grip that swept him under, throwing him into a release so powerful it all but poleaxed him.

*

An hour later, Wynter breezed into the cottage with Cain close behind her. Since Adam upped the bounty a few days ago, Cain had taken it upon himself to escort her to and from work. She hadn't argued, since it didn't bother her and she knew he needed this.

There'd been no further attempts to cash in on the bounty. Also, there'd been no more attempts by her monster to join their souls. Nor had there been any more weird communications between the entity and Kali. All of which was a humungous relief. But she was still on her guard.

"Morning all," Wynter greeted as she entered the kitchen, finding her coven scattered around the room. "Sorry I'm late."

"*Almost* late," Cain corrected. "You've got two minutes before you need to open up the shop."

"Exactly. Not enough time to have a cup of tea and check that nothing's on fire."

Sitting at the table shuffling his tarot cards, Xavier sighed. "I really wish you'd have more faith in us. The cottage is intact. Nothing is broken. No one is injured. Both last night and this morning went without incident."

"Then why is there a scorch mark on the floor?"

Delilah, Anabel, and Xavier all glanced down at the spot where Wynter was pointing. Hattie, however, didn't seem to be paying attention—leaning against the counter, she had her face practically buried in her book.

"Well?" Wynter prodded.

No one responded. They simply went back to what they were doing, keeping their gazes averted.

Sighing, she looked at the witch carefully stirring her bubbling cauldron while seeming overly casual. "Anabel, want to tell me what happened?"

The blonde whirled with a soft curse, wringing her hands. "Why would you automatically assume it was me?"

"Because it was you. When it comes to fires and burns and scorch marks, it's *always* you."

"You and logic," Anabel grumbled. "I'll get rid of it, I swear."

Wynter went to question her further, but then a cup of tea was pushed into her hand. She smiled. "Thank you, Del."

"You're welcome, dear Priestess." Delilah looked from her to Cain. "Since you've both got a well-fucked air going on, I don't have to ask why you're late."

"*Almost* late," Cain repeated.

Pulling a face, Delilah shrugged one shoulder. "It's sort of the same thing, though, isn't it?"

Anabel frowned at her. "No, it's not. There's late. And there's *not* late."

"There's normal. Then there's *you*." Delilah gathered her stock of cosmetics out of a cupboard. "I don't know how you cope with yourself."

"I could say the same to you," the blonde shot back.

Cain drew Wynter close and pressed a soft kiss to her mouth. "I'll come see you at some point today."

Xavier held up a hand. "I'll be standing guard over her the whole time."

Cain gave a satisfied nod and then tapped her nose with his finger. "Be good." He gave her another quick kiss. "I'll see you soon."

Wynter watched him leave, taking a moment to admire all that latent strength and raw sexuality stalking through her home and out of the door.

"That ass . . ." Hattie let out a dreamy sigh.

Wynter whirled on her. "Seriously?"

The old woman lifted her shoulder. "Can I help it if he has such a fabulous behind that there's no ignoring it?"

"Just be glad she hasn't fondled it," Delilah told Wynter. "If I didn't find him so terrifying, I'd be jealous that you have him in your bed. Well, at least someone's getting laid."

Hattie frowned. "I get laid all the time."

"No need to throw it in my face," said Delilah.

Popping a cork into a vial of potion, Anabel turned to the Latina. "You know what your problem is in this department?"

Delilah shrugged. "Enlighten me."

"You're too picky," said Anabel. "No guy quite meets your standards. And you do that typical cat thing where you let only 'the chosen' close. Everyone else? You look upon them with pure disdain most of the time."

"It's true, Del," said Wynter. "Although ... I have seen you slide Dantalion the occasional look when you're sure he won't notice."

Delilah snorted. "The man rarely notices anyone but the other Ancients. I wouldn't get involved with him in any case. The Ancients make me too nervous. No offense, Wyn, but I still don't understand how you can relax enough around one to have sexytimes with him."

"They make it worth it." Or Cain did, anyhow.

Delilah smiled. "Hmm, I'll bet."

The workday went like any other. Wynter had gotten used to having Xavier with her, and it was actually nice to have his company throughout the day. They had a blast exchanging smack talk. The dude plain made her laugh. More, he made her forget just *why* he was there.

Cain came to see her at noon. He ate lunch with her and her coven before then heading off to attend to more business, promising he'd return when it was time for her to walk to his Keep.

Shortly before he was due to arrive, Wynter helped her coven count their earnings and note down whatever they'd received in trade. They preferred to keep track of everything. While the others were debating who'd get what from the selection of traded items, Wynter grabbed the trash bags and carried them out the back door and round to the side of the cottage.

She came to a sharp halt as two male fey abruptly *appeared* in front of her. Before she even had a moment to react, a wave of magick slammed into her, clogging her nostrils and pouring down her throat. It was thick. Sickly-sweet. Cloying, like too-strong perfume.

Her thoughts hazed as a fog built in her mind, insidiously slinking into every corner. A familiar otherworldly breeze washed over her skin, vibrating with urgency. Her monster pushed at her skin, wanting out. But Wynter . . . *damn* if she didn't feel floaty right now. Even a little tipsy. But not in a good way. No, in a way that made her feel weak and weary.

And yet, she felt happy. A silly kind of happy. Like she was caught up in a warm, merry dream.

"It's all right, it's just Cain and Seth," said a male voice.

Her vision swam, blurred into a collage of smudged colors, and then sharpened once more. She double-blinked. Oh it wasn't fey, she realized. It was just Cain and Seth.

She smiled up at them, rocking back on her heels. "Hey. Gotta say, I'm feeling kind of drunk right now. What is up with that?"

"Nothing is up, honey," Cain assured her, resting his hand on her shoulder.

She felt her nose wrinkle. "Honey?" That was a new one. And it made her chortle to herself, though she didn't really know why.

Wynter's head sagged forward. *Whoops.* She frowned as she saw the bottom half of her body. What was with the dress? What had happened to her jeans? And why was the hair dangling around her face auburn?

Questions for the ages.

"The glamor spell won't last long, so let's not waste time getting to the surface," said Cain.

She looked up at him, ready to ask what was happening. But then her stomach did a nauseating flip. "I don't feel so good."

That breeze came again, *slapping* at her skin this time, demanding her attention. Jeez, she was kind of busy here. Freaking deities thought they were the only ones with lives.

"You're just tired," Cain told her, his voice low and full of assurance. "Come on, let's get you home and put you to bed."

"Okay," she said softly, wishing her monster would stop freaking out over jack shit.

Cain curled his arm around her shoulders and *blurred* them across the bailey and into the Keep.

Wynter's stomach lurched. *Oh, fuck.* Convinced she'd puke all over him if they didn't stop, she shoved hard at Cain. They both stumbled to a stop in one of the Keep's many hallways.

Wynter pressed a hand to her stomach. "I think I'm gonna hurl."

"No, you won't, you're fine," said Seth, urging her forward. "We'll just walk at a normal pace now."

Cain frowned. "But—"

"If she spews up her guts, it'll attract attention," Seth said quietly. "We don't want that."

Feeling her brow furrow, Wynter looked up at him. "Say what?"

Seth gave her a shaky smile. "Well, you don't want people seeing you vomit, do you? It's very unladylike."

Okay, that *would* be embarrassing.

A horse whinnied somewhere close by. *A horse?* In the Keep?

She frowned ... and suddenly her surroundings smeared and shifted as the walls peeled away. Outside. She was outside. And she was approaching one of the city's towers.

She blinked. "Why are we ..." She trailed off as the hallway walls slammed back up as if they'd never been gone.

What the hell?

Wynter shook her head hard, unable to properly think. Process. Reason. It was like she had no grip on reality. Like the Keep wasn't solid around her. It made no sense.

Cain stopped near the door to their chamber and briefly touched the wall ... as if pressing a button or something. Seth began tapping one foot like crazy, repeatedly throwing looks over his shoulder. Why was the dude even here?

He'd better not be hoping for a threesome. The thought made her snicker.

Her surroundings briefly wavered, like the flicker of a faulty bulb, and she saw a flash of an elevator door. The image was there and gone *lightning* fast.

Wynter closed her eyes and pressed down on her eyelids. "Why are we waiting outside the chamber?" No one answered. Her monster kept on pitching a fit, and the otherworldly breeze again whipped at her face. *Ow.* "I thought I was going to bed."

"You are," said Cain. "See?"

She opened her eyes and watched the door to the chamber split into two and then each half slid to the side. Split. Into. Two. What the—

A blaring sound made her jump and hunch up her shoulders. An alarm was going off. And it was *loud*. Mega loud.

"Fuck," muttered Seth. "Let's go."

Cain roughly ushered her into their chamber. "Move."

"Don't be snippy with me," she snarked, frowning when he turned and started jabbing his thumb hard on the wall. "You're being *so weird* right now."

Everyone was being weird. Every*thing* was weird. Including her.

She still felt giddy. But it was false. Like the emotion had been planted there. Beneath it, she was confused, uneasy, and frustrated.

The two halves of the door began to meet—again moving sideways—and Cain's shoulders lowered in what appeared to be relief. He looked at her, his eyes dispassionate.

Dispassionate?

She tensed. Not even in the very beginning had he looked at her that way. He looked at most people that way, sure, but not her.

Something was so very wrong here.

His form shimmered. Flashed into something else for the merest moment. Into *someone* else. But then he was normal again. Only not. Because that detached look was still there.

Her uneasiness built, overriding the giddiness. *Not Cain.* No way.

Her surroundings flickered. Furnishings and walls shrank to nothing, revealing—

And then they were back.

She squeezed her eyes shut and shook her head. No, this wasn't real. It wasn't. But when she opened her eyes, nothing had changed.

Her monster shoved her hard, and a breeze swirled urgently

around her. Her vision swam again, becoming a swirl of colors . . . and they reformed into a whole other scene. The chamber walls were gone. The Ancients were gone. She was inside the city elevator, and two male fey were staring down at her.

Her surroundings tried changing again. She gritted her teeth as she mentally *clung* to the reality in front of her. Because it *was* reality. And as that belief firmly cemented in her brain, her uneasiness faded under the weight of a rapidly growing ice-cold rage.

Black ribbons glided over her eyeballs, obscuring her vision.

Both males stiffened.

She punched the emergency button, bringing the elevator to a sharp halt, and felt a cruel smile curve her mouth. "Boys, this was *such* a bad idea."

Her monster took over.

*

Azazel was on his feet as soon as he heard the alarm. Abandoning the mage who'd come to apply for residency, he stalked out of one of the manor's many parlors. This particular distress signal didn't warn of an upcoming invasion. It signaled a local emergency. And Azazel would bet it meant that Wynter was once again missing.

Fuck, Cain was going to lose his mind.

Azazel's step faltered in the hallway as another sound reached him. A roar. A spinetingling, not-of-this-world roar. It was coming from somewhere beneath him.

He quickly tracked the sound, walking further down the hallway, finding himself approaching the elevator. A few men had already gathered outside it, since the new protocol was for the elevator to be guarded if the alarm went off.

Azazel took in each face. The men looked varying stages of disturbed. Who wouldn't be? The roaring was still ongoing, interspersed with crunching sounds. A female cackle sounded, thick with an otherworldly power. *Deity*, he knew.

Azazel turned to one of the men. "Find Cain. Tell him we've located his consort. And be quick about it."

The male nodded and then took off at a fast pace.

Licking his lips, one of the other men looked at Azazel. "What do we do?"

Azazel folded his arms. "We wait."

Minutes went by before the roars and laughs stopped. Soon, the elevator whirred to life, moving upward.

The men shifted nervously, each holding orbs of magick.

Finally, the elevator smoothly came to a stop. A few seconds later, the shiny doors slid open. And there stood Wynter, a vision of blood and gore and battle-rage. Around her were crimson spatter, trails, and puddles. No bodies, though. Her monster had clearly devoured whoever had been stupid enough to tangle with her.

All dignity, she swiped aside her blood-stained bangs as she cleared her throat and stood back to give them room. "Going down?"

Azazel smiled. His friend's consort was nuts. He liked "nuts".

*

Stood in the middle of the street with Azazel while a livid Cain paced in front of the line of fey, Wynter slid her coven a quick look. They stood off to the side with a handful of aides—some in Cain's service, some in Azazel's—all seeming intent on remaining off her consort's radar right now.

It had come as no surprise that Cain went postal on hearing of her attempted kidnapping. He was still in that state now. Well, it was *his* version of postal—he hadn't lost his composure, but he vibrated with a cold, deadly rage that was all the more frightening because it was so unnaturally controlled. Such rage fairly illuminated his eyes, so it was truly understandable that none of the fey would meet his gaze.

He'd been intent on questioning every member of her

would-be-kidnappers' court to be sure they weren't in on the dumb plot. Considering no one would be stupid enough to admit to any guilt, it might have seemed pointless . . . but Cain was exceptionally good at picking up on lies.

They'd all pled ignorance, swearing they would never think to harm his consort. Wynter believed that the majority of them were in fact innocent. But there were a few whose claims didn't quite ring true for her. Cain must have had the same suspicions, because he called for the aforementioned fey to step forward.

The three males didn't so much take a step as *shuffle* slightly forward, sluggish and hesitant. The fey closest to the trio edged away from them, keeping their heads down.

One of the guilty opened his mouth to speak.

"Not a word," ordered Cain, his voice the lash of a whip. "You lied to me. All three of you. You knew of the plot to kidnap my consort and deliver her to the Aeons."

None denied it. *Wise.* There would have been no point.

"It matters not that you didn't aid the two members of your court in trying to snatch her," said Cain. "You could have reported the plan to me. Or to Wynter. Or to Azazel, since you are after all in his service. You could have warned *someone.* You didn't. You said nothing. You *did* nothing. And now, adding insult to injury, you dare lie to me to escape the punishment you deserve."

The guilty fey practically curled in on themselves.

"It may interest you to know that, as part of your punishment, Azazel has invited me to partake in administering that punishment."

Someone whimpered, and Wynter really couldn't blame them. The Shelia incident had made it clear that the Ancients did not fuck around when it came to disciplinary action—particularly Cain. But Wynter felt no sympathy for the fey, because they'd known the risks when they'd held their tongue and they'd done it anyway.

His lips trembling, one of the guilty fey looked at Cain. "We're—"

"*Quiet,*" Cain bit out. "There's not one thing you could say that would make me spare you or lessen the agony I intend to subject you to, so shut. The fuck. Up." He turned to Azazel. "I hope you won't object to my wish not to kill them *too* quickly."

"Oh no, that's good with me." Azazel turned to his aides. "Take them to the dungeon."

The aides were quick to obey, and they weren't gentle about it.

Cain made a beeline for Wynter, his face cold and hard as granite. He swallowed up her personal space but didn't touch her. "I might be a while."

"Take all the time you need." She had no issues with what he was about to do. Especially when she knew he couldn't afford to be lenient in such a situation.

Cain's gaze sliced to her coven. "Do not leave her side."

Xavier saluted him. "Oh, we don't intend to."

Cain gave Wynter one last look and then stalked off with Azazel.

Anabel blew out a breath. "Damn, Wyn, your man is *scary*."

Delilah nodded. "Utterly terrifying."

Not something Wynter could or would deny. She sighed, feeling all icky and tired of drowning in the smell of blood. "I need to go shower and stuff."

As they began to walk to the cottage, Hattie patted her arm. "I suggest a bath. Some hot tea. Maybe even a cupcake or two."

Sounded good. "So long as they're not your 'special cakes.' I'm not feeling in the mood to get high."

Hattie's nose wrinkled. "Not a sentiment I'll ever understand, dear, but all right."

Back in the cottage, Wynter trumped up the stairs and went straight to her en-suite bathroom. As much as the idea of a hot bath held a lot of appeal, she didn't want to soak in the blood and gunk that currently covered her. So after she'd peeled off her gross clothes and plucked any fleshy bits from her body that might clog the drain, she stepped into the shower stall and began to scrub herself clean.

Really, this happened far too often these days.

Stood under the hot spray as gore-stained soap bubbles slid down her body, Wynter tipped back her head and closed her eyes. Only then did she let herself feel the anger she'd boxed away in order to not fuel Cain's; only then did she let it heat her blood, tighten her jaw, and clench her gut.

She wasn't sure who she was most pissed at—those fucking fey for attempting to kidnap her, Adam for putting a damn bounty on her head, or herself for getting caught up in the snare so easily.

None too gently lathering her hair in shampoo, Wynter took in a long breath. Intellectually, she knew it was stupid to be mad at herself. After all, fey were experts at not only creating illusions but trapping people *inside* them. They simply made suggestive comments, and their victim's imagination filled in the details.

A witch from her old coven had once told Wynter how she'd been snared by a fey illusion as a child. It had apparently gone on for *days*. Cilla hadn't eaten or slept within that period, but she'd *thought* she had. If someone hadn't come along and helped Cilla snap out of it, she would have died.

Really, Wynter should probably be appeased by the fact that she hadn't been caught up in it for long. With a few slaps and shoves from Kali and her monster, she'd seen through the illusion and found her way back to reality. But stupid or not, it nonetheless bugged Wynter in a mega way that she'd played a part in her own snare.

The fey had introduced themselves as Cain and Seth, so she'd *seen* Cain and Seth.

The fey had told her they were heading to the Keep, so she'd *seen* the Keep.

Ugh.

Wynter rinsed off the shampoo and watched as pinkish foam slid down the drain. She had to give it to the two fey who came for her, they'd been ballsy as hell to risk Cain's wrath after the fate Shelia met. Well, an offer of two million dollars could make people do stupid things, couldn't it?

After another round of shampoo followed by conditioner, Wynter soaped her entire body one last time and—satisfied she was clean—switched off the spray. Once she'd wrapped a plush towel around her body and curled a smaller one around her rope of wet hair, she exited the bathroom . . . only to find a mug of steaming tea and three large cupcakes waiting on her nightstand.

The backs of her eyes stung. Those crazy bastards downstairs looked after her. They really did. And she adored them for it.

Between sips of tea, she made short work of the cupcakes. Only then did she dry herself off and pull on some clothes. She'd no sooner blow-dried her hair than Cain came stalking into the room. And if the menacing look he wore was anything to go by, the time he'd spent torturing the three fey had made him no less livid.

"Did they cry?" she asked him, setting both her brush and hair-dryer on the surface of her dresser. "Please tell me they cried."

"Cried. Screamed. Begged. Mewled like fucking kittens." Cain rolled back his shoulders and cricked his neck. "I'm so pissed right now I'm tempted to eradicate every member of their court irrespective of those members' innocence."

Uh-oh. "Yeah, it's best you don't do that."

His brow flicked up. "Why not?"

It was an honest question. And she didn't think that telling him "Well, it's wrong" would really make much of an impact while he was in this mood.

"People more easily risk their own lives than they do those they care for," he pointed out as he crossed to her. "If it's made clear that betraying me would lead to not only their own demise but that of their loved ones, just maybe they'll fucking think twice about doing it. My monster agrees it would be a terrific idea."

Well, of course the merciless shit did. "Not all the people in the courts and packs and covens actually care for each other, though. Some have only gathered together because there's safety in numbers." Wynter curled her arms around his neck and melted into him, hoping to calm and soothe him, but it was truly like pressing her body against a brick wall. "Besides, people *are* thinking twice before trying to cash in on the bounty."

He shot her a look of incredulity. "Today's events would suggest differently."

"Before that, it had been a while before anyone tried to kidnap me, though, hadn't it? And it wasn't until Adam upped the bounty that someone was tempted enough to take a chance. Considering the fey dramatically failed, I doubt anyone else will bother to try. But if you really want to be sure of that, torture your new fey prisoners in public the way you did Shelia."

He grunted. "I just might do that." Cupping her hips, he dropped his forehead to hers. "Thank fuck you sensed that you were trapped in an illusion, though I have no idea how you did. Fey magick is very powerful. You shouldn't have been able to see through it."

"I had a little help from my monster and Kali."

"Still, you technically shouldn't have seen flickers of reality around you as soon as you did. That shouldn't have happened for at least a few hours."

Wynter raised and then dropped her shoulder, feeling her mouth curve. "What can I say? I'm awesome that way." She trailed her fingertips over his nape. "Neither of us have had dinner yet, and the cupcakes I ate didn't fully hit the spot. Shall we go eat?"

He lifted his head. "I'd much rather slaughter the prisoners' entire court."

She could tell he genuinely meant it. Worse, he was sincerely considering it. "Hmm, how about you just fuck me instead?"

He gave her an imperious look. "Do you think you can distract me with sex?"

"What I think is that you'd find it a much more satisfying outlet than murdering innocent fey. Am I wrong?" *Please don't let me be wrong.*

The mouth he'd set into a harsh line very slowly began to curl. "No. No, you're not whatsoever wrong."

Thank God for that. "Then do me."

His eyes flared. "It'll be hard. Rough. You'll feel how pissed I am in every thrust, and you'll hurt for me. A lot."

"Promises, promises."

They were promises he lived up to.

Chapter Twenty-One

The following evening, Wynter breezed through the city hall with Cain and her coven as they searched for their allocated seats. The Samhain ball was in full swing. Most people sat at the rows of long-ass tables while others danced to the live folk music.

The decorations were more wicca than Halloween-y. Pumpkins, brooms, candles, and bells were scattered here and there, and some were even used as table centerpieces. The colors orange and black were of course used in the décor—orange to symbolize the dawning of light, and black to represent death and the fading of light.

A bonfire crackled in the middle of the hall. It wasn't natural, of course, it was a product of magick powered by the element of fire. It was thereby harmless, gave off no smoke, and could be extinguished by the click of someone's fingers . . . disappearing as if it had never been. Wynter was impressed.

As they located their seats, Hattie glanced around. "No butlers in the buff tonight either?" She sighed. "These people have no imagination."

Wynter rolled her eyes. "Sit, perve."

As they all claimed their designated seats—placing Wynter between Cain and Xavier—she looked up at the Ancient. His tension was visible in the hard line of his jaw. There was little chance of him being fully relaxed. After all, so many of his current plans rode on whether he was able to punch a hole through his cage tonight. She was a little on edge herself.

She suspected that some of the stiffness in his muscles was also due to the anger he hadn't yet fully shaken off after "the fey incident", as her coven referred to it. Not even torturing their pals in public earlier had eased his rage.

No doubt sensing she was watching him, Cain met her eyes. He splayed his hand on her thigh and gave it a little squeeze. "You okay?"

She nodded. "But you made me a promise before we left, and I've noticed you're not sticking to it," she teased. The promise? That he'd be a lot less tense if she sucked him off.

His lips curved. "I returned a . . . certain favor, though, didn't I?"

He had indeed eaten her out, making her come with his mouth alone. The orgasm had nonetheless been just as powerful as when he used every sexual weapon in his arsenal. Well, the dude had had a millennia to perfect his skills. They were nothing short of top-notch. "You did. And it was very much appreciated."

Delilah took a slice of the complimentary pumpkin bread from the basket in the center of the table. "I hope it's not long before the feast begins. Feeling kind of hangry over here." She bit into the bread and groaned. "Damn, this is good."

Hattie snatched a slice for herself and took a bite. "Mm, very good. Not as good as butlers in the buff would have been, but I suppose I'll have to take what I can get."

Wynter sighed. "Why do you always expect to see them at every celebration we attend?"

The old woman shrugged. "It only makes sense that they'd be included."

"It makes sense that guys would be wandering around naked as the day they were born?"

"It was what the Lord intended when he created us." Hattie grabbed the pitcher of apple cider and poured some into each of their glasses. "I was a nudist at one time, you know. Me and my Derek, God rest his soul, gave it a whirl. It was his idea. He wasn't able to keep it up for long, though."

"Why not?" asked Anabel.

"Well, he died," replied Hattie. "I had him buried naked, he would have wanted that. It meant we couldn't have an open casket, of course, but people understood." Sighing sadly, she slid her gaze to Cain. "I've lost a few husbands in my time. It was tragic that they only lived relatively short lives, but that was evidently God's plan for them."

"Or *yours*," said Delilah with a snort.

Hattie notched up her chin. "A divine power of some sort could have intervened on their behalf. None ever did. The only force that came for them was death itself."

"Did you feel its breath?" Anabel asked the old woman.

Her hand tightening on her glass, Delilah leaned toward the blonde. "*No one* feels it."

Anabel tossed her a teacher-to-student look. "Just because you haven't personally experienced something doesn't mean it isn't real."

"But you *didn't* experience it." Delilah tapped her temple. "It's all in your head."

Hattie turned to the blonde. "Very dismissive at times, isn't she? And so disapproving. As if it's her right to sit in judgment over the choices and actions of others."

"It is not only my right, it is my calling," insisted Delilah.

"Because a one-eyed, child-eating, human-sacrificing, bogey-witch said so?" Anabel let out a derisive snort. "Excuse me if we place no weight in her words."

As the two females continued to bicker, Wynter exchanged an amused look with Cain. It was as she began to turn away that she caught sight of some witches eyeing him warily. To be fair, quite a few guests were sliding nervous glances his way. It was no doubt thanks to the public punishment he'd earlier administered. Well, it had been pretty brutal. A statement that any who even *heard* of plans to harm her would be dealt with harshly if they didn't report it.

A message that had been very clearly received.

Not wanting to think on negative stuff right now, Wynter turned her attention back to the ball. The overall celebration had begun at dusk with a parade that featured lots of lavish floats and scary costumes. Not all magick-users had attended. Some preferred to hold private feasts or even threw by-invitation-only house parties. To each their own.

A loud groan erupted out of Xavier, who glared at Anabel and Delilah. "For the love of all that's fabulously unholy, can we please be done with the arguing? It's *Samhain*. We're supposed to be celebrating. You're shitting all over it."

Anabel folded her arms. "Fine," she clipped.

"Fine," Delilah bit out.

Xavier rolled his eyes. "*Thank* you. Oh hey, Hattie, there's George."

Hattie tracked his gaze and smiled. "My, my, my, the man wears a suit well." She tipped her glass in his direction, and he returned the gesture.

Anabel's brow pinched. "Who's the guy next to him? They're sitting pretty close. Almost intimately close, really."

Hattie patted the back of her hair. "Ah, well, he's one of George's swinger friends."

Wynter blinked. "Swinger friends?"

The old woman cocked her head. "You don't know what swinging is?"

"I do, yes. I'm wondering if *you* do."

"Well, of course." Hattie sipped her cider. "I had a most fascinating introduction to it."

"Hold on," began Delilah, "on top of everything else, you're into swinging now?"

"A girl should try everything at least once," said Hattie. "According to George, the man sitting next to him is into Cognitive Behavioral Therapy. Though why he felt the need to tell me that I don't know."

Anabel tipped her head to the side. "Cognitive Behavioral Therapy? He said that?"

"Well, he abbreviated it to CBT, but Xavier explained what it stood for," said Hattie.

Her mouth tightening, Anabel rounded on him. "*Xavier.*"

He laughed silently, his shoulders shaking.

Hattie straightened. "What? It means something different?"

"Cock and Ball Torture," explained Delilah.

The old woman's brows lifted. "Oh. That explains a few things."

Anabel looked at Xavier, her face hard. "You're going to hell. You know that, don't you?"

Grinning, he lifted his glass of cider. "I've *always* known that."

Wynter snickered and then took another sip of her drink. The conversation turned lighter as time went on, though there was some playful shit talking here and there. Delilah and Hattie hit the dance floor a few times, always huffing at Anabel's refusal to join them.

Neither Wynter nor Cain were particularly fond of dancing, so they mostly amused themselves by watching Xavier flirt with server after server, adopting a different identity each time.

The music came to a stop when it was time for the feast to begin. First, a bell was rung forty times to call the dead the guests wished to honor. Only after that did the food arrive.

The feast consisted of three courses and offered different selections. Wynter went with potato soup, pot roast, and apple pie. Every single course was utterly fricking delicious.

Shortly after the feast, the folk music started up again. There was then more dancing and laughing. At one point, most of the guests tossed a list they'd written in advance of emotions and habits they wished to purge themselves of right into the bonfire.

It was just as Wynter burned her own list that Cain gently cuffed her arm and said, "I need to leave now."

He hadn't said "we", she noted. He was giving her the choice to stay behind and continue to celebrate with her coven. Which she appreciated but, yeah, that wasn't happening.

"I'm coming with you."

He searched her eyes. "If you're sure."

"I'm sure."

*

Cain waited near the table as Wynter explained to her coven that she'd be back in a while. As he'd expected, they weren't surprised by her leaving. He knew she'd warned them of it beforehand—though, of course, she hadn't broken Cain's confidence and explained just *why* she'd be leaving.

With that done, he led her out of the hall and over to his Keep. After making their way to the surface via the mirror in his chamber, they left the manor and walked to the northern boundary of the transparent cage, far away from any residents.

There, they exchanged greetings with Ishtar and Inanna, who were waiting somewhat impatiently. Maybe it was due to the seriousness of the situation, but Ishtar didn't pettily shoot Wynter any "I hate you, please die" looks for a change.

The other Ancients soon arrived, along with Eve and the twins. Rima had apparently decided to help after all. The three Aeons seemed surprised by Wynter's presence but made no comment.

A subtle hum of restlessness in his blood, Cain rolled back his shoulders and said, "Let's get this done."

"Have you tried puncturing the cage before?" asked Eve.

He nodded. "Many times." Particularly in the beginning. They'd attempted it on a daily basis for a long time. It took a while before any of them were prepared to accept that they were forever trapped.

Noah squinted. "Even though the cage was created by Aeons, I don't see it."

"They didn't want us to be able to see it," Azazel told him. "They wanted us to be taunted with how it *seemed* we were free."

An "Ah" expression washed over Noah's face.

"It worked," said Dantalion, his voice sober. "A person can get used to the sight of bars. They eventually come to view the space within it as their world. They will come to feel safe only while surrounded by four walls, in many instances—even if only as a psychological defense mechanism. But if they are no walls, no bars, only a view of places that are so close yet so far … I would liken it to being stuck on a small island in the middle of the Caribbean.

You can see the world beyond it. You simply can't get there. It is maddening at times."

"Especially when we know that our own blood was used to reinforce our cage," said Lilith, flexing her fingers. "It makes it feel as if we are partially responsible for our own imprisonment."

Eve swallowed. "I'm sorry this was done to you. I'm sorry I was not able to help."

Seth briefly touched her arm. "You're helping now."

Rima looked at Wynter. "As are you, apparently." It wasn't said with attitude, it was simply an observation. Which meant Cain didn't have to tell her to watch her fucking mouth.

"I might not be needed," said Wynter. "I'm just here in case I am."

Cain half-expected Ishtar to snort in disdain at his consort, but the female Ancient paid her no attention. She was focused on the prison she couldn't see. Good. He wanted them *all* fully focused on the matter at hand.

He swept his gaze over each and every person. "I'm assuming everyone remembers just what it is they need to do and when they need to do it?" They'd already discussed it the previous night.

People answered in the affirmative. They all then lined up, fully facing the transparent cage. Cain looked at his consort, who stood between him and Abaddon. She gave Cain an encouraging nod, her eyes practically yelling *You can do this.*

Azazel raised his hand. A narrow beam of shimmering power shot out of his palm and crashed into the forcefield, making a small portion of it flicker, showing its honeycomb pattern.

Aiming power at the construct wasn't like throwing a dart at a board, because the wall wasn't hard. It was flimsy like gossamer and swayed like a cloth in the breeze, but it was tougher than any steel.

Azazel kept the needle-thin flow of power concentrated on one spot. Dantalion went next, focusing his own blast on that exact same spot. Lilith added her own power, as did Seth. Then the sisters. Then Cain. Soon the needle was so thick it was more of an arrow.

"The cage definitely isn't as strong as it once was," said Azazel. "But it's still like poking a finger at a damn veil—all you do is stretch the material, nothing breaks."

"Not *yet*," corrected Noah, more confidence in his voice than Cain might have expected.

The three Aeons then acted. Cain *felt* their elemental power fuel and interweave itself with the "arrow", causing the construct to throb and hum.

Cain glanced at his uncle. "We've put as much of a strain on this part of the wall as we can. Now you go."

Abaddon flooded the "arrow" with his own power, visibly amplifying it. The construct thickened, sharpened, and glowed more brightly.

Cain's pulse jumped as he felt a slight *give* in the ethereal wall. Like a stitch was being strained. He looked at his consort and nodded.

Wynter let out a surge of dark, rippling magick. It crackled as it hit the arrow and then curled around it, smooth as a snake. There was something very predatory about the flow of magick as it slinked its way closer and closer to the tip of the arrow, like a serpent creeping fast toward its prey.

"Now," Cain ordered, speaking to everyone at once. He dug deep into his reserves and boosted his own wave of power. The others did the same and then, at once, they gave the arrow an abrupt, forward shove.

Seams stretched. The wall tautened. The arrow vibrated.

A stitch popped.

Satisfaction curled his lips. "Again."

They drilled the arrow forward once more. Another stitch broke under the strain, followed quickly by another. And another. And another. The wall bounded backwards as a perfect tear formed, long and wide enough for a person to step through.

Everyone pulled back their power and stilled. The prison was now once more transparent, but it didn't matter. They all knew *exactly* where that tear was. And, having craved the sight of one for so long, there was no danger of them ever forgetting its location.

Ishtar moved first, her hopeful expression almost childlike in its vulnerability. She tentatively tried poking her hand through the gap they could no longer see. "I feel it, I feel its edges brushing my skin." Her face lit up as her arm stretched all the way through the tear. Laughing to herself, she stepped through the hole. Then she was jumping on the spot, urging her sister to join her.

Like the other Ancients, Cain slid through the gap, feeling a soft brush of *something* . . . like the swish of a curtain. As he planted both feet on the ground beyond the prison's boundary, a smile pulled at his mouth. Free. He was fucking free. Finally.

He let out a quiet exhale and then drew in a long breath through his nose. There was a lightness in his chest. As if a weight, a restriction, was gone. Warm energy trickled through him, leaving him feeling ultra-alert.

His creature basked in its freedom, raring to do one thing only— destroy those who'd taken that freedom from it in the first place.

All in good time.

The other Ancients were grinning, their eyes glowing with elation.

"It's a little strange to know I can now go anywhere I want whenever I want," said Inanna, looking up at the sky.

Ishtar tipped her head back and stretched her arms out wide. "Is it just me, or is the air so much fresher here?"

"It's just you," Rima deadpanned, making Wynter snort in amusement.

Ishtar threw the Aeon a dirty look but then went back to reveling in the moment.

Noah elbowed his sister. "Maybe you could stop annoying Ancients. I like you *alive*."

His sister only rolled her eyes.

Turning to Cain, Wynter smiled up at him. "I'll bet you can breathe easier just knowing you're not trapped anymore."

He felt his mouth curve. "That's exactly how it feels."

Eve bit her lip. "There's no way the hole will mend itself, is there?"

"No," replied Seth. "Just as a tear in a sweater wouldn't fix itself. The damage is done."

"And if it *did* by some miracle close up, we'd just undo it again," said Lilith.

"I think I'll sleep out here tonight." Ishtar let out a wave of power that formed a translucent, plump rectangle. She flopped back onto it, chuckling when it jiggled like a waterbed. "Come, Inanna, we can sleep together like old times."

Rima folded her arms. "Okay, so you're all officially free. Now what?"

It was Azazel who answered, "Now we refine our plans to invade Aeon, because we're *definitely* fucking invading it."

"I long to head there right now." Abaddon held up his hand to halt any objections. "I won't. It would be foolish to act alone, I know. Still, it's tempting."

"Very," agreed Dantalion. "But I'm not about to ruin everything now by moving too soon. We should do as Azazel said and refine our plans. We can do that here and now, in fact."

"I want to be part of the battle," Rima blurted out.

Cain blinked, taken off-guard. "You wish to not only see your childhood home destroyed, but partake in its destruction?"

"You were initially very much against the idea of another war," added Seth, his eyes narrowed.

Rima flexed her fingers. "I do not *like* the idea, but the place will soon be a wasteland anyway. I want Adam to pay for what he did to my mother."

Noah reached out and squeezed her hand, his expression grim. "We both want some part in making it happen. And we agreed that there is only one thing that will truly hurt Adam—seeing Aeon, a place he thinks of as his kingdom, fall."

"If we have to join you in order to ensure that, so be it," Rima added.

Noah nodded hard in agreement.

"I, too, would like to come along," announced Eve, twiddling her fingers. "I am no fighter, but I am still an Aeon. I am not weak. And I *need* to see Adam be brought down. He must suffer for all he put me and my children through."

Cain exchanged a look with each of the other Ancients, seeing the same suspiciousness in their gazes that he felt. They'd planned to somehow coax the Aeons into being part of the force of troops, because to leave them behind would also, essentially, leave Devil's Cradle in their hands. Sure, the Aeons could be confined to a dungeon. But Saul had once been imprisoned in such a way, and he'd been freed.

Cain and the other Ancients would rather have the Aeons where they could see them, but they hadn't thought that the trio would actually volunteer to take part in the war. Particularly *all three* Aeons. It was a little too suspicious, but it also suited the Ancients, so Cain said, "If you're very sure that this is what you want, you may come."

Rima's brows dipped. "You're not going to argue?"

Cain gave a fluid shrug. "Why would I? You have as much right to seek revenge as anyone else. Now I say we do as Azazel said and refine our plans." The Ancients as a whole would merely be careful not to say *too* much in front of the Aeons. It would be foolish to trust them with every little detail.

Rima cleared her throat. "Well. Um. Thank you."

"Yes, thanks, we need this," added Noah while Eve gave a smile of gratitude.

Since none of the Ancients were in a rush to return inside the cage, they started a small campfire and gathered around it to hold their discussion.

"I can help with the plans," said Wynter.

Ishtar's upper lip curled. "You? How so?"

Wynter gave her a sweet smile. "You once lived at Aeon, but I'm betting many changes have been made to the place since you were last there. The layout may be different in various ways. As someone who lived there up until several months ago, I can give an accurate description of the place as it currently stands."

"So can Eve and the twins," Ishtar pointed out.

"But I'll bet they can't tell you about the non-Aeons who live there," hedged Wynter, and neither Eve nor her grandchildren objected. "*I* can. It only makes sense to know what kind of force you'll be facing."

"She's right," said Dantalion. "Eve and the twins can give us details on the underground utopia and the people who live there, but not the town above it or its residents."

"How many people live in the town?" Abaddon asked Wynter.

"Nowhere near as many as can be found in the town here," she replied. "Especially since some died in recent battles or fled Aeon to seek safety elsewhere. There won't be many underground either. Aeons don't have several packs and covens and conclaves etc. below the surface. They only permit one of each group to reside down there."

Azazel frowned. "Why only one?"

"They consider it an honor," Wynter told him. "It's an honor they'll only bestow to few. Every member of each group *has* to be trained to fight, protect, and defend. No individuals who they consider a weak link are allowed to live among them, so they must either be cast out of their group, or said group must accept that they will never directly serve the Aeons."

"So they're still all about 'perfection'," said Abaddon. "I suppose they still view themselves as holy and expect to be treated as such."

Rima bristled. "Not all are like that."

Noah sighed. "Most do expect mortals to worship them, though. They don't claim to be gods, but they want the awe, fear, and devotion that gods receive."

"Which isn't something I see a present need to complain about," began Lilith, "because the limitations they have on how many can reside among them in the underground city works for us quite nicely. I suspect we will meet more resistance when on Aeon's surface than we will beneath ground."

"*If* you can get down there," said Rima. "Aeon itself isn't preternaturally shielded, but the entrance to the utopia beneath it is—it had to be to protect Eden's place of Rest."

"Yes, we know," Cain told her. "But there must be another way in and out of the underground city. I heard that there was a separate entrance, but I was never able to learn where it was. I firmly believe it exists. Adam would want a bolt hole."

Rima blinked. "There were whispers of another entrance existing, but I never met anybody who claimed to know if it truly exists, let alone where it could be located."

"Same here," said Noah, who then slid his gaze to Eve. "Do you know of one?"

Eve shook her head. "If such an entrance does in fact exist, Adam would not share it with many. He certainly wouldn't share it with me. He never trusted me with any information he wished to keep private. He knew my loyalty would never be to him."

"I never heard whispers about there being a second way into the city," said Wynter. "But that doesn't mean there isn't one."

"We could search for it while there," Inanna suggested. "And if we fail to find one, we will simply have to do our best to flush the Aeons out."

"I have an idea of how we might do that," said Cain.

Abaddon gave a satisfied nod. "Then let us all talk war."

Chapter Twenty-Two

Pulling on her boots the following evening, Wynter looked up as Cain stalked into their chamber with a casually menacing grace, a sense of battle-readiness clinging to him like a cloak. This was so *not* the time for her hormones to get all excited, considering they were about to invade Aeon, but her body gave not one single shit about that.

She'd known he'd gone to speak with an aide who, along with some other hirelings, would watch over the Keep while he was gone. There were a number of residents who wouldn't partake in the battle—it was important not to leave Devil's Cradle vulnerable, and not all who lived here were fighters anyway.

"Any issues?" Wynter asked.

Cain shook his head. "All is moving along exactly as it should." He slowly raked his gaze over her in a very predatory and assessing way, as if searching for weaknesses. "I see no weapons. You assured me that you'd be armed."

An unnatural breeze brushed over her skin, humming with amusement. Kali found it laughable that he would be so overprotective of a being that was almost impossible to kill. Wynter found it sweet. Until he started doing dumb shit like threatening to keep her confined "for her own safety" when, really, it would be to give him peace of mind.

Cain narrowed his eyes. "I don't like how often She intrudes on our private moments."

He was getting much better at sensing Kali's presence, though he didn't always pick up on it. Wynter was so used to the deity being close by that she didn't think much of it. "I wouldn't bother whining about it, if I were you. It would be a waste of time. Deities do whatever they want—the end."

He mumbled something beneath his breath.

"As for your worry that I'm unarmed, don't be fooled. I have plenty of concealed blades tucked here and there. Also, I'll be able to conjure my sword at will. There's therefore no sense in carrying it on my person. And don't forget that my magick is a concealed weapon, in a sense." She stood. "Speaking of magick . . . Is my coven here yet?"

"Yes. They're waiting outside the Keep. And, for once, they're not bickering with each other about anything."

"They can be serious when they need to be." Staring into Cain's eyes, she didn't need to ask if he was ready to leave. Those dark pools were lit with determination, bloodthirst, and anticipation.

She'd bet his creature was just as raring to head to Aeon. Both had waited too long for the moment they could wreak vengeance on those who slaughtered their loved ones, all but annihilating their species, and then jailed the eight survivors here.

Cain skimmed his hands up her arms and then rested them on her shoulders. "Are you sure I can't persuade you to remain here?"

"As I told you last night, I'll stay if you will." And they both knew he wouldn't.

He let out a soft curse, his nostrils flaring.

Wynter stifled a smile. "You had to know you'd never convince me to remain behind."

Yes, Cain had known that he was wasting his breath. No warrior would hang back at such a time, and his consort was a warrior through and through. More, she'd no doubt been instructed by Kali—who seemed to have some interest in ensuring that Aeon fell—to not remain behind.

Still, he'd had to at least *try* to convince her to instead stay and defend Devil's Cradle from any would-be invaders. How could he not want to take every precaution when it came to this witch, who

THE MONSTERS WE ARE

was his world? Who was the only person to ever love him in a way that was so simple, so easy, so unconditionally?

Having her in his life had changed him in subtle ways. Positive ways. Losing her would change him once again, but not positively. No, he'd become the very thing that the Aeons preached the Antichrist would be. The ultimate evil. The bringer of pain, death, and destruction.

She placed her hands on his chest. "Don't worry about me. You can't afford to be distracted. Concentrate on doing your thing, and trust me to do mine."

"Oh, I fully trust that you'll be alert and focused. I know you have an edge over most people, given what you are and that a deity looks out for you. Just the same, I know that going into war isn't new to you. But we're about to walk into a battle that is like nothing you've ever before experienced."

"I know that."

He sighed at her smile. "Only you would be so excited."

She snorted. "Like you're not raring to get moving so you can take Adam down. And he *will* go down."

"Yes, he will. The other Ancients and I will settle for nothing less. In the meantime, do as we pre-agreed and focus on taking out his people. Leave the Aeons to us."

"I already assured you that I wouldn't deviate from our plan unless put in a situation where I had no choice but to go off-script."

Still, he worried that she'd be tempted to take on Adam herself. Not only to avenge her mother, but to avenge Cain. His consort had commented many times on how much she longed to see Adam pay for all he'd done to Cain. The need to wreak vengeance was at the core of every revenant, after all.

Although she wouldn't break her word and seek out the last ruling Aeon, she might well engage in a duel with him if given the chance. The very thought made Cain's blood run cold. Wynter was a being that was built to defy even death itself, but Adam was not only tremendously powerful, he could call on the elements. If he realized that he was in fact dealing with a revenant, it would be easy enough for him to conjure iron and use it to weaken her. Adam would then pounce, and he wouldn't do a half-assed job of trying to kill her. He'd take her out for certain.

His chest tightening at the idea, Cain caught her face in his hands and pinned her gaze with his. "Stay safe for me. You can't know what it would do to me to lose you. You can't know the suffering that both me and my creature would inflict upon the world if something were to happen to you. So you ensure that nothing does."

"Right back atcha."

"I'm serious, Wynter."

"So am I." She sobered. "I'm a revenant, Cain. There isn't one single thing on this Earth that would live through the plagues, pestilence, and curses I'd unleash if you were taken from me. Don't doubt that for a second."

"What a pair we make." He rested his forehead against hers and slid his hands from her shoulders to her neck. He didn't say anything. He just held her close for a few moments, breathing deep. Then he very gently squeezed her neck and stepped back. "It's time."

Wynter slowly dipped her chin. "I'm ready." She allowed him to lead her out of the Keep, where they found her coven and Maxim waiting. Each of them looked equally eager to get moving.

Curt nods were exchanged and then, as planned, they headed to the surface and walked to the town's vehicle storage facility. Many people stood around—residents, Ancients, aides, and Aeons—all ready to pile into the modes of transport that would soon be brought out of the warehouse one by one.

Wynter watched as some residents cast the Aeons wary looks. No one trusted the trio's motives for coming along, and that was understandable. But no one had objected, so maybe they weren't fond of the idea of leaving the Aeons here unsupervised by any Ancients. Some of the aides had been instructed to keep a very close eye on the oblivious trio during the battle.

Soon, people were filling the assorted vehicles available—SUVs, station wagons, sports cars, motorcycles, minivans, pick-up trucks, all-terrain vehicles, and even a few Winnebagos—and then they were driving through the tunnel to make their way to Aeon.

Wynter, Cain, and her coven had claimed a six-seater jeep. The dominant, commanding bastard probably would have insisted on taking the wheel if he'd had any driving experience. He rode shotgun while she drove. Her coven sat on the two rear passenger rows, not saying much.

Wynter couldn't help but notice how Cain's gaze drank in whatever they passed. He'd had ways to "see" the outside world from his prison, but it wasn't the same. She wished he wasn't getting these in-person sneak peeks for the first time when on their way to a damn battle.

Considering Adam could "see" beyond Aeon in much the same way, there was of course a chance that he would spot them coming. But it didn't seem likely that he would carve out time to spy on the land that lay between Aeon and Devil's Cradle—he would never expect that they would escape their prison. Still, it was a risk they had to take.

The drive to Aeon was no quick journey. Over the course of the next two days, they stopped a few times to rest, eat, change, refresh themselves, or to use the "bathroom".

It wasn't until they were a mile away from Aeon that they parked the vehicles in a forested area. Dead leaves crunched beneath Wynter's feet as she slid out of the jeep. The evening air was fresh, cool, and laced with the scents of dirt, moss, and sweet cedar. There were no bird calls or the chattering of squirrels, as if the wildlife had stilled in uneasiness at the sudden presence of so many predators.

Although dusk was beginning to fall, it wasn't so dark that she had trouble seeing. Peering between the tall, weathered trees, she could spot the fringe of the woods up-ahead; could make out the vast and familiar prairie land beyond it.

Cain slid his hand up her back and gave her nape a squeeze. "I'll be back in a moment," he said before making his way toward the other Ancients, who'd gathered into a huddle a few feet away and were waving him over.

Taking a slow glance around, Wynter said, "I remember this forest well. I had to traipse through it after freaking Shelia teleported me to the prairie land over there."

"Bitch," Delilah mumbled. "May she rot in hell."

Well, given she'd sold her soul to an actual gateway to that plane, Shelia was definitely in hell. Wynter knew that much for certain. And if any of her coven died tonight, the same would have happened to them if Cain hadn't promised her that he would release their souls to be reborn if they died.

She gave each of them a hard look. "You'd better survive this battle. I mean it."

Xavier snickered. "Well, if you mean it . . ."

She gave his arm a light punch. "I'm serious."

He raised his hands. "We'll be fine. I'll call on Asmodeus if all goes to shit."

"That's not actually reassuring."

"Oh, give the poor demon a break; he's not so bad."

"Annis will have my back," said Delilah.

Anabel frowned. "How? She's in the spirit world."

Delilah only smiled.

"Avian shapeshifters, move!" Dantalion called out.

"That's me," said Hattie. "In a witchy-sense, of course."

"Remember, don't get too close to the keepers," Wynter told her. "They're often armed. We don't want them shooting you out of the sky."

Hattie gently patted one side of Wynter's face and smiled. "I'll be fine, dear. I'm too mean to die." She cackled at that and then, with a colorful burst of magick, shifted into a crow. Like the other avians, she took to the sky to scope out the area surrounding the entrance to Aeon.

"She'll be all right, Wyn," said Delilah before gulping some water from a bottle. "She's tough as old boots."

Wynter rolled her shoulders. "It doesn't stop me from worrying."

While they waited for the spies to return, they joined many other people in stretching or walking up and down. Despite that they'd taken breaks during their journey, Wynter's ass hurt, and her legs felt cramped.

Finally, a few avians returned. Then a few more. And a few more. And eventually came a cluster that included Hattie.

A relieved breath slid out of Wynter. She didn't get the chance to speak with Hattie. The eight Ancients rounded up all the spies and questioned them.

Close enough to overhear the conversation, Wynter learned that the Aeons hadn't upped their level of security—no doubt feeling confident that their only worthy adversaries would forever be trapped in a cage. Keepers still went out in groups of two. Altogether, twenty patrolled the outskirts, and each duo was situated at a different distance away from Aeon.

Although they were all armed, it wouldn't be hard to take them out. Not if everyone stuck to the pre-agreed plan. Wynter would certainly enjoy the part she played in it.

Walking toward her with Dantalion, Cain narrowed his eyes at her, his lips twitching. "There's that hunter stare."

She felt her mouth curve. "It's not directed at you this time."

Dantalion studied her expression. "The next move is yours. Are you sure you want to go ahead with this?"

"Positive." She didn't fail to notice the look of disappointment that crossed Cain's face. He'd tried talking her out of it several times already but, unable to deny that her little plan was their best move, he'd eventually relented. Begrudgingly. And sulked for a full hour.

"Then I'll get the others into position," said Dantalion, who then began barking out orders.

Wynter gave a nod to both Anabel and Xavier. The two quickly got to work putting a protective spell on the jeep. The keepers had a tendency to shoot first and ask questions later, so it seemed only sensible to make the vehicle bulletproof. Other magick-users would likely do the same to their own modes of transport before approaching Aeon.

Cain sighed. "For the record, I still don't like this plan you came up with."

"I know, but I've walked into far more dangerous situations," Wynter told him.

His brow pinched. "I'm sensing you think that's supposed to in some way comfort me, but it doesn't."

She cast him a sheepish smile, trying to hide her amusement. "Sorry." To be fair, he was right to be concerned. The plan *could* potentially blow up in their faces. But she had faith in herself and her coven.

Once Xavier cemented the protective spell on the vehicle with a little blood magick, he let out a satisfied sigh. "Done."

Wynter climbed into the trunk of the jeep and curled up on its carpeted bottom. Her monster probably would have grumbled its disapproval if it wasn't asleep.

Delilah puffed out a breath. "Fucking confined spaces." She reluctantly shifted into a housecat and leaped into the trunk, where she then curled up beside Wynter.

"Ready?" asked Xavier, his thumb hovering over a button on the key fob.

"Ready," Wynter confirmed.

He pressed the button, and then the trunk lid slowly began to close.

"See you soon," she mouthed to Cain, keeping her eyes locked with his until the lid finally closed.

The vehicle jiggled slightly as the rest of her coven settled into it. Wynter knew that, as planned, Xavier would be driving while Anabel rode shotgun and Hattie hid beneath the front passenger seat in her crow form.

Soon, they were on the move. They couldn't have been driving for longer than fifteen minutes when Anabel said, "We can see two keepers up-ahead. They're coming our way, and they're armed to the teeth."

A spike of adrenaline pumped into Wynter's bloodstream. "Keepers usually are." Thankfully, none would be Aeons—those arrogant shits wouldn't take on such lowly positions.

"We're being flagged down," Xavier announced.

Wynter felt as the jeep began to slow. She kept her breathing steady and remained still, her senses seeming hypersensitive courtesy of the adrenaline.

Unfurling from her ball, Delilah stood in front of Wynter, facing the trunk's lid.

The vehicle came to a halt, and the engine switched off.

"State your business," someone called out.

Wynter narrowed her eyes. She recognized that voice. It belonged to a werewolf who'd once regularly shared the bed of Wynter's old Priestess. Truthfully, Tito was a bit of a prick. Hence why he and Esther had made such a good match.

"We're here to cash in on the bounty," Xavier declared. "We brought Wynter Dellavale."

There was a distinct pause.

"Where is she?" asked Tito.

"In the trunk," Xavier replied.

"You're managing to keep a witch contained in a trunk?"

"She's bound and gagged with magick. She's not going anywhere or she'd have escaped by now."

Another short silence. "Out of the vehicle. Both of you."

Metal creaked as the doors opened, and the jeep rocked slightly.

"So you're from Devil's Cradle?"

"Yes," Xavier simply replied.

A grunt. "Your girlfriend will stay right here. Quick warning, if she does anything stupid, my friend over there will put a bullet in her brain. Now move."

Wynter heard two sets of footfalls make their way to the rear of the vehicle, so she had to assume that Tito had gestured for Xavier to head that way. Her pulse kicked up, and she licked her lips.

"Open it," said Tito as the footsteps paused outside the trunk.

"I need the key fob for that," Xavier told him.

An annoyed sigh. "Wood, use the damn key fob to open the trunk."

Wood, huh? Wynter remembered him, too. The mage had been a friend of the boys who killed her when she was just a child.

There was a jangle of keys, a slight *snick*, and then a low whirr as the trunk slowly opened, moving higher and higher.

Delilah pounced in a flash of movement, shifting mid-air into a monstrous cat and slamming Tito's body to the ground, burying her iron claws into his chest. Screaming, Tito fired his gun, but the shot went wide.

Wynter moved a mere millisecond after Delilah, lashing out with magick, sending an ultraviolet orb smashing into Tito's skull. Still a cat, Delilah tore out his throat before he had the chance to retaliate.

Wynter turned to see Xavier impaling Wood on his rapier sword. The keeper had claw marks on his face that she guessed came from Hattie's talons. The crow was now perched on Anabel's shoulder.

"Anyone hurt?" Wynter asked, relieved when everyone responded in the negative.

Hearing voices calling out in the distance, they looked to see a cluster of people racing their way who'd no doubt heard the shot firing. Good. Because that had been the whole point—lure keepers their way and take out as many as possible before they stormed Aeon.

"Move," Wynter barked out.

She and her coven quickly huddled behind the jeep—and not a moment too soon. The vehicle jiggled as bullets and orbs of magick crashed into it again and again. Her heart pounded in her chest as footfalls thundered along the ground toward them.

Anabel squeezed her eyes shut. "So this is how we die."

"Don't start with that shit. The plan will work." Wynter looked at Xavier. "How many are coming at us?"

He peered through the windows. "Eight."

Knowing some would carry swords that she'd enchanted, Wynter briefly chanted beneath her breath to swiftly disable the runes. *No one* got to use her own magick against her or her coven.

Xavier launched two balls of magick over the jeep and then ducked down again. The colorful flashes of magick would wonderfully act like freaking flare guns to any nearby keepers.

Her monster stirred menacingly, wanting to surface and attack. But a cautioning brush of air from Kali stayed it.

Xavier and Wynter took turns tossing orbs of magick at the approaching men, managing to take out two. Hattie and Delilah returned to their human forms and joined in, their magick more feral in nature—it bit and clawed, scoring and puncturing flesh.

Wynter looked to where the forest lay behind them. It looked so small from here, but she knew the army hiding there could get to them fast if necessary. It *wouldn't* be necessary, though. She and her coven had this.

"Do you think Cain will definitely hold back until *all* the keepers are close?" asked Anabel, using the sword she'd conjured to deflect bullets and orbs.

"Yes," replied Wynter. "He's protective, but he knows better than to let the army's presence be noticed too soon."

After all, if the keepers saw a small cluster of enemies, they wouldn't bother to sound an alarm; they'd come to help their fellow keepers handle the situation. But if they spotted an army, well, things would go differently. No one wanted the Aeons to yet know just how close their home was to being invaded.

"These shitheads are almost on us," said Xavier even as he blasted them with more magick. "And I can see more in the distance now heading our way."

"Then it's time," said Anabel. "Call her."

Wynter leaned forward and sang into her ear, "Mary, Mary, please come out."

A glimmer of madness sprung to life in the blonde's eyes. The sounds of magick crackling, bullets firing, and men shouting out challenges made her face light up. She looked fondly at her sword. "We fight?"

"In about, oh, ten seconds," replied Wynter, calling to her own blade. She hurled a few more blasts of magick while counting down in her head. "Okay, now!"

Delilah and Hattie shifted into their animal forms once more as they all broke cover and attacked. A few keepers skidded to a halt, clearly not expecting the bold charge. They recovered fast, aiming their weapons.

Wynter concentrated on the one directly in front of her. She blasted his gun with a ball of hot, toxic magick, heating up the metal until he was forced to drop it with a hiss of pain. He charged at her, shifting into a coyote, moving too fast for her to impale him on her sword.

She hit the ground hard, her breath whooshing out of her, inwardly wincing as a rock dug into her spine. *Well, ow.* Looming over her, the coyote snapped his teeth but didn't move to kill.

Not that he would have managed it in time, because she was already moving.

His head whipped to the side as she punched him with a ball of dark, rotting magick. She would have repeated the move, but then a blur of black fur barreled into his side, knocking him off Wynter.

She leaped to her feet, lifting her sword to take out the coyote. Anabel/Mary beat her to the punch, slicing off his head, singing "Everybody Walk the Dinosaur". As you do.

A hard impact slammed into Wynter's shoulder, sending white-hot pain lancing through her. *Bullet.* Heat grazed her upper arm as another skimmed her flesh.

"Just come with us, Wynter," said the shooter—a lycan who was something of a bully. "I don't know what your plan is, but you don't have a prayer of taking on all of Aeon. Come quietly. Don't make us kill you."

She smirked. "Ah, don't forget, Adam would kill *you* if you did."

A crow swooped down on the lycan's head and flapped her wings, obscuring his view and clawing the motherfucking shit out of his face. Wynter all but flew at him, burying her sword in his gut.

The fight raged on. Bullets fired. Animals lunged. Magick blazed through the air. Bodies fell, but more keepers came. Which was totally fine, because it meant that plan A was a raging success.

The keepers never tried to kill Wynter, but they tried to disable her. They failed. With her blade, she sliced, stabbed, and impaled. With her magick, she burned, infected, and destroyed.

Even though the keepers knew her blade was enchanted and that insects weren't really crawling all over their bodies, the illusion nonetheless distracted them—something she pounced on. Again and again, actually.

Wynter braced herself as yet another keeper rushed her. A severed head came out of left-field and hit his skull hard, causing him to stagger to a surprised halt. Anabel/Mary was then there, hacking his own head clean off.

Hot pain punched Wynter's leg, and her knee buckled. Hissing in agony, she tracked the shooter with her gaze. Before she had the chance to retaliate, a surge of Xavier's magick crashed into the asshole's arm, causing him to drop his weapon with a loud cry. Ha.

Wynter hobbled over to the piece of shit. "He's mine," she told the large cat who went to charge him. Wynter swiped out with her sword, disemboweling the prick in one smooth, cruel motion ... and he dropped to the ground like a stone. Dead. Just like every other keeper.

She heard the gunning of engines coming from behind her. She didn't need to look to know that the army that had been hiding in the woods had now *poured* out of it.

Skirting the corpses and dismembered body parts that littered the ground, Wynter looked at each of her coven. "Everyone okay?"

"Fabulous," sang Anabel/Mary, even as blood poured out of a wound on her thigh.

Wynter didn't panic for two reasons—the injury wouldn't be

fatal for an immortal, and it was already closing over much like Wynter's own bullet wounds.

"I'm good," said Xavier, panting. "Got shot a few times but healing fast."

Delilah and Hattie shifted to their usual forms. Their skin streaked with blood, they prodded at the few non-lethal injuries they sported and then announced that they too were fine.

"Then it's time for us to get back in the jeep," said Wynter, crossing to the driver's door. "We have a town to invade."

Chapter Twenty-Three

As the SUV Cain rode in whizzed past the spot where Wynter had fought the keepers, he noticed that the jeep was gone. Which meant she'd already joined the sea of speeding vehicles. He hoped she wasn't in the front, but he wouldn't put it past her to lead the charge.

There was no way to creep up on the town. Not when there was nothing but prairie land up-ahead, giving them no cover, making it easy for the people in the watchtowers to spot them. As such, they'd all chosen to drive toward Aeon at top speed, using the vehicles as shields of a sort.

Despite the rumbling of so many engines, Cain heard bells ring in the near distance. "The alarm has been sounded."

Sitting beside him in the rear passenger row, Azazel nodded. "I wonder if they'll guess it's our people who's coming at them."

"Whatever the case, they won't guess that any Ancients are part of the army. Our presence will take them off-guard for certain."

Azazel grinned. "Which makes this all the more fun."

Cain studied the curtain stone wall—one covered in rotting moss, thanks to Wynter—that shielded the town. It wouldn't be necessary to take it down in order to enter Aeon. Which was good, because it was solid enough to withstand blasts of power and even the impact of crashing vehicles. The grand wooden doors in that arched opening, however? Not so much.

"Arrows," said the aide in the driver's seat.

A thin wave of flaming arrows flew through the sky and rained down on them. They bounced off metal and windows, harmlessly hitting the ground courtesy of the protective spells cast by the many magick users.

Everyone sped on. And so more arrows came. And more. And more. Then came bullets and blasts of magick, all of which did no damage to the vehicles.

Cain sometimes heard the screech of metal grinding against metal coming from somewhere outside, suggesting that maybe riders of bikes had been hit and subsequently lost their balance. But most everyone continued making a direct beeline for Aeon.

And they were almost there.

Near the entrance, a harsh wind abruptly built in the air and then came racing toward the vehicles.

Cain pushed open the roof hatch and released a surge of power. It crashed into the wind and turned it into a spinning vortex. A vortex that soon shifted into a horrendously large swarm of angry wasps. Wasps that then zoomed toward Aeon.

"The keepers are abandoning the watchtowers," said the aide riding shotgun, a smile in his voice. "Shit, they can't move fast enough."

Cain returned to his seat. "It won't matter. Those were killer wasps. Their stings are fatal."

Azazel looked at him. "After that show of power, they'll know the Ancients are leading the army—or at least suspect it. Adam won't want to believe it."

Cain shrugged. "They'd have learned it soon enough anyway, because we're almost there."

"Hey, I'm not complaining. That wind would have tossed the vehicles here, there, and everywhere. We can't afford to lose people."

"Here comes the first line of defense," said the driver as the wooden doors burst open and troops hurried out of it.

The troops didn't charge at the vehicles. They formed three lines and gathered in front of the entrance, guns raised or orbs of magick in hand. They didn't attack, though. Cain suspected they were waiting for the invaders to exit the vehicles and expose themselves.

Close to the entrance now, the vehicles began to slow ... with the exception of the cars in front. They charged right at the troops, mowing many down but stopping short of the curtain wall.

Mere moments after all the vehicles came to a halt, passengers were hopping out and then racing toward the troops. There were roars of fire, crackles of magick, whooshes of power, and the thunder of bullets. The troops fell quickly, ridiculously overpowered.

Abaddon led the charge as everyone poured through the arch or—in the cases of dragons and many avian shapeshifters—cleared the curtain wall. From outside it, Cain heard battle cries, the firing of yet more bullets, and the roaring of animal shifters ... which meant many troops awaited them. The arch was only wide enough for five people at a time to barrel through the gap, which meant those in front were going to meet with the resistance without much backup *initially*. He hoped it didn't mean they were taken down.

When Cain was finally inside the walls, he almost rocked back on his heels. The once lush landscape was a sad sight. Trees were black and gnarled. Grass was brown and covered in fungi. Shrubs were leafless and thin. Ponds had dried up or become swampy bogs.

Excellent work, pretty witch.

Turning his attention to the battle, Cain resisted the urge to seek out Wynter. They'd already agreed that it didn't make sense for them to fight alongside each other. The Aeons and their troops would most want to capture Cain and Wynter, so remaining separate would force the bastards to divide their attention. She had her coven, not to mention Kali. They'd do what they could to protect her.

The residents of Devil's Cradle flooded every corner of the town. The Ancients walked among them, fighting and killing even as they made their way to the entrance of the underground city.

Cain hurled balls of power, smiling in grim satisfaction as they cleaved into people and buildings. The other Ancients made similar moves, wreaking havoc. They weren't only there to kill. They were there to destroy the town itself. So they demolished houses, knocked down buildings, upturned vehicles, and set fire to the rotting trees and underbrush.

Most troops refused to get close to him, striking from afar. Cain took them out easily—they stood no chance against Ancients, though they might have done if Aeons were among them. Those bastards were nowhere to be seen. They'd no doubt sought sanctuary beneath ground, just as he and the other Ancients had anticipated.

Cries of pain filled the air again and again as Cain's people attacked with a fury. Berserkers charged. Lycans and shifters pounced. Dragons breathed wind, fire, and ice. Fey, witches, and mages took troops down with magick and weapons. Vampires, demons, and other preternaturals fought with both their bodies and their combative abilities.

The people of the town put up a strong resistance. Cain caught glimpses of Devil's Cradle residents being knocked to the ground by shifters, slayed by weaponry, and assaulted hard with magick. He intercepted where he could, saving some but sadly not all.

It was easy to tell that the residents were shocked to find their home under siege. It had likely never occurred to the Aeons that it would actually happen, so they'd never trained their people to deal with such an eventuality. He had no sympathy for them—they would have invaded his town if he hadn't gotten here first.

A group of troops came toward Cain, one of whom held a net that crackled with power. He almost rolled his eyes. They thought they could catch him like a fucking fish? Really? He flicked his hand, plucking a dead tree out of the ground and sending it sailing at them. They fell like skittles.

Two jumped to their feet and fired at him. He raised his hand, stopping the bullets with a wave of pure power. The troops cursed and fled. Wise decision.

He heard a familiar laugh. It seemed that Ishtar was having fun. So was Azazel, if the smirk he wore while pummeling troops with smoky spheres was anything to go by.

Well, what was not to like about the current situation?

Maybe if he'd been a sentimental person, Cain would have felt saddened by the sight of the smoking and broken buildings and the fire spreading along the ruined landscape. But Aeon had never been a place he was truly happy. Besides, it was already dying. The Ancients and dragons were simply speeding up the process.

Another cluster of troops advanced on Cain, exchanging looks, trying to position themselves to come at him from several angles. He waved his arm, sending clumps of heavy rubble from a fallen house flying at the troops. Most collapsed to the ground while others retreated.

Seth sidled up to him, his eyes lit with the effects of the adrenaline coursing through his veins. "It's possible that we have a problem."

Cain frowned, hitting yet another building with a ball of lava. "What kind of problem?"

"Eve was supposed to stick with me, but she's gone. I didn't see her slip away."

Cain felt his expression harden. "If she's betrayed us, she'll die here tonight. You know that, don't you? You won't have a say in the matter. Neither will I. Wynter will butcher her before we have the chance."

*

Battle adrenaline bubbling in her blood, Wynter slammed up her sword to parry the blow that came her way. Much like every other troop she'd come across, he did his best not to kill her. He simply aimed to defend and disable, clearly planning to haul her off to his leader.

She was having none of that shit.

Wynter whacked him with a surge of scorching hot, toxic magick, aiming for his open wounds so it would enter his bloodstream. He fought on even as his flesh blistered, blackened, and cracked. But when his skin began to peel and decay, leaving festering holes in his face and arms, he freaked the fuck out.

299

Distracted by the sight of his pinky finger withering, he didn't see Wynter coming. She speared her blade through his heart and gave it a merciless twist. Once the life left his eyes, she withdrew her sword, allowing his body to slump to the ground.

She blew out a breath, feeling the sting of many superficial wounds. The air was hot from the fires and static from the potent power of the Ancients. She spared a quick moment to check on her coven. All had minor wounds but were otherwise fine. And they were still fighting hard.

Back in her huge cat form, Delilah consistently lunged, swiped out with claws, and bit into throats. Anabel/Mary swiped and parried and slaughtered, currently singing the Backstreet Boys' "Everybody" as she did so. As a crow, Hattie not only repelled magickal hits but repeatedly attacked, distracted, and blocked the view of any troops who came too close. When Xavier wasn't raising the dead, he was fencing while also lashing out with his magick, lacing the air with its distinctive smell—the combined scents of death, mold, and decay that could make anyone retch.

God, she had the best coven *ever*.

So far, she hadn't seen a single Aeon. None had come to the surface to fend off the Ancients, even though they had to know by now who'd descended upon their home and that their people would be helpless against the eight beings, who were launching power in all directions.

Most troops admirably, albeit stupidly, stood their ground. They also fought *hard*. And well.

Her heart squeezed each time she caught sight of a Devil's Cradle resident meeting their end—throats were slit, bodies were ravaged, heads were lopped off, vampires burst into ashes, a dragon came crashing to the ground. It was devastating, but she couldn't spare more than a passing sad thought for them; couldn't afford to shift her focus from the battle.

It helped that some of the troops had wisely retreated. She'd bet that they hoped the Aeons would allow them to hide beneath ground with them. She doubted the arrogant fuckers would permit it, but she'd soon find out.

Two troops bypassed Anabel/Mary wickedly fast, heading right for Wynter. She swiped out with her blade, slashing at one. The other fisted her hair but just as quickly released her with a loud cry as Xavier stabbed his sword through the dickhead's side. Wynter concentrated on the other troop, burning and infecting him with her magick even as she fenced, eventually taking him out with a brutal and fatal blow to the throat.

Xavier swiftly used his magick to reanimate the two corpses, just as he'd done to most of their victims—hence their current army of the undead, which sure came in handy. The zombies quickly joined it.

"I really should not like that you use your magick this way, but I damn well do," she said to Xavier, needing to talk loud so that he'd hear her above the horrendous din.

The guy grinned. "Awesome, aren't I?"

A troop rushed Wynter, his sword raised. With a soft curse, she quickly whipped up her blade and blocked the blow, their weapons clashing with a distinctive clang. She moved fast and fluid as they fought. He was good. Clever. Fast enough to catch her off-guard. Heat sliced her chest as the tip of his sword scored her, tearing cloth, drawing blood.

Gritting her teeth, Wynter all but flew at him, expertly slicing and dodging. He staggered backwards under the pressure, and an opening finally came. Wynter wasted no time in taking him out with a hard thrust of her sword through his gut.

Her monster snarled, sulking at only being allowed to watch as opposed to fight—well, to eat and maim. Kali repeatedly cautioned it not to surface. Thankfully.

The buzzing of insects joined the many other sounds of battle. *Cain.* A smile built inside her at the confirmation that he was alive, and some of the tension left her muscles. She hadn't let herself wonder if he was okay. She couldn't afford to lose focus. She couldn't—

Wynter frowned. "Mary, no, we don't drink blood!"

Pouting, the blonde dropped the severed head she'd been about to drink from while holding it upside down . . . like it was a fucking mug of soup.

Unbelievable.

Wynter and her coven kept moving forward, hacking through troop after troop with the help of their undead friends. Before becoming immortal, she'd have been tiring and slowing and sporting far more injuries at this point. But now, her blows were still strong, her reflexes were still sharp, and her breathing wasn't yet labored.

Tag-teaming an unfortunately powerful telekinetic vampire, Wynter and Delilah managed to reduce him to ashes with their combined arsenal of teeth, claws, magick, and sword. Which was right about when Wynter realized that Xavier was knocking back one of Anabel's healing potions . . . and sporting one fuck of an injury to his chest.

Her heart leaped. "You okay?"

He nodded, rolling back his shoulders. "Punctured lung. I'll be all right now."

Anabel/Mary pressed a kiss to his cheek even as she thrust her arm out to the side, stabbing a troop right in the face. *Well, ow.*

Wynter's peripheral vision yelled a warning. She ducked, evading the energy ball that then sailed over her head. She turned toward her attacker, noticing he was chanting under his breath. Before she could strike, a heavy blast of magick punched her right in the damn solar plexus. The breath left her lungs in a rush, and she felt her hand spasm around the hilt of her sword.

Oh, she was gonna destroy this fucker.

She didn't get the chance. A glass vial shattered as Anabel/Mary threw a potion at his feet. Smoke puffed upward and surged down his throat. He stumbled backwards with a choking sound, scratching at his neck, his face reddening to the extreme. Eventually he hit the ground hard, dead.

Wynter gave Anabel/Mary a nod of thanks, who went back to

singing, only adding to the awful level of noise. Clangs, screams, roars, and explosions fairly *vibrated* in the air.

The Ancients were still hurling blasts of power everywhere. The buildings in the town were all but demolished. The number of troops had gone down—partly because so many were dead, and partly because many others had given up on fighting and were seeking cover. Wynter had stumbled upon a fair few of them. And she might have let them be if they hadn't tried to nab her. Idiots.

Hearing a hissing whistle, Wynter turned just in time to lift her sword and deflect the fireball that came her way. She spun to face her attacker, who charged at her in a *blur*. She backpedaled fast, bringing up her blade to slam it against his own.

They fought hard. Fast. Skillfully. But it only took one nick to his skin for the guy to rear back. He slapped and scratched at his flesh, seemingly unable to fully ignore the scuttle of phantom insects courtesy of the sword's enchantment. Taking advantage, she slit his throat in one clean, devastating swipe.

Hearing a squawk of pain, Wynter felt her breath catch. *Hattie.* She twisted quickly to—

A heavy weight slammed into the back of her head, dazing the fuck out of her. Pain wracked her skull as her vision blurred and dimmed. Then everything went black.

Chapter Twenty-Four

It was blistering hot pain that woke her. *Seriously* hot pain. Like her blood was actually boiling. The agony pulsed through her veins, as rhythmic as a heartbeat.

It took everything Wynter had not to whimper. Especially when, moreover, the back of her head ached like a mother. *Blow to the skull*, she remembered. She suspected she had a real nice goose-egg back there.

Taken. She'd been taken.

Keeping her eyes closed, she used her other senses to process her situation. She was lying on a cold, hard, rough floor. Stone, if she had to guess. A heavy metal weight was clamped around her neck—a collar of some sort. *Bastards.*

The smells of dust, iron, and rust laced the cool air, making her nose wrinkle. She could hear the flickering of flames that made her think of the wall torches in Cain's temple. There were also muffled voices nearby, and she was sure that one of them belonged to Adam.

Her monster was *livid*, but Kali was keeping it calm and cautioning it to wait. Really, with how rough and drained Wynter felt, she wasn't sure she could release her monster. There was something very wrong with her right now. She felt weak and bruised and stiff, like she'd been starved for weeks, forced to run marathons, and subjected to more than a dozen beatings.

She subtly tried conjuring a small flame of magick in her hand. Said magick purred against her skin, answering her call, but didn't follow her request. Not good.

Shoes scuffing stone.

Her pulse jumped as several sets of footfalls came her way. They halted a short distance from her, but no one spoke. She didn't move, wanting to get a better sense of her situation before—

Cold power slapped her face hard. The shock of it made her body flinch and her eyes snap open. She stared at the four Aeons standing outside her cell. Yeah, she was in a fucking cell. *Those motherbitches.*

"I would imagine that you are wondering what's causing you so much pain," said Adam, his lips curved in a cruel smugness. "Liquid iron. My grandson injected you with it."

Noah smirked at her, his eyes drinking in her face as he awaited her response, as if wanting to feed on whatever shock, anger, or betrayal she might feel. So his smirk dimmed somewhat when she gave him no reaction.

Dismissing him with a look, she clenched her teeth as she pushed herself onto her elbows . . . hearing a jangle of a chain. She only then realized that one was attached to her collar. Anger tore through her, but she set it aside, not wanting to give these assholes the pleasure of a reaction.

Without even looking to see *what* she'd been chained to, Wynter forced herself to sit upright. Every muscle protested and cramped so painfully it took everything she had not to moan. She shelved the pain, more concerned about the spots dancing in her vision as lightheadedness crept up on her.

Dammit, she would not blackout. Not again.

She leaned back against the stone wall, going for casual. Which wasn't easy when her eyes watered, sweat blotted her skin, and there was a slight tremor in her limbs.

Using only her peripheral vision, she took in the scene. She was in a dungeon or prison, by the looks of it. There were no torturous instruments that she could see. Just rows of cells. It was hard to tell due to how dark it was, but she didn't think there were any other prisoners here.

Rather than demand answers to her questions, Wynter sat very still, making no sound, showing no fear. She swept her eyes over each male face, boldly meeting their gazes head-on. She recognized the two flanking Adam as his younger brothers, Emmanuel and Jude. Oh, the Ancients would have some fun butchering these dudes, especially Emmanuel since he'd killed Abaddon's eldest son right in front of him.

Adam folded his arms. "Noah tells me that you are Cain's consort." A sadistic delight flared in his eyes. "Oh, how he will loathe breathing his last breath knowing that I have you in my possession."

Wynter didn't respond. She merely stared at him, keeping her expression unreadable. Which didn't seem to please the Aeon. Yay.

"I can understand now why he point-blank refused to consider surrendering you to me. He wanted to protect you." Adam let out a dark chuckle. "He failed."

The others grinned and snickered. Wynter ignored them all. It wasn't hard. They were a bunch of dicks.

Jude, who was basically a leaner and shorter version of Adam, rubbed at his bristly jaw. "I wouldn't have thought that Cain would ever claim anyone as his own."

"I would not have believed it of him either," said Adam. "I certainly would not have thought that any woman would allow him to claim her." He narrowed his eyes on Wynter. "You *do* know what he is, don't you? Noah believes you must."

Again, she said nothing. She kept meeting his gaze steadily.

A bright white sphere flew out of his palm and crashed into her chest with the force of a punch. *Motherfucker.* It was like a mini explosion went off inside her chest and someone poured acid into the wound. She would have cried out if her breath wasn't trapped in her throat.

Dragging in air through her nose, she gritted her teeth and clenched her hands tight. That rat bastard was gonna pay for that. Dearly.

"Your pain tolerance is impressive," Emmanuel told her. Broader than both his brothers yet roughly the same height as the eldest, he was all brawn with *some* brain.

Adam nodded. "It is indeed. I am rather pleased about that. It will make it so much more satisfying when I break her during our upcoming sessions."

Okay, she had to snort at that.

His brow lifted. "You do not believe that I can?"

"Kali won't even let you try." The deity was currently pissed—Wynter could feel it.

"If She cares so much, where is She?"

Wynter only smiled.

"You know, I still have a difficult time believing that you are a revenant. Even with the mark on your face. Noah assures me that it is true, however. And it is telling that the liquid iron has proven effective."

Wynter's head snapped up as the land far above them seemed to vibrate and rumble. She let her lips curve. "Ah, they're here."

Adam's expression hardened. "They will not penetrate the shields that protect the entrance."

She flicked up a taunting brow. "You sure about that? Personally, I wouldn't be. But then, I'm not quite as arrogant as you are."

"If I were you, I'd watch your mouth," Noah said to her.

Continuing to blank him, she spoke again to Adam. "I mean, they broke out of a prison you constructed. Why wouldn't they be able to pierce a shield?"

Adam gave an arrogant flick of his hand. "They had the aid of Aeons, then. This time, they do not." He said it as though the Ancients were nothing when not backed by his own kind.

She snickered. "You people believe you're so damn special and superior. I cannot think why. Hell, you couldn't even get rid of a little rot."

His nostrils flared. "You will do that for us."

"I will do *shit*." She choked on a breath as power streamed from his fingertips and slammed into her stomach, making it feel like she'd been impaled on four roasting hot swords. God, it hurt, it burned, it made her fucking *pissed*.

307

He briefly looked upward as yet more vibrations ran along the city's surface. "Wrong, witch. You will do whatever I tell you *when* I tell you."

She shot him a daring smile. "You'd have to take the collar off first, and I don't think you have the guts to do it."

More white-hot stabbing pain rammed into her, sinking straight into her shoulders. She locked her teeth, refusing to make a single sound of pain.

Inside Wynter, her monster pressed forward and merged with her soul before she had the chance to stop it. Power punched into her, but it didn't surge through her body this time or whip through her like lightning. It *trickled*, slowly filling up every corner and extremity . . . as if a foreign force had taken a slow, languid stretch inside her and fitted perfectly into her very being.

Even so, the power was too much to bear. She couldn't hold back the moan as her eyes prickled, her blood bubbled, her teeth rattled, and her head swam.

Distantly, she heard the deep chuckles of males who no doubt thought she was buckling under the brunt of Adam's petty strike.

A breeze, cool and otherworldly, danced over her face—reassuring, soothing, distracting.

And then everything began to settle as the discomfort faded. She flexed her fingers, feeling charged and restless. Her senses had sharpened. Her nerve-endings were all fired up.

Her monster gently withdrew . . . and she realized then that the pain from before was gone. Just the same, she no longer felt weak, sore, or stiff.

The monster's power had evidently neutralized the liquid iron. And now she felt hyper-awake and energized—which was hard to hide, but there was no need for the Aeons here to know about it.

"Finished making unwise remarks?" asked Noah.

Again, Wynter pointedly ignored him. Hearing yet more rumblings from up above, she slowly reached up and tugged at the collar. "It's only a matter of time before they get in here," she told Adam.

He made a dismissive sound. "Our shields are impenetrable, but feel free to believe whatever makes you feel better." He rolled his shoulders. "I shall be back later once the Ancients and their people are dead. Then you and I can get better acquainted." He cut his gaze to Noah. "Stay with her." He and his brothers then strode off.

Noah took a step toward the cell, sneering. "I hope you don't *really* think that anyone's coming to save you."

Wynter flashed him a patronizing smile, planting her hands on the floor either side of her. "Of course they're coming."

Noah let out a derisive snort. "The entrance is blocked and shielded."

"The *main* entrance, sure. But there's another way in and out, isn't there? It's how you got me here, and I'll bet it isn't guarded."

"Doesn't matter. Outsiders don't know of it."

"*You* claimed to not know of it, as did Eve and Rima."

"They were telling the truth. I once saw someone access it. I knew I could use it to bring you down here to my grandfather. He was very pleasantly surprised. He truly didn't send me, Rima, or Eve to Devil's Cradle, so he wasn't expecting me to arrive with an unconscious you in tow. I knew that the only way to get you here was to help the Ancients escape their prison so that you would all declare war on the city, and so that was what I did. And it worked."

The prick sounded so very proud of himself, like he'd outsmarted everyone. He was clearly also certain that she wasn't going to escape or he wouldn't be so chatty.

Wynter cocked her head. "How do you think your grandmother and sister will feel when they hear of your betrayal?"

"They'll understand," he said with utter surety.

"Hmm, I think not." She paused. "Where are they?"

"Somewhere safe."

"Meaning you stashed them someplace against their will?"

He jutted out his chin. "It's for their own good."

"Nothing you've done here is for anyone's good but your own. Not that it matters. You won't survive this night."

309

He chuckled. "Oh, is that a fact?"

"It is, actually." Drawing her knees up, she balanced her crossed arms over them. "You always meant to betray the Ancients, didn't you? But not for Adam's sake. You want him dead. You also want the Ancients dead. You figure they'll all kill each other here and now. You intend to lead whatever Aeons are left standing." She snorted. "I can't imagine what makes you think they'll bow to *you*."

His eyes blazed in indignation. "You know nothing. And if you want my advice, you should worry more about what's going to happen to you than about my motivations." His mouth kicked up into a smirk. "I'll bet waking up here came as a shock, didn't it?"

She shook her head, sadly. "Oh, Noah, Noah, Noah. You honestly think this came as a surprise to me? Nah. I knew you would betray me."

"Really?" he drawled, his voice dripping with humor and skepticism.

"Yes. Kali warned me that you would. She and I had a conversation after I last died. She told me many things. She told me a few more things in a dream I had just last night." Wynter tipped her head to the side, seeing no harm in explaining all—Kali wouldn't let him leave; he'd be dead in a matter of minutes. "Did you know that Kali, Apep, Nyx, and Nemesis were sent to oversee parts of the netherworld after they failed to watch over the guardians and gatekeepers?"

He snorted. "Of course I knew."

"What you probably don't know . . . is that being made overseers of the netherworld isn't really what bothers the deities. The reason it's such a terrible punishment for them is that it means they're separated for eternity. Kali can therefore tragically no longer be with her consort, Apep. And the sisters, Nyx and Nemesis, are equally devastated at being forced to remain apart. I can tell by your expression that you didn't know that the deities were connected in such ways—I didn't either. But with this little bit of knowledge in mind, you can see that the punishment truly is one motherfucker, right?"

He blinked, shrugging. "Well, they earned it."

"Oh, yes, they acknowledge that. But they're also mightily pissed at the race that caused the war and, in doing so, led to that punishment. And the more time has gone on, the more that anger has grown and deepened. The more it's been twisted into resentment and bitterness. Oh, and scorn—so much scorn directed at your people. There's even a streak of insanity threaded through it all.

"Hey, I can understand it. If I was kept apart from Cain, I'd be nothing more than the living embodiment of fury. It would eventually twist me all up inside. Yeah, I'd go a little crazy over time, and I'd be looking to avenge us both. I'd need someone to blame, someone to hurt, someone to *destroy*. I'd crave revenge, just as the deities do. God will probably punish them for what comes next, yes, but at this point they don't care. All they want is vengeance."

Noah swallowed. "Well, then, I guess it's too bad for them that there's not a thing they can do about it," he snarked.

Wynter felt her lips tip up. "The deities found ways to communicate while in the netherworld, despite being kept apart. They came up with a plan. Having no physical form when in this realm, they needed to use others to achieve their goals.

"Kali found a witch She could use as Her own personal revenant. Nyx sent Kali the perfect netherworld entity for said revenant to host. Nemesis used oracles to indirectly communicate with the Leviathans—manipulating them, really, by informing them of only what She wanted them to know. And Apep led the revenant to Abaddon's resting place so that the Ancient could be woken, allowing the Leviathans to free themselves—being the most powerful of the deities, Apep was the only one who could unlock the gate to the resting place."

"You lie," Noah accused, a slight shake to his voice that said he wasn't truly so certain. "They couldn't have done all that."

"They could. They did. Kali told me *all* about it. She also told me that you'd take me to Adam."

He scoffed. "Bullshit."

"Nope, pure truth."

"Yeah? Then why didn't you do anything to stop it from happening?"

She smiled again. "Because I wanted to come down here, silly. She said that Adam would dump me exactly where I need to be. Yes, I've learned that there genuinely is a reason that you Aeons fear the fall of this place."

Noah stiffened, and his mouth opened and closed a few times. "I don't know what you are talking about."

Wynter leaned forward slightly. "I know what's here," she said quietly, as if confessing a secret. "Or, I should say, *who* is here. He's beneath us right now, in Eden's old resting place. And he. Wants. *Out.*"

Noah's eyes flickered.

"I think it's about time he gets what he wants, don't you?"

"You can't free him. You can't even free yourself."

Wynter tugged ever so slightly on the iron collar, and it split into several pieces as it fell from her neck. Enjoying how his jaw dropped, she asked, "You didn't notice me touch it earlier? I infected it with a little rot . . . much like I did the floor beneath me." She pushed to her feet, brushing off any pieces of the collar, and walked toward the front of the cell. "That rot is spreading and spreading throughout the foundations of this place as we speak."

Paling, he shook his head and backed up. "You . . . no. No, you wouldn't—"

"Of course I would. I do *all kinds* of crazy shit."

His face flushed in anger. "You don't know what you—" He cut himself off as a tremor ran through the building. Beneath them, something roared.

"Ah, it shouldn't be long now until he escapes."

"Are you fucking stupid?" Noah demanded. "He'll kill us all!"

"It *is* a possibility, I have to admit." She bit her lower lip. "But then again, maybe Kali's right and he'll just go after the people who've kept him here all this time. I guess we shall see."

A breeze whipped around the space, blowing out the torches, carrying an otherworldly laugh that bounced off the walls.

Noah sucked in a sharp, shaky breath.

The breeze returned only to smash into the cell door, which unlocked with a *snick*. Wynter whipped it open, slamming it into Noah, hearing him hit the floor hard.

She was on him in a blink.

*

A growl sawed at Cain's throat as he once more failed to penetrate the shield before him. It was little more than a bubble of power. A bubble that surrounded a single door. And yet, his strikes hadn't made even so much as a dent in the shield.

Unlike with Devil's Cradle, a building didn't sit upon the entrance to the city beneath Aeon. There was merely a small hill featuring a thick wooden door. So easy to penetrate if only it wasn't protected. Powered by the blood of both Aeons and Ancients, it was built to keep all intruders at bay in order to protect Eden should she be Resting.

Only Inanna and Ishtar weren't helping attack the shield. They were searching for another possible entrance. There had to be more than one way in or out.

Really, Cain and the others weren't battering at the shield in the hope of breaking it. Their purpose was to provoke Adam. They knew him. Knew how his mind worked. Knew that, being as arrogant as he was, hiding underground would be poking at the man's ego.

Adam would hate that the Ancients might think he was too scared to face them. He'd hate that they were essentially pounding on his front door while he remained inside where he was safe. More, he would detest what it said about him that he'd left the people on the surface to handle the invasion for him. It showed a cowardice that Cain himself had often pointed out but that Adam had refused to acknowledge he possessed. And so Cain and the other Ancients were playing on that.

In the meantime, many of their aides were currently watching their backs, fighting off any enemies who thought to attack while the Ancients were preoccupied. As for the people of Devil's Cradle . . . they were still fighting hard, and they were winning.

Azazel chucked yet another sphere of power at the shield, grunting when it had no effect. "I didn't think he had it in him to hide this long."

"Neither did I," said Dantalion. "It will certainly be an awakening for him."

Seth scratched at his nape. "Do you think we should try something else?"

Cain shook his head. "If you keep banging on someone's front door long enough, they'll do something sooner or later."

"Especially if they are anything like Adam," Lilith added.

Abaddon frowned, his gaze moving to something behind Cain. "Isn't that your consort's coven?"

His brows snapping together, Cain turned. And yes, the Bloodrose Coven was hurrying toward them. His heart jumped. Because Wynter wasn't among them . . . and Xavier was carrying her blade. "Where is she?" Cain bit out the moment they reached him.

Delilah grimaced. "You're not gonna like this, and you're probably gonna be pissed at us. But Wynter made us swear we'd stick to the plan."

The bottom dropped out of his stomach. "Tell me."

Delilah licked her lips. "Noah took her to Adam."

The breath gusted out of Cain's lungs, and panic exploded in his gut. *No. No, no, no, no, no.* As the owner of her soul, Cain knew that she was alive. But he was also very aware that she'd suffer at the hands of the Aeons.

"She knew that Noah would do it," Delilah quickly added. "Kali warned her—"

"Wait, Wynter *knew* she'd be betrayed and hauled off to the city below?" asked Cain, a growl in his voice as anger bubbled through both him and his monster. Anger at her, at Noah, at Kali, at Adam.

"Kali made it clear that Wynter *needed* to allow it," Xavier cut in, a crow perched on his shoulder.

Cain bared his teeth, contracting his fingers like claws. "Why?"

"We don't know," said Anabel, not seeming as unstable and bloodthirsty as she had earlier. "Wynter wouldn't tell us anything more. She only asked that we watch out for the moment Noah took her so that we could follow him and find out where the other entrance to Aeon is. Then we're supposed to tell *you* where to find it. So that's what we're doing."

"Now do you all want to see where it is or not?" asked Delilah.

Urgency thrumming through his body, Cain called out to two of his aides, both of whom were mages. "I want you both to blast this shield over and over. It won't crack, but don't stop." He wanted the Aeons to think that the Ancients were still pointlessly slamming power at the shield. Otherwise, Adam would wonder what they *were* up to.

Once both aides took over, the Bloodrose Coven led Cain and the Ancients to the other side of the hill. It wasn't until Delilah pointed to a well-hidden doorknob that Cain even realized that a door was cleverly concealed by the hill's decaying grass. Much as he yearned to try smashing it to pieces, he couldn't afford to draw attention to his presence.

Silently cursing his need to be subtle, he tugged on the handle. Nothing. It didn't even rattle the door, let alone open it. As he'd suspected ... "It's locked somehow," Cain ground out, his pulse thudding with dread as he tried and failed to push aside thoughts of what Adam would do to his consort—because, yeah, Noah would tell his grandfather just who she was to Cain. "Did anyone see how Noah opened it?"

"I did," said Xavier. "He sliced into his palm with a small knife, dipped his finger into the blood, and then carefully drew some symbols on the doorknob like this." The male witch carefully replicated Noah's movements. "The blood seemed to soak into it, and then he just pulled the door open."

Azazel went to speak but then glanced at the coven. "We need Inanna and Ishtar before we can proceed. They're searching for a second entrance. Bring them to us."

The coven didn't look too keen on walking away, but they did as asked.

Azazel then said, "Aeon blood must be needed to unlock the door. It could even be that only the blood of an Aeon related to Adam will work. It would be just like him to ensure that only those who are part of 'his legacy' are able to use this door."

Dantalion nodded. "Seth might have changed in many ways when he became one of us, but the blood that runs through his veins is still celestial. More, he's Adam's son."

Cain's brows lifted. "That's a good point. My blood has celestial qualities, but that's not the same, and I'm not related to Adam." He looked at his brother. "Try it."

Seth shrugged, sliced into his palm with pure power, and then repeated Xavier's exact movements. He leaned forward, twisted the doorknob, pulled on it . . . and the door opened.

Abaddon grinned. "Wasn't so hard."

His muscles tight, Cain cricked his neck and rolled his shoulders. His creature writhed and hissed and *demanded* that he find their consort. The only thing keeping both him and his monster from losing their motherfucking shit was that they knew Wynter was alive.

"She'll be all right, Cain." Seth quickly whipped up his hand. "I'm not being dismissive of the situation. I just mean that if Kali truly wants her down there, the deity will be with her. She'll watch over Wynter and do what She can to aid her."

She'd fucking better. Deity or not, he'd find a way to rain fresh hell on Her if She didn't.

The coven quickly returned with the sisters.

Ishtar looked unbelievably put-out at the sight of the open door. "We examined every inch of this side of the hill and found *nothing*."

"Should we gather some of our people to accompany us to the underground city?" asked Inanna.

"If there are non-Ancients with us, we will . . ." Lilith trailed off, casting a quick look at the coven. "There will be a certain something we cannot do when we fight."

Inanna's frown smoothed out as she nodded in understanding. "Ah, true enough."

Cain turned to the coven. "You four need to stay here."

"Sorry. Can't. We have very specific instructions from Wynter, and they include us being down there," said Delilah.

"We get that there's stuff you'd rather we didn't know about your kind," said Xavier. "But you have our word that we won't talk to others of what we see." The crow squawked, as if to back him up on that.

"Wynter told us that you'd want us to remain up here," Anabel interjected, "so she also asked us to tell you that she literally *needs* us to be down there. She didn't explain beyond that."

Cain cursed, swiping a hand down his face. "Fine."

Ishtar gasped. "Cain—"

"We don't have time for debates," he snapped out. "We have to move. My consort is currently in Adam's custody, and fuck knows what is happening. What makes it more important to move *now* is that we're going to have to move slowly."

Inanna's lips parted. "*Adam* has her?"

"Yes, courtesy of Noah," Cain bit out. "Who I would happily torture for a fucking lifetime if there isn't one thing I know for certain."

"What's that?" asked Abaddon.

"He's already dead," replied Cain. "Wynter will have ensured that by now."

Chapter Twenty-Five

Cain stepped through the door and straight onto a stone platform. The other Ancients and the coven hurried inside and quickly shut the door before sounds of battle could filter down to the city below.

Blocking out his creature's enraged hisses, Cain held up his hand for silence and listened carefully. He heard nothing. Not even muffled voices. Good. If no noise was trickling upward, it meant none would trickle downward.

Seth lifted his hand and conjured a faint sphere of light, illuminating the spiral staircase, dust motes, and rough-hewn walls. They were clearly in a cylindrical tower. A *narrow* tower.

"God, I *hate* tight spaces," Anabel whispered. "Stay in your crow form, Hattie. This staircase will otherwise be a nightmare for you."

Ishtar made a quiet sound of complaint as she studied the steps. "There couldn't be an elevator, no, there had to be a staircase."

Still holding the ball of light, Seth led the way as they all quietly began to descend the compact staircase, careful not to let their shoes noisily scrape the stone steps. The scents of dust and stale air were strong, aggravating Cain's senses and the back of his throat.

Considering that Seth's white sphere didn't cover much radius, Cain suspected a few other Ancients had conjured their own source of light. He didn't look back to check. He kept his focus on the steps before him. He had to. It would only take one person to slip and lose their footing for several others to be knocked down like dominoes.

It *killed* Cain to move so slowly when he knew his consort was somewhere down below, possibly suffering at the hands of Adam.

It seemed doubtful that the Aeon was currently torturing her—the bastard had bigger things to concern himself with right now. But the whirl of violent emotions inside Cain made it difficult for him to cling to that piece of logic.

He felt pumped up. Restless. Charged with a dark energy that demanded release.

He kept it all bottled up, still moving slowly. They came across no windows, or even any cracks in the walls that would allow thin shafts of light to beam through. Which was good, because it meant they had a better chance of moving undetected.

The staircase seemed to go on and on and on. The constant twisting and turning aggravated his sense of equilibrium. The slow pace threatened to make his creature lose all patience, even as it understood the need for stealth.

"*Finally*," said Seth as they eventually reached the bottom of the staircase and came upon a door. He pressed his ear to it. "I hear nothing." He gripped the handle and went to open it, but a quiet "Wait" came from Delilah.

The witch hurried over to the door and chanted while drawing a brief pattern in the air. A glistening wave of magick ghosted over the door and then disintegrated. "Now the hinges won't creak when you open it."

Seth's brows hiked up, and he nodded in thanks. He then twisted the handle and inched open the door, peeking through the small gap. "The coast seems to be clear. And there's plenty of cover we can use."

He wasn't at all wrong—a cluster of massive willow trees would help conceal them. It turned out that the staircase was built *inside* the rock wall of the city, which was covered in a sheet of moss and trails of climbing plants that very cleverly veiled the door.

It wouldn't have been so hard for the Aeons to create and hide the staircase—they were experts at calling on and using the natural elements, after all. Experts at moving and manipulating earth, rock, and stone.

The last to exit, Dantalion closed the door behind him. Everyone quietly padded over the carpet of grass and took cover behind the trees. Cain could hear Adam's voice—he spoke loud, as if giving a speech, but his words were indecipherable from that spot.

Cain quickly but quietly advanced through the maze of willows toward the sound, conscious of the others following him. It wasn't difficult for him to navigate the area because the landscape hadn't changed since he was last here. It was still much like a giant botanical garden that was dotted with various buildings—not many of said buildings were new.

It was strange to be back in this place where he was born and raised. There were no feelings of nostalgia. For him, it felt like the memories he had of Aeon were from a different life. A life in which he'd never felt truly *alive*. A life in which he'd merely existed, always feeling somewhat detached from everyone else.

As such, he felt no joy at being here. Just the same, he felt no sadness in noticing the signs of decay. It was nowhere near as prevalent here as it was above the city, but it soon would be.

The once lush greenery was dry, thinning, and turning a brownish shade. Fruit and vegetables were rotting, and many littered the floor. Water sources were dirty and gradually drying up. The old-style stone houses he came across featured cracks and dents. More, the few gold temples he passed had lost their shine, looking a dull bronze that possessed streaks of black.

As Cain neared the center of the city where the large temple that sat above Eden's old resting place was situated, Adam's words finally became audible. Yes, he was making a speech.

"Soon enough, the Ancients will have worn themselves out after expending so much energy on pointlessly attempting to break through our defenses," said Adam, his voice ringing loud and clear. "Already, we can tell that less power is behind their strikes. They are weakening, and this is our time to act."

Cain halted behind a tree that gave him a clear view of Adam. The bastard stood on the top step of Eden's temple with Jude and

Emanuel flanking him. Rows upon rows of people stood in a tight formation as they listened to the last ruling Aeon.

There was no sign of Wynter. Cain felt his mouth tighten. Unless Adam took his captives to a different place nowadays, she was probably being kept inside the temple's dungeon. Which was the one reason he didn't dare try to kill Adam there and then with a wave of sheer power. If the man ducked, the temple would take the hit. If it collapsed, Wynter might be crushed—at the very least, her escape route would be blocked.

"But although the time to move is now, it is not yet the time to attack," Adam went on, looking every inch the pompous asshole. "While we wait for them to weaken further, a large number of you will use the second entrance to leave the city—Jude will show you where it is and unlock the door. You will stealthily make your way around the hill so that you can come at the Ancients from behind. When they are too weak to defend themselves, you will attack."

Beside Cain, Abaddon grunted and said, "The man doesn't have an honorable bone in his body."

A quick glance around confirmed for Cain that the other Ancients were close, all taking cover as they glared at the Aeons ahead of them. But the Bloodrose Coven was nowhere to be seen.

A faint rumble came from Eden's temple. Like an earthquake rattled its very foundations.

Adam looked over his shoulder. Nothing more happened, but he exchanged a quick glance with Jude before turning back to the crowd and clearing his throat.

Cain smiled. He'd bet his life that his consort was responsible for whatever just occurred in that temple. She'd never stay still and quiet like a good little captive.

Adam set his hands on his hips as he swept his gaze over his troops. "I trust that those of you who head up to the surface to blindside the Ancients will do the rest of us proud. You know every inch of the land. You know how to remain unseen. You know how to defend yourselves against these creatures."

"Do you want Cain to be kept alive and brought to you?" one troop called out.

"No," replied Adam. "You need not worry about him. Once the Ancients are distracted by you, I will come to the surface and deal with Cain—he will not see me coming. His death will come at my hands."

Abaddon let out a quiet snort. "He always was an overachiever."

"As for the other Ancients, they will also die tonight," Adam continued, his voice hard. "Every last one of them. Then the witch will restore our home to its former glory, and we will be what we always should have been—the most powerful race to have been born on this Earth."

Cain's creature hissed at the brief mention of Wynter. It kept pushing and shoving at him, tired of waiting for him to seek her out.

"He is so very at ease with sacrificing his own people, isn't he?" said Abaddon. "There are over a hundred troops out there. Most appear to be Aeons." He paused. "I remember there being far more of them."

"Many Aeons died in the original massacre," said Cain. "Yet more died when Lailah and Saul brought an army to Devil's Cradle. Abel also led some Aeons into battle, though not a great number of them."

Another rumble came from Eden's temple. A crack zigzagged its way down one side of the building. Another skittered down one of the thick columns.

Adam tensed, eyeing the latter crack with unease. He whispered something to Jude, who then strode into the temple. Facing front again, Adam began barking directions at his troops.

"It would be so easy to kill Emmanuel right now," said Abaddon.

Cain tensed. "Don't. If you strike and miss, you'll damage the temple. It's already unstable—"

"And you don't want to risk your consort being trapped inside, I know." Abaddon sighed. "Even so, it's a . . ." He trailed off as yet more vibrations came from the temple. Worse this time. So much worse.

Cain's heart leaped. Shit, it was about to collapse in on itself.

Adam and Emanuel rushed down the steps using the enhanced speed of their kind, and a shimmering protective shield quickly encompassed them both.

Cain fisted his hands, needing to move, needing to—

Jude came barreling out of the temple. He wasn't alone. Another figure was a short distance behind him. *Wynter.*

Relief fluttered through Cain like a warm breeze. She raced out of the building in a blur of speed and jumped down to the base of the steps, her hand fisted in the hair of Noah's severed head.

That's my girl.

"Get her!" Adam ordered.

Several troops rushed her, but then they skidded to a halt. Pretty much everyone stilled. Because the collapsed temple was quivering. Shifting. As if something was caught beneath the stone blocks.

"No," Adam gasped, his eyes on her. "You didn't."

"Oh, I totally did," said Wynter, her lips quirking.

"Stupid girl, you have no idea what you've done!"

Her eyes hardened. "Of course I do. Just as I know you've kept him here since the massacre all those years ago. You tortured him. Endlessly. Until you felt sure that there was nothing of him left; that he was reduced to a feral, insane *thing.* And I gotta tell you, Adam, I have a real problem with that. Not just because it was a straight-up evil thing to do, but because he once saved Cain's life. There was no way I'd ever not repay him for that."

Cain's scalp prickled as a possibility drifted through his mind. No. No, surely not.

"He'll kill us all—you included," Adam snarled.

"Noah was of the same opinion." She tossed the traitor's head on the ground. "I guess we'll see if you're both right." She blurred out of sight.

Stone blocks went flying as something surfaced from the fallen temple. Cain felt his face go slack. People stumbled backwards, crying out in horror as a mammoth-sized serpent stretched its upper

323

body high, its golden scales glittering even through the layer of dust that coated them. It released a hissing shriek that carried screams directly from hell itself.

A Leviathan.

And not just any Leviathan. Cain recognized the distinctive scar on its head.

"Baal," Abaddon whispered.

Yes, Baal. Cain's own uncle. A man they'd all thought dead. A being who, if the light of insanity in his monster's eyes was anything to go by, truly was now only a creature of rage.

With yet another shrieking hiss, the serpent breathed a long, wave of fire. Any person it touched literally melted out of existence, their soul heading straight to hell. So there was little wonder that the troops scattered in a blind panic.

Several explosions abruptly went off all around, knocking people off their feet, and causing blue smoke to balloon in the air in various places. *The coven.*

Cain and the other Ancients chose that moment to make their move. It was *Adam* he wanted. But—as proven by how the Leviathan's fiery breath harmlessly hit the shield—the Aeon was currently protected. The only saving grace was that neither Adam nor Emmanuel could attack anyone while within the shield, so people were just as safe from them.

For now, Cain would settle for taking out the other Aeons. He tossed a frisbee of power that sailed through the air, cleaving into several troops like a chainsaw. Their broken bodies dropped to the ground like sacks of spuds.

Thanks to Baal's flames, it took a few moments—and several deaths—for the Aeons to realize they were under attack from the Ancients. But once reality hit them, they retaliated fast. Power was launched from almost every angle, coming in waves, blasts, flames, whips, and orbs of all kinds as the two sides went head-to-head.

Not all troops stopped to fight. Some ran for the staircase that would take them up to the main entrance, determined to flee from the serpent now slithering through the city, exhaling fire and wiping out several people in one swoop. Every one of the fleers screamed in terror when two silver-scaled Leviathans appeared in front of them, blocking their path of escape. *Inanna and Ishtar.*

Cain's own creature wanted out. *Not yet*, he told it. He wanted to pick off more of the Aeons first. As the only Ancient who could twist their elemental power and turn it back on them, he was the best form of defense the Leviathans had against this race. So that was what Cain did over and over and over. He twisted water, earth, fire, and air into swarms of locusts, bees, wasps, hornets, and mosquitos that targeted only the Aeons.

Cain occasionally caught peeks of the Bloodrose Coven. Wynter, Xavier, and Anabel fought with both sword and magic while a crow and monstrous cat brutally tore into troops as a unit.

A scorching heat licked at Cain's temple as a fireball skimmed the side of his head. He hissed out a curse. The scent of blood made his creature snarl.

Cain retaliated swiftly, hitting his attacker with a crackling stream of power that curled around her like a snake, contracting and squeezing as it shattered every bone in her body. He didn't bother to stick around and watch her die. He turned his attention to the nearest troops and fought on.

Soon, Dantalion and Lilith also released their inner creatures, ramping up the level of chaos around them. And it truly *was* chaos. There were yells. Cries. Blasts. Animal howls and snarls. Hissing shrieks of Leviathans. Hoarse groans of revived corpses. The shatter of glass vials, which were promptly followed by explosions.

He also heard a female voice singing in a Scottish accent— something about walking five hundred miles. He thought it might be Anabel but couldn't be certain.

Cain never strayed far from Adam and Emmanuel, who were still safe within their shield. Smoke puffed out of the Leviathan's mouth as it repeatedly tried and failed to bite through the protection forcefield. For Baal to concentrate so hard on Adam, he apparently had enough awareness to at least know who his true enemy was. That was promising.

A troop conjured a ball of pulsing energy and went to sling it at Cain. But then an electric tentacle sliced through the air and struck him down. *Seth*. The confirmation that his brother was alive made Cain breathe easier.

He knew that Wynter, too, was alive but didn't let himself worry about her. He couldn't. He instead concentrated on wiping out as many of the troops as possible so she'd have less people to fight.

Again and again, Cain traded long-distance blows with the troops, taking out several. Orbs or gusts of magick occasionally came at him, but he effortlessly obliterated the witches and mages. They were simply no match for him.

"I have one of your fellow witches, Wynter!" yelled Jude.

Cain swiftly turned to see Wynter standing ten feet or so away from Jude, who held a sword to Anabel's throat. The blonde didn't seem at all fazed—in fact, she was weirdly smirking. But Wynter? Fury was etched into every line of her face.

"You really should let her go," said Wynter, her voice hard.

"After all you have done to *my* home?" Jude shouted, spittle flying from his mouth. "After you killed Saul—*my friend*? No. Not a chance."

Her fingers contracted as thin, black streaks moved along her eyeballs. "That's a shame. For *you*."

"Say goodbye to your friend here." He moved as if to slice his hostage's throat.

Wynter's body seemed to *burst* as it lifted into the air and shifted into a black, cloaked, oily-looking shadow. A shadow with a gaping mouth, skeletal arms, and clawed hands. Tatters dangled from the ends of its fluttering, hole-riddled cloak. It was grotesque and chilling and gave off a feeling of dread to any who looked at it.

Cain gaped, his pulse kicked up. This was no mere beastly entity. Not even close. And he was reminded of something he'd said to her in his temple when he revealed his secrets.

"God has a liking for banishing souls to purgatory. He did the same with the souls of the Nephilim, even those who were unborn, meaning the only existence they ever knew was that of the mists of darkness and so they became *darkness; were branded the Rephaim, the dreaded ones."*

His consort was a vessel for one of the Rephaim. Mother*fucker.*

The ground beneath the monster rippled and flowed, becoming a puddle of dark water. The entity leaned back its head and let out a croaky, spinetingling screech. It was a call. A summons. And then two of its kind crawled out of the water. Then more. And more.

And, yeah, everyone in the Rephaim's general vicinity quite simply bolted.

The screeching entities winged through the air, biting and mauling and killing everyone they came across—Jude included, who'd abandoned Anabel with a scream while she'd merely laughed and then run for safety.

Between the Rephaim and the Ancients, the troops didn't stand a chance—especially since Baal, Inanna, and Ishtar were melting enemies with flames. Their number was being decimated fast, which meant Cain could turn his attention to Adam—always mindful to avoid the Rephaim, since they didn't distinguish between friend or foe. Cain knew his fellow Ancients would remember that they'd need to do the same. He hoped Kali helped keep the Rephaim focused on the Aeons.

Crossing to the shield within which Adam and his brother still stood, Cain saw that Abaddon was hurling shimmering orbs at the forcefield while baring his teeth at a very pale Emmanuel. Baal's creature was elsewhere, but Seth was aiding Abaddon in trying to penetrate the forcefield.

Cain caught Adam's eye and smiled. The Aeon kept his chin high, but it was easy to see that he was nowhere near as undaunted as he was attempting to appear.

"Such bravery," Cain mocked. "Your people are being slaughtered all around you. And what do you do? Hide like a coward; leave them to suffer."

Seth's mouth quirked. "Are we really that surprised, though?"

Pursing his lips, Cain shook his head. "No, we're not."

Adam sneered at them. "You think you have won."

"So do you," said Cain. "And here's what I *know*. I know that it's only a matter of time before you begin to run out of steam. The shield will then falter, and the weight of our attack will crush it. You'll be so weak from trying to keep the shield intact that you won't have a prayer of defending yourself against us when it's down. You'll die, writhing in unbearable pain."

Seth cocked his head. "Just visualizing that makes me smile."

"There is another way this can go," said Cain before Adam could snap out a livid response. "You can drop the shield now, while your level of strength isn't low, and have a one-to-one duel with me."

Adam scoffed. "Like the others would stand back and do nothing."

"I didn't say they'd do nothing," Cain pointed out. "In fact, Abaddon will do his utmost best to wipe out Emmanuel. And I'd imagine that Seth would fight off any troops that might attempt to save you or your brother—not that there are many left."

"If I dropped this shield, the three of you would attempt to kill us both."

"It's going to drop at some point. You need to decide whether you wish to be weak when it does. Your best chance of survival is to lower it now. You know that. The question is . . . are you too damn afraid to do it?"

Adam's upper lip curled. "I do not fear you."

Cain felt his mouth curve. "Prove it." Sensing that the Aeon was going to do exactly that, Cain backed away, putting a distance between them that was appropriate for a duel.

The moment the shield went down, Adam struck hard and fast, directing a tidal wave of fire at Cain.

So predictable.

Cain slammed up his hand and sent out a burst of power that engulfed the flames. The gust of fire spun faster and faster and faster until it became a blur. A blur that soon began to buzz as it formed into a swarm of bees.

The duel then officially began.

In between zapping the buzzing insects with power, Adam threw everything he had at Cain. The Aeon was the best living wielder of elemental power among his kind, and it clearly showed. Cain repeatedly found himself dodging spears of light, showers of little rocks, harsh blasts of air, and also hails of shards that were ice cold and scalpel-sharp.

Cain met each violent surge of power with one of his own. He also made a point of continually twisting Adam's elemental strikes—both aggravating and mocking him.

Adam had always been an expert at shutting off his emotions when it suited him. But the ability appeared to be alluding him at this moment. Was that any surprise? The city was falling apart around him, his people were screaming and dying, and the one person he loathed above all others was now using his own power against him.

A silver shockwave rammed into Cain's body hard enough to make him rock back a step. He acted fast, pitching a ball of dark flames right at Adam. It connected with the Aeon's side, burning through cloth and blistering skin. Adam let out an animal cry of anger.

Cain might have smiled, but then orbs of fiercely bright light bulleted through the air toward him. He ducked and dodged, but one slammed into his chest, knocking the breath out of him—it was like being hit by a steel door. Hissing at the burning sensation it left in its wake, he sharply flicked his hand, whipping Adam with a heavy blow of power that sent him staggering backwards.

They traded yet more long distance blows. Soon, both sported burns, cuts, deep slashes, blisters, and shallow stab wounds. Adam was also covered in bee stings.

As he fought, Cain was distantly aware of his uncle still battling Emmanuel close by. The Aeon was buckling under the weight of the Ancient's assault, but Abaddon wasn't capitalizing on it. No, he was playing with the Aeon, inflicting as much pain upon him as possible, dragging it out.

Cain jerked aside just as a beam of white-hot light dived toward him. Before he had the chance to return the blow, a bitterly cold wind flared out and pummeled him, snatching his breath, breaking a rib, and sending ripples of pain up his side.

Grinding his teeth, Cain tossed dark smoky orbs at the Aeon. Adam coughed as they hit him full-on in the face. Taking advantage, Cain swiftly followed up his attack with balls of boiling hot power that punched Adam's head and body, leaving horrendous burns that sizzled and crisped.

Just then, Emmanuel stumbled backwards, crashing into his brother. Adam fell to the ground, whacking his head hard, dazing himself . . . completely vulnerable to a killing blow. And so, conscious of his promise, Cain allowed his monster to surface.

Firmly in the backseat now, Cain could only observe as his creature took over, shifting in a blur of motion. It unfurled its body, glaring down at Adam, a cruel anticipation swirling in its blood.

Paling, the Aeon gaped up at the Leviathan, his face a mask of sheer unadulterated fear. A fear the creature greedily drank in. Cursing in panic, Adam shakily whipped out his arm.

The creature shrieked out its fury as waves of cold air blasted its armored scales. In no mood to duel, only to destroy, the Leviathan opened its mouth and exhaled a roaring flame of fire right at Adam, melting his body and sending his soul straight to the place it belonged.

The creature then let out a hissing shriek in triumph. One that was answered by the other Leviathans. More than satisfied, the monster didn't fight Cain when he pushed for control.

Once more in the front seat, Cain rolled back his shoulders.

"He's gone," said Seth, staring at the spot on the ground where Adam had once lay. There was now only scorched grass. "And I can't tell you how delighted I am by that."

Taking in the rest of the city, Cain saw that few troops still lived, just as few buildings still stood.

Abaddon swiped a hand over his brow, looming over a very dead Emmanuel. "Now I need to go see if I can coax Baal to shift back. I know he's feral, but we can't kill him. He's been through enough."

"If anyone can make him listen, it's you," said Cain.

His uncle nodded and then hurried off in a blur ... just as one of the Rephaim came sailing toward Cain and Seth, a bloodthirsty screech clawing out of its throat.

Shit.

A strong otherworldly breeze washed over it, and the entity stopped abruptly. It stared at Cain through eyes he couldn't see and then cocked its head in a bird-like movement.

Cain's gut prodded him. "Wynter?"

It let out another screech. It wasn't one of bloodthirst this time. It was a summons. And as the floor beneath it became dark water, the rest of the Rephaim soared toward it and dived into what could only be a portal to the netherworld.

"I guess the Rephaim feel that they're not needed anymore," said Seth.

Only once the others were gone did the calling Rephaim shift in an explosive movement that sent blood and gore bursting outward before rebounding back on Wynter. And as her body began to fall to the ground, his heart slammed in his chest. Because the portal was still there.

Fuck, no.

He tore across the space between them and grabbed her hand just as she sank halfway into the black water. Seth rushed to his side, and they both hauled her completely out of the portal, which then finally closed.

Blowing out a breath, Cain hovered over her unconscious form. He had no clue if her monster had returned to the netherworld with its brethren. The only thing he knew for sure was that it hadn't taken her soul with it, because Cain could still vividly *feel* her. Not like with Annette, a berserker who Wynter had tossed into the netherworld—his connection to her soul felt muted.

He brushed Wynter's blood-soaked bangs aside, murmuring nonsense to her, wanting her to wake. She boasted a lot of injuries, but none were severe.

He sensed others gathering around them, including her coven, but he didn't look at them. His only concern was for his witch.

Cain stilled as her eyes finally fluttered open. The pools of quicksilver went soft with relief when they locked with his, but they quickly turned shuttered as she studied him warily.

"I don't care what you host," he told her, sensing what made her uneasy. "You should know better than to think I would." He helped her sit upright and pressed a hard kiss to her forehead.

"You're pissed at me," she sensed.

"I'm pissed that you didn't mention that Noah would betray us. That's something you should have shared. However, we'll discuss that later."

"Sure," she easily agreed as she pushed to her feet. Grunting, she rubbed at her lower back. "But don't expect an apology. Things had to happen the way they did. Kali insisted on it. And you can't claim that Her plan didn't come together." Wynter caught a vial that Anabel tossed her way and then quickly chugged the potion down. "Well, to be fair, it wasn't merely Her plan. Apep, Nyx, and Nemesis were in on it, too."

"Why?" asked Dantalion. "What was their motivation?"

Leaning against Cain, his witch then launched into a short story that she claimed to have earlier relayed to Noah before killing and beheading him.

"I had no idea that Kali and Apep were consorts," said Lilith. "To be separated like that for eternity ... What an utterly cruel punishment."

"I'm sorry I didn't tell you about Baal," Wynter said to Cain. "I couldn't. Kali was sure that if your focus shifted from vengeance to freeing your uncle—which would only be natural—things wouldn't play out as they should, and many lives would be lost."

Cain couldn't even deny that the deity was right. He and the other Ancients would have been so determined to help Baal that they might even have made a move too soon as opposed to take the time to make a proper plan of attack. "So She had *you* free him."

Wynter nodded. "As an apology for the deities' neglect that led to your kind almost being completely wiped out." Her eyes drifted to something behind Cain. "And it seems that Abaddon managed to convince him to shift."

A serpentine screech of pain rang out, making Cain's head snap to the side. He watched as a silver Leviathan slumped to the ground, causing vibrations to rumble through it. It lay too still, unnaturally still. And then it shrank, altered shape, and eventually went back to its usual form.

Inanna.

She drew in a sharp, rattling breath. And another. And another. And—

Her chest stopped moving. Her body sagged. Life faded from her eyes.

Cain felt his mouth drop open, his gut twisting.

The other silver serpent stilled for the merest moment ... and then it let out a roar-screech of agony streaked with rage and grief. A billow of flames burst out of its mouth and lit up what seemed to be the last Aeon standing. Then the serpent shifted, and Ishtar was dropping to her knees beside her sister.

"No!" She shook Inanna hard, ordering her to wake up, get up. "You can't leave me!" Ishtar slammed a fist on her sister's chest, as though it might restart her heart.

Lilith took a step toward her. "I'm sorry, I—"

Ishtar bared her teeth at the other Ancient, such pain in her eyes. "Don't you tell me she's gone! She isn't!" Ishtar went back to shaking and punching her sister, until finally she balled up her fists, sobbing wildly.

Lilith looked as though she might make another attempt to approach her, but then Ishtar tossed back her head and screamed like a banshee, her grief still raw with fury. Jumping to her feet, she hurled power around—striking buildings, trees, dead Aeons, and even the walls.

Seth cautiously approached her, repeating her name again and again. But she didn't seem to hear or see him, lost in the madness of her grief. He touched her arm. "Ishtar—" He cut off as she yelled in his face and punched at his chest again and again ... until she sagged against him, sobs erupting out of her.

Seth rubbed at her back, murmuring into her ear.

Cain swallowed, pity for her swirling in his belly, grief for Inanna thick in his blood. He hadn't been close to Inanna, but he'd respected her. Her death was a blow even for his creature. For Ishtar, it would likely be worse than losing her own life.

Wynter leaned into him in a gesture of support. No one spoke for long moments, the air alive with shock and pain and sympathy.

Cain only broke the silence when he saw his uncle stalking toward them with Baal tossed over his shoulder. "He's unconscious?"

"Yes," replied Abaddon. "The bastard's creature is stubborn, so it took a little time to convince him that he was no longer in danger and would be safe with me. Baal spoke a few words and then collapsed. I suspect he will wish to Rest for some time."

It would be the best thing for him. Baal needed time to emotionally heal.

Abaddon looked at Inanna, his face grim. "I had told myself that no Leviathans would die here today; that we wouldn't allow the Aeons to kill any more of us." His gaze moved to Ishtar. "I know what it is to watch a sibling you love so dearly die. She will never truly recover from this. A piece of herself is now gone."

Cain nodded. Inanna had been Ishtar's anchor, protector, and— in many ways—her conscience. Without her sister at her side, Ishtar would no longer be the same person.

Wynter's coven quietly surrounded her, insisting on trying to clean her up with vials of liquid that Anabel produced. They then just as quietly whined at their Priestess for not telling them the story of the deities. And as Cain realized they must have always known she hosted a Rephaim yet were loyal to her anyway, he developed a newfound respect for them.

Crossing to them, Azazel tipped his head back. "Much as I hate to sound insensitive, we can't afford to stay down here—we left many of our people up on the surface."

"I'll be surprised if the battle isn't already over," said Cain. "But if it isn't, we'll finish it."

Chapter Twenty-Six

Wynter was relieved to discover that the battle was in fact over. The residents of Aeon were completely wiped out, but they'd first managed to eliminate a fair number of the people from Devil's Cradle. Her chest squeezed each time she came upon the dead body of someone she recognized.

She'd known in advance that there would be casualties—it was sadly inevitable at times of war. She'd also known she might even be one of those casualties. That didn't make the sight in front of her any easier to bear. And the loss of Inanna . . . damn, that was a heavy one for every Ancient.

Wynter would never like Ishtar, but her heart still broke for the woman. To lose someone so close to you, someone who had been at your side through the passings of eons, who was the only person you ever truly loved . . . yeah, Wynter wouldn't wish that sort of pain on anyone.

Passing her old home, seeing it burning to the ground, wasn't easy either. She had some good memories of that house. Memories of the time when Davina still lived.

No one wanted to just *leave* the corpses sprawled around like their sacrifices had meant nothing. As such—aside from Inanna's body, which Ishtar carried around and quite simply refused to part with—the Ancients incinerated each one . . . which sounded cruel, but it was done very respectfully, as if honoring every life lost. And no, they didn't send the souls to hell. Some people gathered the ashes of those who were cremated, intent on scattering them back at Devil's Cradle.

It was while injuries were being tended that some were-coyotes reported they'd found Eve and Rima in a cellar. Both Aeons were sleeping deeply, and the efforts to *fully* wake them failed. The clearly drugged females would stir, flutter their eyelids, mumble crap, and then fall right back to sleep. Seth gave up attempting to rouse them, sure they'd wake properly on their own at some point.

Once wounds were taken care of, the Ancients blasted the land with fire, flattening the ruins, leaving it a clean slate—just as they'd done to the underground city.

Aeon had officially fallen.

For the sake of the land itself, Wynter put a hand to the ground and halted the spreading erosion caused by her curse, knowing the rot would then die off.

Outside the walls, everyone piled into the waiting vehicles and then began the long-ass drive home. Again, Wynter claimed a jeep and rode with Cain and her coven. Not a lot of chatting went on. People were tired, achy, grieving, and dealing with adrenaline crashes.

After the two-day drive was over, vehicles were returned to the warehouse, ashes were scattered, and people went home.

Wynter followed Cain and Abaddon to the grotto, where they settled a sleeping Baal into the water. He'd slipped into a state of Rest during the journey home, and the Ancients hadn't bothered trying to rouse him; they felt it was better to let him sleep.

"Do you think he'll wake any time soon?" she asked.

Cain moved to stand beside her. "No. And it would be best if he doesn't. The Rest is what he needs for his mind to heal." He sighed. "If I'd known that he was still alive—"

"There was nothing you could have done."

"Your consort is right, Cain," said Abaddon. "You were just as much a prisoner as he was."

Cain scratched at his temple. "I don't understand why Adam never told us about Baal. Why didn't he boast that he'd captured and tortured my uncle?"

"He got off on the fact that you *didn't* know," said Wynter. "It made him feel like he'd got one over on you."

Abaddon nodded and settled a hand on Cain's shoulder. "Take comfort in this: Now that Adam is exactly where he belongs, your father will subject him to even worse torture than what Baal received."

Cain's frown smoothed out, and his brows lifted. "Yes, there is that."

"You two go on," urged Abaddon. "I'm going to sit here awhile."

And Cain's frown was back. "Do you wish to Rest again?"

"No, that is not why I hesitate to leave. I simply don't feel ready to walk away from my brother just yet." Abaddon gave him a faint smile and settled on a stone ledge. "Go. I will be fine."

Cain gave him a nod, took Wynter's hand, and led her out of the grotto. They headed up the stairs and then began making their way out of the temple.

"So, it's finally over," said Wynter. "With the exception of your mother and Rima, the guardians are dead. Aeon has been leveled. And you and the other Ancients are free."

"I spent the entire journey back to Devil's Cradle processing it all. Or trying to. My mind has not yet fully absorbed this new reality, or that Inanna has gone, or that my consort hosts an actual Rephaim."

"But you meant it when you said that you're not freaked out about the latter, right?" Because it would be a problem if he was. And she'd be tempted to punch him in the junk, considering she'd accepted *his* creature without a qualm.

"Of course I meant it."

Junk-punching averted. "I'm kind of bummed that I didn't get to see your monster. It's not fair. You saw mine." She knew she sounded like a whiner, but whatever.

He draped one arm over her shoulders. "I'll let it free sometime soon so that you can officially meet it."

"Awesome."

"I don't think many people would find the thought of being face to face with a Leviathan 'awesome'."

"We've already established that 'normal' and I long ago got divorced."

His lips twitched. "I suppose that's one way to put it."

As they exited the temple and began walking along the garden's twisting path, Wynter cast him a sideways glance. "Are you truly not mad at me for keeping so much from you?" she asked, her voice unintentionally hesitant.

"I'm pissed that you withheld things from me, but I'm not pissed at *you*. I'm pissed at Kali for giving you so many conditions." He jerked slightly as the deity then brushed over them both in her breeze-form in a sort of *tsk, tsk* gesture. "Wait, She's still hanging around?"

"Don't worry, She has no other plans for me. She just . . ."

"Cares for you in Her way and wishes to be near you," he guessed.

"Kind of. I think She's also lonely. Anyway. As for Her imposing conditions on me, I didn't like it much either. But She swore that things had to happen a certain way. And I was *not* going to cross Her on that, because She also said that She'd allow me to stay with you after the battle was over if I followed Her orders to the letter."

Cain blinked, his brows snapping together in affront. "*Allow* you to stay with me? As if She had a choice in the matter?"

"I didn't like how She worded it either. But you and I both know that, while it doesn't seem fair, She *did* have a choice in the matter. Anyway, Her original plan was apparently to bring my soul back to the netherworld after I'd achieved Her goals so that it could move on and begin a new life. But She promised that She wouldn't if I did as I was told, although it would mean I'd have to permanently keep the entity I host."

"Why?"

"Without a monster inside me, I wouldn't be a revenant anymore. And if I wasn't a revenant, I'd be nothing at all. Dead rather than undead."

"Ah, I see." They slowed their pace as a snake slithered across the path in front of them. "So it was Apep who repeatedly called you here, hmm?"

"Yup."

"It explains why the snakes stayed close but didn't harm you while you were sleepwalking. Apep is a serpentine deity; He can communicate with any serpent. He would have ordered them to leave you alone."

"Kali told me a lot about Him. There was *such grief* in Her voice when she spoke of Him." Wynter swallowed. "She mourns Him, in a way. Mourns what they once had until they were separated. All that grief and rage and bitterness and spite brewed inside Her until She couldn't take it anymore. And I get it. I'd have become just as twisted up inside if someone took you from me."

Cain gave a soft nod, lightly squeezing her hand. "As would I have been if someone dared try to separate us. What the deities did to avenge themselves ... I wouldn't have done any differently in their shoes."

"Me neither."

"And it was Nyx's idea to put one of the Rephaim in you?"

"According to Kali, yes. The deities needed something powerful. Fearless. Monstrous. But also obedient. The Rephaim inhabit the area of purgatory that Nyx oversees, and She sort of leads them. She sent one Kali's way, ensuring that it knew it had to obey Her." Wynter felt her lips faintly curve as a snake lunged at a white moth and missed.

"Did you know it was one of the Rephaim?"

"Yes. I just didn't know that Nyx basically gave it to Kali. Not until recently, anyway."

Reaching the gate, he pushed it open and waved her out of the garden. "Will it bother you to keep the entity with you permanently?" he asked as he closed the gate behind them.

"Nah, I'm used to it at this point. Plus, you said it didn't kill you when it might have tried, which I find very reassuring. I wouldn't have believed it would ever have hesitated to hurt you or anyone else. All I can think is that it recognized you. Recognized that you're mine. Or something. Maybe."

"I think it did, but not before Kali all but barreled into it. She might have told it who I am to you. My creature likes that you have something so powerful inside you." While Cain personally had nothing against the Rephaim, he would prefer—for her sake—that his consort wasn't a vessel for something that was pure darkness. Leading her into the Keep, he asked, "Does it usually call on other Rephaim like it did tonight?"

Her nose wrinkled. "I don't think so. But then, I black out when it takes over. I'm a little jealous that you see everything your monster does when you set it free. So, when do I get to meet it?"

He felt his lips quirk at her eagerness. "Soon. It will be more than happy to spend time with you. *And* bind with you, which you won't fight us on."

"No, I won't fight the binding."

He blinked. "You won't?" He hadn't expected such easy capitulation, given he hadn't uncovered the answers to her questions.

"Kali made it clear to me last night that twining my life-force with that of your monster would have no ill-effects on it or you. She was also adamant that your death wouldn't drain or weaken me as, given I'm undead, death doesn't really have as much of an impact on me as it does others."

Both Cain and his creature settled on hearing all that. "Good. Because I won't be satisfied until the binding is done." Once they were inside their bedchamber, Cain tugged her close. "Why didn't you tell me that Kali promised not to drag your soul back to the netherworld if you followed Her orders?"

"Two reasons. One, I knew you'd get all cranky at the whole Her 'allowing' me to stay with you thing—you hate that She feels She has more of a claim to me than you do."

"Because she doesn't," he clipped.

Wynter rolled her eyes at his tone. "Easy there, I'm not disputing that. Anyway . . . my second reason was that it would have felt like I could be giving you false hope, since I wasn't sure I could trust that She'd live up to her promise. Deities are a law unto themselves."

"That they are," he conceded. "Ishtar accused me more than once of playing games, using you and others as pawns and positioning you all exactly as I pleased. But in this instance, the chessboard was never mine. It was the deities' board. They were in charge of the game all along."

Wynter wrapped her arms around his waist. "But the game is now over. We're not pawns anymore. Our choices are our own. So . . . what do you want to do next?"

"Honestly?" He slid a hand up her back. "Toss you on the bed and fuck your brains out."

She chuckled. "Okay, let me rephrase. What do you want to do now that you're free? Or, more to the point, where do you want to go?"

He pursed his lips. "I haven't quite decided. As I've said before, not all the Ancients can be away from here at one time. I do wish to travel, but I'm not in any rush, so I'm fine with letting some of the others go first."

"You're worried about Abaddon," she guessed. "You don't want to leave him."

His consort read him well. "My uncle's need for vengeance gave him a sense of direction. He no longer has that. Though the relatives he lost have been dead a long time, their loss still feels very fresh to him. All he has left of his family are me and Baal, and heaven only knows when Baal will rise. So, yes, I'd like to keep an eye on Abaddon for a while."

"Understandable. In truth, I'm a little concerned for the guy myself."

"I would also prefer to keep watch on Ishtar—I don't know just how she'll react while processing her grief. She has been known to fly into irrational rages over small things, after all."

"Rima's grief will be just as deep and strong," said Wynter.

"Rima might not blame me for killing him, all things considered, but she'll still hate me for it. I wouldn't even be able to judge her for that. Noah was her *twin*, and they've been alive since almost the beginning of damn time."

"*I'd* judge her. You did what you had to do. And it would never have happened if he hadn't betrayed us." Cain brushed her bangs away from her face. "You're fine with waiting for other Ancients to return from their travels before we head off anywhere?"

"Sure. I'm not terribly fond of the outside world. What I saw of it wasn't very impressive. Plus, I love it here. It's our home. It's my coven's home, and God knows the world is safer when they're tucked away here. So, no, I'm not hankering to leave."

"Then we'll content ourselves with weekend breaks here and there. Couples do that sort of thing, yes?"

"Yes, they do."

He pulled her closer and brushed her nose with his. "You know something else that they do?"

"Fuck each other's brains out?"

He blinked.

"You weren't going to say that? Sorry. You put the thought in my head a minute ago, and it *really* isn't going anywhere."

Humor warmed his gut. "Giving you what you want will be my pleasure. Literally."

"I was hoping you'd say something like that."

Chapter Twenty-Seven

Waking to the feel of his consort dragging her tongue up the length of his cock would never get old.

Cain threaded his fingers through her sleek hair, drinking in the sight of her straddling his body, wearing only his shirt, and fisting his shaft with blatant territorialism. "I do love that tongue of yours." Seeing her lick and touch and play with his dick, knowing he owned that beautifully lush mouth, made his possessiveness unfold and stretch out inside him.

Locking their gazes, Wynter swallowed his cock.

He drew in a breath through his nose. "Suck, baby."

She did, her eyes still fixed on his. Resisting the urge to take over, he watched as she worked every inch of him, length and girth. *Christ*. It seemed as if, over time, she'd learned and filed away every little thing he liked—just as he'd done for her.

The wet heat of her mouth, the tight stretch of her lips, how hard she sucked, the rasp of her tongue against each ridge and vein ... It was utter perfection. "My pretty little toy knows just how to make me feel good."

Her eyes flared with heat. She upped her game, sinking down faster, sucking harder, eating at his control. Until he had no choice but to snatch up her head, since he wanted to come deep inside her body, not in her mouth.

He used the head of his cock to paint her lower lip with drops of pre-come. "Don't lick them off. Leave them there. I want to see them while I take you."

"All right." She began pumping his cock, her grip sure and bold.

He thrust into her hand with a grunt. "Put my dick inside you."

Oh, gladly. Wynter dropped down hard, impaling herself in one smooth move. Her breath caught. Jesus, he *filled* her—so thick, his shaft pushed against her inner walls with such pressure it stung; pressed on and brushed against every nerve-ending, making her feel overly stuffed.

"Don't move," he said when she went to ride him, removing his shirt from her so she was utterly naked. "You just stay right there like that. I'll move you as and when and where I want you."

Well.

"Quick warning. My creature is done waiting."

She'd thought as much. It had risen during their bout of shower sex last night to bite her. As it took three injections of its venom to perform the binding, she'd known the monster would likely bite her again very soon. "Then it'll be pleased to know I don't need it to wait any longer."

His lips curved into a pitying smile as he cupped her hips. "Sweet witch, it wouldn't have let you make it wait."

He began slamming her down on his dick, thrusting upwards each time to ram himself deep. He used her in that way he often did, handling her like she was merely a toy that existed purely to get him off—nothing more, nothing less. And she'd long ago accepted how insanely intoxicating she found it.

Wynter dug her nails into his chest, letting him have his way. He took her savagely, his pace furious, his grip on her hips so tight she knew he'd leave bruises. Wynter didn't care. Not when every upward slam of his cock hit her *just right*, winding her body tight.

Pure pleasure ghosted along her soul, soft but so electric it snatched her breath and made her feel so fucking *alive*. Hot. Charged. Then it came again and again.

Her heart raced. Her breaths came sharp and fast. Her nipples pebbled. Her skin turned so ultra-sensitive it felt like buzzing little sparks skipped along it, sending a sea of little bumps sweeping over her. "Cain ..."

"Don't come. Not yet." Cain ground his teeth at the sight of his cock, all slick and shiny, disappearing into her body over and over. Christ, she was a fucking vision. Her lips were swollen, the lower one damp with pre-come. A pretty flush had swept up her body, reddening her cheeks. Her tits bounced in an almost hypnotic rhythm, her nipples dark and tight with arousal.

His creature slid beneath his skin, fairly quivering in anticipation. It didn't push Cain to hurry, content in the knowledge that it would soon bind Wynter to it.

He sent more pleasure sweeping over her soul, so it would feel like a warm, static hand had given her entire being a firm, drawn-out stroke. She arched into the sensation, like a cat would arch into a full-body pet, and pricked his skin harder with her nails.

"Come when you're ready, pretty witch."

Her breathing sped up. Her inner walls fluttered. A whimper slipped out of her.

Cain rolled her clit with his thumb, and that was all it took. She came hard, her eyes glazing over, her pussy squeezing him tight. Remaining inside her, he rolled them both over and left all restraint behind as he powered into her, brutal and primitive.

She took it, curling her legs around his hips, scratching at his back. The sting made his balls tighten.

He dragged the siren song of her scent into his lungs. Laced with need and magick, it made his head swim. Wynter Dellavale had been his drug since the first time he'd fucked her, and he knew that would never change. He didn't want it to.

He gripped her breast and held it still so he could latch onto her nipple. She moaned, her pussy rippling around him. Her nails scored his back again hard enough to sting. And he figured that turnabout was fair play.

Wynter gasped as pain-edged pleasure spanked her soul like the flat of a hand. And then came another spank. And another. Some were more like light taps. Others cracked down hard. Some felt like the flick of velvet tassels.

The tempo of the sensations repeatedly went from slow to fast then back again. There was no rhythm. No way to time when the next spank would come or guess just how much of a sting it would carry.

The assault to her soul continued even as he kept fucking in and out of her. Soon, she was drunk on pleasure and pain and feel-good chemicals. God, she was close to imploding.

But then the strikes to her soul turned soft, silky, and ultra-light. As if ribbons were being trailed along her very being. Which wouldn't get her off right now. And he damn well knew it.

A sob of frustration caught in her throat. "You gotta make me come."

"Since when do toys get to demand anything?" He bit into her jaw. "Your only purpose at this moment is to get me off. Something you're so very good at."

On and on the torture went. He manipulated her body using every tool at his disposal. Until she was coiled tight, both inside and out.

She shook and whimpered and clawed at him. He didn't take pity on her, though. He plied her soul with yet more sensations. Little pinches. Tiny scrapes. Suckling bites. Velvet lashes.

She sank into the pleasure and the pain. More, she lost herself in it. Sounds dimmed, as if the physical world was so very far away. Only Cain's weight and the slamming of his cock kept her anchored.

"You feel me everywhere, don't you? Don't you?" he pushed when she didn't respond.

"Yes." Her voice broke on a sob.

He snarled. "There's no part of you I can't touch. No inch of you I don't own. No fragment of your soul that's free of me."

She narrowed her eyes at him. "That goes both ways."

"Of course it does." He switched his angle and pounded harder, striking her sweet spot with each feverish thrust. "Come. Break for me."

His eyes changed as his creature surfaced, and then it bit her neck hard. The stab of his teeth hurt, much like the venom that slipped into her bloodstream. But the pain triggered the orgasm that had been looming so close.

Wynter broke, tears springing to her eyes. She screamed as her release clawed its way through her, ripping her apart with its intensity. She dug her nails deeper into his back, arching into him, sunk deep in pure bliss ... which was when something seemed to latch onto and twine itself around her—she couldn't quite explain or describe it, since the sensation faded so quickly. She was so caught up in it all that she was barely aware of the hot streams of come filling her pussy as Cain's monster exploded above her.

She flopped to the mattress, her arms spread wide. Her throat was bone dry, and her body was a happy mass of trembling muscles. *Yowza.*

Bracing himself on his elbows, Cain pressed a kiss to the bite on her neck. It was done now. She was officially bound to his monster. *Good luck with that, little witch.*

His creature merely sniffed at that mental comment, too pleased with itself to be truly annoyed with Cain. All along, it had felt somewhat on the sidelines—particularly since she'd been unaware of its existence for some time. It had even felt jealous that Cain owned her soul. Now that it had its own claim to her, the creature was content.

She looked up at him through eyes that were soft and languid. "I don't feel any different."

"Did you think you would?"

She shrugged. "I don't know, really."

"You're not bound to my monster in a way that forms a metaphysical bond. Your life-forces are tied, that's different." He dropped a light kiss on her mouth. "By the way, that bite won't heal much."

Her lips parted. "Ever?"

He shook his head. "The third bite is an official claiming mark. The skin will close over, but the bite will always look fresh. Also ..."

He swiped his tongue over the brand, and she bucked in his arms with a gasp. He smiled. "Such marks are allegedly extremely sensitive to the point of being erogenous. If your reaction is anything to go by, it seems that that is in fact the case."

Her brow flicked up. "You don't think this is maybe something you should have told me before I let the monster have its way?"

"Probably. But it's more fun to surprise you."

"Surprise me, or fuck with my head?"

"Aren't they essentially the same thing?"

"No. No, not at all."

He merely shrugged.

She looked at the ceiling, mumbling something he couldn't quite make out.

Cain felt his mouth kick up. He hadn't smiled anywhere near so much until Wynter came along. Well, she gave him plenty to smile about, especially when she so often did the unexpected. He doubted any other woman would have dared curse his cock so that it would wither and rot if he ever betrayed her. Only Wynter. *His* Wynter.

Their lives had so easily *clicked* together. She was a Priestess. He was a ruler of sorts. They had different responsibilities and duties. Yet, there had been no push and pull, no struggle for balance, no difficulty for either to keep a foothold in their own "world". He wouldn't have expected that. Wouldn't have thought it could work that way.

But then, he wouldn't have thought a lot of things until Wynter. More, he wouldn't have believed that anyone could become part of him, until there was no way he could exist in this world without them.

He combed his fingers through her hair, letting his gaze drift possessively over her face. "I forgot to tell you something."

Her gaze flew back to his, her brows slightly inching together. "What?"

"I realized something when you almost fell through the netherworld portal right before my eyes."

She slid her hands over his shoulders. "It would be nice if you didn't glare at me like I did that on purpose. I was kind of unconscious."

"I know." He pressed his forehead to hers. "I thought for sure I wouldn't get to you in time. My heart was in my throat. My creature was frozen in horror. Fear . . . I could taste it, smell it. Even though I caught you and hauled you to me with Seth's help, that fear didn't leave right away. I could feel your soul, I knew I hadn't lost you, but relief didn't really hit me until you opened your eyes. And I realized that, fuck, I love you."

Her face softened. "You do?"

"I do." He lifted his head. "I didn't know that the emotion could be so intense and raw. Didn't know it could be so dark that it straddled the line of obsession and could make a person so much more dangerous than what they already were before. I am more dangerous for loving you, because to lose you would be to lose myself. You're as much a part of me as my own soul."

Ignoring the ache in her throat, Wynter swallowed. "Well, that's . . ." Dammit, she got all choked up and awkward and flustered. She'd never be good with expressing how she felt, or at handling hearing how deeply he felt for her. And she could tell that, sensing her struggle, he *really* wanted to laugh right now. Asshole.

As she suddenly remembered something he'd said before, she frowned. "Hold on a sec, you realized you love me, but you 'forgot' to tell me? How? How does one forget that?"

"Perhaps 'one' was waiting for the right moment." He bit her bottom lip as he withdrew from her body. Rolling them both onto their sides so that they faced each other, he added, "Now here's where you give me the words back."

"You've already heard them many times."

"I want to hear them again."

"So spoilt." She gave him a quick kiss. "I love you."

"I hope for both our sakes that you never stop, because I will still keep you here. In chains, if necessary."

She sighed. "What is it with you and chains?"

"Why are you so opposed to them?" He cupped her pussy but didn't stroke her, as if he just wanted to hold her that way. "Being a sexual captive wouldn't be so bad."

Yeah, in Hattie's world. "It wouldn't be anywhere near as exciting for you as you seem to think. I would make a *terrible* captive. Defiant. Bitchy. Totally uncooperative—"

"All of which would give me reason to punish you." He hummed. "I do like to punish you on occasion."

"Yeah, well, I'd also do whatever it took to get free, *and* kill whoever stood in my way—including you." She probably shouldn't have been surprised at how heat flared in his eyes. "God, you're so weird."

"Now really, little witch, are you in a position to be throwing stones like that?" he teased, sliding his hand from her pussy up to palm her breast. "You come back from the dead. You host one of the Rephaim. You gave yourself to the son of Satan. And you lead a coven of people who wouldn't know 'sane' if it skewered them with a sword."

"What's your point?"

His lips hiking up, he kissed her. "Would you prefer if we pretend I don't have one?"

"As a matter of fact, yes, I would."

"Then that's what we'll do. Back to what we were speaking of before . . . So, being chained up would truly be a problem for you?"

She made an exasperated sound in the back of her throat.

"I'd make sure they weren't made of iron. You wouldn't have to worry that they'd weaken you."

"Oh, well that changes things."

"Does it?"

"Honestly? Honestly, no." She held up her hand. "Chains are *out*. And don't think I don't know you're enjoying how huffy and frowny this topic makes me."

He smiled. "Of course I enjoy it. Why else would I keep bringing up the subject?" Releasing her breast, he slipped his hand further down to palm her ass. "It's as if you *still* sometimes forget that fucking with your head makes me hard."

She exhaled a long breath. "I guess there are worse kinks."

Epilogue

Khloë Wallis jerked back from the toddler in her arms, evading the little hands that struggled to grip her throat. "Dammit, kid, what is your problem?" Demons didn't need to morally contend with the concept of killing, not even as children. But this young, they generally didn't attempt to mindlessly murder whoever they came across. "If you really want to kill someone, there are quicker ways than strangling them. For instance—"

"No," Devon cut in on the park bench beside her.

Khloë blinked at her friend. "What?"

"Do not corrupt my daughter with your messed-up imp ways."

"Imps are not messed up."

Devon took Anaïs into her arms, her green gaze still on Khloë. "So you'd call them sane? Really?"

"And you'd call a hellcat mating a hellhound sane?" Khloë shot back. "See, this here is what happens when you go mixing breeds that aren't supposed to produce offspring together. Shit goes wrong. Psychopaths are born. Deaths soon after follow."

"Anaïs is not a psychopath. And she doesn't try to kill people, she just plays rough. She . . . what's the matter, baby?" Devon asked the hellpup as she melted into her mom's chest with a scared whimper.

Khloë tracked the path of Anaïs' gaze to see a couple stood a few feet away. A very pretty dark-haired woman sighed up at a hot-as-fuck dude who looked the epitome of bored.

"You don't like the place, do you?" the woman asked him.

He spared her a quick look. "It's . . . not unbearable."

A snort. "That's probably the nicest thing you've said about anywhere we've been. I kind of thought that Vegas would be a hit with you." Exhaling heavily, she lifted her hands. "I'm just gonna take a wild guess here and assume that you aren't all too enamored with the wider world so far."

"You assume correctly."

She leaned into him. "Why don't we just head back home, then? I miss the place. Miss the Keep."

"And your coven," he pressed.

"Them, too."

"And you want to ensure they haven't set the cottage on fire or gotten themselves killed," he hedged.

"Either is a very real possibility. Honestly, I can't even say that potential threats to them will only come from outside sources. It's highly possible that they've tried to murder the shit out of one another. But we can keep traveling for a little while longer if you're open to it, or just go on another trip at a later point. You can come and go anytime you please now, remember?"

Satisfaction blotted his dark eyes. "I can." Those eyes skittered over to the bench, as if he sensed their scrutiny. He honed in on Anaïs, his expression unmoved.

His woman nudged him. "Don't even *think* about trying to scare children because you're bored. It's beneath you."

He frowned at her. "Sadist, remember?"

The two then walked away.

Khloë hummed. "Well ... they were weird. And powerful. A little *too* powerful." She'd been able to feel it rolling off them.

Devon kissed her daughter's head. "Did they scare you, baby?"

"She has good instincts. *Killer* instincts."

Devon's eyelid twitched. "You just had to add that, didn't you?"

"I'm not wrong."

"My daughter is not a—" Devon's words cut off as the hellpup wrapped her little hands around her mom's throat.

"She's not a what?" asked Khloë, watching dispassionately as her friend choked.

Her eyes widening, Devon moved her lips as if trying to communicate something.

"Sorry, can't hear you."

Fury flashed in those cat-green eyes, and her lips moved faster.

"*Still* can't hear you."

Devon thrust her daughter away from her just enough to escape her grip. She coughed, glaring daggers at Khloë. "I loathe you."

"Hate is part of your love language, so I'm good with it."

Her nostrils flaring, Devon angled her daughter toward Khloë. "Anais. Kill."

"You can't use her like she's an attack dog on a—" Khloë cut off as the toddler grabbed her throat tight.

Devon grinned. "Sorry, I can't do what?"

Acknowledgements

A billion thanks to my family for supporting me so fully and choosing to simply ignore how I zone out frequently and spend far too much with the fictional people in my head. They love you as I do.

More thanks must go to my PA, Melissa, and social media manager Bev—you guys keep me sane and take on so much so I can simply write.

Thank you also to the wonderful team at Piatkus, especially my editor Anna Boatman. You're all so fantastic and I'm forever boasting how I have the best people ever behind my books!

Last but certainly not—and never—least, a huge thanks to all my readers, I hope you enjoy the trilogy despite that it's bonkers.

Take care,
S :)